GOOD STORY

THE FORGOTTEN PLACE

THE FORGOTTEN PLACE

JOHN FORES

COWARD-McCANN, INC.
NEW YORK

COPYRIGHT © 1956 BY JOHN FORES

All rights reserved. This book, or parts thereof, must not be reproduced in any form without permission.

The characters in this book are entirely imaginary and bear no relation to any living person.

Library of Congress Catalog Card Number: 56-10501

MANUFACTURED IN THE UNITED STATES OF AMERICA

CONTENTS

I	THREE PARTINGS	7
II	AT WESTONMILLS	12
III	FARUDA	23
IV	HOME	51
V	NIGHT IN THE DESERT	68
VI	THE BOAT	92
VII	THE AFTERNOON	133
VIII	THE EVENING	164
IX	THE NIGHT	191
X	AND THE MORNING	222
XI	THE CHANGED PEOPLE	240

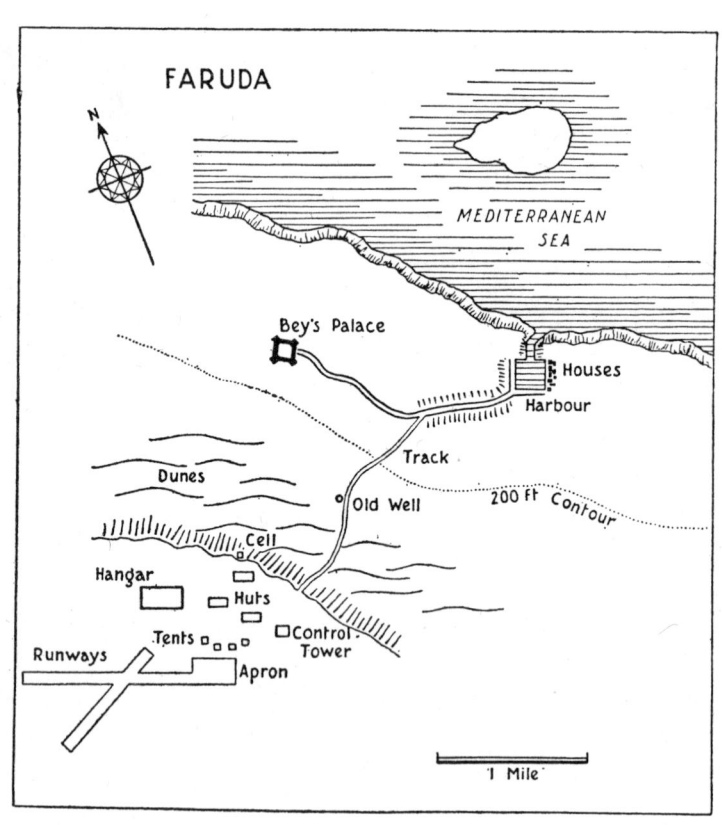

CHAPTER I

THREE PARTINGS

AT five o'clock Kingsley awoke and lay listening to the unceasing bird voices which came from the garden below the bedroom's open windows.

He turned his head and saw that the sky was clear before the coming sun, bright with promise of the new day. It was the kind of day when anything might happen.

Beyond those of the birds, another voice, distant and grumbling; the airfield stirred too, groaning in its awakening. With a kind of sliding roll which scarcely disturbed the sheets Kingsley got up, knowing vaguely that he wanted to and that the day's impending load was never made lighter by lying in bed. His wife's sleeping face was pale and faintly worried, in complexion something between the whiteness of the pillow and the light brown hair which fell over it in curly-ended strands. In three weeks the baby would be here. He couldn't believe it was only three weeks.

The bathroom's soaped and powdered air met him with a warm embrace; while the bath was filling he stared with a touch of smugness at his reflection in the cabinet mirror and the familiar morning stranger looked back curiously from his vitreous cavern. In the bath he stretched his long body in the water; all his skin was burned to a medium and even brown except for the white abdomen like a bleached stripe across him.

When he returned to the bedroom he was Captain William Conrad Kingsley. His dark blue uniform carried three gold rings on each sleeve, gilt buttons impressed with a beaky eagle, and a pair of small gold wings on the left breast. He wore it well and easily, as though he had long been used to it.

His wife was awake. Her head rolled over on the pillow and she looked up almost as if she did not recognise the tall man by the bed, her eyes half closed and still empty from sleep.

"What time is it?" She spoke quickly.

"Five-thirty. A fine morning."

"It should be for once. . . . You'll have to go soon."

"In a minute."

"I might as well be married to a commercial traveller. You're always away." Her voice was cultured into insipid flatness.

"Not always, Carol. This is only a short one, and we'll be back tonight. I told you. . . ."

She bit off a yawn, stretching her legs under the covers. "You like it, though, don't you? You like being away more than you like being at home. You flyers. . . ." She smiled suddenly, a sort of weary liveliness springing to the pale face. "I think at this time you ought to be at home."

"I will, if they'll let me," Kingsley said seriously, watching her. "Are you all right? Can I get you anything?"

"No, I'm all right. I never feel sick at all." She paused and then put out her hand to his. He felt how nervously tight her grasp was. "I'll get up soon. Is your bag packed?"

"Yes. All ready."

The silence before she spoke again seemed to be a wait for strength to come. At last she said, "Is it dangerous this time?"

Kingsley laughed. "You know it's never dangerous." He stopped short, considering the brightness outside. "It's only unusual sometimes—not very often."

"Often enough," she said. "I can remember those times —times when the unusual was dangerous. It could be again."

"Now don't worry, Carol. I'll be back tonight. It's not long." He spoke slowly and soothingly, returning the pressure of her hand.

"No. . . . I'm glad this is a short one."

"So am I. I don't want to be an absentee father."

"I hope it will be a boy," she said suddenly, smiling directly and almost triumphantly into his eyes. "Now we both want a boy."

Kingsley's face was stiff with surprise. "Why, I thought . . ."

"I've changed my mind," she said. "It's settled."

Her words and the pale, unemphasised form of her face thrust all at once against this moment, forcing it aside, and he was back with her as they had once been, long ago, when love and happiness was new and would last for ever. He bent

over her and they kissed, and then it was time. She watched
him go, heard his footsteps on the stairs and then the garden
door closed with its little, final snap of the spring lock. There
was a sudden strong, urgent movement inside her, and she
knew that she was still afraid. When the movement ceased
she turned her face into the pillow and the light hair fell
over it so that not even the probing sun could see it then.

*   *   *

The engineer was called Gleason. He was a medium, compact man with a quiet and regularly handsome face, twenty-
nine years old, but looked younger except when he was
frowning. He was frowning now at the girl in the bed, and
deep down in his eyes lay a curious and baffled hesitation.

Light came uneasily into the hotel room, a square cabin
which was allowed only a slit of the washed morning sky above
the grey wall of a warehouse opposite. From beyond the
wall came the sound of hammering. Hammering, Gleason
thought, at half-past five in the morning. . . .

He put on his jacket, dark blue, with two gold rings. The
girl stared at him. Her full breasts were above the sheets,
her arms spread, the fingers with their scarlet nails clutching
upward at the room's faintly scented air. The long golden
hair fell over a wide and sensual face, arched brows, a broad
nose. Her eyes were bottle-green and knowing, and she looked
impatiently sulky although the generous lips were parted over
big square teeth that filled her mouth like white peas in a
split pod.

"You *are* coming back tonight?" she said. The words were
slow and a little slurred, with a west-country accent. "You
won't hang me up?"

"Tonight," he replied briefly. He turned away and began
to pack clothes into a hold-all on the low table beside the
window. If he looked at her too much he wouldn't go. "It
may be pretty late."

"Well, I'll be here. Don't be too late, Bob."

He yawned. The tiredness was all in his head now.

"I suppose it's one way to earn a living," the girl said, still
watching him. "But I wanted you here today. My birth-
day. . . . And I'll have to spend it alone."

"Sorry, Della, but I can't help it, can I? What will you do?"

"I don't know. . . . Stay in bed and feel lonely, I suppose. What else is there to do?"

There were lots of things, he thought, but Della wouldn't be interested. He folded the hold-all and zipped it up, then turned to face her. Immediately she held out her arms to him, and when he came to the bed she kissed him and her mouth smothered his, her body moving in the bed.

"I don't want you to go," she muttered.

"I must—now."

He forced himself away. The clothes were almost off her, and her body was a white and slenderly curved magnet on the bed.

"I must." He was convincing himself. He picked up the bag and it was heavy.

"All right then." The girl put out her tongue at him, childlike, and rolled on to her side, and he backed towards the door, away from this scented temptation. "Go away and work. Why do I have to want a man who's always going away?"

He stopped by the door.

"What about me?" he said with sudden harshness. "Do you think *I* want to go? You know I need you and you know I have to go, but you don't help me."

Della Harris smiled sadly and pulled the bedclothes over her body, covering it.

"There," she said. "Does that help?"

He closed the door quietly and went down the corridor towards the staircase. Between the inadequate patches of carpet the bare boards rang under his feet. His face was still, a doubt pulling at his tight mouth and smearing itself across the eyes. It was always with doubt that he left her. He knew that it was not Della that he left, but Della's body. There was no Della; but this lovely, empty thing which she gave so eagerly was all he wanted, all he deserved when he was with her. There was only work and women, and all women were flesh and possession.

Now there was work. As he descended the stairs he lifted

his head and saw for the first time that the morning was bright.

*   *   *

"It's wash day, idiot," Mrs. Barthell said loudly. "*That's* why I'm up early. You're not the only one who can get going at five."

"You don't have to start so soon just because . . ."

"Try washing for five people some time, Harry Barthell. You'll see. If I hadn't been fool enough to carry three kids for you . . ."

"All right." Barthell grinned at his big and cheerful wife. "I'm going."

"Go on then. The sooner you're outside the better. I want to get started."

Their kiss was quick and noisy.

"Out!" Mrs. Barthell cried, and pushed the man along the hall to the front door. "Bring me back a box of dates."

She slammed the door behind him with a bang that shook the house, and was singing and rolling up her sleeves before she got to the kitchen.

CHAPTER II

AT WESTONMILLS

If you had been at Westonmills on that particular morning, early, you might have thought that sometimes even an airfield can look pretty handsome. Later on it began to rain, and then it didn't look so good at all.

Left over awkwardly from the war, Westonmills was one of those airfields which had been leased to charter companies like Bond's to enable them to clear up the crumbs of air transport work which dropped from the tables of the big public corporations and which afforded them an adequate if not luxurious living. It consisted of the usual runways—three of those broad and striding roads which seem to lead nowhere but to a belt of trees or a fence and yet are highways to all the world—and a motley collection of depressed and inconvenient buildings strung out beside a fairly wide concrete apron. But it was less than thirty miles from London on a main road to the south-west; and though it had little of the importance and only a fraction of the size of the great city airports, two or three times a year Westonmills came into its own when the larger fields lay uselessly under cold shrouds of smog. Then the big machines would come down in clear skies to the airfield on top of the hill, and the passengers would wonder why it was that a little smoke and water vapour could still, in an age of diabolical scientific intelligence, disturb the careful and expensive schedules of their journeys.

Now, at half-past six, the whole field was dawn-washed and bright with sunshine so that even the two slaty hangars, angular twins lying side by side, looked as though someone had lacquered their dirty flanks, and the squat control tower was like a white ivory cube, reflecting the brilliant light. On the field the grass was growing high, smelling warm already, and to the south the beech wood—that one which the pilots thought was just a little too close for comfort to the long runway—was a straight wall of green, the trees packed close and shouldering one another like tight ranks of soldiers on parade.

You wouldn't have found a cloud in the sky, then, but high up the moon hung thin and pale like the last wafer of a saline tablet before it dissolves.

Behind the control tower a long black Nissen hut squatted at the end of the apron, looking like a fat caterpillar with a white head where the tower was, and over its one door the hut bore a slightly crooked sign on which the legend " Briefing Room and Meteorological Office " was painted in faded letters.

When Kingsley stepped from this doorway his first thought was that it seemed already a long time since he got up—much longer than the ninety minutes it actually was. His second thought was that it was almost too fine a day to be leaving England, especially for a country where the sun seldom shone with benevolence, but blazed virulently from dawn to darkness. He paused, waiting for the navigator, and looked first at the bed of wan and weed-haunted flowers beside the hut wall, then at the crooked notice over the door. He always looked at this notice before going on a trip and had got into the habit of wondering when he would see it again; for it was not until he passed beneath it on each return home that he knew the journey was really over, that his responsibilities were then at an end. Until the next one. . . . Somehow it had become almost a kind of talisman, he thought, through familiarity and because of its marking of the start and the end of every journey. He wondered if they would ever straighten it and renew the paint. Most of Westonmills could do with a coat of paint.

If Kingsley had been an inch taller his attenuation would have looked grotesque. His was one of those spare and flexible bodies which long-distance runners have, tapering down thinly from a deep chest. He had a decisive, bony face, full of a kind of questing vitality, long and solemn under a cap of straight dark hair, but its gravity was tempered by the humour round his mouth and the restless eyes, so that a smile would make a big change in his face, but not an unexpected or infrequent one. Though the uniform suited him, it somehow did not help his leanness but rather emphasised it. His hair needed cutting.

The burly man who came from the door to stand beside

Kingsley dropped the green canvas bag he carried in his left hand and put down more carefully the box in his right, and tipped his cap over his eyes as he looked over the apron.

"Well, skipper," he said, "here we go again. Fair winds and all the world's sun. It's a flying day."

His voice was husky, rumbling up from somewhere deep in the broad chest which bore a navigator's wing. His eyes were small and bead-bright, set in a face that looked as if at one time it had been pushed up hard against a wall. The big ears seemed to have been thrown at him, not very accurately, and had somehow stuck. Great muscles bulged everywhere; in his face, under the tight uniform, on the backs of his hairy hands. He grinned with an ugly cheerfulness at Kingsley, and when he moved his powerful body showed a curious delicate poise that was unconscious as an animal's.

Kingsley lifted his hand to shade his eyes, gazing up at the bright sky and the defiant wafer of the moon, questioningly, as though they might contain the answer to a problem. There was a deft economy in his movements, like that of a man who is conserving his energies for some grave and special use. Already the sun was warm on his back.

"It's a flying day all right, Harry," he said. "Most days are, for members of the air tramping profession. But today, well . . ."

He smiled quizzically at the navigator who gave his cap another prod and grunted, "I know. Always harder to leave when it's like this—better when it's raining catfish and you get through to the sun at five thousand or so. Still, I'm not worrying. It's wash day at home, and that's always hell. How's Mrs. K.?"

"Pretty well, thanks. Three weeks now."

"Soon as that? Wait till you've got three of them—you'll wish you were away all the time."

Kingsley laughed. "We'll see how we manage with the first one. Well, Harry, if our tame weather experts know what they're talking about we ought to have a good trip. Ten thousand?"

"High enough. Made out the flight plan for that—best winds there according to met."

"Fine." Kingsley hesitated, looking narrowly at Barthell's

rugged face. They had been flying together for a long time now.

He said, " What do you think of this one, Harry? Strange stuff for us, isn't it?"

" Well, I don't know." The navigator smiled, and his features were oddly softened. " It's another job to be done, that's all. We've had a few queer ones in our time."

" We have. The world set-up being what it is today makes the queer ones necessary now and then, I suppose. But it's not our job to worry about reasons. . . ."

" Well, y'know, skipper, I've found that people who fly a bit are usually pretty simple types," Barthell said, " liable to be concerned more with their flying than with the why or wherefore. And right now my own concern is about the condition of a certain runway at a place called Faruda. . . ."

" You've got it, Harry. Anyway, we'll know all about it when we get there. For the moment I can think of nothing better than breakfast."

Harry Barthell sighed gustily. " Let's go. I'm starving."

He picked up his canvas bag and the strangely shaped box of the kind in which aircraft sextants are carried and walked with Kingsley round the end of the hut to where the canteen crouched alongside one of the hangars—a single-storey building like a squashed packing case. It was very hot inside, and the smells of cooking food were crammed tightly under the low ceiling.

Kingsley saw that the rest of his crew were already there. Sitting together at a long table in the middle of the room, they had an air almost of resignation, Kingsley thought, and certainly little of expectation. Here was David Tarrant their young radio operator, the stewardess whom he knew only slightly, Gleason, and the co-pilot who was called Lester Cummings and was conspicuous with flaming red hair and a straggling moustache of identical hue which was a pride of the Handlebar Club. Three men in civilian clothes sat in the corner nearest the service door, and at another table Kingsley recognised two of the airfield mechanics who must have been on night duty. It was still too early for the morning crowd which usually arrived a little before eight.

"Attention, crew! They're here," Cummings said, standing up and bowing gravely. "Our revered captain and respected navigator—well briefed and raring to go." He sat down and gave a wolfish grin which jerked up his moustache unevenly, one end higher than the other.

"After breakfast," Barthell rumbled laconically, taking a chair beside the stewardess. "Even we who are briefed must eat. Co-pilots, being unimportant, just eat."

"When?" inquired Cummings, stroking his whiskers and his slightly pop-eyed look turning expectantly towards the service door. "My importance, or lack of it, is trifling compared with the prospect of food."

At that moment the door opened and a perky young waitress began to serve them.

The stewardess sat quietly, watching the men. Her round grey eyes travelled from face to face as though she weighed each character in some balance of her mind but was not sure of its accuracy. She knew them all, but had never flown with this crew before. Her face had a sensitive and underlying strength; it was clear-skinned, not without its lines of laughter and sadness near the mouth and on the high forehead which showed its latent mobility. But it was still now, without any set expression, waiting in serenity which was a foundation of the beauty which it did not quite achieve. Her blue uniform was trim and unobtrusive, relieved by a white blouse open at the neck, the collar turned down over her tunic. She had short, curly hair that was neither brown nor gold but a fineness between. She did not say anything unless it was to answer one of the others. Tarrant sat opposite, and he was quiet too, glancing occasionally at the stewardess; he hadn't been flying as long as the rest, and he was not yet used to stewardesses.

After they had begun to eat it was some time before anybody spoke. Charter crews were accustomed to flying off to almost any part of the world at a moment's notice, and Kingsley could not help smiling to himself at the thought that although his crew was aware that the trip was a short one, only he and Barthell yet knew where they were going, but no one had troubled to ask.

Gleason spoke first, and he merely said quietly, raising dark eyes, "Who are the three bodies in the corner?" and looked as though he didn't really care about an answer.

The three men in dark suits were eating in an absorbed and determined manner, in silence. They were in three well-defined sizes—a large and fattish bald man, one tall and thin, the third small and wiry with a sharp red face. Kingsley threw them a curious glance and said after a moment, "They must be our passengers. Rogers says we've got three. They're French."

"Passengers. . . ." Tarrant grinned widely at the captain and then across the table at the stewardess. "Three won't trouble you too much, Miss Wells."

Susan Wells smiled briefly and, it seemed to the radio operator, indulgently. He looked down at his plate with a feeling of having said something unaccountably foolish. Kingsley said, "I'm not sure where these people are going to sit. The kite's packed to the roof, and it's a freighter."

A shadow of uncertainty passed across the stewardess's face. Kingsley saw it and went on quickly, "It's all right, Miss Wells. There is a galley."

"Oh, I'm glad. Is it like those on the passenger machines?"

"Just the same. This is one of the passenger machines with the seats and fittings ripped out. You'll probably find it very inconvenient, but you know the Bond policy is to carry a stewardess whenever there are passengers, even if they have to be tied to the wings."

"Best place for passengers," Cummings decided. "They're only trouble. Did I ever tell you how a passenger tried to murder me once? It was back in fifty-one when I was doing some hack work for the Kuwait oil people. . . ."

"All right, Lester, cut it short," Barthell pleaded. "Did he succeed in the attempt, or not?"

Cummings treated the navigator to a glare of ineffable contempt. "I must apologise for the puerile humour of some of my colleagues, Miss Wells," he said. "Also I have no doubt that you would be interested to know why we are gathered here this morning. I don't want to appear inquisitive, skipper, but do you think we might have a hint of where we're going, and why?"

Kingsley rubbed his ear and looked round as though afraid that he might be overheard.

"Well, it's a fair question, Lester. Harry and I just had it all at briefing, and it's a nice short trip, as you know. Something new, too." He waited, then spoke more slowly. "Working for a charter company, we all know that queer jobs are likely to come our way now and then, though this one isn't exactly *queer*. . . . We're going to take supplies for the survey of a derelict war-time airfield on the North African coast."

There was a silence while the crew stared at him. Then Cummings tugged hard at his moustache and said, "Derelict airfield?" He was incredulous. "Whose bright idea is this, skipper? How are we going to land if the place is derelict? And what are . . .?"

"Hold it, Lester," Kingsley interrupted. "It's not quite as crazy as it apparently sounds to you."

"I certainly hope it isn't."

"Rogers says the place is okay for landings. Naturally we're not going to take any more risks than necessary, and I shall have a good look at the field before we pancake. We're not staying. We're dumping the stores and passengers and then coming straight home. We ought to be able to fly back here without refuelling, but if necessary we shall land in France for petrol on the way."

After a pause Gleason said, "Then this place is being opened up again?"

"I understand that it may be, but I wasn't told very much. Our passengers are going to survey it and generally check up on the shape it's in, and the stores are to keep them going while they're doing so. The place is called Faruda."

The co-pilot's face was that of a man upon whom a great light has broken. "Ah, I see! The free nations' build-up of defences, and all that. Is that why it has suddenly occurred to someone that the place may be worth a look?"

"Well, Lester, officially I wouldn't know, but I think you might bet that this survey is all tied up with Faruda's possible strategic importance in case of war."

"It will be crawling with strategic importance," Cummings grunted. "Everywhere is, nowadays."

"It's rather strange that we should have got the job," Kingsley said thoughtfully. "I suppose there just weren't any French machines available. We're actually on charter to the French Government."

"Well, it's happened before, skipper. Captain Barker and his crew did a trip to Dakar for them a few months ago, ferrying out engines and spares."

"Yes, I remember now. Well, it's our turn today, and we're going out again in five days' time with a final lot of cargo."

"They surely think up some wonderful jobs," Cummings said. "What's the dope on this Faruda?"

"It's in French territory—hence the Frenchmen. It was a fighter-bomber station during the war, and a good bit knocked about I believe, so there probably won't be much left apart from the runways. It's miles from anywhere, way off air and shipping lanes and, frankly, nobody seems to know much about it."

"No town or harbour?"

"Rogers didn't know, and there's nothing on our maps. The place may be entirely uninhabited, and that's why we're taking all this stuff. They don't seem to have missed a thing —we've got food, water, tents, petrol, cookers, bedding, radio gear, medicines in the cargo—the lot." Kingsley paused. "If the weather's bad we divert to Tripoli and have another go when it clears."

"It will be a change from carting civil servants to Nice and mining machinery to Pakistan, anyway," the engineer said in his quiet voice. "But it doesn't sound so attractive, this Faruda. I'm glad we're not staying."

"So am I," said Barthell. "I don't envy these Frenchmen if Faruda is only half as grim as it sounded at briefing. How long are they going to be there, skipper?"

"Two or three weeks, Rogers says—depends how long the survey work takes. It seems to be something of a rush job altogether, as far as I can see." Kingsley sat back and his mouth closed up into a thin line. He looked round the table for several seconds, his eyes lingering on the composed face of the stewardess, and then said, "There's just one thing which I think you all ought to know now. We've been given three Sten guns and a couple of automatics. . . . Just in case, Rogers said—in case anyone unfriendly turns up, which I don't for a moment anticipate."

They watched him in silence. He went on, "We have to get the right idea about this, and we shouldn't attach too much importance to what is only a wise precaution. The place may be uninhabited, as I've said, and if it isn't I've not been told any reason to expect that the natives may be hostile. Faruda is isolated and our information about it is pretty sketchy, that's all."

"There's been a lot of unrest in North Africa generally, hasn't there?" Tarrant said doubtfully.

A gloomy Cummings said, "They're going all nationalist from Cairo to Casablanca. Nastily nationalist, some of them."

"Cut it out, Lester." Kingsley waved an irritated hand at the co-pilot. "Because we're going prepared for trouble it doesn't mean that we shall run into it. Rogers certainly doesn't expect any."

"He's not going," Tarrant grinned.

"Well, it sounds a crazy sort of trip to me," Cummings said, fingering his moustache and determined to see nothing good in the whole prospect. "Do we get danger money?"

"The rest of us do for flying with you, Lester," Barthell grunted. "Personally I'm looking forward to going to a place where we shan't be badgered by souvenir sellers or oily gents who try to interest us in a little smuggling."

Gleason nodded towards the navigator, smiling a little. "Journey into the unknown. It's a rare experience nowadays."

"Well, that's it," said Kingsley, stuffing tobacco into a well-used pipe. "You know as much as I do now, which I admit isn't an awful lot. Final thing is that we're not supposed to talk about Faruda too much, outside. I think that's something we all understand."

"Ours is certainly not to reason why," Cummings remarked. "They would keep it a secret if we were flying out bangles for Basuto belles. . . . And now—a derelict airfield. It's the dreaded end."

A short-legged, balding man in a grey suit entered the

canteen. Captain Rogers, the operations manager, was stout and a little anxious of countenance, and as he came to stand beside Kingsley's chair he was sweating slightly as though he had been hurrying. He seemed to have no neck, his face bulging out from a tight collar, globular and pink and shining.

He spoke in a quick and high-pitched voice. " Is everything all right?" He looked at the crew defiantly, as if expecting someone to challenge him. " You've briefed them, Bill?"

" I have." Kingsley looked up. " We've finished here and just have to see Customs. Is the loading complete yet?"

" Yes. All properly stowed and lashed. I've got the load sheets here, and she's full."

" Good." Kingsley took the sheets from Rogers and stared at them for a minute. " Four thousand gallons of gas, too —that brings us to the all-up limit. Trust Bond's to fill 'em up."

" It's a habit," Donald Rogers said. " Even when pay-load doesn't count they have to fill them up." He sucked his teeth quietly and moved over to the corner table and returned with one of the passengers.

The passenger was the smallest of the three, a little dark man of about forty with a red thin face and cropped hair which came to a point low in the middle of his forehead. His eyes were sharp and watchful, clear as a cat's, but long afterwards Kingsley could never remember what colour they were. He had an air of conscious but softened authority. The top of his right ear was missing, sliced off straight and clean, and he walked quickly and eagerly beside Rogers with his right hand a little extended and ready for action.

Rogers said, " M. Yves Garraud—Captain Kingsley. M. Garraud is in charge of the little party for Faruda—he is to survey the airfield."

Garraud's hand was strong and cool. He said, " How do you do, captain? I am happy to meet you," with the too perfect diction of the foreigner who speaks English well, and bowed slightly.

" How do you do?" Kingsley introduced his crew. " I hope you will have a pleasant trip with us."

" Thank you, captain. I have no doubt that I and my

colleagues will enjoy it." He inclined his head towards the other table. " Richer there is our radio operator "—he indicated the thin man—" and Tarollier is the *fonctionnaire*."

" I'm afraid that there won't be much comfort for you. She is only a freighter, you know."

" She? Oh—I understand." Garraud laughed, raising his hands expressively. His laugh was genial, exposing one gold tooth among several very white ones. " It does not matter —we did not expect luxury. I will probably sleep, and knit up the ravelled sleeve of care, as Shakespeare has it."

Kingsley smiled. Without knowing precisely why, he was already beginning to like Garraud. The Frenchman had a kind of regulated yet careless energy and a sufficiency about him that made Kingsley feel that he was a big man in all but the physical.

" We shall make the journey as comfortable as we can, of course. Miss Wells will be looking after you."

" That will indeed be delightful." Garraud bowed towards the stewardess, smiling gravely. As he turned to go back to his table he paused and the smile suddenly vanished. He said, " We are going soon—very soon?"

" Take-off is in half an hour," said Rogers.

" Ah, thank you." Relief flickered for an instant in Garraud's clear eyes, he hesitated for a second more and then moved away.

Rogers said, " Miss Wells, I—er—I was speaking to the station manager yesterday. This trip is something of an unknown quantity and there is just the possibility of—well, an incident. We felt that in the circumstances if you would rather not go there would be no objection to your transferring to another flight. . . ."

Susan Wells's face was pale and very firm. " I would like to go, Captain Rogers," she said.

" Well, that's all right then." Rogers nodded, his round face looking more cheerful. " I think you've got it all now, Bill—we covered pretty well everything at briefing. See you tomorrow, then. Have a good trip."

CHAPTER III

FARUDA

As they walked out into the sunlight, Kingsley was thinking about Faruda. Even in twelve years and almost nine thousand hours of flying in all parts of the world, there hadn't been any Farudas. I've landed in some odd places, he told himself, but never on a derelict desert airfield with a fully laden machine. Rogers was certain that it was fit for landings. It must have been landed on, probably by the French, and declared safe for a heavy aircraft. Had they seen no sign of habitation there? —probably they had not stayed long enough or their information had been lost in transit to Westonmills. It was eleven years since the place had last been used by fighter-bombers during the war, which was long enough for any field to silt up. According to Barthell's map there was a good runway, more than two thousand yards long, and another shorter one; but there was not much detail of the coast or the surrounding country. Still, how could you show detail of a desert? Harry would have to drop a smoke bomb to get the surface wind for landing. And—if anything went wrong with the kite they would have the radio which the Frenchmen were going to set up. But why should anything go wrong?

He thought suddenly of the co-pilot's panacea for all flying troubles, and laughed out loud in the sun.

Their machine was the middle one in a row of three on the tarmac. The petrol bowser and the loading trucks had gone and now only the energiser stood under the nose, already plugged in to start her up. Kingsley felt again, as he never failed to before any trip, the tingling and always fresh anticipation of flight and the warm knowledge that soon, again, he would be looking down upon the earth from a giant's viewpoint as he sped powerfully through the clean vastness of the sky. Flying is for me, he thought, my only skill, and I have no want of any other. Was it true, as Carol had said, that he liked being away more than being at home? Sometimes a man had to get away; and being away meant flying. But he wanted to be at home when the baby came.

The aircraft was fat, four-engined, a little down by the tail, "BOND AIRWAYS" in big blue letters above the row of cabin windows. The tail fin raised its slender shaft to the sky as though pointing out a star, and the silver body was bright with reflected needles of the sun. Her name was Peter Fox.

Kingsley climbed up the steps and into the cabin. The long cylinder was dim after the sunlight, and it was filled tightly with piled packing cases and water drums and fibre boxes roped to metal rings in the floor, and near the tail was a great pile of petrol cans, crated up, and bales of something that might have been bedding or tents. Opposite the door a small petrol generator was lashed securely, close to the neat and polished complexity of the galley. There was just enough room for a man to pass along the narrow gangway which had been left between the stacked freight; and at the front of the cabin, under a hanging cliff of boxes, three seats had been fixed for the passengers. The silvery metal ribs of the machine curved up above the gangway in regular, concentric arches.

Once he had settled in the pilot's seat Kingsley forgot all about Faruda in his concentration on the preparations for take-off. Take-off—so easy and yet so difficult, so much to do that had been done a thousand times before and still must never be neglected, never missed. He sniffed again that peculiar smell which aeroplanes have, that subtle alloyage of oil and metal and fabric dope and rubber. He admitted shamelessly that to him it was the smell of all adventure in a tin can; it was as sharply evocative as any of those scents pressed into dark and sombre dockside sheds—scents which could transport the mind to far countries on frail component breaths of spice and gum and sandalwood and sundust. . . . The flight deck was warm, sunlight liquefying inside it.

He looked without haste along the rows of dials on the dashboard and on the engineer's panel behind him. Cummings climbed awkwardly into the co-pilot's seat, subsiding with a sighing grunt. Between the two pilots the block sprouted its coloured levers like flower heads—four throttle flowers and four pitch blossoms, landing gear and flaps and auto pilot.

When they were all aboard a mechanic removed the red-painted safety locks on the wheels and control surfaces. Kingsley strapped the broad canvas safety belt tightly across his thighs and put on his headphones. Looking from the side window he held up his hand, and the man standing by the nose lifted his in reply.

" All right, Bob. Three, four, two, one."

Gleason switched on number three and pressed the starter button. The propeller blades revolved reluctantly for a few seconds, there was a loud bang and a cough, then the sudden roar and fume of blue smoke from the exhausts as the motor started.

Two minutes later Gleason said, " Right, skipper. Four ticking."

" Let's go, then."

When Kingsley waved his hands one across the other the mechanics ran beneath the wings to pull away the chocks. He opened the throttles slightly and the machine belched sound and lurched forward, and he turned her to the right and across the apron, past the bulking hangars to the end of the runway. He could feel the great weight of her behind him as she duck-waddled on fat tyres. She was heavy, all right.

The run-up was all sound and tremor, clouds of swirling dust behind. Gleason crouched, his hands on levers, watching the flickering needles that danced the motors' tune. A final lever came back, and a strange and minatory silence coiled about the slow propellers.

" All okay, skipper. No snags."

" Right. Everybody set? Fine pitch, twenty degrees of flap. Boost pumps on, Lester?"

" On, skipper."

Kingsley spoke into his microphone.

" Peter Fox to Westonmills tower. May I go, please?"

The voice in his earphones was loud and gritty and seemed to have been de-sexed on the way. " You're clear to go, Peter Fox," it said. " Have a good trip. Out."

" Roger. Out."

Like a wide grey river the runway stretched between grassy banks, its far end invisible below a slight rise in the middle of the field. Kingsley worked the stick and rudder pedals to make sure they were free; here we go, he thought, and we're top weight. . . . He released the brakes and then opened the throttles slowly as she rolled. All at once he had pushed the throttles wide, the motors screamed and a great gale battered furiously at the flanks of the machine and the ground was rushing past the windows, faster and faster, and now he could put both hands on the stick and hold her straight with the rudder. He felt the powerful shove of the motors as their force was unleashed, pressing his head back against the seat cushion. He saw a green blur of grass and trees and from the corner of his eye looked quickly at the airspeed needle. A hundred, a hundred and ten. . . . He pulled back firmly and smoothly at the stick, but she wouldn't come. Too heavy. How much runway left? God! Is that all? A hundred and twenty. Now. . . . He pulled again and she came off at last, touched once gently, and then was airborne, howling.

"Wheels up," he said calmly to the engineer, and the boundary fence flashed past thirty feet below. Gleason moved the undercarriage selector and throttled back the dreadful howl and they turned on to course and began to climb, east of south.

When she had settled Cummings looked down, back to the airfield, already tiny and insignificant behind them. The bunched buildings by the road seemed to have been driven into the ground by the pressure of the great sky.

"Not too much runway there, skipper. I began to think we wouldn't make it."

Kingsley set the auto pilot and switched it in. He sat back and touched his face and found that it was wet.

"Yes. . . . We needed full power that time. And there was no wind, which didn't help."

"Well, you've got to keep going," Cummings said wisely. "Half-way down a runway is no place to start thinking about turning back for another go. I knew someone once who did. . . . He's not with us any more."

The co-pilot groped in his pocket and pulled out a small grey-furred thing which he placed carefully on the window shelf above the crash guard where he could see it. Then he leaned back and unbuttoned his jacket while the ridiculous whiskers took up their crooked elevations.

Kingsley said, " I don't know why you have to carry that unhygienic stump around. It's probably riddled with myxomatosis."

Cummings smiled affectionately at the sad and mangy object.

" On the contrary, it came from a female animal of rude health, who died by my own hand. I called her Flo. Did I ever tell you how Flo's foot saved my life in forty-four? It was . . ."

" You told me. You plugged a hole in the dinghy with it, and you've carried it ever since."

" Why, that's right," the co-pilot said with the air of a man surprised. " I thought I'd not . . ."

" Many a time, Lester. And now you'd never travel without it."

" Bad luck if I did. Know it in my bones. Skipper, you're fortunate to have that foot in this machine."

" Bunkum!" Kingsley said sharply. He felt suddenly angry with Cummings and his foot. " I don't believe in this superstitious nonsense. Knowing your job is a damn sight better than a whole bagful of rabbits' feet."

He stared ahead at the approaching coast-line. Cummings looked at him and opened his mouth, but closed it again without speaking. He gave the foot a long and tender look and then gazed down at the fields and woods below. The skipper was entitled to his opinions, he thought, but I *know*. . . .

The engineer had finished setting the throttles and pitch levers. More by habit than conscious action Kingsley looked again along the rows of dials, noting the revs., oil temperatures and pressures, the course and airspeed. The altimeter needle crept slowly upward, recording their steady ascent.

The Channel. . . . A blue, calm lake far below where little ships made white partings in the water and they could just see the dots of following sea-birds. Far out to the west was the only cloud—a long white bank of cumulus which shone in the sun like the ramparts of a snowy mountain range rising from a vast blue plain. It was hot now on the flight deck, the sun making square, groping patterns from the windows as the machine swam in the lifting air towards it. Kingsley's solemn face was satisfied as he looked back and saw the airscrews, synchronised and rotating evenly about their blunt spinners, the round motors hanging beneath the upswept silver wings. The sunlight came to him and he was happy to be above the earth in these clear, empty, limitless plains of air, in the immense fields of the sky.

They were well over France when Kingsley levelled out at ten thousand feet; because of the weight it had taken a long time. The auto pilot flew the machine with little precise and formal movements of the stick and rudder pedals, holding a course and height against the shifting winds.

The cabin door opened and the stewardess came on to the flight deck with a tray of coffee cups. She walked with an easy confidence in the narrow gangway between the crew positions, and as she passed the radio operator he thought that she looked even more distantly composed than when he had seen her in the canteen. She handed Kingsley his cup first and he said, his eyes slanting up at her, " Thank you. How're our passengers, Miss Wells?"

" Quite comfortable, captain." She spoke with a faint smile, as though passengers were somehow quietly comic objects.

" Any complaints?"

" No. I've given them coffee and magazines."

" See that they don't smoke. With that load of gas in the tail we can't take any chances. I'll pay them a visit myself in a few minutes."

The stewardess looked thoughtful, and gave coffee to the remaining crew men. Tarrant said, " You're not lonely back there in that galley, are you?"

" Not a bit, thank you."

" Time doesn't drag?"

Susan Wells smiled sweetly. " Oh no. I brought my knitting."

" Knitting!" Tarrant muttered. " A stewardess—knitting. . . ."

When he had finished his coffee Kingsley said, " Watch her, Lester, will you? I'm just going back to have a look at things."

"I've got her, skipper."

Kingsley climbed from his seat and moved back past the engineer who sat sideways before his tall instrument panel; Gleason's head was bent, his face absorbed as he wrote carefully in his log. Tarrant seemed to be holding a solemn conversation with the black features of his transmitter, and across the gangway Barthell, jacket off and shirt sleeves rolled up over strong hairy arms, was drawing in a course on his chart.

"Paris says the weather is good right across France," Tarrant announced suddenly. "I've just sent a signal giving our position." He glanced slyly at the navigator. "That's if Harry has got it right, of course."

"It's always right, and you know it," Barthell grunted, dropping his pencil and sitting back. "How about some bearings for a change?"

"You don't need bearings on a day like this—why, you can see fifty miles. Use your map."

Barthell appealed to Kingsley. "How can I do my stuff if I'm to be frustrated by tired radio ops? Tell him to get me a bearing, skipper."

Kingsley grinned at them. He was used to this. "All right, you two. How are we doing, Harry?"

"Better than flight plan, so far. A twenty-knot wind on our tail—makes ground speed two-forty knots." Barthell put his eye to the drift meter, peering at the ground below as it passed along the grid wires in the instrument. "Hardly any drift—maybe a degree to port."

"Not bad." Kingsley nodded, leaning over Barthell's shoulder and staring at his chart. "I'll push the revs. up when we've shed some more weight."

The voice behind him was not that of any of the crew. Kingsley turned quickly and saw the man standing inside the door to the cabin. He was speaking to Tarrant in a voice that was faintly accented and stumbling with urgency, the radio operator looking up at him with a mask of surprise on his face. It was the man who was called Richer; he seemed to be agitated, his hands moving up and down in a curious sort of pumping motion.

Richer's thinness made him appear taller than he was, and

he stooped. Like many thin people his head was big, too big for his body. His eyes were large and bright and sunk deeply in the face as though shrinking from all they saw, and round them the skin was tight over its bony frame and with a uniform glossy pallor. The hair was thick and black, brushed straight back over the domed head, and he wore a thin streak of black moustache which followed faithfully the upper of two bloodless and sucked-in lips. His age was difficult to fix—anything from thirty-five to well over forty.

Kingsley faced the Frenchman and said sternly, "What are you doing here, sir? You must know that passengers are not allowed on the flight deck."

Richer drew a deep breath and his hands became still.

"I am sorry, captain," he said in a more controlled voice. "I—I merely wanted to ask something of your radio operator."

"If you require any information you must ask for it through me. What is it?"

Richer said, his eyes staring, "It is about something I left behind in London, a—how do you say it?—a briefcase. I was wondering if it was possible that you had received a message since we left about a man coming to Westonmills to see me. . . ."

"A man bringing the briefcase, you mean?"

"Yes, that is it. I thought perhaps the friend with whom I stayed might have come to Westonmills hoping to give it to me before I left, you understand, as the airfield is so close to London."

Kingsley turned from the fulgent stare towards Tarrant.

"Have you received any messages from Westonmills about anyone coming to see M. Richer?"

Tarrant shook his head. "No, skipper, nothing. Only the routine signals."

"Does that answer your question?" Kingsley asked, gazing directly at the Frenchman.

"Thank you, captain." Richer smiled faintly, and all at once his eyes were veiled. "I am sorry to have troubled you. If the case is lost it does not matter—it contained nothing of importance."

Kingsley was still looking hard at Richer. He paused, then

said, " Very well. Now I must insist that you do not come to the flight deck again. You will find a bell by your seat and you have only to touch it to summon any assistance you may require."

" Thank you, captain. I will remember."

Richer bowed his big head and went out, closing the cabin door carefully behind him. Kingsley, Barthell and Tarrant looked at one another and the navigator said dryly, " Interesting type, eh?"

For some time Kingsley stood in silence. Presently he said softly, " Very interesting, Harry—especially as I'm pretty sure that Richer never had a briefcase at all."

Barthell stared. " Never had one? How d'you know that?"

" Because Richer said so himself. As I was leaving Customs I overheard Rogers asking the passengers if they had forgotten any of their baggage, and he happened to mention briefcases specifically. I was behind Richer—he didn't know I was there. I heard him tell Rogers that he hadn't forgotten anything and carried all his personal kit in one large *suitcase*. . . . Well, what do you make of that?"

Barthell stroked his chin. " Nothing, at the moment."

" Nor I. But it's queer, Harry. It sounds like an excuse to get to the flight deck for some reason. Why?"

" I wouldn't know, skipper, but we do know that flying turns some people bug-brained. Something to do with the altitude. Anyway, watch yourself when you go back there."

When Kingsley opened the cabin door and passed through it he saw that the eyes of Garraud were already on his, as though his coming had been expected. Richer was in his seat on the opposite side of the gangway, the big man beside him. Kingsley nodded to Garraud and suddenly decided that he would speak to the passengers later, after he had examined the cargo. He moved down the narrow passage towards the tail, testing the freight lashings as he went. The cabin was hot and drumming with the noise of the motors—more noisy than the flight deck had been. When he touched the bare skin of the fuselage shell it was trembling and strangely cold, its icy but vital movement sending a tingle to his fingertips. The crated petrol cans smelled faintly.

The cargo was secure. Susan Wells was standing in her small galley, erect over the sink where she was washing coffee cups. She looked cool and almost frighteningly capable, Kingsley thought as he watched her from the door; a blinding patch of sunlight from the small window touched her hands as they moved economically between the sink and the racks above it. She looked up and jumped as she saw him in the doorway.

"I'm sorry, Miss Wells. I didn't mean to startle you."

"It's all right, captain. I hadn't heard you come."

"These freighters are very noisy after the passenger machines, aren't they? Is everything all right?"

She was surprised at what she thought was an urgency in the captain's voice. "Yes, quite all right."

"Good. Have any of the passengers rung for you lately?"

"No, none," the stewardess answered, her eyes wide.

"They haven't been wandering about the machine, or anything like that?"

"No."

"Good." Kingsley was about to tell her of Richer's excursion to the flight deck, but he checked himself. "I'll go back, then. Press the buzzer if you want us, Miss Wells."

The stewardess nodded briskly, and Kingsley did not see the touch of bewilderment in her eyes. As he went back to where the passengers were sitting he noticed that Garraud was peering down intently through the small round window beside his seat. On the other side of the gangway Richer and the big man seemed to be asleep. Below lay the wide brown fields, the dull green of great woods and the straight white roads and little villages of the Loire valley. Then Garraud turned with a quick movement and saw Kingsley standing beside him.

"Hello, captain." He displayed the gold tooth. "This is a fine smooth flight you are giving us."

"Thanks to the French weather."

Garraud paused, his cat's eyes on the wings on Kingsley's jacket, and then he said, "This will be a strange assignment for you, perhaps?"

"Strange? I don't know. Unusual, certainly."

"Of course—unusual."

Garraud spread his hands, still smiling. "But I underestimate your knowledge and experience, captain," he said quietly. " No doubt you will be familiar with the unusual."

" To an extent," Kingsley said non-committally, " though this is something new, I think, even for an air charter crew."

The Frenchman nodded. " You know, captain—I have been thinking about this flight, and about what lies at the end. . . ."

" And what have you thought?"

" Small things, I am afraid. . . . One is that at Faruda, anything may happen." Garraud laughed, and Kingsley caught an undercurrent of nervous excitement beneath his words. " We are together in this machine, on our way to an unknown place—or a place that was once known but is now forgotten. . . ."

He paused, his eyes bisected by reddish lids as he looked up at the captain. " Now," he said, " now we know nothing about it except that it is there. . . . In such a place what might not happen?"

" Anything, indeed," Kingsley murmured, adding with a touch of malice, " though my experience is that these places seldom live up to our expectations of them."

Staring down through the window again, Garraud did not answer. Kingsley saw that Richer was awake now and flicking idly at the pages of a magazine. Beside him the man called Tarollier lay back with closed eyes. He was as tall as Richer, but bore no other resemblance to him. Tarollier was almost bald, only a fringe of brown hair encircling his pale skull, and his heavy body was running to fat yet still strong. There seemed to be more of the sandy brows between the eyes than above them. His face was flat and pale, the features small and close together so that they appeared to have a border of bleached flesh round them; the mouth was red like a woman's, tiny and pouting.

Suddenly Garraud said, " We are coming to the Loire, eh?"

" Very soon. You know this part of France?"

" But of course. It is my own part—I was born at Tours."

All at once they saw the river below. It was broad and muddy, and they crossed it where a great curve flowed out of the haze that was Orleans, away on the port side.

" The Loire. . . . My part of France," Garraud repeated,

gazing down at the river. For an instant Kingsley thought he saw the Frenchman's face change—saw a quick darkening of it as a twist of the wind will darken a patch of water. The straight sliced-off top of his ear was a yellowish white. " Mine is a beautiful country, captain, beautiful. But, like much that is beautiful, there is often ugliness beneath."

" That might be said of many countries, if not all."

" Perhaps—but not necessarily in the way I mean. I was thinking of the ugliness of weakness, of indecision.

" In government, in leadership," Garraud said, a harsh note all at once ruffling the smooth nap of his voice, " weakness is ugly." His lips drew back from the gold tooth, and he pointed to the window. " Down there we are drifting, because there is no strength, no leader who can command his country's loyalty and obedience."

" You must forgive me if I am not very well up in French politics," Kingsley remarked. " We are lazy about politics in England—so much so that we even leave them to the politicians."

Garraud laughed. " In France everyone is a politician. We have too many, just as we have too many governments, weak and tremulous governments which must rely on the support of parties who will lend it only so long as it suits them." Now Garraud's tones were persuasive and compelling. " We flatter them by calling them governments, for they are too sickly to live long, let alone to govern. They are always coming and going—always. And where there is no strength . . ." His voice stopped abruptly and the last words hung like an execration in the hot cabin.

It seemed to Kingsley that almost every time Garraud spoke he rang some subtle change of manner, of voice or expression or mood, to show a differing facet of his mind. It was a restless mind, for now he appeared to have erased the instability of governments from it as he looked down with a little expectant and even contented smile at the wide pattern below. He had been eager to leave Westonmills, Kingsley thought; surely a strange man, as in a different way was this other who lied about briefcases. . . .

As he was about to move on, Richer spoke behind him.

The thin man's words were slow and careful as he said, "Excuse me, captain, but when may we expect to arrive at Faruda?"

"In a little over four hours," Kingsley answered briefly.

Richer's big head wobbled an acknowledgment. "That is good. You—you hope to find it without trouble?"

Kingsley laughed. "We certainly do. I have a very experienced navigator, and I shall be surprised if we miss it."

There was a short silence, and then Richer said deliberately, "You will be coming out to Faruda again soon, I believe?"

"Yes, in five days' time—that will be on the twenty-sixth. We shall be bringing the final batch of stores, and the jeep, which there wasn't room for today."

Richer turned to look from the window. "On the twenty-sixth. . . . We are keeping you busy."

"It's not too bad. We are short of crews at Westonmills at the moment, and we're lucky to have five days between trips."

"I see. Will you be coming in this plane, or another?"

"In this one. All the others are either in the hangars or booked for other work."

"So—if anything happened to this one," Garraud put in, smiling, "we would have to sing for our stores, eh?"

"Well, until another machine became available."

"It is a long time since I was flying," Richer said. "You do not carry parachutes any more, captain?"

"Parachutes?" Kingsley gave a surprised laugh. "I haven't seen a parachute since my R.A.F. days."

Richer smiled quickly. "Oh—excuse me." He raised a tapering hand, smoothing his thick hair. "In case of emergency, I wondered whether . . ."

"Parachutes would be so much dead weight these days." Kingsley looked at his watch. "Well, I hope you will be fairly comfortable. We are doing well for time. If you want anything, just ring for the stewardess. I will see you again before we land."

"Thank you, captain."

As he passed through the door to the flight deck Kingsley shot a final glance at his passengers, and both Garraud and Richer were staring at him, the former with a kind of fierce curiosity, while in Richer's eyes he thought he saw the fretted tail of anger or pain before the Frenchman turned his head away. He was aware of a brittle tension in the cabin's atmosphere which he had not noticed when he first entered it. Was it Faruda that had laid some strange twisting grip on the minds of these men? There they had to stay, and for these three it was even more a place unknown about which they knew nothing, " except that it is there. . . ."

It was very hot now on the flight deck. Kingsley climbed into his seat beside the co-pilot and the motors drummed out their low, monotonous note as though they would keep it up for ever. Each slicing revolution of the airscrews thrust them on; another mile, another flight, more hours in the log, more knowledge and experience. Experience to sit in and know the sky, to see the dawn earlier and the sunset later than people with their clogged feet in the dust, experience to feel detached from things sodden with familiarity and repetition. But because we are high, Kingsley thought, we are not mighty. The brilliant sky which is just the other side of this thin shell is a humbling sky, powerful as the sea and yet more vast. It allows you to climb in its cold breath only so long as its laws are respected; like the sea, it is merciless with the contemptuous and the foolish. It will take up the wise and humble and show them things which it keeps only for their eyes, and which they will never forget. He turned his head from the immaculate brightness which knew no end, down to the earth. This, too, shone, reflecting the power of the sky. He saw a little village on a white road, the red roofs clustering round a tiny market place; what village was it, what kind of people lived there, what were they doing on this clear morning? Because he would never know these things, this was a village of enchantment, a magic ephemerality which he would never find or see again.

He thought about Faruda, over the great curve of the world lying ahead, and a small finger of anticipation touched him. Every journey was a new adventure to which flight was the key. . . . Then his mind jumped inconsequently back to his home and to Carol, and he was ashamed of his happiness which seemed to increase with his distance from them. But soon there would be a difference—there must be a difference.

Kingsley looked out at the motors, then carefully and methodically at the instruments on the engineer's panel. Gleason sat with his arms folded and his eyes closed before it, and he was concentrating on not thinking of Della. They flew on, now high over the central mountains of France which were seamed with deep and narrow valleys like a face marked with years and suffering.

* * *

Sardinia was far behind, the Mediterranean blue and still below—so still that no wind lanes could be seen on the glassy surface, and Barthell found that he could not get a drift sight from this featureless sea which was like a clotted desert beneath their wings; and they flew alone in the centre of an empty azure world that changed from paleness high above to night indigo at the fellow-travelling horizons. It seemed that the sun had burned up everything but their winged cylinder, quelled the sea with a vitreous enamel of its own. Kingsley stood beside the navigator, and a map was spread on the table before them.

Barthell scowled across the gangway at the radio operator and said, " I've been getting fairly good bearings from him for once—and I took a sun shot a few minutes ago, skipper. . . . I don't think we'll have any trouble hitting the coast near Faruda." He placed a thick forefinger on the map. " There she is. Forty minutes to go."

Kingsley nodded, eyeing the map. "We're lucky that visibility is so good. I'm starting to let down soon."

Barthell rummaged in his canvas bag. " Here's the large-scale map of the place. The longer runway is more or less parallel to the coast, practically due east–west. Hope we can see it—if it's not covered with sand."

" So do I hope. Have you got the smoke bomb?"

" All ready. There shouldn't be much wind at all, if the sea here is any guide."

" No, but we'll have the bomb. Let me know when you expect the coast to show up."

" Right. Keep steering one-six-two degrees."

Kingsley resumed his seat. The sun had moved across his sky and hot whiteness stabbed through the windows from the aircraft's starboard bow, but the outside air temperature was below zero. Kingsley turned the elevator control of the auto pilot and the machine tilted her nose in a shallow dive; he watched the airspeed needle creep up the dial.

He thought about the landing, hoping that the runway was safe. They would make a low run over it first—there could be deep sand or obstructions of some sort—and there was nothing like having a good look before you land. It was like jumping on ice, this landing, when you didn't know how thick the ice was. When they were down to three thousand feet Kingsley levelled her out, altering course on Barthell's instructions five degrees to starboard.

He was still trimming the machine level when Barthell called, "Got the coast on the radar screen, skipper. I can see the island off Faruda, dead ahead. You ought to be seeing it any minute."

"Right, Harry. Lester, keep your eyes open—target coming up."

Cummings grunted and stretched himself. "I can hardly wait to clap eyes on this fabulous place." He peered ahead, caressing his moustache. "Wonder what'll be there—the desert sands or a nice new estate of bijou villas for aged Bedouin? What do you expect, skipper?"

"Anything," Kingsley said crisply.

The co-pilot was the first to see the island. It stood off the coast of Africa, brown and kidney-shaped like a new potato in blue water. Behind it the coast lay insubstantially in a bed of haze, a pale irregular line that at first had looked like the shadow of a cloud on the sea. Nearer, the coast resolved itself into grey rocks and cliffs, not very high but dropping sheer to the water. There were no beaches. From the coast an undulating and barren shelf stretched away to hills low and vague in the southern distance. And to Kingsley's surprise they saw the airfield almost at once and without difficulty where a little huddle of sand-smudged buildings stood two or three miles in from the shore.

He said, "I'm doing a left-hand circuit. David—send a signal that we have arrived and are about to land. . . . Ready with the smoke bomb, Harry, but don't drop it until I tell you."

A minute after crossing the coast Kingsley banked the machine in a steep turn to port. Faruda lay impaled on the wing tip, brown and dusty, silent with the stillness of a decay which he could feel even as he looked down upon it.

Staring pop-eyed down the slanting wing Cummings said, " There's the runway, skipper, and a shorter one crossing it."

Kingsley nodded silently. The straight black scar was blurred over with blown sand, but nevertheless unmistakable. The other crossed it near its eastern end, and close to this intersection stood the two or three dusty shacks, the stumpy control tower and the arched roof of a hangar with sand piled at the sides—the buildings which they had seen when first approaching the coast. Faruda looked dirty and forlorn, with a dismal hopelessness about it, as they flew now to the south of the field, and Kingsley felt a sudden pang for Garraud and the other two who were condemned to stay here.

He turned again to port, and all at once Kingsley saw the hidden village and the harbour.

The harbour was very small, with a narrow, dog-leg entrance opening to the north-east, shielded and concealed by fairly high cliffs. A cluster of tiny white houses—not a dozen—fringed its eastern wall, and from the other side a track in a dry valley ran up towards the airfield. Two squat fishing boats were tied up in the harbour, beneath the houses. To the west, between the airfield and the coast, there were some square cultivated fields, a pale track or two, and small plantations of olives or dates. Here, not far from the sea, a big flat-roofed house stood alone, square and with a forbidding greyness, and a high wall with little watch towers at the corners enclosed the house and its courtyard.

" Well, well," Cummings remarked. " Quite a tight little community. Our passengers will have company after all."

" Looks like it." Kingsley trimmed the machine's nose down once more. " It will be Garraud's job to get to know whoever runs the place."

" I expect the locals will turn out for us. Shouldn't be surprised if we make the front page of the *Faruda Times*."

Now they flew westwards, close to the coast, and Kingsley gave the order for the smoke bomb to be dropped. Barthell released it through a small hatch in the floor of the flight deck; he shouted, "Bomb gone!" and Kingsley banked the aircraft hard over, and he saw when they came round again the thick yellowish smoke belching up and drifting very slowly over the field.

"Just a light westerly breeze, skipper."

"Landing to the west, then. I'm doing a low dummy run, then a circuit for landing if it looks all right. Did you get that signal off, David?"

"Yes, skipper. They heard us."

Kingsley took the machine in low over the runway. Sand had washed over it so that its edges were obscure, but the sand was thin and had not piled into drifts on the flat surface, and the broken white line along the runway's centre was still faintly visible.

"It looks all right, eh, Lester? Everybody strapped in—stewardess too? Right. . . . Well, here we go."

When they came down-wind the machine had climbed again and was at a thousand feet.

"All set?" Kingsley turned back to the engineer. "Okay, Bob, wheels down, revs. up to twenty-seven hundred. Boosters on, Lester."

The machine jerked painfully as Gleason moved the undercarriage lever, and the landing wheels dropped from their housing in the wings to hang huge and black beneath the inboard motors. Green lights flashed on the engineer's panel. Gleason sat motionless, watching the panel, his face still. He said, without turning his head, "Wheels down and locked, skipper. Revs. twenty-seven hundred."

"Flap twenty-five."

"Flap twenty-five," Gleason repeated.

The drumming of the motors mounted to a threatening pitch, and as the air flaps came out speed was suddenly checked as though the air in which they flew had congealed about them. Kingsley trimmed the nose down and turned for the end of the runway, losing height. For one desperate moment he could see only sand under her nose, but then there was the blurred scar coming up towards him, a little to the left. Was there ever a runway which didn't look dangerously short on the approach? Faruda's was no exception.

"Full revs. Full flap."

The motors screamed as Gleason opened the pitch levers wide, and speed decreased again as the flaps came full out. The runway came at them, rushing up to the machine's nose. It seemed that they must fly right into it when Kingsley snapped the throttles shut and pulled back firmly on the stick. There was that curious floating sensation, the ground rushing below, and he pulled again and a terrible squeal came from the tyres and there was only a little bump and then they were rolling along, slowing, and the pale sand was all round them like a brown still sea.

As they taxied back down the runway Cummings reached forward and retrieved the mangy foot from the window shelf.

* * *

A solid heat blasted at them from the sky and up from the crackling sand, and the air was still, fiery.

In the shadow of the aircraft's tail they ate a meal which the stewardess had cooked in the galley, sitting on boxes and the folding chairs which had been brought in the cargo. The food was ready almost as soon as the motors had been cut off, and Susan Wells served the eight men with an unhurried deftness. It was a good meal, Kingsley thought, prepared under conditions that might well have defeated some women. But if the stewardess had been at all concerned over its preparation she showed no sign of it. The Frenchmen, apart from Tarollier who ate noisily and said little, were gallantly appreciative, lamenting the impending departure of so admirable and attractive a cook. There was even sadness in Richer's deep, bright eyes as they rested upon the girl's calm face.

As soon as he had finished eating Garraud stood up, looking at the silver bulk of the machine above his head, and a sudden urgency seemed to gather itself in his small frame, giving it an appearance of sinewy readiness.

"I would like to begin the unloading, captain—now." He spoke quietly and firmly, smiling. "If we might have a little assistance from one or two of your crew. . . ."

"Well, it's scarcely our job to unload stores," Kingsley said doubtfully. This was a point which seemed to have been overlooked even by the tidy-minded Rogers.

"We might as well lend a hand, skipper," Gleason said, eyeing Garraud. "There's no sense in wasting time here."

"Include me," Barthell said deeply.

"Ah—thank you, gentlemen. You wish to go as soon as possible, eh?" Garraud swept a hand round the silent, baking desert. "It is no wonder."

"Nothing to stay here for," Cummings agreed. "I'll help."

"And who's going to help Miss Wells?" Tarrant asked suddenly.

"You are," Kingsley said. "Get this stuff back into the galley, David."

Tarrant rose at once and the stewardess looked at him briefly and without enthusiasm as he began to help her gather the used crockery together. Inside the galley he piled it carefully beside the tiny aluminium sink. The sun's fierce blaze coming through the window above the cooker filled the compartment with a tight and cruel heat; the very air was scorched to a suspended, almost unbreathable ash. He looked round the galley appreciatively, seeing its ordered and utilitarian brightness, its collected and unobtrusive efficiency. Just the place for Miss Wells.

"You needn't stay if you don't wish to," the girl said briskly as she brought in the last tray. "There isn't much to do."

"There'll be less if I help," Tarrant said reasonably.

She looked at him with round, doubting eyes. He was young, she thought, fair and downy and immature, with a wide pink face that would reflect every motion of his mind; a young man happy because he had not yet considered sadness or fear or disappointment, sound and healthy in construction. His hands were almost chubby, but strong, with short square-tipped fingers. Each thumb was short and flat as though it had been hit with a hammer.

She said, and all at once her voice was kinder, "Thank you, Mr. Tarrant." Her face was pale, as if all the blood had been squeezed from it into a single pucker of redness where the mouth was, and her nostrils were dilated.

Tarrant stared at her. "You're feeling the heat?" he asked, knowing that she was, yet wondering if she would deny it.

"A little. It's very hot—I'm not really used to it yet."

"Why don't you sit in the shade outside? You'll get more air. I'll fix these things. . . ."

"No—thank you." She swung almost fiercely to face him. "This is *my* job. I can do it."

"Yes, but if you're not feeling well. . . ."

"I am quite all right now, Mr. Tarrant," she said, deliberate with finality. "Shall we get on with the work?"

A perverse child, Tarrant thought as he turned on the hot water, like so many of these stewardesses. If only they weren't so consciously conscientious, if they wouldn't encase themselves in this hard glaze of efficiency with which they tried to hide inexperience. . . . He sighed; she was a pretty new stewardess. He supposed that she would learn in time.

Garraud, Richer and Tarollier were soon busy in the cabin, unloading the cargo with the aid of the small crane inside the freight doors. They moved quickly, and Garraud had a little, set smile of ferocious satisfaction on his face. On the dusty and decayed concrete below Barthell stepped lightly and in silence, and Gleason and Cummings sweated in the sun to remove the stores to a dump a few yards away, the co-pilot keeping up a steady and monotonous grumbling. Kingsley had watched them for a time, and now he let his eyes roam over the scorched and featureless plain upon which the airfield lay.

Faruda's desolation was complete. He had parked the machine on the sandy apron at the end of the runway, not far from the crumbling ruin which had once been the airfield's control tower. From here the sea was out of sight, hidden by a great field of sand dunes; there was no vegetation but some scattered tufts of pale grasses with pointed tubular blades, each tuft sitting upon its own little hillock of sand in desperate defiance of the desert's erosion. To the south the sand was hard and flat, a dun plain reaching to a ridge of low hills in the shimmering distance. Kingsley could feel the heat of the ground coming up through the soles of his shoes, and when he looked at them he saw that they were already powdered whitely from the dust.

It seemed that in the way of architecture Faruda, like wartime airfields all over the world, had not been particularly fortunate if what was left of its buildings was a fair sample of the whole. Nearest to the apron stood the tower; beside this and a little behind it, close to the dunes, three low, bleached huts in varying stages of decay appeared to be sinking into the sand, and to one side the hangar humped its metal back. One or two dusty concrete bases showed where other erections had once been and the body of a rusted petrol pump, like a sun-fossilized man, still leaned in eternal muted conference with the sand; nothing else but the brassy sky and the heat-flayed and pulverous carcase of the earth beneath it.

He lit his pipe and walked across to the control tower. It scarcely deserved the name tower, he thought, for it was only two storeys high, squat and grey and decayed. The doors were missing and the metal stairway to the upper floor had come away from the walls and lay uselessly in the sand. Inside the two windowless lower rooms sand was piled thickly: was it from these gritty caverns that this field had been directed, its loaded machines sent out to bomb and strafe the enemy? All at once the empty silence depressed Kingsley, and at that moment he could not imagine that this had ever been a busy peopled place, or ever would be again. The three surviving huts a little way off seemed to be in fairly good condition, though without windows or doors, but the hangar was no more than a curved rusty roof, its holes making strange patterns of sunlight on the sanded floor.

Kingsley left the hangar. Now that he had satisfied some of his curiosity about the place he was ready to go home. He would have liked to see the harbour and village, but there was not time. Approaching the apron he looked at his machine standing beside the growing pile of stores which it had disgorged, and it was the only live and friendly thing in sight; it waited, blinding silver, strength amid wreckage, and to him beauty in ugliness. Suddenly he thought, what if she were to fail us, to strand us here? He felt then that there would be no escape from Faruda, that they would be rooted here always on the hem of a desert. No one would come, ever. Of all the world's places Kingsley had seen, it seemed that Faruda was the most undiscoverable and the farthest from home.

It struck him then how brooding, how silent and empty the place was. It was now nearly two hours since they had landed. He guessed that the village was no more than two or three miles away, and yet nobody had appeared, not a single curious native; outside their own, no life of any kind was apparent in Faruda.

Could anyone be watching, from the shelter of the dunes? He looked towards them, but the crumpled hillocks were void and lifeless under the heat-enamelled sky.

Kingsley moved his shoulders impatiently—there would be a simple enough explanation, he told himself. None the less there was something almost threatening in the awful silence of Faruda—the silence which he had first noticed and which had so depressed him at the control tower. . . .

Barthell's shirt was sticking in dark patches of sweat to his broad back. He had been working. Whenever Harry did anything, Kingsley thought, he put his heart and soul into it. The navigator said, " That's nearly all, skipper. Full of enthusiasm, this Garraud."

" Looks like it." Kingsley watched the darting little Frenchman in the cargo doorway. " He doesn't seem to want to delay us."

Barthell damned Faruda with a glance. " He's welcome to this dump. I was stationed in a place like this once, and I've still got the scars."

The last sling of cases was out, and Tarollier and Richer descended the ladder from the cargo doors. Garraud's voice came to them from somewhere inside the cabin.

" I am just making sure everything is out," he called.

In a short time he appeared at the door and came down the ladder. He stood in front of Kingsley, mopping carefully at his forehead which had the point of black hair in the middle.

" It is all unloaded, captain. We need not detain you any longer."

" Do you want any help to stow this stuff under tarpaulins? We could . . ."

" No, no. It is nothing. We shall put the tents up now."

" All right. These buildings are not in very good shape, of course, but you may be able to use one of the huts. You'll be fixing the radio up soon?" Kingsley paused. " You have your arms too in case anything . . ."

" Yes, captain, we have our arms." Garraud spoke sharply, as though the subject was scarcely worth discussion. " And

Richer here will see to the radio at once. We shall be all right."

Kingsley looked at him narrowly. This man Garraud—yet again he seemed to have changed. Since they had arrived here he had been nervous, though showing a new touch of command, almost of contempt, in his manner. The gold tooth remained covered. Richer stood behind him, silent, stooping a little, and now he was wearing an old khaki sweater which clung tightly to his spare body; how could anyone bear a sweater in this heat? Kingsley wondered. And why had Richer lied about the briefcase in the plane over France? He gazed directly at the Frenchman, and Richer's eyes were bright and level on his own, but telling him nothing. In the background Tarollier hung about awkwardly, still morosely silent.

"Well, if there is nothing more we can do, we'll go now," Kingsley said. He glanced at his watch. "We ought to be well over France before it gets dark."

"Good." Garraud paused, and then he said, "So you expect to be back here on the twenty-sixth?"

"Yes—five days from now, at about the same time."

"The twenty-sixth," Richer said, as though repeating a lesson.

Garraud shook hands all round and the two others followed with that punctiliousness which the French observe on every greeting and parting. "Thank you, gentlemen, and you, m'selle." His voice was quiet, solemn. "I am happy to have met you. Goodbye."

"*Au revoir,* we hope. See you in five days."

Now that the big shell of the cabin was empty Kingsley thought that it looked like that of another machine and not the voided body of trusty old Peter Fox. The petrol smell was stronger now, and there was a damp smear of spirit on the floor near the tail. No smoking on the way back, either. With an empty machine Kingsley expected to be able to reach Westonmills with plenty of fuel and there ought to be no need to land in France. He was suddenly very glad to be going; and they would all have had enough flying for one day by the time they got home.

She started easily when Gleason pressed the buttons, as though anxious to go herself, and the familiar throaty growl of the motors as they taxied to the end of the runway was a reassurance and a promise of home. Kingsley moved the stick and the controls felt taut and good as elevators and ailerons responded, and Gleason ran up his engines quickly, sending great roaring clouds of sand to swirl away in the brittle air.

And then, on the take-off, the roar of the motors became a scream and a huge wind pounded at their metal shell as the machine bounded forward. From his window Barthell had a flashing view of their late passengers waving beside the pile of boxes, but it seemed that between the others Garraud had his hand up, motionless, in some kind of awkward salute. Suddenly the runway was gone, and turning on to their north-westerly course they saw again the little village and the harbour, and above these the big walled house that was like a guarding fortress.

They climbed in the sun above the sea, faster now because the load was gone, and soon the pale rim of Africa had dissolved behind them.

*   *   *

The evening was well advanced when they flew in over Marseilles. Down by the harbour the tall pale houses were washed in rosiness from the late sun so that they looked like the pink buildings of some old Moroccan town, and the hills behind were grey and pink too, ready for the night. Westward the great low arc of the Languedoc coast swept away towards Spain, an arm cradling the flat sea. The air was smooth, and there was no cloud.

Kingsley looked down at the coast and at the level plain of the Rhône delta, the Arles canal an unswerving furrow in the plain. He yawned, stretching.

"I remember lobbing down here about the end of forty-four," Cummings remarked. "Istres it was. All busted up —Jerry hadn't left two bricks stuck together. A few Huns had been captured and were patching the place up. A tough little Aussie was in charge of them, and though he was less than half the size of the smallest prisoner they were all scared to hell of him. *Les girls* were set up in a big house on the way to the village. . . ."

"Convenient," Kingsley put in, grinning.

"Never had time, myself. They seemed to be carrying on business as usual—such old-established professions survive wars and foreign occupation with no trouble at all." Cummings stopped abruptly, feeling his pockets, his great whiskers drooping lower with every movement of his hands. He swore quietly and then said, "I've lost the foot. It's gone."

"Just as well," Kingsley said shortly.

"It must have dropped from my pocket while I was helping with those blasted stores." The co-pilot's face was taut, his eyes more protuberant than ever. "This is bad, skipper. . . ."

Kingsley laughed. "Don't be a fool, Lester. We'll do all right without it."

"That's what you think. But I'm damned sure something will go wrong now."

Cummings stared down moodily at the fading land. Looking at him Kingsley was surprised to see the pale wash of unfeigned alarm on the co-pilot's face, and now even his flaming hair seemed to be less stridently coloured. Kingsley was annoyed with himself then, because something unbelieved and yet strangely potent had communicated itself to him. He turned his mind from it, turned it ahead and homeward as they flew on in their vain attempt to outpace the night's stealthy westward creeping.

"How's fuel, Bob?" he asked presently.

Gleason said, "All right, skipper. Enough to get home and an hour over. All motors behaving."

"Fine. David, send a signal that we're not stopping to refuel, but going home. No, wait a minute—what's the E.T.A., Harry?"

"Twenty-two twenty-five, Greenwich. Two and a half hours to go."

"Weather at Westonmills?"

"Fine now. Rain's stopped and there is only three-tenths cloud, visibility fifteen miles."

"All right, David, start sending."

Tarrant adjusted his dials and began tapping at the morse key with rapid flowing movements of his wrist. The engineer watched Tarrant's hand on the key for a moment before turning back to his panel. The rows and blocks of dials and switches and lights flickered and quivered and spoke their strange language. The small table beneath them was a sounding board for the heart and lungs of the machine, and by touching it and listening he could feel and hear every small tremor and pulse and sway of the metal thing which bore him in its hollow belly. Well, not just a thing. She had a heart, after all. She . . . No, aeroplanes were not women, although sometimes they had woman's unexpectedness and perversity, woman's capacity for raising the trivial to heights of dangerous importance, such as when a tiny fuse blew and you didn't know whether your wheels were locked down or not. But most of the time they were more reliable and less demanding than any woman.

Gleason tapped his teeth with a pencil; his fine and regular face was contracted, still faintly doubting. In a little more than three hours he would be back, back with Della. He wondered what she had been doing. It was likely that she had spent much of the day in bed; there was no doubt that Della was at her best in bed, and this ought to have been the attainment of most women but wasn't. Some were at their best in bars, on horseback, humiliating their friends, rearing children or in the kitchen. What would Della be like in a kitchen? He had never seen her in one, and somehow he didn't think that she would look at home against a background of pots and cookers and sinks and dishcloths. The thought made him pause. It was only a clamorous, ready passion with Della, but it was a kind he had never known before and had come to need. He wanted nothing else from her, and he knew that he did not deserve anything else. It was enough now; it would not always be enough, but it was such that no future doubt could scratch its hard and sufficient texture. What else had women to offer, or he to give?

In the co-pilot's seat Cummings roused himself from a surly contemplation of the evening. "Hell, I'm tired," he said, closing his eyes. "And I feel as sticky as a new fly-paper. That Faruda—all heat and sand. Strange that none of the locals turned out." He opened his eyes and stared down at the valley stretching away dimly to the north. In the fading light it seemed very far below.

"Glad we're safe up here," Kingsley said. "We might have

been stuck there with a sand-filled motor or some such. I wonder how they're getting on?"

"The Frogs? Friend Garraud will be pushing the other two around, I expect. An enthusiast for toil, that one. I hope he picks up Flo's foot."

Kingsley grunted. "He didn't want to keep us. I don't know, but he seemed different, somehow, after we got to Faruda. Notice it?"

"Can't say I did. He looked all right to me, but I was busy, anyway."

"I don't know what to make of him, or of Richer and his non-existent briefcase. They're a queer lot. . . . Well, if anyone is going to use Faruda again it will take a lot of knocking into shape."

Cummings nodded sleepily, looking at his watch. "Over two long hours to go. Ain't flying hell?"

Kingsley smiled. "Think so?"

"Well—sometimes. It's a job, and sometimes all jobs are hell."

The stewardess came to the flight deck and began to hand round coffee, smiling impersonally at each man. The Cevennes loomed ahead, dark in the lee of the sunset, and all the western sky was aflame with the funeral pyre of day.

There was no warning before the explosion.

It travelled along the machine in a dark shock of sound and hit them there on the flight deck so that they sat momentarily frozen in whatever movement they had been making. It sounded to Kingsley as though a gun had gone off above his head, but somehow he knew that it was from the tail. The aircraft gave a horrible fluttering convulsion and seemed to pause in its flight with a tired, sickening indecision. And then the nose fell slowly, and Kingsley could hear a new noise, a strange distant roaring like water falling. He heard a pallid Cummings say "God! What's happened?" and instinctively he grabbed at the control column and pulled.

It moved uselessly in his hands, an awful flabbiness in the feel of it, and the nose fell further, bringing nearer the death-quiet valley below.

CHAPTER IV

HOME

SOMEBODY was yelling hoarsely.

"What is it? What's hit us?"

Again Kingsley pulled back desperately on the stick. Above the new roaring that flooded the machine, a jangling voice. . . . "I don't know. Hold on. . . ."

A sudden dreadful calm fell upon them, and nobody spoke or moved. Must get her nose up, Kingsley thought wildly, or we're done, but the awful looseness of the controls made sick fear well up from his stomach to his dry mouth, to his brain, and in it reason was drowning. This dive—he had no command over it. The finger grips felt like icicles in his hands. Beside him Cummings crouched, white-faced, clutching the padded crash guard. The stewardess was in the gangway between Tarrant's place and the navigator, and she was holding with one hand to a bracket by the radio, the other stretched out before her as though to push something away, her knees bent. Kingsley's mind plunged with his machine into a vault of madness, screaming that this was the end for them all unless the unresponsive thing in his hands could carry its message to the elevators. The dive was steep, a long dive, unalterable. And now the ground seemed very close, so that there would not be long to wait. . . .

But then, suddenly, something happened. It was as though a great hand came up from below, lifting them back into the sky. As the stick came fully back into Kingsley's stomach the machine ceased its terrible downward slide and slowly the nose began to move upward, up to the black horizon. Kingsley held the stick hard into him, body straining against the safety belt which he had automatically clipped on when the dive started. Still the nose moved up.

As the first shock of fear began to recede within him he found that he had some strange and casual control over the attitude of the machine, but there was a horrible elastic slackness in its response to the stick and the response came only reluctantly and without certainty, long after he had called for it. The rudder seemed all right. Now the nose was almost up to the horizon again and he reached out and pulled back the throttles, reducing speed.

Swallowing, he attempted words. "Is everybody all right?" The question mocked him as they replied in the strained voices of strangers. They were safe only for this moment; but afterwards . . .? His heart convulsed, shrank, clutching at the present's flimsy levels beyond which could be the final drop of death.

"I think I've got her now." Got her—with this loose, futile thing? "It was in the tail. . . . Stewardess, strap yourself in the spare seat—don't go back to the galley."

Tarrant put a shaking hand to the bruise over his eye which he had got from the transmitter when the explosion hit them. As the stewardess passed him he looked up and said, "You're all right, aren't you?" His eyes were dull, vaguely curious on her.

She made a stiff nod, pale face jerking oddly.

"We'll get down safely," he said. He didn't believe it, and he was so frightened that his tongue could scarcely form the words. "Strap up tight." She nodded again without speaking and went back to the seat just inside the cabin door. Gleason was perfectly still before his instrument panel, staring at it with a kind of stunned fascination; it gave no sign that there was anything wrong.

Kingsley called over his shoulder, "I want one of you to go back and see what's happened. We may be able to do something. . . ."

A wait. Then, "I'll go, skipper."

Barthell slid from his seat and went back into the cabin. Silent, they watched him go and he stepped warily, like a man walking in darkness on an unknown way. The machine was now solidly level, flying on as if nothing had happened, but still the new roaring shook and threatened it from behind. Kingsley saw that they had dropped more than four thousand feet. He turned his head.

"She's flying," he said wonderingly. "She's still flying."

Nobody else spoke, as though one more sound could shatter life's fragility. It seemed a long time before Barthell returned and stood beside Kingsley. His strong face was stained with a sickly pallor.

"It's near the tail." His voice shook. "There's a great hole in the side—starboard side, where the petrol was."

"The controls—what's making them so slack?"

"The crank to the elevators. . . . It's bent, and the pivot with the control rod is loose."

Kingsley tasted a filthy sourness. "Is she going to hold—hold together?"

"I think so." Barthell did not think so, but there was nothing to be gained by adding to the fears of the crew his own sick foreboding. "Better go in at Istres, skipper."

"We'll try. Can we do anything back there?"

"Don't believe we can. I tried the crank and although the pivot is loose I don't think it will come out. The split pin has held."

Kingsley drew a long, whistling breath. "So long as the tail doesn't fall off," he muttered. "Now—everybody at emergency stations, and prepare for crash drill." He felt better as he gave the orders. "See the stewardess is strapped tight, and tell her not to worry. David! Call up Istres—tell them we're in trouble and are trying to get in. Top priority."

Tarrant shook himself and reached for his microphone. Would she turn? Kingsley wondered. There was no time to waste—turn slowly, to save strain on the tail, and let down. Slowly. . . . The machine came round obediently on rudder and ailerons, came fully about so that they now flew southward, aiming at the dusky plain that spread from the river. Closer now and yet still so far away, on solid earth which they must soon meet with killing force or with gentleness, the snapping red pundit light of Istres issued its mocking and bloody invitation.

When the crash drill had been carried out and the emergency escape hatches opened they all sat silent, tense as the straps that held them, men hanging on a fraying rope above a dark and merciless pit, borne precariously by the torn and twisted body of the stricken machine. Once it gave an unaccountable and nauseous lurch downward, like a small boat dropping suddenly into the trough of a wave, and then straightened painfully, flying on.

Istres was waiting, and they knew that all the grisly accoutrements of rescue would be there—the fire engines and ambulances and crash teams. Into Kingsley's fear-softened mind came the memory of how he had watched these lining up beside the runways of more than one airfield, waiting for machines in trouble to land. Now, he thought, it is my turn, my responsibility. . . . It was suddenly necessary that he should look at his crew. He turned his head and saw their set, glaucous faces—strange, deranged faces of men he knew, who were relying on him, as they must, trusting in what he had to give.

He prayed that it would be enough, that the tail would hold and the elevators respond for a few more precious minutes.

He dared not risk flying round the airfield to use up fuel. He must land—if he could—for soon it would be quite dark and he must use what light was left. He tried to thrust the terrible thought of fire from his mind. . . . The slipstream was rushing through the hole in the tail with the distant, menacing roar of a Niagara, building up a pressure which might tear off that fragile and shuddering plane as the autumn wind would tear a leaf from a tree. Now the airfield was close. All other machines had been held off so that they would have an unobstructed landing. Kingsley saw that they were down to three thousand feet—he would make just one more turn for a long run in from the east, a judged final run. There would be no second chance.

Again she turned without difficulty, wheels and flaps down to reduce speed. In the gathering darkness he saw the runway ahead, now picked out by two rows of lights, like some great wide street leading to the afterglow of the fallen sun. As they flew at it the street seemed to come to them very slowly, drifting up with a lazy casualness that belied its terrible importance. Kingsley's hands were slippery on the stick, and he rubbed his palms, one at a time, hard on the material of his trousers. Nearly there.

"We're going in!" His shout was harsh, tuned to the clamour of the motors, as though they had howled the words. But he felt strangely calm and detached now, as if outside himself, watching the trial of another. The motors whipped themselves, screaming, to full revs.

"Hold on. . . . Power off—OFF!"

Gleason jerked back the throttles. The engines sobbed in strangulation, propellers windmilling. The big machine floated, hovering between the lights like a silver, blinded bird feeling for earth. They had a glimpse of fire engines and ambulances lined up as if for inspection. . . . Kingsley pulled smoothly and strongly at the stick but he was an instant late and the machine flew on, down into the runway. There was a fierce shocking crack like wood splintering and it still went on, forward and downward, then a huge screaming and a kind of tearing shudder. He saw a shower of red and white sparks from the propellers and his body was snatched harshly forward against the safety belt as the machine slewed to the left. It skidded for what seemed minutes on end and then all at once became still, quietly, as though it had had enough and wanted only to rest. Involuntarily Kingsley reached out and snapped off the ignition switches.

Within seconds they were all out, standing vacantly in a gesticulating crowd. Already they found it difficult to remember exactly what had happened. It had all been so quick. Apart from Tarrant's bruised head they were uninjured; but Peter Fox was not.

She was a silent wreck. As he looked at her Kingsley felt a sense of pain and loss which shocked him with its intensity; it was like being parted from an old and well-tried friend.

The undercarriage had collapsed, and now the wheels lay splayed out unnaturally behind the wings. The belly of the machine was torn and ragged underneath where it had been gashed open as it skidded along the concrete. The propeller tips, biting into the ground, were bent back at right angles like some strange agricultural tools.

And right aft, on the starboard side below the tail plane, gaped the great hole that the explosion had made, a hole nearly big enough for a truck to pass through, and inside were the shattered and twisted ribs of the broken thing, loose wires and torn skin, and a dark petrol-smelling silence. The front wall of the galley had been flattened backward like a piece of cardboard. That the whole tail had not come off in the air was something against all probability or reason. She had been true to the end, Kingsley thought; she had not burned, she had got them down alive and had died herself in the achievement.

Even Cummings was silent, watching the smashed carcase beside the runway, knowing that this was no time to tell them what he knew. Soon the warm darkness came, covering the field.

* * *

"Tell me about it," Rogers said. "But take your time."

Kingsley nodded, pulling hard on his pipe. "You rang my wife, Don?"

"Yes, and the rest of them. I told her you'd landed in France for re-fuelling and were staying the night." Rogers paused, his face a shining pink roundness sitting on a white collar. "I didn't say anything about trouble."

"Just as well, I suppose," Kingsley said, frowning. His bony features were even more solemn than usual as he looked through the window. Outside the operations manager's little office the early afternoon sun lay warm and bright over Westonmills, just as it had on the day they set out for Faruda; was it only yesterday? It seemed long, long ago.

He told Rogers about Faruda, about the explosion, about the landing at Istres. Rogers leaned back in his chair, his legs crossed and a foot jigging restlessly, and his eyes never left the captain's face.

At last Kingsley said, "So that was it. They flew us back this morning, and here we are. Mission completed, as the Americans say, but not quite according to plan."

"I'm damned glad to see you all safe, anyway," Rogers said slowly. "I heard Marseilles radio put out some story that you were all believed killed. I don't know how they got that, but you've had a hell of a shaking. . . ."

"I was a second late in holding her off. I couldn't tell when the elevators were going to respond or even if they'd answer at all."

"Never mind. It was damn good work to get her down as you did, Bill." Rogers seemed to hesitate, shifting the little silver model aeroplane which stood on his desk. "But Peter Fox appears to be a complete write-off, except for the engines. Losing a machine is a serious matter for the

Company, and there'll be an inquiry and so forth later, of course. . . ."

"I know." Kingsley made smoke. "I'm sorry, Don."

Rogers smiled painfully. "My dear chap, it's certainly not your fault. What we have to discover is the cause of this explosion, if we can. It *was* an explosion, I suppose? Now what's your idea?"

Kingsley had been standing by the window, and now he moved round the desk and sat down beside Rogers.

"Well, naturally I hadn't time to inspect her properly, and anyway that's a job for the accident people. But I do think we can rule out any external cause—another aircraft hitting us, gunfire, or something like that—and so I can only assume that it must have been an explosion, inside. And the petrol was stowed there."

"Was anybody smoking, at any time?"

"No—I can vouch for that. I forbade all smoking both on the way out and back, and you know how easy it is to spot tobacco smoke in an aircraft. That's out."

"All right. Now, did you notice anything about the petrol cans at Faruda, or on the way out?"

"There was a faint smell of petrol all the time. When we had unloaded at Faruda I saw a smear of petrol on the floor in the tail, and the smell was a bit stronger than it had been on the trip. I can only assume that a can was leaking and some petrol had penetrated beneath the floor and perhaps collected in the fuselage well. It's possible that a spark might have been made by friction from one of the control rods. . . . That might have caused the explosion."

"I don't know. It's just possible, of course," Rogers said doubtfully. He twiddled the little aeroplane in his fingers. "All the cans were properly stowed, under my supervision. It's inevitable that they would smell a little, of course. and not impossible that one might spring a leak. It's this ignition business that worries me. A spark—now, just where would a spark come from? Well-greased control rods don't make sparks, Bill."

"It was just a theory. I don't know what else to suggest."

"No. . . . Well, I shall be going out to Istres as soon as

I can to have a look at her myself. There isn't much we can do until then."

"You know, Don," Kingsley said suddenly, "things haven't worked out all that well on this charter, have they?" He laughed shortly. "Cummings lost his precious rabbit's foot for the first time at Faruda, and he thinks that's the cause of all the trouble.... Well, this is the first time I've ever lost an aircraft."

"And it will probably be the last. Don't worry about it."

Easy enough to say that, Kingsley thought. He felt unhappy and ashamed. After a time he said, "Those passengers—strange lot."

"How?"

"Well—Garraud—I don't know what to make of him. I thought he seemed anxious for us to leave Faruda, as though we were an embarrassment to him there. His manner was always changing.... And on the way out Richer came to the flight deck with some story about losing a briefcase...."

"He had no briefcase. I asked him."

"I know. It sounded like an excuse to try to find out if anyone had come to Westonmills for him after we'd left."

"No one came as far as I know."

Kingsley lifted his shoulders. "Well—I don't know what it's all about.... Anyway, what's the programme for us now?"

"This crack-up will delay any return trip to Faruda for a bit, of course. You won't be sorry to have a few days off, I expect. By—let's see—by the twenty-seventh, if I hurry up the engineers, Peter Easy should be ready, and you can take her then. So we'll say the twenty-seventh, provisionally. You can all have leave until she's ready."

"Survivors' leave, eh? But—Peter Easy!" Kingsley groaned in mock despair. "That old crate is always misbehaving herself—seizing bearings or bursting oil pipes or something. Can't we have another?"

Rogers grinned at him. "Sorry, Bill. She's all we've got for the job."

"Oh, well.... Let's hope the bitch isn't going sour on the twenty-seventh. We shan't get away with it if *she* blows up." Kingsley sighed. "Poor old Peter Fox."

"Yes—she was one of our best kites. I was fond of her too."

"By the way, have you had any signals from Faruda?"

"Oh, yes." Rogers picked up a message pad. "We had one this morning, but I shouldn't think we'll be getting any more as it isn't their job to report to us. They're all okay, and Garraud is about to start the survey work. It was very short and to the point. We acknowledged it."

"Did you tell them about our—our little mishap?"

"No. We don't want it advertised, and it won't do them any good to know. If they haven't heard before you can break the news when you make your return trip." Rogers looked directly at Kingsley. "Are you sure you're all right, Bill, and the others? What about the stewardess?"

"She's a cool young woman. She says she's ready for another trip any time."

"Um. . . . You've had a bit of a shake-up, you know. If you don't feel like doing Faruda again I can recall Barker from leave."

"You'll do no such thing, Don. We're perfectly all right, and anyway we have a few days to get over it."

"Okay, if you're sure. I'd like you to do it again if you can, of course, because you know the place now." Rogers rose from his chair with a heavy movement. "Well, I'll see you on the twenty-seventh, unless anything unexpected happens in the meantime."

"Will you be going to Istres before then?"

"Don't know yet. I've a lot to do just now, so I wouldn't think so."

Kingsley nodded, rising. "Right, Don."

"Have a good rest, mind."

"Oh, I will. But it will be long enough for me to be on the ground."

"By the way," Rogers said. "When is the baby due?"

"A bit under three weeks." Kingsley hesitated. "Er—any chance of being at home then?"

"Well, it's difficult to forecast." Rogers looked up, stroking his chin and smiling knowingly. "But we'll try, Bill. Babies aren't always on time, you know, but we'll try."

Suddenly Kingsley wished that he hadn't asked about being

home. It sounded foolish now. He went out slowly into the sunshine. From the nearest hangar an engine-less Peter Easy poked out her blunt nose at him with a motionless and silent derision.

*   *   *

Driving home he was wondering uneasily if Carol might have guessed that something more than what Rogers had told her was the reason why he had not returned the previous night. He didn't want to tell her the real cause—not now. Perhaps it might be in the papers, but it wasn't often that Carol read the papers.

She was sitting in the garden in a deck chair, and the maid had placed tea ready on a small table beside her. She looked up at him as he bent to kiss her, a slow and achromatic smile touching her straight mouth, and she said, " Hello, Bill. I waited for you."

" That's fine." He sat down on the opposite side of the table, regarding the tea things with a solemn appreciation. " How are you feeling, Carol?"

" All right. A lot better than I felt in the winter."

He knew how she had felt in the winter. The garden was quiet, and at the bottom a bank of limes in new leaf hid the village housing estate's raw brick. Kingsley took the cup from her and stirred the tea. It was very weak tea, he thought, just as Carol liked it.

He said, " We're lucky. This is the best time of the year to be having a baby."

" Oh, yes. I couldn't bear it in the cold weather." She made a wry face, and he saw a tiny muscle jumping in her cheek. You would have to bear it, he thought, his mind smarting under a sudden annoyance; other women can, and are glad to. She raised her cup in a thin hand and when she put it down it banged on the saucer so hard that he expected it to break.

" It was after eleven when Captain Rogers rang up last night," she said in an injured tone. " I thought it was you. Were you all right?"

Kingsley's bony jaw moved for a second before the words came.

"Yes, we were all right. We landed at Istres—for petrol. There was a snag on the machine and I decided to stay the night. I'm sorry, Carol, but . . ."

"It doesn't matter. You're back now. Where did you go?"

"A place called Faruda, on the North African coast. Pretty desolate. It's an old war-time airfield which may be opening up again, and we took some people out to survey it." He saw that she was watching him as he spoke, her eyes bright with a kind of strained and flickering interest. Was it interest, at last? The pale mobility of her fine, regular features all at once touched some raw nerve within him and he said flatly, "I haven't got the right job for you, have I, Carol?"

She gave a little surprised laugh.

"What do you mean? It's a good job, and you like it."

"But you don't. You're not really interested in it, and this isn't your kind of life."

He noticed the pause before she said, "Not one I would choose, perhaps."

"No." He smiled faintly; she had always been frank. The sun was pleasantly warm, so different from Faruda's torrid glare. "Unfortunately I don't know how to earn a living any other way."

"And you wouldn't want to, Bill. But there's no need. . . ."

"I know all about that," he burst out. "But I've got to do it. I can't be kept, living on your money."

"Of course not," she said soothingly. "It's just that—that you're always dashing off, and half the time I've no idea when you'll be back. There's no permanence, no security about it." A lot of little parallel lines appeared on her forehead. "Sometimes it seems as though we're in some strange, uncertain state which is neither marriage nor single life, but a kind of uneasy suspension between. It doesn't suit me, I'm afraid."

"You're too much alone," he said, and he was suddenly gentle. "But things will be different soon."

"I hope so." The words were unsure; then she smiled. "Well, I couldn't imagine you being tied to some office chair, my dear. Nine to five, the morning paper and a rolled umbrella isn't in your line."

"Scarcely." He hesitated. "I don't think I could be an

employee, not in the usual sense. I know I'm one now, but only when I'm at the field. Once we're away I'm the boss until we come back. It has its advantages, Carol. I get plenty of time off. . . ."

"That always seems to make it worse," she said, touching her hair with a flaccid, unnecessary gesture. "When I've got used to your being here and everything has become settled and nicely regulated you're away again. How long is it this time?"

"Five days, then Faruda again." Five days seemed a long time. Kingsley looked round the well-kept garden and at the low, pleasant house with its flagged terrace and wistaria-hung walls. Everything was here—every material thing, but not that something else which he seemed able to reach only when he was away; it was something essential to his life, and it was not here. Perhaps, one day, he might learn the secret of bringing it with him, bringing it home.

The church clock chimed four, its slow, cracked *bongs* floating over the trees from the village; and distantly then, the sound of the airfield.

"Drink your tea," Carol said coaxingly. "It's getting cold."

He murmured an apology and tasted the cool, weak liquid. He looked down at his uniform and it seemed out of place here, and he promised himself that he would change immediately after tea.

"Would you like to go anywhere tonight?" he asked.

"I'm a little too big to go out now," she said, glancing down and smiling faintly. "No—I think I'd rather stay at home."

All at once Kingsley's mind went back to the previous evening, to those terrible minutes in the staggering machine above the valley of the Rhône, the valley which might have been death. His head dropped and he began to feel tired with a creeping mental and physical numbness which was strange to him. Perhaps five days wouldn't seem so long after all; perhaps he needed them.

"Yes, we'll stay at home," he said.

A small cloud had covered the sun when they got up to go into the house. Inside the french windows leading to the lounge they stopped for a minute, as though by some mutual and expected compulsion, and Kingsley saw his wife. She was slim and tall, her body bowed a little to the child's weight so that her pregnancy was less noticeable than it might have been, her light brown hair smooth and curling at the ends. She looked somehow younger than she had in the garden, even happier.

He said quietly, "Do you still want a boy?"

"Yes, I do. I've come to want a boy. Are you glad?"

He nodded. "What about you? Are you afraid still?"

"No," she said doubtingly. "I don't think so now. It's something I can't really believe yet." She spoke carefully, considering her words. "I think it's something we both need. I hope you will be here."

"I want to be here." He smiled and put his arm round her thin shoulders. "It doesn't happen every day, Carol."

She laughed nervously, leaning against him.

"Thank God it doesn't," she said, and began to cry.

* * *

"Where are we going?" Della asked.

Gleason looked at her from the corner of his eye and then turned his gaze back to the road.

"I thought about that little beach.... I've forgotten its name. We've been there before."

"I remember. It's quiet.... I feel like a swim. Oh, Bob, isn't it a lovely day?"

Della was happy, and it was good to see her happy. Her yellow hair streamed back in the wind that blew round the windscreen of the small sports car, her full lips were parted over the big square teeth. She smelled beautifully—a strong, healthy, woman smell which came to him even through the artificial scents which she always found it necessary to wear. It was the smell of the essential Della, he thought, unalloyed and uncomplicated as she was herself. There was no deviation, no mystery about Della; anyone who said that women had to be mysterious to be desirable didn't know what he was talking about, nor did he know Della.

"Can't we go any faster?" Her voice was pitched high above the wind's rushing. "We'll have more time there."

"We're doing over fifty now."

"Fifty!" she cried scornfully. "You should have let me drive—my driving is unique."

"That's just one word for it."

Della laughed and put a bare arm across his shoulders. Her green dress had been carefully chosen to match her eyes, and it was full skirted and cut low in a boat-shaped line at the neck. She lay back in the bucket seat, her slim legs crossed and the knees drawn up and uncovered almost to the tops of her near-invisible nylons. Della, with good reason, was proud of her legs, and as objects of admiration saw no cause to conceal them unduly, especially when the chief admirer was by her side. She was happy now that Bob was back. Men were a constant necessity to her, and he happened to be her favourite man; it was all as simple as that. He was beautifully and gravely handsome, she thought, his shirt open at the neck and his brown hands resting easily on the wheel. He looked much too romantic to be an engineer.

"You were naughty not to come back on Monday night," she said, her mouth close to his ear. "I missed you."

"Couldn't help it, Della. You know what happened."

"I know. Oh, Bob, you must be careful. I need you." She leaned closer.

"Hey—stop that! You'll have us off the road."

She giggled delightedly. "All right. . . . Later."

The small, enclosed beach was scattered thinly with rocks, eroded fragments of the low cliff behind it, and the sand was fine and embedded in it the smaller water-worn stones were islands in the little pools left by a receding tide. It was still too early in the season for many people to be on holiday, and the beach was almost empty, but the sun's strength seemed to have been borrowed from full summer. Fat white clouds rode the horizon like a circling armada, all its canvas clutching greedily at the lightest wind.

They undressed behind a rock and it was only after a thorough display of her lithe, creamy body that Della consented to its partial eclipse under a swim suit. She swam with effortless speed, easily outstripping Gleason in a race out into the deeper water. The sea's touch stung their flesh, its cold exhilaration bubbling over them in astringent currents.

Della was laughing, her head thrown back and her hair

flying as they ran hand in hand up the beach. Gleason lit cigarettes and they sat leaning against the warm, smooth rock face, watching the sea.

"You can't beat the old Channel on its day," Gleason said. He shook water from his hair and screwed up his eyes against the strong light. "Most other places the water's either too hot or too rough or too filthy, or you have to dispute every few gallons with the sharks."

"Oh—sharks? Well, there's only a siren here, except that she can't sing."

He smiled, watching her as she fluffed out the golden cascade over her strong shoulders.

"But that doesn't matter, my sweet—not with us," Della murmured. Her mind was never far from the immediate and basic things.

"Aren't you beautifully brown," she said after a pause. "I wish I was, but I go all blotchy if I get too much sun. You wouldn't want to make love to a blotchy girl, would you?"

"No. You'd better be careful."

She laughed and tickled his ear. "I'm glad you like me, Bobby. I wish we could always be together like this—close, where I can reach out and touch you. . . ."

"We could be," he said. Why not say it now?

"No—you're always going away." A sulkiness dropped on her mouth and she stretched out her long legs, digging her heels in the sand.

"But it's never for very long, Della." He was on the defensive already.

"It was nearly a fortnight once. Don't you call that very long? It was too long for me."

"And for me. But since we've known one another, that was the only trip which has gone over six days."

"How long have we known each other now?" Della asked, beginning to count on her fingers, her lips pouting. "Three . . .?"

"Exactly five months."

"It's gone very quickly," she said slowly, regretfully. "And —in another five months . . .? I suppose it can't be the same. It can't go on always."

"Why shouldn't it?"

"You know it can't. Nothing ever does."

"But why not—for a long time?" His dark, almost mysterious eyes searched hers, and she did not look away. "Why not, Della? We know one another now. We're both simple people, aren't we? We don't ask for more than this. I know that I need you, that I'll go on needing you. . . . After what happened over France, somehow I need you more than ever."

"Yes, Bob, I know. But . . ."

"We're not fooling ourselves, Della, because we know the extent of our need, and its limitations. If there is anything that we don't give one another, it can't be important to us." He waited, and then said slowly, "Why don't we get married?"

She was silent, but her body moved uneasily beside him.

"I know you'll not be there when I come back one day," he said, as if speaking to himself. "I want to know you'll always be there."

Della said derisively, "Don't be silly. We're happy like this, and why shouldn't we go on until we're not? Are you happy?"

"Yes. But it's not right that . . ."

"What's not right?" she asked angrily. "It's right with me. It's selfish and immoral and everything else—so what? We're not harming anyone else. We haven't to answer to anyone else—I'm alone, and so are you. As things are, if anything happened, later, there would be nothing to regret and no knots to untie.

"I can't be bound," she said. "Not yet, Bob. Some day, maybe. . . . I'm very fond of you, you know that. And we *are* simple people—simple, selfish people—shallow would be a good word for me. Oh, I know—I am. I don't want intellectual companionship, and companionship isn't much use to me anyway. I want what we give and what we are to one another." Her green eyes slanted mischievously towards him. "And I've found that you don't have to get married for that."

He was morosely silent. "Later," she said, "you'll be glad. We can't give each other any more than this, but one day it won't be enough, especially for you, Bob."

"I've never been given anything more," he said sulkily. "I don't expect any more."

Della giggled. "That's not very flattering to your old girl friends, is it? But it just proves what I've said."

"Why?"

"Why, Bob? Because they've gone. Where are they now?"

"You're different. I've never felt like this about anyone else. You're more necessary every day."

"Suits me," she said. Her eyes were bright and knowing, no hardness in them, and she stretched her shapely arms upward and outward to the sea and the sky; it was the gesture of an appeal and an embrace. "Look—everything is beautiful today, and it's all ours. Why bother about tomorrow? It may still be beautiful, or it may rain, or never come. . . . Today is everything."

Everything, he thought, only because he was with her. Again he was ashamed of his need, ashamed that he could feel nothing beyond it, see no finer repose of spirit and no final haven for it. To him love was the physical difference between man and woman; and it seemed that it would always be like this.

"I'll be burned soon," Della said, touching her shoulders gingerly. "I'd better get dressed."

She peeled off her swim suit and sat looking at him, behind the rock. And he suddenly knew then that Della was too beautiful to be anything but what she was, too lovely for him to care that she was no more, or he either.

"Hurry up," he said jerkily. "Someone might come."

She leaned towards him. "I can grab the towel. Kiss me first, Bob. I want you to kiss me now."

In a minute she stood up and drew her dress over her head. Her eyes were filmed, and she was trembling slightly.

"Come on, slow-coach," she said, prodding his chest with her bare foot, "we're going. I'll put my stockings on in the car."

"If that's all you're going to wear, you'll freeze."

"'I've got my love to keep me warm,'" she sang, skipping lightly round him while he struggled into his clothes, "all the way home."

"Home," he mumbled from behind his shirt. "A hotel room. . . ."

"Well, there's a bed in it, isn't there? What else do you want?"

CHAPTER V

NIGHT IN THE DESERT

It was exactly the same as before, the same pure and Mediterranean weather. The same tallow shore moved up under the Africa-sniffing nose of the machine, hardened and kinked, shed its island, its ball of heated rock to fall hissing into the sea; the boiled water about the ball was white, the rest a cyanic salt-pan throwing back the sun's stares.

There was no promise in this shore, no forecast of what might lie beyond it. It was another edge of land, another border which could be the rim of a continent or the pinched and scraggy pipe of an isthmus. AFRICA, the map said boldly; you can keep on flying for five thousand miles and you'll still be in AFRICA, so the map said. But maps were liars—anyone who flew knew how they could lie. This place, here, this shore from horizon to horizon was not Africa's. It was Faruda's, and Faruda was a country bounded by the shore and the hills beyond, a hot, dead, silent, forsaken country which they were trying to bring back to life; some kind of life.

So Kingsley thought as they flew over the last miles of sea. They all knew something about Faruda now, this same crew, but most of what they knew seemed to be only a kind of negative apprehension of it, a wonder of whatever such a place could bring this time. Somehow it had been better before, when they had known nothing. Now it was still to be discovered, this small, deep empire of sand, ruled by the barbarous sun.

On the flight something had grown in the machine. Kingsley had felt it develop behind him, a slow, impalpable thing. Expectation—and something more; uneasiness in it, a laggard finger rubbing its inflamed spots on their minds. Were they not returning to the strange land, to the three strangers they had left there?

And now this other stranger was with them, the unexpected and hastily-produced man whose name was Smith.

His coming had been the only surprise on an uneventful trip. At Westonmills that morning Rogers had introduced him, Arthur Smith, a meteorologist; he would also act as relief radio man at Faruda when necessary. It had been decided at the last minute, Rogers said with an unwonted vagueness, that accurate local weather observations would be desirable so that the survey should be as complete as possible, and to save time Mr. Smith had been loaned by the Air Ministry, thus overcoming the need to await the arrival of a French meteorologist.

He sat alone and quietly in the cabin, the saturnine monarch of a rumbling, half-filled canister. He was about thirty-five, fairly tall, with a hard-looking athletic body. His thin face was keen, carrying an expression of ill-tempered inquiry, and he seemed to have few words. Kingsley had thought that Smith was not very pleased to be going with them to Faruda, but he had been anxious to learn as much as possible about the place before they left Westonmills and had questioned Kingsley closely about it and about the Frenchmen and their work. During the flight he had scarcely spoken, however, except to assure the stewardess that he was comfortable and once to complain about not being allowed to smoke.

The load was lighter this time, consisting mainly of a jeep and more food and water. Peter Easy had behaved immaculately, never causing Kingsley the slightest uneasiness.

Now Faruda waited below. When they came over it they saw that three green tents had sprouted near the control tower, a radio mast rose above the tents and a new windsock dangled limply at its pole. The small harbour with its village was quiet, baking in the sun; above them the big house brooded, watching from behind its square grey walls.

Barthell stared down at Faruda as he stood between the two pilots, his flat face compressed into a kind of muscular distaste.

"Here again," he grunted. "And I hope for the last time —until we have to fetch all these people away."

"I wonder how they've been getting on," Cummings remarked. "My guess is that the local bandits have murdered them all." He stroked his long whiskers, his protruding eyes resting hopefully on the brown wastes unrolling below.

"But if they are still alive I certainly hope one of them has found Flo's foot...."

"Never mind that," Kingsley cut in. "Now—all ready for landing? Have you been able to raise them on the radio telephone, David?"

"No, skipper. There's no reply."

"Well, we'll go in and wake them up. Landing to the west. All set, Bob?"

Gleason turned his head. "Ready when you are, skipper."

Kingsley took the machine in, losing height, and then she touched smoothly and rolled along the sand-blown concrete, slowing as he braked. He turned her and they taxied back to the tarmac where she stopped, and Gleason cut the motors.

The silence was like a hot, close-meshed net tangled about them.

Kingsley said, "Now, as we've lost one machine, Rogers suggested that it might be a wise precaution to put a guard on the kite, just in case—well, in case any unfriendly natives turn up." He looked at the co-pilot. "It's not a bad idea, at that. We'll be in a jam if anything happens to this one. I want you and Bob to stay with her for a time while we see how things are shaping here, and then we'll relieve you. Keep the artillery handy and your eyes open. All right?"

The little party stood together in silence beneath the machine—Smith, the stewardess and the three crew men. At first they saw nobody on the hot strip of the apron; but then, suddenly, as though he had risen out of the ground near the little cluster of tents, Garraud was there. His sunburned, wiry body was bare except for boots and a pair of khaki shorts, and there was a slack, gaping surprise on his face as he stared at them. Something else was there too, embedded in the surprise, and it could have been fear or even fury. A small muscle twitched nervously in his jaw, and the level top of his mutilated ear was a muddy yellow.

Kingsley took a step forward, his eyes intent on the Frenchman's face.

"Good afternoon, M. Garraud."

It was several seconds before Garraud spoke. He moved slowly towards them, like a man who suspects a trap, and Kingsley noticed that he did not attempt to shake hands.

"You are back," Garraud said at last. The surprise was beginning to leave his face. "I was not . . ." He stopped, swallowing.

"Not expecting us?" Kingsley prompted quietly, but Garraud did not answer, and he went on, "I'm sorry that we are a day late. We had a little—accident on the way home last time. Perhaps you heard?"

"Yes. . . . We heard by radio from Marseilles about it. We could not get much information and the signals were poor, but—but I understood that all were killed. . . ."

"Not quite," said Barthell grimly, "but as near as we want to get to it."

"Were you not told that we were coming today?" Kingsley asked.

"They said that there would be a delay, and a new machine would be coming." Garraud shrugged; he was more composed now. "We were given no details of crews, and after what Marseilles said it was a little shock, eh? But I am very glad that you are safe, gentlemen—and m'selle. Very glad."

Kingsley said, "By the way, we have brought an addition to your little company—Mr. Smith. He will make weather observations while you are at Faruda. We have extra rations and equipment for him in the cargo."

Eyeing Garraud levelly, Smith said briefly, "How d'you do?" He shook hands with the Frenchman whose face was suddenly puzzled and faintly apprehensive.

"Ah—a colleague," Garraud said after a slight pause. "It is unexpected—we did not know that anyone else would be coming, not to stay." He seemed to collect himself. "But welcome, Mr. Smith. Welcome to Faruda." He said it, Kingsley thought, almost as though Faruda was his personal property.

"But I forget myself," Garraud went on, snapping his fingers in front of his face. "You will be hungry and tired, no doubt. I shall call Richer and we will prepare a meal for you at once."

The stewardess said hesitantly, looking at Kingsley, "I thought that we would be eating from the galley. . . ."

"No, no! You must allow us," Garraud insisted. He was suddenly brisk and smiling, the gold-capped tooth flashing and his clear eyes travelling from face to face. "It is our responsibility and our pleasure." He led them towards the tents.

Then, outside the largest of these, they saw Richer standing. It seemed as though he had been watching them for some time before they became aware of him; and it seemed too that on his taut, yellowish face there was the fading residue of astonishment and anger. Richer's eyes were very bright, like eyes which are about to shed tears. Tension stooped in his thin body, the long arms hanging stiffly before it. He was dressed in drill slacks and the old, long-sleeved sweater which he had worn when they last saw him, and now he was looking not at the crew or at Garraud, but with a fixed and curious intensity at Smith.

"See, Richer," Garraud said. "Our friends are safe after all—they have come back again."

"I see." Richer's oversized head nodded ponderously. "I am glad that you and your crew are safe, captain. We heard of your unfortunate accident. . . ." He hesitated, moving his hands and feet uncertainly. "You have another crew member this time?"

"A passenger. My name is Smith," the meteorologist said crisply. "I have been sent out here to make weather observations."

"To stay?"

"Yes. How else could I make them?"

"Ah. . . ." A spasm passed across Richer's gaunt features and his sucked-in mouth was oddly slack. "I see. . . . Mr. —Smith."

"It will be pleasant to have another with us," Garraud said. "Do you not think so, Richer?"

"Of course. But—Faruda is not the most charming of places. And surely Mr. Smith will have little to do. The weather here seldom changes."

"It might," Smith said imperturbably.

They followed Garraud into the tent, sitting on folding canvas chairs in front of a trestle table while he and Richer busied themselves outside where a spirit stove and insulated food and water containers had been collected under a tarpaulin cover. Kingsley was thinking that after his initial surprise Garraud looked and behaved now as though he was glad to see them; but with Garraud that could change in an instant. Smith said nothing. He seemed to be feeling the heat and mopped continuously at his face and neck with a large blue handkerchief. For the first time Kingsley noticed how the man's forehead bulged; it overhung his brows like a jutting cliff, giving him an air of frowning and surly erudition.

They waited. The stewardess, sitting erect, still carried wonder and defence in her saucer eyes, but it was a softened light. She seemed more ready to smile now, Tarrant thought. They all had something more now—a common experience of fear which could bind more firmly than love or hate. They had all been afraid, recognising fear in each other, but it had been the sudden, pressurised fear of surprise and shock. It was drawn-out and relentless suspense that would be the sterner test. How would I acquit myself then? Tarrant wondered. He looked covertly at the stewardess. He was beginning to know and feel things beyond the ordinary business of work and pleasure, he thought. Fear was experience, and experience made you think. If you didn't, you didn't deserve it. He suddenly knew that he was beginning to think, but it seemed that Susan Wells had been thinking for a long time.

"Tarollier is unfortunately away in the village this afternoon," Garraud called to them. "But we will start the unloading while you have your food. Please do not hurry on our account."

When the meal of canned meat and vegetables, fruit and coffee had been served, the Frenchmen went off to begin the unloading. They had been gone about five minutes when Gleason came into the tent, wiping the sweat from his forehead.

"Bob . . .? What's going on?" Kingsley asked. "I wanted you to stay. . . ."

"I know, skipper." The engineer looked worried. "But I thought I should tell you at once. It's that damned kite." He jerked a thumb in the direction of Peter Easy. "I thought she was being too good to be true today. . . . We've got an oil leak."

"Oh, hell! Not *here*."

"It's on number four—a bad one. I found it as I was doing the check just now. I think a gland must have gone just before we landed. The cowling will have to come off."

Kingsley drew a long breath. "All right," he said resignedly. "How long do you think it will take to fix, Bob?"

"Can't tell until I've seen it. Any time from a couple of hours to a day. You know what these leaks are."

"I know, well enough. David, when you've finished go and stand by the kite so that Bob can eat. If he doesn't get going on this motor soon we shan't be off today."

The man Smith watched them with hooded eyes, eating his food without interest. In a short time Tarrant went out and Barthell said, "Well, if we have to stay the night I'll begin to think there's a jinx on this place—for us." He sighed loudly, rubbing a protruding ear. "Who'd work for an air tramping outfit?"

"Nobody with any sense," Gleason answered. When he had finished a hurried meal he rose and said, "Well, skipper, I'll go and tear that motor apart."

"Let us know if you want any help. You can send Lester in to eat."

The afternoon went by, a stretched tedium of comfortless waiting. It seemed that even the sky was tarnished with its own heat—a pale, acidified sky that robbed the air of all freshness and vitality, pressing down relentlessly on this barren border of Africa, so that all movement was borne with difficulty and even the act of drawing breath was unsatisfying and laborious.

Garraud worked quickly and with a heat-proof energy on the unloading, as he had done before, his wiry body glistening with sweat, assisted by Richer. Even now Richer had not removed the sweater which he had been wearing when they first saw him outside the tent, and Kingsley wondered how he could bear its clammy press. But Richer too seemed impervious to the heat, and he paused in his work only once, briefly, to watch Smith enter the machine to collect his weather recording gear.

Still Tarollier did not come.

Soon it became apparent that Gleason, sweating in the sun

at the top of a ladder on number four motor, would not complete his work before nightfall. The leaking gland was in a difficult position and would take several hours to strip down and replace. When the unloading was finished Kingsley asked Garraud to signal Westonmills with a message to say that they would not be home until the following day, for the engineer estimated that it would be midday or later before the leak was repaired.

They had a final meal as the sun began to cool in the still evening. Richer had sent the signal from the radio tent and it had been acknowledged. Helped by Tarrant and Cummings, Gleason worked on the motor until dusk.

The two Frenchmen sat with Kingsley and the navigator and stewardess outside the mess tent, drinking coffee and smoking. Nearby Smith had set up a small tent; there was a dim light inside it and they could see his distorted shadow on the canvas making odd, sporadic movements as he arranged his bedding. It was less oppressive now that the gory sun was setting over the flat western horizon, and soon the cold North African night would be upon them.

At first Garraud and Richer were not talkative, answering questions briefly as though their minds were occupied with thoughts which drew them to far distances, perhaps to France and home. Kingsley thought that they both seemed a little on edge, but alert, listening for something. He found himself listening too, but could hear only the terrible silence of Faruda, its waiting breathlessness. There was no breeze, no movement, all life was stilled. And the stillness held some vague tension of expectancy—something that was almost sinister, a faintness of evil working within it.

"You have been unfortunate with your visits to Faruda, captain," Garraud said at last. He was taking short, quick pulls at a flattened cigarette, drawing the smoke deep. "First your accident in France, and now a bad motor. Your families will never know when to expect you home, eh?"

Kingsley laughed. "No. But I hope Westonmills will have told them about this. They're used to it—they have to be."

Barthell said cheerfully, "The longer I'm away the better my wife likes it."

"Oh, I don't believe that," Susan Wells smiled.

"It's true. She can get on with cleaning the house when I'm not in the way. She's so house-proud that she just hates the idea of anyone living in the place at all."

"My wife is the same," Garraud admitted. "Always cleaning, polishing, moving the furniture. Sometimes I must not smoke, and there is often nowhere to sit in comfort. That is no kind of home for a man, eh? I tell you, I was not sorry to get away."

"It's good for both husbands and wives to part now and then," said Barthell. "It can put a shine on almost any marriage where the tarnish isn't too deep."

"Or, in our beautiful modern usage, it makes a nice change," Kingsley said. "But it could have the opposite effect. There are some married people, you know, who don't like being parted."

"Then they make a prison for themselves." Garraud showed the precious tooth. "And many are in prison their whole lives and never know it. They do not see the bars or feel the cold cell walls. . . . Marriage is good for a man if it is not his whole life, but wives cannot see that. Ah— it is true, m'selle," he said as the stewardess made protesting sounds. "They think that because a correct dose of the drug is beneficial it follows that an overdose must be more so."

Richer was staring at Garraud, his thin mouth open, and he looked startled. Garraud saw him and laughed. "What do you think, Richer?" he asked. "Is that not a woman's logic?"

Richer licked his lips with a long, pale tongue.

He said, "I do not know if that is true. I am not married, and therefore I know little about these things." He smiled, the lips drawing back painfully. "I have no woman to consider, and it does not matter where I go or how long I stay there. My home is wherever I am. . . . But I do not think that marriage is a prison to so many people as poverty is. For millions poverty is the dark cell from which they will never escape, for there *is* no escape." Richer had turned his head as he spoke, and they could not see his eyes.

The pause was sudden, uneasy. All at once Richer laughed and said, "Marriage, poverty—these are great human problems, and it is for every man to deal with his own as best he can. But the greatest problem to the individual is always that which is most immediate."

"In our case, a dud motor," Barthell said gruffly.

"How are you progressing with the survey of Faruda?" Kingsley asked Garraud.

"Well enough. I have completed a preliminary survey, and now I must continue in more detail before I begin to collect the main facts for my report."

"I see. How long are you expecting to be here?"

Garraud shrugged, a completely Gallic gesture. "Two more weeks, perhaps. I do not know. It depends on many things."

"Of course. . . . Have you made any contact with the people? We saw the village, but nobody seems to approach the field."

Richer answered. "I think they are—what is it?—shy of us, perhaps. There are a few fishermen in the village. They are quite friendly and do not bother us here." He paused, his thin body leaning forward, still. "How did your plane come to crash in France, captain?" he asked quietly.

Kingsley looked at him. "There was an explosion," he said briefly. "We do not know what caused it."

"The petrol?" Richer said. "It was all stowed near the tail. . . ."

"It may have been the petrol. Did Marseilles radio say the explosion was in the tail?" Kingsley watched the two Frenchmen, his eyes dark and alert.

"We understood that it occurred there," Garraud put in quickly, "and the petrol seems to be the most likely cause, does it not? There was a strong smell in the machine."

Kingsley nodded without speaking. "Well, we are very glad that you escaped," Garraud said. Faruda's oppressive silence filled each gap in the conversation, and every time it seemed stronger and more difficult to disperse.

Presently Susan Wells asked, "Who lives in the big house above the village? It looks like a Foreign Legion fort."

"That is the Bey's palace, m'selle," Garraud said. His voice was more animated and persuasive than it had yet been that evening. "I made a call on him when we first came here. He is a charming man."

"What does he think of the possibility of this airfield being re-opened?" Kingsley said.

Garraud paused. Richer was looking at his colleague attentively, his eyes luminous.

Garraud said slowly, "Well, I do not think he—he can be expected to like it very much, but "—he shrugged again—" what can he do? He would like to be left in peace, to live quietly among his people. I cannot help allowing him some sympathy. He will not, of course, cause us any trouble."

"A large base here, though, might bring him a great deal of prosperity."

"Prosperity!" Garraud ejected the word as if it was a foul thing on his tongue, and his face was angry. "Perhaps he does not care about prosperity. There are other things in the world—better things. . . . He is naturally not very pleased with the prospect of having an uninvited foreign army at his door."

The stewardess's serene face broke into a smile in which there lay the cast of mockery.

"Poor fellow!" she said. "Half Europe has foreign armies at its door, and some are already over the threshold. And I don't remember that any were invited."

"Some may be more welcome than many people imagine," said Garraud shortly. "In Europe such occupation is still necessary."

"The East Zone Germans showed quite a dislike of their brand of occupation in June fifty-three," Barthell remarked.

"Bah!—those *Boches!*" Garraud snapped. "Any kind of occupation is better than none for them. And now we are putting weapons into their filthy hands again, after all they have done to us."

Barthell nodded, his shrewd little eyes on Garraud's red and angry face. "Yes. It is unfortunate, but unavoidable."

"Unfortunate?—a poor word, m'sieu. It is a dangerous and stupid thing. Who trusts a German when he has a gun?"

"Nobody, least of all myself," Barthell said in an unemotional voice, and he smiled his strangely gentle smile. "I have no reason to trust them, and I am anything but ashamed to say that I helped to kill a few in the war. Arming them now is only the lesser of two evils."

"A matter of opinion, m'sieu," Garraud said, lighting a fresh cigarette.

"Well, if this airfield is re-opened eventually I don't think the Bey need fear any interference from it," Kingsley said levelly. "The possibility may be a shock to him, but he must know that it will be done not from choice but because of world conditions."

Garraud retorted, "North Africa is already over-full of French and American bases. It is inconceivable that there is to be yet another." He shook his cropped head. "But it is not for us to ask questions, eh, gentlemen? We have our orders, our work to do. I shall do mine."

Looking at him, something told Kingsley then that Garraud would do his work to the best of his ability whatever his opinions of its usefulness or necessity might be. Again he thought what a strange and inextricable mixture the little Frenchman was, a medley of moods and thoughts and expressions which seemed to have been ever changing since they first met. And now Garraud was smiling, his gold tooth glinting in the light of the spirit lamp which Richer had placed on a box at the tent door.

"Here we are, m'selle, gentlemen," Garraud said suddenly and softly. "A few people—alone on the edge of a desert. We are far from home, and sometimes in the last day or two it has seemed that there is no such place. Sometimes it seemed to me that I should never see my home again." He paused, his cat's eyes gleaming in the fast-fallen darkness. "I am sorry. . . . In strange places strange fancies take the mind and seize it so that it bangs inside the skull like a pebble in a tin. But then I am not used to such unusual assignments as this. Not now."

"But once you were, perhaps?"

"Once—yes. Once I was used to walking with the unknown, to going forward in the dark," Garraud said tonelessly. "I was a courier with the Resistance. . . . I was caught, and I finished the war in Buchenwald. That is one reason why I do not love the Germans, M. Barthell." He laughed, a sad sound. "And when I came home France was a different country—for me. My friends were gone, and the spirit of the Resistance was gone also. I could find nothing to help me rediscover the heart of France. It is there, somewhere, strong and faithful, but it still has not been discovered. . . ."

Kingsley looked about him. All around the field was in a darkness complete but for the birth-light of the young stars. Garraud had spoken almost reluctantly, he thought, but with simple truth. What were this man's beliefs? He embraced some kind of vague ideology concerned with strength in and obedience to government, but this did not mean that he was a communist. Perhaps Garraud himself did not know completely where his mind lay. . . .

"And so we are here now," Garraud was murmuring, "here because someone in Paris, or London, or New York has made a decision. That is why we are sitting in the desert, our task to turn the relic of one war into an instrument for another. We . . ."

"Not to do so would increase the possibility of another," Kingsley interrupted, an edge to his voice. "Faruda will become part of the *defensive* system of the free nations. And we are not here because someone in Paris or New York has made a decision, M. Garraud. We are here because someone in Moscow has made decisions, and if those decisions were altered there would be no need of any Farudas."

"Perhaps." Garraud spread his hands and smiled in his most genial and engaging manner. "Perhaps we search too deeply for causes with which we need not, after all, concern ourselves. What matters to us is that we are here, and our work here must be done. It will be done, eh, Richer? A few days more. . . ."

Richer nodded, smiling thinly. "A few days more. That will be enough."

Garraud looked at his watch. Suddenly his quick interval of good humour was gone, and he said abruptly, "You will be tired, gentlemen. Come, Richer, it is time that we sent our evening report. I believe that you are sleeping in your machine, captain. I am sorry that there is no other accommodation. . . ."

"Thank you," Kingsley cut in decisively. "We carry some emergency bedding in the aircraft, and Miss Wells will have the spare tent we brought today."

"Ah—good. I hope you will sleep well. Good night.

Good night, m'selle." Garraud bowed formally, and he and Richer walked quickly away across the dark field.

In a few minutes the stewardess rose. "If you will excuse me I think I will go now, too," she said. She looked tired, her calm face pale, deeply shadowed in the lamplight.

"We'll be keeping a watch," Kingsley said, "so you can sleep well. Good night."

When the stewardess had gone Barthell flexed his powerful shoulders with an impatient movement, jerking his head towards the radio tent which the Frenchmen had made for.

"Queer pair," he said economically.

Kingsley was thoughtful. "Garraud seems like a different man every time we meet," he said. "And Richer—well, what can you make of a man who talks about non-existent briefcases and wears a sweater in this heat? I wonder...."

"Wonder what?"

"What the set-up is here. Garraud gives me the impression that he distrusts Richer, and Richer seems jumpy. And where's the third man—Tarollier?"

"Perhaps he's found a girl friend in the village," Barthell suggested, grinning.

"I don't know. Anyway, it's time we got some sleep."

"If we can, in that old crate. But I'm tired enough to sleep anywhere—even in a tin can on the edge of a desert. What about these watches?"

"An hour and a half each will be enough. I'll take first watch and Bob had better take the last so that he can get going early on that motor. There may be more hours' work on it than we bargain for, and we don't want to stay here longer than necessary."

"We do not," Barthell said feelingly. "Personally, I've had more than enough of Faruda already."

They walked over to the dark hulk of the machine. Neither noticed the still figure of Smith outside his tent, watching them go, as he had watched Garraud and Richer go into the radio tent a few minutes before.

When the captain and navigator had disappeared inside the aircraft Smith moved quickly, a silent gliding wraith in the faint light of the stars. He made straight for the tent nearest the control tower, paused for a moment, staring round intently in the dimness, and then bent down and slid through the flap.

His hand was already shielding the electric torch before he switched it on. He looked quickly at the three low camp beds and their tumbled blankets, the scatter of clothing and toilet articles, the suitcases pushed casually beneath the beds. Dropping to his knees he pulled out the first suitcase; there were two white-painted initials on the cheap fibre of which it was made.

"Right first time." The murmur was lost in eternal silence.

The case was not locked. Smith examined its contents, and his search was experienced, his hands moving fast but with an amazing deftness. Then he closed the case and replaced it beneath the bed. He rummaged quickly through the blankets, feeling the pillows, his thin ill-tempered face absorbed and the eyes sharp, missing nothing. When he had finished with an article it was replaced exactly as it had been found.

Smith frowned as he came to the end of his search through the clothes which had been left on the bed, and then he turned his attention to the groundsheet covering the floor. He leaned across the bed and pulled back the edge of the rubber sheet where it was close to the tent wall, and the frown on his face suddenly melted into a grim and satisfied smile.

He drew out a folded newspaper and a black canister about six inches long which had been pressed into the loose sand beneath the sheet. Both these articles he examined carefully and without haste, and then replaced them and turned back the sheet as it had been before.

Snapping off the torch he moved quickly through the tent flap. Outside the silent darkness was unchanged, and nobody came as he waited briefly beside the tent. His walk back was light and sure, making no more sound than the falling of the stars' faint light upon the desert.

Garraud and Richer had left the radio tent for their sleeping quarters when Kingsley descended the ladder from the machine and sat in a folding chair beneath the tail, a Sten gun across his knees. The final, shrieking silence of night was all around—not even a cicada chirped. He wished that he could see the village from where he sat, for even one dim light from it would have been a ray of friendliness and hope in the silent darkness. To hear the sea would have been a comfort. But there was nothing—nothing to draw the mind back from its fearful explorations in the dark and lonely labyrinths of imagination. As he sat there Kingsley thought of his many years of flying, of the strange far places he had seen in those years, of the adventures of a life that was all change and movement. But few of these adventures had been so strange, surely, as this one which had led him to sit at night, with a gun by a broken-down aircraft, on a derelict airfield in a brooding desert, waiting—for what? He did not know.

There was no moon, but the stars hung huge and close as if woven into a lowered gossamer net, snapping their blue-white sparks in the stillness. He looked up at them, identifying the great constellations and the bright navigating stars—Sirius and Rigel, Capella and Regulus and Polaris. They swam regally in the night, the only life and hope in the decaying silence that was Faruda. They cast a pale glow like candle-light over the field, and Kingsley could just pick out the crumbled mass of the control tower and the vague bulk of the hangar. Beyond the hangar the sand dunes rose, twenty or thirty feet above the level of the field, undulating faintly against the star-dusted sky, and where they began was the small depression that must lead down to the village. . . .

It was another unexpected night away from home which Rogers would have to explain, but at least he could tell the truth about this one. Still, what would Carol say? She was sure to complain—she had complained a lot lately in a quiet, genteel and hurt way which was harder to take than any outburst. But what can I do about it? Kingsley thought wearily. I must do my job, and you can't run a charter company to any kind of regular schedule, and anyway aeroplanes have their temperaments; I don't *choose* to squat in a desert rather than lie in my own bed—it has just happened that way. But it would be difficult to show it that way to Carol. Perhaps the child would make a difference. . . . Poor little devil!—he didn't know what swollen expectations hovered over his unborn head. Only a fortnight now. It would be good and right to be home then.

Time passed, slow as the clock of pain. Kingsley felt the coldness of the night on his shoulders, and he pulled his blanket closer. He had almost fallen asleep more than once before he yawned massively and looked at his watch and saw that there was fifteen minutes to go until he called Tarrant to relieve him. Everything seemed so quiet that he wondered if he had been a little officious in placing a guard on the machine; but it was the safer way. Anything could happen in an isolated place like this, and they had lost Peter Fox already. Rogers was flying out to see her tomorrow.

A sudden sound from the direction of the control tower made him turn sharply.

It was only faint, but in that vast stillness it came clearly to Kingsley's ears, and he could make out a dim figure passing slowly by the tower. . . He watched carefully, not moving. And then he recognised the gross shape of the third Frenchman, Tarollier. The figure came on, walking with a tired, shambling gait, hardly bothering to glance towards the machine, so that Kingsley thought it was unlikely that Tarollier noticed him sitting in the shadow of the tail. Tarollier went directly to the far tent and opened the flap, bending his big body to crawl inside.

Kingsley sat through several minutes, motionless and watchful. There was no sound or movement from the tents. And then he got up and climbed the ladder into the cabin to wake Tarrant.

*   *   *

Gleason had been working since dawn, and now they knew that he would not finish the repairs until the middle of the afternoon. The crew heard the engineer's forecast with renewed dismay; the afternoon seemed heat-years away, and there was nothing they could do to bring it closer.

They had changed into khaki tropical uniform, and now they stood in the elongated shadow cast by the machine, all the crew except Gleason, aloft on his ladder, and Cummings who was wandering unhappily on the dusty apron, searching for the lost rabbit's foot. Above, the same burnished sky poured down its candent malice; a sky which would be the same tomorrow and all the other tomorrows. All the promised, equal days the sun would shine, probing endlessly to wring any undiscovered drop of moisture from the earth's corpse.

This morning the stewardess was among them, not a little apart as she had appeared to keep herself before. She seemed ready for anything the day might bring, as calm and neat and capable as ever, but deep in the large grey eyes there was some tiny weakening of self-reliance, the faintest shadow of anxiety or uncertainty. Susan Wells looked almost as though she had taken one on her firm chin, but wasn't sure just what had hit her. It gave her a softened and essentially feminine appeal that did not fit so exactly with the well-cut but unimaginative khaki uniform. Her brown hair shone, hard brushed, and as she turned her head from Kingsley to Tarrant and Barthell it was as though she was looking to these men as a searcher for reassurance, a seeker for a lost faith.

Staring up at the exposed engine, Barthell had been uttering restrained and rasping execrations upon the state in which they found themselves. Inactivity was anathema to him, as it was to Kingsley in a lesser degree; possessing a strength and vitality far greater than normal tasks required, doing nothing built up a pressure of physical energy within him that needed eventual release.

"I knew something would happen to this old crate," he grumbled. "She's not acquired her reputation for nothing. Why couldn't we have pranged her, instead of the Fox?"

"I wish we might, if we had to prang one," Tarrant said. "But Lester tells me that we can't expect anything other than trouble until he finds that foot."

"Then I wish he would find it. I've a good mind to help him look for the thing."

Kingsley was stroking his bony chin, staring thoughtfully over the field. Cummings came up to them, looking morose, his whiskers hanging limply.

Tarrant grinned. "No luck, Lester?"

"No. It's the same colour as this blasted sand. But I'll find it, and then we'll be all right."

"You've a touching faith in that thing, haven't you?"

"Well, look what's happened since I lost it," Cummings said seriously. "We nearly bought it over France, and now we're stuck in this dust-heap. Before that I flew for years without any trouble to speak of. Now we're in it up to our ears."

"You'll find that helping Bob is more likely to get us out of this spot than looking for a mangy rabbit's foot," said Kingsley grimly. "Do I make myself clear?"

"Yes, skipper." Cummings grinned faintly. "Well, it *was* pretty hot out there."

"Right. Now, we've no alternative but to stick around until the motor's fixed, so stay here and give Bob any help he wants. No wandering off and getting lost or anything like that." Kingsley looked slowly from face to face, his own impassive. "It will be best to send another signal to Westonmills, I think. David, find Richer and get him to send it—say we shan't be away until this afternoon, about three o'clock Bob reckons."

"Right, skipper."

Tarrant went off to find Richer. Kingsley began to pace slowly up and down in the aircraft's shadow; he saw Smith near his tent, and the weather man had just sent up a small yellow balloon which he was watching carefully through a theodolite, and he made notes in a book every few seconds. Richer and Tarrant passed by on their way to the radio tent, and Richer was staring at Smith with distrustful eyes. The Frenchman seemed to find it difficult to believe in the necessity for weather observations at Faruda, Kingsley thought. Smith's arrival had been unexpected, certainly, but even here in weather so apparently predictable, accurate data must be collected. Smith appeared to be handling his instruments with a deliberation which did not entirely match his usual quick sureness of movement. He was dressed in a white shirt and well-creased drill trousers, his head shaded by an old brown trilby with a turned-down brim.

As the two radio operators disappeared into the tent Smith all at once closed up his notebook and came over to Kingsley.

He said, "You will be going home this afternoon, captain?" His eyes were steady on Kingsley's, but veiled, so that it was difficult to be sure of their expression. The two men were a little apart from the rest of the crew, facing each other beneath the machine's tail.

"We hope so. About three o'clock."

Smith nodded and extracted a sealed envelope from his hip pocket.

"Would you mind sending this letter to the Air Ministry when you get back? It is rather important."

"Of course."

"It is something I forgot to tell them. . . . You will send it—without delay?"

"Certainly, if it is important," Kingsley said, wondering at the sudden urgency in Smith's voice.

"Thank you. Please do not forget—the Ministry will be expecting it."

Smith smiled briefly, a little sour smile, and went back to his instruments. Kingsley stuffed the letter into his pocket and began to fill his pipe. Couldn't Smith have sent a radio message instead? Perhaps he hadn't thought of it.

Richer would be sending their own signal now. Although radio was a familiar and unremarked thing to him, Kingsley looked up then with a grateful wonder at the telescopic mast which reared skywards beside the radio tent. It was their only link with the world while they were stranded at Faruda, for the aircraft's radio was useless while on the ground, without enough height or power to transmit except over very short distances. This slender mast was their mouthpiece, from which would issue any call for help—if ever help was wanted. The thought made Kingsley shake his head in annoyance. Why, and against whom, should help be needed? They had passed safely through the night; why should the day bring dangers which darkness had failed to produce?

The jeep which they had brought yesterday stood by the tents and Garraud was packing it with the equipment for his day's work. He put in a large canvas bag, a wooden box and a tripod. A camera was slung round his neck and he wore a khaki shirt and shorts and a battered greyish sun helmet, aslant, which seemed to rest on the clipped top of his right ear. He climbed into the jeep and started off down the runway without a glance at the aeroplane or its crew.

They had not yet seen Tarollier that morning; Smith's yellow balloon had disappeared into the vast caverns of the sky and the weather man now stood a little awkwardly by his instruments, staring at the machine.

Now Gleason's head was inside the engine cowling and he was whistling quietly to himself, while in the wing's shadow Barthell and Cummings squatted in attendance, facing one another like two sleepy old men playing an interminable game of chess. Inside, the stewardess was doing something in her galley. Even in the shade the air pricked like white-hot needles, and Kingsley suddenly felt restless and impatient—with the machine, with Faruda. It was yet only mid-morning.

" I'm just going to have a look round for an hour or so," he said. " See you later." He had seen all of Faruda before ; but there was nothing else to do.

Nobody spoke. Kingsley turned away and walked slowly across the dusty apron and the heat of it came through his shoes, burning his feet. Though the sun had a new ferocity on the shadeless concrete, the machine had been like an oven and the tents were bags of some foul gas which was not air. It was better just to be fried, and to move. Looking up he saw that the stiff new windsock hung motionless like a corpse at the gibbet.

He approached the control tower, and it was surely the symbol of all Faruda, grey and ruinous with silence. It was as he remembered it from their first trip—the empty, windowless rooms, the piled sand undisturbed in the corners, the rusty fallen stairway lying in the sun.

He moved on to the hangar. It seemed bigger this time, a great corroded hall with an arched metal roof supported by steel spans from the concrete floor. There were little swirls and mounds of fine sand on the floor in curiously regular patterns designed by the winds which must sometimes blow here, perhaps in winter; in one corner lay a pile of rotting timbers, old iron girders tangled together and a sand-crusted tractor minus wheels rested on its side. The roof was a sieve of jagged holes, the sunlight pouring through like jets of amber liquid to the floor.

The three huts were near in a small depression at the edge of the sand dunes. The first had no windows or doors, and most of the wooden roof lay in the sand, some inside and some outside the hut. Kingsley's long face suddenly smiled as he looked at the rotted structure, his eyes shrinking in their creases, and he was thinking that only a fool would brave this heat just to inspect a jumble of ruins, to explore this crumbling camp which had once been so alive with men and machines. . . . But something new seemed to drive him on, something apart from his curiosity about Faruda and his desire to picture in his mind what it had once been like, and so what it might one day become again. Kingsley himself was hardly aware of this other compulsion, for he was thinking about Faruda. If it ever was to become a great air base, re-born, he knew that he would have some satisfaction in remembering his own part in restoring it from desolation—a very small part, but the first step in this conception. And if Faruda was to be needed for the defence of the free world, he would have helped a little in the building of that defence.

The second hut was in much better condition, though like its fellow without benefit of windows or doors, but the roof was intact and it seemed to have escaped the full onrush of the desert's enmity. On the wall at one end Kingsley saw some faint lettering, and when he looked more closely he could make out a few words in faded red characters. " ADIEU FARUDA! Sept. 19 . ." The rest was indecipherable. He wondered who had written these words; where was he now?

He turned aside from the hut entrance and walked round it on the side away from the apron and tents, and he could not see these above the lip of the depression in which the buildings lay. It was a remote place here, between the huts and the dunes, a place of blown sand and loneliness under the empty, brittle sky. The last hut and one or two concrete bases where other erections had been were there, marking those man-made follies which the desert had destroyed or which man himself had demolished when war was raging here; there was still some tattered evidence of bombing. The dunes were close—high piles of loose, fine sand with little ridges and valleys in them, and here and there ribbed in curving furrows ploughed by the wind.

Once again, as on the first trip, Kingsley had the curious and uneasy sensation of being watched. But there was no one anywhere in the blazing silence. Where was the world —his crew, the Frenchmen, the people of the village? That world was gone, and he was alone in another, and he knew then that it would show him something.

The thing was there before him when his eyes looked again towards the dunes. It was a row of footmarks, faint and blurred by shifting sand, but unmistakable, and it seemed to lead only to the foot of a dune.

As he placed his own feet in the blurred holes Kingsley was aware that his appetite for discovery would never allow him to turn back now, but with each step he took he felt an increasing and causeless sense of danger. He thought suddenly of Carol. She had always laughed at his passion for wanting to know how things worked or for searching out what lay round the next corner. She would laugh now. Perhaps, one day, their child would laugh too.

He came closer to the dune. Quite suddenly the footmarks disappeared at its base, and there was only the pale sand sloping upward in a high bank, the crest twenty feet above his head. But it was different sand here from the rest of the sloping wall. It was less dusty and old-looking, and there was a slight but regular depression from top to bottom in it; here it was sand that had been recently disturbed.

Kingsley bent down and thrust his fingers into the sand. It burned them; but there was something solid beneath it. He began scraping at the loose stuff with his shoe and all at once a small avalanche rolled down the slope like liquid, piling silently into a smooth mound at his feet.

Concrete was there beneath, flush with the dune's exposed face, old and flaking stuff, and some deeply grained woodwork. He scraped again, and as more sand fell away he saw that the inset door was about four feet square with a rusty iron ring fixed near the bottom, rusty hinges and a loose hasp. He had no thought of stopping now. He grasped the hot ring and pulled sharply, and the door came open so easily that he almost fell backwards, expecting a stronger resistance.

The mouth that gaped dimly behind it held a short flight of concrete steps leading downward into webbed and filmy shadows. For a moment Kingsley hesitated, and then he moved through the door, crouching.

Inside it was cool, the air heavy and faintly musty, still. There were only five or six steps down to a level, gritty floor.

He stood motionless at the bottom of the steps while his eyes became conditioned to a light dim only by the standards of Faruda's glare, hearing nothing but the jerkily expectant thumping of his heart. He was in a small underground room; it seemed to be about ten feet square and just high enough for a man to stand upright. It was more than half filled with sealed metal boxes stacked from floor to ceiling, each a little bigger than a couple of biscuit tins. One near the steps had been torn open, and he saw what looked like small black cans inside. There was some faded white lettering on the boxes and a mark like a fleur-de-lis emblem. For a minute Kingsley peered closely at these marks and then stood back, and his pent-up breath was expelled in a long, shivering hiss.

The quick rushing scramble on the steps behind him was so sudden and unexpected that Kingsley had no time to do more than turn his head towards it, and then it was too late to avoid the blow. It was like a screaming explosion in and behind his ear, and Tarollier's contorted face swam in ink for an instant before the red-shot blackness and pain closed above his head.

CHAPTER VI

THE BOAT

The man who was called Arnold took the binoculars from their box by the wheelhouse door and stared through them intently at the thin brownish patch which was daubed on the horizon to the south-east. Then he put the glasses down on the shelf beside the throttle levers and turned the wheel, altering course a point to starboard.

That was the island all right. Beyond it lay—should lie—Faruda.

The smile which lifted the corners of his well-shaped mouth was nervous and yet it contained something of insolence and self-praise. He was nearly there, the hardest part of the business done; what with the storms and engine trouble, getting here had been pretty bad. But—was it the hardest part? The smile became more nervous, faded. He still had to get in, and get out. And he didn't know anything about Faruda except what he'd been told in Marseilles that time and it had been vague enough then and seemed more so now. He'd never been as far east on the African coast before. Tangier and Oran and Algiers and the score of little harbours between—he knew them all, better than most. But this Faruda. . . . He hoped he could get her in without ripping the bottom out of her.

Reaching forward he opened the throttles slightly, and the hum of the two powerful diesels rose higher from the engine room aft of the wheelhouse. Late—two days late because of a broken shaft and the storms farther west; they wouldn't like that. They wouldn't like the girl being on board either, but that was his business, not theirs. He felt brave about them, now. It was his boat too, wasn't it?—and he could do what he liked with his own boat.

The sea was clear and deeply blue, calm, only a slow, glassy swell rolling down square to the boat's stern so that she pitched a little and easily, with no hint of a roll. But she could roll, like all these narrow ships when they got it on the beam. She was a converted motor torpedo boat, long and low and fast, she carried no name and wore no flag but was painted a dull and patchy grey all over the hull, and her upperworks were grey too, from the short mast to the squat wheelhouse and cabin skylight aft. She had no wish to court recognition, and hers was the dress of anonymity and camouflage at sea.

Since dawn the sun had blazed down from an empty sky, oiling the sea and making the pitch between the deck boards soft and glossily black. It was the pure Mediterranean weather, Arnold thought, the real stuff, it was why a man wanted to stay here. Sure, it was bad sometimes, like it was off the islands the other day, but no one who knew it like he did would want to go, not when there was the wide sea and a boat like this under your feet. She was a good ship and he had looked after her, and you could tell her class and her power from the way she moved and sat the water. He wished for two things then—that he could scrape off this filthy coat of dockyard grey, and that they should get out of this Faruda without damage.

Arnold stared ahead at the island, above the slowly rising and dipping bows of his boat, above the heads of the two disreputable Spaniards who formed his crew and who lounged indolently on the fore deck in dirty singlets and dungaree trousers, and saw it now loom above the water in a clearer and more definite form. Soon the coast would appear behind it; when he was a bit closer he would be able to take bearings on the island and shape a course for the harbour entrance. It might be difficult. . . . They had said that the entrance was very narrow, with a dog-leg in it, a mere slit in the cliffs. All at once his hand slipped on the wheel. He took out a clean, folded handkerchief and wiped his hands, then his forehead with it, a jerky motion. When he had done that he pulled a comb from his hip pocket and drew it slowly, sensuously and lovingly, through the thick, arranged waves of his yellow hair.

He turned his head to look aft. Something had made him turn it, and he knew that the girl would be coming along the deck. She picked her way carefully, for she was not yet used to this motion beneath her, her hand on the rail, and there was a sulky droop to her full red mouth. She was tall for a woman, her slender and beautifully moulded figure clothed in a sleeveless cotton shirt and white linen shorts, her slim arms and legs were an even pale brown from the sun, and the chestnut hair hung down in soft, shining coils to her shoulders. This chestnut frame surrounded an oval face of fine, clear features, the skin smooth and fair, but it seemed that the wide blue eyes were faintly wary and touched with a shadow of knowledge which, too soon, had brought its disillusions. Her lips were heavily painted; she looked tired.

As he gazed at her Arnold felt again the recurring tenderness that was anchored in desire rise up within him. She was coming to him now, his beautiful Jo. . . . To hell with them at Faruda, he thought savagely. She was his girl, and she would stay with him. Perhaps, after all, she would not want to go home. She might want to stay here. His heart began to work with heavy and quickened thuds, and he found that he was silently praying that she might want to stay.

The girl came into the wheelhouse and sat down on top of the flag locker behind Arnold, stretching her long, shapely, dancer's legs out before her.

She said, " Give me a cigarette, Jim, will you?" Her voice was husky, faintly sharpened by a Cockney accent. Arnold took a packet of American cigarettes from the shelf and gave her one, lighting it.

She looked at him dispassionately over the flame of the match. He was good looking all right, she thought, in a fair and weak sort of way. His chin and mouth were weak, but there was still a jaunty and insolent assurance about him, and the wide eyes and forehead and the sun-bleached wavy hair saved his face from meanness. He was very proud of his hair. His tall strong body was deeply tanned; he wore a clean white shirt, open at the neck, and neatly pressed grey trousers. A locket hung on a fine gold chain round his neck under the shirt.

He had been good to her these past few days, though—and a little sad smile parted her lips—she supposed she had paid for it. There was not much else she could have done but go with him. A small-time touring revue actress, stranded and broke and wanting desperately someone to cling to and to go home, had little choice over the means or the price of rescue. And it had not been such a price, she thought; it was the only way and he was kind, and so—here she was. He was in love with her now, she knew that, but it was nearly all a physical love. She knew about him; he was the unthinking, physical man, and that was the only kind of love his sort wanted or understood. And she had come to want him too, physically, for he was attractive, attentive and kind in his loving. But, more than this, she wanted to go home.

Suddenly she looked up, glancing quickly over the bright sea in the direction of the sun. Arnold knew that she had not yet seen the island, and he knew what she was going to say too. Again his brown hands slid nervously over the wheel's smooth spokes.

"What time is it?" she asked sharply.

She was intelligent, he thought, too intelligent. "Nearly eleven," he said, trying to make the words sound casual and unimportant.

A wait. "Then we're not heading for Malta, are we?" She spoke quietly, looking directly at him, and he had to turn his head from her to stare over the bows of the boat.

"Not yet. I . . . I haven't told you about—about this."

"You haven't," she said, still quiet. "Why aren't we going to Malta?"

He licked his lips. "Because I have a little job to do first. I must do it, Jo."

"You told me that you would take me to my friends in Malta so that I could go home. You promised me, didn't you, Jim?"

"Yes—I promised." He swung round to face her. "And I meant it. I *will* take you to Malta."

The girl pulled hard on her cigarette and ran a hand slowly over her chestnut hair. She was angry, he could feel it, but she was holding it down. Arnold shivered in the hot wheelhouse; if she knew what the job was she'd murder him.

"You knew I had to come with you," she said. "Why didn't you tell me?"

He was shifting his feet uncomfortably on the slatted platform. " I thought you wouldn't come if I told you. You know how much I wanted you to come."

She smiled slowly, her painted lips curling up over even teeth. " And what is this so important business that you must do before we go to Malta?"

" I have to meet someone—pick something up," he said carefully. " You know what I do."

" Yes, I know. And this job is more important than getting me home."

" Look, Jo, I have to do it, *have* to. Things are pretty bad—I must have the money. When I get it I can give you enough to go home. . . . The Tangier run is about finished, it's too dangerous and overcrowded. There was nothing else but this."

" I see."

" You know," he went on quickly, " I can make enough from this to pack up. . . ."

" Pack up?" Her laugh was spiked with scorn. " You'll never pack up, Jim—not until you're caught or drowned."

" I'm not going to be caught *or* drowned," he said, sulkily defiant.

" All right. Where are we going?"

" To a place called Faruda. We'll be there in less than an hour."

The girl rose and stood beside Arnold, flicking her cigarette almost disdainfully into the sea. Her sudden nearness made his blood ardent, and again he felt a desperate and commanding urge to embrace her. She smelled faintly of some flower fragrance, not all the time, but now and again it came to him, crested pulses which matched and mounted with his own thudding desire. He held her and bent to kiss the painted mouth, and her hair was a floating veil about his face like a life germ's husk and the germ was here, in them, and her soft body was poured warmly against his. For a time she clung to him, and for her too there was nothing else. Then her hands dropped suddenly and though she did not move or speak he knew that her passion was past. Arnold released her and stepped back, seeing her rigid face, a dread of this new coldness growing within him.

She was gazing over his shoulder at the island which was large and clear now on the port bow, and behind it the low mark of the coast had risen doubtfully from the sea.

He said at last, "It's on the coast, behind the island."

"What are you going to pick up there, Jim? It's something big, isn't it?"

"Yes. Pretty big."

"What is it?" She spoke insistently.

"It's better that you shouldn't know, Jo. It won't do you any good to know."

"I want to know!" Her voice was suddenly shrill and angry, her blue eyes blazing at him. "I'm on your ship, and if anything is going to happen I want to know what I'm being mixed up in. . . . I've a right to know."

Arnold's face twitched nervously and he reached down to the locker beside the wheel for the brandy bottle which he kept there, then thought better of it and straightened up, empty-handed. Yes, he thought, she had a right to know, and anyway she would find out sooner or later, and he had got her into this, after all. But he couldn't tell her what this job was, not yet. She wouldn't like it—there was a straightness in her that would make her hate it. He didn't like it himself, but even a smuggler had to live, and it was big money. If there was going to be any trouble with her at Faruda Pedro would see that she didn't leave the ship. The anxiety passed from Arnold's vagrant mind, and then his mouth was hard with the obstinacy that weakness can set against reason.

"You've a right," he muttered, "but it will have to wait. I'm sorry. . . ."

She stared at him, anger and something near to loathing twisted on her face.

"So you won't tell me?"

"Not yet."

"And you won't take me to Malta?"

"I will—afterwards."

"I don't like this now," she said in a tight, breathless voice, "because you won't tell me about it. You've always told me about everything else. . . . Do you love me?"

Their eyes met in a long gaze. And then almost in wonder

Arnold said, "Yes . . . I love you. I want you and need you, Jo. You know it, don't you?"

She nodded, the chestnut coils dancing about her face.

"When we're holding one another I love you. But not touching you I can just as easily hate you. Don't make me hate you, Jim."

"I don't want to," he said hoarsely.

She came closer. "You will if you do this. Turn back, Jim, now. I don't want to be mixed up in something bad. It *is* bad, isn't it?" Her words rushed at him. "You mustn't do this to me. Turn back—*please*, Jim."

Again his mouth was stiffly set, and he was not looking at her but ahead, at the shore of Africa.

"There's still time," she went on quickly. "Can't we turn back?"

"No," he said. "Don't you see?—I have to do it. We're broke, and I don't like being broke, Jo. I'd have to sell the ship even to pay what I owe those two cut-throats on the fore deck. And we're nearly out of food and water. That's why we can't turn back now."

A deeper loathing returned to her face and eyes. He moved his head and saw her, and knew that his only chance was to take her to him again. He left the wheel and reached out towards her, but she stepped back quickly to the wheelhouse door and her cold, elusive figure slid away through it and along the deck to the cabin.

Arnold's face was still as he stared after the girl and soft, futile curses fell from his tongue. He thrust his head through the open window above the wheel and called "Pedro!" and one of the ruffianly Spaniards hoisted himself to his feet and shambled leisurely towards the wheelhouse. Arnold spoke to him quickly in Spanish, pointing to the coast and then to the cabin aft. Pedro grinned slyly, exposing blackened teeth, and nodded. Reaching into the pocket of his dungarees he pulled out a crumpled cigarette which he lit before slouching back to join his companion on the fore deck.

Arnold grabbed the brandy bottle from the locker and took a long drink, putting the bottle on the shelf beside the compass and dabbing his lips delicately with the handkerchief.

Soon after the drink he began to feel better—more hopeful

and confident about Faruda, even about Jo. She would change her mind, and he could help her to change it; she must, because he needed her, and he had been too long without a girl. Now the island was abeam, a brown boss of rock rearing from the sea like the crusted shell of some submarine monster. The coast lay ahead, a straight depressed cliff beyond which he could see nothing but a range of hazed hills far to the south. There was a headland on the western side of the island, and he felt in his pocket and brought out the chart which they had given him in Marseilles and stared at it doubtfully. It was a rough job, drawn uncertainly on flimsy, yellowish paper, but it was all he had. Then he took a bearing on the headland with the hand compass and laid it off on the chart, and a quarter of an hour later another, marking his position.

Again he altered course. Now the coast of Africa was close, but still he could not see the harbour entrance. He knew that it was a mere slash in the cliffs, angled to the coast so that the harbour itself could not be seen from the sea. Arnold pulled back the diesels to half speed and turned the wheel, shaping the boat's course eastward so that it lay parallel to the coast and about half a mile offshore. For several minutes the grey-brown flat-topped cliff and the fallen chunks of rock below it that were eternally bathed in white foam passed by like the endless walls of some great unconquered fortress.

Suddenly the entrance was there, and Arnold's face was glassily pale as he saw the little V-shaped gash. It opened north-east to the sea, and seemed to lead only to another wall of rock behind the shore.

He put the wheel hard over and the bows came round to point at Faruda. Arnold shouted to the Spaniards, throttling back the motors still more; Pedro shuffled past the wheelhouse with a leering wink at the brandy bottle and disappeared down the companionway to the cabin, while the other stood in the bows peering over the side with a heat-mesmerised stare at the clear blue water which creamed away from the boat's stem. It was best, Arnold thought, that Pedro should watch the girl—anyone could be here and it might be easy to start trouble.

The entrance didn't look quite so bad when he got closer

to it, and afterwards Arnold wondered why he had worried about getting in. It was tight enough, but there was plenty of water and the jutting rocks at the mouth were natural breakwaters which cut off the swell from the dangerous part where the mouth met the sea. The cliffs rose forty or fifty feet above the water here, and the long narrow boat slid quietly between the rocky jaws, but there was less than a dozen feet to spare on either side. It was like taking her into a crumbling and disused lock whose function was no longer necessary, but whose level waters might hide danger.

The cragged walls leaned and closed above the channel; now the boat was in black shadow, the sky only a fractured splinter of a greater sky which was gone. When they were a little more than the boat's length inside Arnold could see that the rock barrier ahead was offset to their course and the channel made a sharp turn to the left.

There was very little way on her now. He waited, watching as the bows came slowly up to this wall, and when it seemed that they must strike against it he spun the wheel fast to port and the boat went into a slow swing, round the corner, but he had to use the engines too, starboard motor ahead and the other in reverse. There was no room to spare between the jutting rocks as she came round, and then she seemed to glissade down a slope of broadening water and the little harbour all at once opened before them.

It was almost square, a low stone quay along the side to the right from which a sandy track led up through a depression towards the west. A rusty corrugated iron shed leaned for support against the rocks close behind the quay, rocks which made a wall growing up to the level edge of a low plateau. On the opposite side of the harbour, which was about fifty yards across, a small huddle of flat-roofed houses stood, ten or a dozen of them, and they were of whitened mud and stone with holes for doors and windows, and one or two had tin roofs and nets hung up to dry on the walls. The sun blazed harshly on this whiteness, and Arnold's eyes hurt when he looked at it. Two squat black fishing boats, wood built and about thirty feet long, were made fast beside the houses, their brown lateen sails furled, and he saw two dark-skinned men with tattered cloths about their middles working on one of them. They glanced up briefly as the grey boat crept into the harbour and then hurried on with their work with heads averted as though it might be dangerous to look too much at this long, strange craft which had suddenly come to Faruda. And for a second Arnold caught a glimpse of a naked child in the open doorway of one of the houses before the little figure seemed to be snatched away into the darkness behind; there was no other sign of life.

Arnold eased the boat slowly towards the quay, touching the bows gently, then went ahead on one motor with the rudder hard over. Better have her ready facing the entrance, he thought. She swung round in the blue water, and as he looked over the side he could see that the harbour bottom was of sand, not rock as he had expected, and the water was deep and so clear that patches of weed and small stones were easily visible on the floor which must have been twenty feet below the boat's keel. The Spaniard in the bows leaped ashore with a rope and tied it to an iron post which protruded from the uneven stones of the quay. When the stern had been made fast Arnold middled the rudder and cut the motors, then stood motionless in the wheelhouse, listening to the new and strange silence of Faruda. Usually you could smell Africa, but here there was no smell but the sea's scent; nothing but the heat and the silence.

As he stood there a man, bulking and slow, detached himself from the shadow thrown by the sagging tin hut, and moved across the quay towards the boat. It was the remembered figure of Tarollier.

The Frenchman's heavy form moved clumsily over the rough surface of the quay, and it seemed to expand as it came, a kind of reeling power in it. Tarollier was dressed in a loose khaki shirt and slacks, a sort of peaked beret on his head, and Arnold noticed the black sweat stains at the armpits of the shirt. Although he could see no bulge, Arnold somehow knew that Tarollier carried a gun. He was the type who would.

Tarollier heaved himself over the rail and stumbled into the small wheelhouse, filling it. Inside the border of pale flesh which surrounded them the squeezed-up components of his face were surly and accusing; they made a velvety, compressed thing that did not belong to this big body, like a child's face with evil grafted upon it. It was not the expression but the face itself which all at once struck fear into Arnold, and he wanted to get away from the little, soft, evil thing. He retreated across the wheelhouse until his back came up against the sharp corner of the flag locker, and the sudden pain shocked away the fear. He grinned then, almost laughed, at the big man.

"You're here at last, then," Tarollier said abruptly by way of greeting. His voice was high and thin, and the English fell easily from his tongue. He removed the beret and mopped at his bald head with a soiled handkerchief that smelled of stale sweat, and trickles of sweat ran down through the sandy brows which were thicker between the little eyes than above them, irrigating the flat, fleshy nose. Arnold had not remembered how small and red his mouth was.

"Why were you not here on time? You are two days late."

Arnold shrugged. "I know that. I couldn't help it—there were storms off the islands and I had to shelter. . . ."

"Shelter!" Tarollier snarled contemptuously. He leaned towards Arnold, towering above him. "It was going to be very easy. . . . But just because you are late everything is a thousand times more difficult."

"I told you. I had engine trouble too."

Tarollier said, "Listen—this is a big job, and there is trouble already." He paused, jerking his head towards the track leading up from the quay. "He won't be very pleased with you, my friend."

"He is here?"

"Of course he is. But there are others."

"What others?" Arnold's voice was sharp, surprised.

"The plane crew is here," Tarollier said softly. "That does not help, eh? We saw you coming. Why did you have to come in broad daylight?"

"Try getting into a harbour like this in the dark," Arnold said sardonically. "You want a ship, not a wreck, don't you?"

"Bah! It is a pity that you have to be here at all."

Arnold ran his hand slowly over his yellow hair and laughed. He had no fear of this gross and sweaty Frenchman now. "You can't do without me or my boat, and you know it. There's not a seaman among you." He lit a cigarette without offering one to Tarollier and leaned with studied unconcern against the wheel.

The hostility faded slowly from Tarollier's eyes. He said, "We are all in this together. We need one another, eh?" He was suddenly ingratiating. "Troubles shared are smaller troubles."

Arnold smiled insolently, the cigarette dangling from the corner of his weakly handsome mouth. "Anyway, what does it matter that this crew is here? Won't they be off soon?"

"Unfortunately, no. They have something wrong with their machine. But it is not that. . . . It is this so inquisitive captain."

"What about the captain?"

Tarollier said, his voice soft again, "What about him, my friend? He has found our cargo, that is all."

The cigarette trembled and dropped from Arnold's lips and he bent slowly, groping, to pick it up. The slatted platform creaked weirdly under his feet.

"He's found the cargo? How did he find the cargo?"

Tarollier held up his hand. "He is a very inquiring man, this captain. He was prowling round the airfield this morning while waiting for his machine to be repaired. I followed him. Someone was careless—there were footmarks in the sand, our captain followed them and found the cargo."

"My God! What happened?"

A look of genuine amusement spread over Tarollier's pale little face.

"I hit him," he said, and the small red mouth that was like a woman's curved in a smile. "I flatter myself that I did it well—one blow behind the ear. He groaned a little as he dropped."

"Why did you do that?" Arnold was whispering the words. "His crew will be looking for him. . . ."

"What else could I do?" Tarollier said carelessly. "And the crew—they will be all right for a little while, and we can deal with them, I think."

"Where is he now—the captain?"

Tarollier laughed. "He is safely locked up in the Bey's

palace. I had to fetch one of the Bey's men to help me take him there on horseback. Then from the watch tower I saw you coming. You can see that I have had a very busy morning, and in this heat...."

"Why wasn't the cargo left in a safer place?" Arnold demanded. "Were you crazy—storing it where anyone could stumble over the stuff like that?"

"It is in a safe place, *mon ami,* safe from all except those who prowl, and there will be no more prowlers," Tarollier said smoothly. "It was just bad luck that our captain found it—it might not have been discovered in a hundred years. And I said it was big—there is nowhere else to keep it in Faruda."

"What about the Bey? Couldn't he have held it?"

"The Bey!" Tarollier laughed again, a small high sound that whistled mirthlessly from his thick throat. "Much as we love our friend and partner the Bey it is best that we should keep it out of his possession. It is of no use to him, of course, but it is as well that he should not be tempted to—ah, acquire it. He will be paid for his co-operation, and that is all that will concern His Excellency."

The silence between them was thick and stagnant like a toxic smoke before Arnold destroyed it. His voice seemed to be pitched curiously on two different keys at the same time, as though two voices spoke through the single mouth.

"But—the captain.... What about the captain?"

"Ah, yes." Tarollier smiled, his tiny features a central knot of cold and terrifying anticipation. Arnold was suddenly afraid of this face again. "It is unfortunate.... He knows too much now, and the Bey will not want his own part in this made public. There has been no time yet to think about our captain." The Frenchman paused, looking absently across the harbour, and then said without change of his casual tone, "Perhaps the most simple way would be to take him with us when we go."

Whiteness beneath the sunburn turned Arnold's irresolute face a smudged yellow. He saw Tarollier's eyes, and knew what he meant.

"Not that—no!" Again the two voices were there, but

shrill and frightened now. "I don't want any part in a killing, d'you hear? There will have to be another way."

"Don't excite yourself," Tarollier said mildly. "Nothing has been decided yet, but my personal preference would be to dispose of him at sea. So easy—and so final. It is probable that he would never be found. . . ."

"There will have to be another way!" Arnold almost shouted. He was trying to draw courage from the loud sound. "He's not to be brought aboard my ship!"

A grimace, angry and impatient, suddenly rippled Tarollier's soft face, and slowly he thrust a big hand into the pocket of his drill trousers. It was a simple and natural gesture, but somehow it drove a keener blade of fear into Arnold than any he had known before.

Quietly Tarollier's voice drifted across the wheelhouse. "I said that nothing has been decided yet. But I think that you must do what you are told. . . . Do not forget one thing—if you had come on the right day all this trouble would not have happened. We made arrangements for dealing with this crew should they return at an awkward time. But it was you who arrived at the awkward time, my friend."

"I couldn't help it," Arnold muttered. "The storms . . ."

"The storms!" Tarollier spat contemptuously through the door. "Are you so frightened of a little wind and water? Now, is the boat in good order? Is everything ready?"

"Yes. There is plenty of fuel, but I need food and water."

"I have thought of that. It will be arranged, tonight." Tarollier glanced up and down the decks. They were empty but for the Spaniard lounging in the shadow of a hatchway near the bows. "The fewer who are in this the better. You have a crew—how many?"

Arnold straightened himself painfully and tossed his cigarette into the water. Growing inside him there had been a desire to delay Tarollier's knowing about the girl. She need not be discovered yet—not until they were at sea again, and then it would be easier. They would be on their way then, with the cargo, and once they were away with it the girl's presence wouldn't matter so much. And she was safe enough with Pedro, locked in the small room off the cabin alleyway. But he realised now that he had been a fool about her, a fool to bring her on his ship when there was this job to do; yet a woman like that could make a fool of any man. . . .

"Well, I have asked you," Tarollier said sharply. "How many are on board?"

"I have two Spaniards as crew—that one by the hatchway and another down below."

"Is that all?"

Arnold's hand pecked at the wheel. "That is all."

Tarollier grunted and looked at his watch.

"There is a lot of work to be done," he said sourly. "And in all this heat. . . . Chasing this fool of a captain delayed me. I must go to see the Bey and tell him we are almost ready, and make final arrangements about the loading—we need his assistance to transport the stuff. And then I must pacify the crew about their captain, if I can. If not . . ." Tarollier shrugged his heavy shoulders expressively. "Where is the cargo to be stowed?"

"In the storeroom below this wheelhouse. There is a space in the forepeak too. How many cases are there?"

"About sixty—so big."

"Sixty!" Arnold whistled. "You did a good collecting job, didn't you?"

Tarollier fixed a smirk on his wet little mouth.

"I did well. But it was not too difficult. The only pity is that it has taken me so long to return. Now—at last—I have succeeded. I have waited a long time for this, and nothing is going to stop its completion."

The unnatural glare in his eyes made Arnold feel sick. The girl, and the captain—they would not be allowed to stand in this man's way. Arnold knew then that Tarollier felt nothing about the captain's disposal—nothing but a little terrible anticipation, and later it would be gladness to be rid of him; and I, he thought, I shall be in it just as much as Tarollier. He was trembling like dead leaves then, the sickness foul in his mouth and stomach. Tarollier was saying in a slow and almost dreamy way, "You will never know how I endured the years of anxiety and fading hope, my friend. Nor will you know the frustrations and disappointments, the hundred schemes which rose and crumbled in my mind before today. For years my life has been centred on Faruda, and yet I was miles away. . . . That is why nothing will be allowed to interfere with this thing which we are about to do."

Arnold tried to beat down his fear. " The stuff," he said hoarsely. It helped to talk about the stuff. " It must be worth millions of francs, many millions. . . ."

Tarollier said gently, " I do not know yet how much it is worth. But I suggest that we leave these—these surmises until later. Our cargo is here, it is all in good condition, and your boat is to take it away."

" Where?"

" You will be told that later."

" When are we going?"

" Tonight. We are late already, and we cannot risk any more of these people at the airfield finding things out. And there is another little matter—something which they may connect with us if their suspicions are aroused. I am afraid that you will have to take your boat out of here in the dark whether you like it or not. The stars will give a good enough light, and we must be well out to sea by dawn."

" Now," Tarollier said, " I must go to see the Bey." He looked at Arnold, his little eyes intent and calculating. " And you, my friend, had better come with me."

Arnold's head jerked up in surprise. " Come with you? Why? What good will it do for me to see the Bey?"

" No good at all. But let us be frank. I do not trust you, Arnold. You are frightened, because of this captain, eh? and frightened men do strange things, such as taking boats away when no one is looking. That is why I want you to accompany me."

Arnold gave an unconvincing laugh.

" I shan't run out on you. And I'm not frightened either. . . ."

" All the same, you will come." Again Tarollier's hand was in his pocket, but it wasn't necessary; he knew that he was in control now, and that Arnold would do as he was told.

" I must tell my crew that I'm going ashore, then," Arnold said.

He left the wheelhouse and walked forward to speak in

low and rapid Spanish to the man who was propped against the fore hatch, and then he came back to join the Frenchman. They set off across the quay and up the track that led from it towards the west, climbing between eroded outcrops of sandstone that rose on either side and made a little valley of the road; its surface was fairly smooth hard-packed sand, wide enough for a car to have passed beside them as they walked abreast. The high sun was merciless on their sweating bodies.

It was merciless too on the man who watched from the concealment of a rock on the outcrop's lip. There was no shadow anywhere at this hour, and all Faruda was naked to the sun and consumed by it. But Smith did not feel the heat now as he saw the two men leave the boat and come up the track towards where he stood above it. His hooded eyes and thin face were as still and compacted as the sand beneath his feet, and carried no more expression. From this point of vantage on the little plateau above the harbour he had seen the boat arrive and Tarollier meet it. Things were moving here, and moving fast, he thought; it had been worth coming after all.

The two came nearer, Tarollier lurching along with clumsy and undirected power, but Smith's eyes lay unwinkingly on his companion. He saw the slim body in its spruce and particular clothes, the handsome sunned face with its cap of wavy yellow hair, and then surprise released the tautness of his mouth and lit a candle of amusement and understanding behind his stare. Jim Arnold! Our old friend Arnold, of all people, here in Faruda. . . .

Well, he mustn't see me yet, Smith thought, or I'm cooked. Now it was all becoming clear, beautifully clear. The reflex that carried his hand down to the gun in his pocket was automatic and fast. But it wasn't time yet—there were a lot of things to find out first. Smith allowed himself a grim and anticipatory smile, and for the first time in minutes his body moved, sliding round the rock so that he could keep Arnold and Tarollier in view as they passed. Arnold looked pretty sad, he thought. Things couldn't be going right, or perhaps Jim was just scared. It didn't take very much to scare Jim.

He wondered where they were going now. Well, there was nothing like finding out.

When they had passed he stretched himself and then slipped

cautiously down the smooth, grainy sandstone slopes to the track below, moving quick and lightly between the scattered boulders which lay beside it. It would be difficult, but he must try to keep them in sight.

At the top of the climb the two men were on an undulating plain, and away to the right the ocean's turquoise immensity lapped the sky's distant shore; and to the south-west, in the direction of the airfield, another sea of brown dunes which humped and rolled and spilled in vague and hazy spaces showed the desert's edge. Tarollier's pale face was sweat-bathed, the dribbles of moisture running down it and inside his shirt, rank and black on the cotton; his breath came fast with a peculiar forced hiss through his flat nose, and his feet slurred on the sand and raised white dust. They walked on in silence for some minutes, and Arnold scarcely noticed the heat and his own sweat because he was thinking of the girl back there in the little room with Pedro, and of this pilot. He would never have touched the job if he'd known about the pilot; whatever I am, or have been, he told himself, I am not a killer or an accessory to killers. Perhaps even yet there might be a way out. . . .

The road sank into a shallow depression and after about half a mile another joined it from the left, a prominent white rock like a big milestone marking the junction. Tarollier pointed a thick finger.

" That is the way to the airfield."

He said nothing else. Soon they were passing a plantation of date palms, then the arranged patterns of olives and small fields of corn where the soil had been scooped out round the plants to make troughs for the conservation of dew or what moisture might fall from the hostile sky. No one was in the fields or among the trees. To Arnold there was something disturbing in these sudden cultivations in a barren vastness of rock and sand. These plants seemed to be living here without human aid, growing in some awful geometric and self-controlled husbandry, auto plants which fruited and reproduced and tilled their own soil. He was glad when they ceased and the desert returned; and then, round a bend in the track, he saw the Bey's palace.

Its walls were grey and buttressed, with small watch towers

at the corners; it stood alone in a desert of its own, and the track led directly to a high arch in the centre of the facing wall which was flat at the top and so tall that Arnold could see nothing above it but the sky. The heavy iron-studded door beneath the arch was open but guarded by a sentry who wore a burnous of a saffron hue, and the man held a long-barrelled rifle. He looked at Tarollier and Arnold intently as they approached the gate but silently allowed them to pass at a sign from the Frenchman.

They were in a square, open courtyard round which ran a raised balcony supported on worn sandstone pillars. Arnold was surprised to see an almost new motor truck in a corner of the courtyard, its chromium fittings and glossy paint flashing incongruously against the old, sun-flaked stone of the pillars. It was quiet and hot inside the walls, and the shadows beneath the balcony were black grease beside the sun's rigid glare. As they went across the stone-paved yard an old Arab moved slowly from these shadows to meet them. He smiled in bare-gummed silence, vacantly, and inclined his head, and they followed him through a small door on the far side from the gate.

The old man led them through a long, empty corridor with infrequent narrow windows which let in a filtered yet dusty something which might have once been light. Arnold had a strange feeling of being dragged on invisible traces through a warm, dim, endless tunnel; but then their guide turned off to the right and they were in a high, square room with open archways at one side, a mosaic floor of rich colours spread with thick rugs, some low Moorish tables and divans deep in silk cushions. A frieze of gold-embossed Arabic characters on a blue ground encircled the walls. The old man indicated a divan and bowed, moving from the room through one of the arches.

To Arnold the wait seemed like an age. Tarollier did not speak, standing uncomfortably and staring at the floor.

They heard a deep, quiet voice, and the man stood not in the archway through which the old Arab had left but by the door from the empty corridor.

"Good morning, gentlemen," he said in English.

There was no trace of hesitancy or accent in the Bey's even

tones. He was slim and not very tall but there was a latent strength about him, and in his eyes no welcome, nothing but a far-looking stare of remorseless determination that touched the two men briefly and then went on and away under some driving pressure of mind. His face was fleshless, fine and dark, the aquiline nose and small pointed beard like two talons set for striking. He was well under forty, and wore an embroidered white burnous and gold-piped head-dress, and the jewelled hilt of a dagger protruded from his waistband.

He moved towards them, and Arnold saw that he had a slight limp. Tarollier said in French, " Excellency, I have brought M. Arnold."

The Bey regarded Arnold with a dark and haughty stare, silently, and motioned to one of the divans. At the moment they seated themselves a servant appeared with black coffee in small cups on a great brass tray, and then withdrew. The Bey remained standing, his arms folded and his head back like a man listening.

" Mr. Arnold will take your cargo?" the Bey said abruptly. He looked coldly at Tarollier, faint distaste on his thin lips, and Tarollier knew that he had been reproved for speaking in his own tongue.

" Yes, Excellency. We would like to leave as soon as possible after dark."

" You may leave when you wish," the Bey said. He touched the jewelled hilt at his waist with thin strong fingers. " Always provided that you bring the payment due to me."

" I shall bring it."

" Your cargo is of no value to me, but do not be tempted to try to take it without paying for the services of myself and my men."

" I would not attempt it, Excellency."

" Good." The Bey's eyes narrowed, and craftiness sidled in the slits. " I need this money, Tarollier. You know why I need it—that is no secret between us, eh?"

Tarollier nodded, staring unhappily at the small table before him, and the Bey glanced indifferently at Arnold. Arnold could find nothing to say, but he was aware of a curious magnetism in the Bey's face and scarcely moved his eyes from it.

The Bey said, "My truck will be at your disposal. When shall you require it?"

"I would like to collect it at seven o'clock tonight."

"Very well. You will bring the money with you, and you will take the captain away." The Bey frowned, and a nervous spasm pulled at his firm mouth. "He must be disposed of—finally, you understand? He will be ready, in the truck. Two of my men will go with you as guards, and they will wait until the boat leaves Faruda before returning with the truck."

"Yes, Excellency."

"This pantomime of a prisoner in my house is distasteful and degrading," the Bey said acidly. "It would have been almost impossible for things to be handled in a more incompetent manner. . . . Troublesome inquiries are certain to be made soon about this pilot, and I shall have to ensure that there is no evidence of his being here. This man, and what happens to him—that is your responsibility altogether. Is that understood?"

Tarollier said in his high voice, "Yes, Excellency. But the immediate thing is this crew—they are still here, and soon they may cause trouble when their captain does not return. It would help us if . . ."

The Bey silenced him with a quick movement of his hand.

"That is your business," he said harshly. "You should have arranged for the boat to come when they were not here."

"It was arranged, but things went wrong," Tarollier muttered, glowering at Arnold. "The boat is late, and the crew was not expected back. . . ."

"I have said that it is your business—to dispose of the captain and to handle his crew. I know nothing, and I shall do nothing against them which might reach the ears of the French. And much as I detest the upstarts who oppress my country and who deny us our rightful political responsibility, I want no trouble with them—yet." The Bey seemed to grow in stature, his eyes two prisms to the sudden fires within him. "That will come—and this money will strengthen my arm in the fight for freedom. . . ."

He went on more quietly, "But now I want no dispute with the—the authorities. If there is any trouble between this crew and my men, the French will garrison my village and throw me out of my own house. You will deal with this problem yourself."

Tarollier was humble, bowing his bald head.

The Bey said, "I have ordered my people to stay away from the airfield and to keep to their homes while you are here. I have even, with great reluctance, housed this captain whom you so stupidly allowed to discover your cargo. And if this money was not necessary to me in my struggle against the French oppressors I would never have made this bargain with you. However, I have given my word, and I shall keep it. But I will do nothing more."

A silence. The big room rested in time and space, filled with the silence. The Bey still stood, arms folded, head back.

At last he said, "One may do much with money, eh, Tarollier? With it one can purchase many things—arms, men, ideas, obedience, power. And the sum is power. How did you get this money, Tarollier?"

The Frenchman's pale little face smiled briefly.

"Does it matter, Excellency? I have it."

"No, it does not matter. It is very little in comparison with what you hope to get, is it not? But you are lucky, Tarollier. You knew that what you came for would be safe —that we would not touch what was not ours. Have you thought of the damage it can do?"

"No," Tarollier said indifferently.

"You possess a ruthlessness and a determination which I cannot but admire. You have cunning also. It was a clever scheme, all those years ago, and well carried out. And you are lucky too that none of those who fought here then know anything about it. If they did, I think they would kill you. . . . If not for themselves, for those who died because of you."

"They do not know," Tarollier muttered, fear jumping in his small eyes. "Nobody knows but ourselves."

A stiff smile moved the Bey's lips. "It is as well. Soldiers sometimes have long memories."

"Those days are far away now."

"But they may return," said the Bey quietly. He paused, and gently stroked the pointed beard. "I have never been consulted about this air base, gentlemen. When it is rebuilt we shall be in the front line of any future war. We do not want that, for we are the same as all those voiceless millions in the world, the little people who hope and pray and struggle feebly against war. We in Faruda will be a target. . . . That is why I shall fight my own little battle against those who would draw us into war, against those who, although they have never seen it, would seize and employ my land for their own ends and ambitions."

The Bey dropped his arms to his sides. He said abruptly, "You will come tonight, at seven. Good morning, gentlemen."

He clapped his hands once and then disappeared through one of the archways; the old man who had shown them in suddenly stood beside them, and they followed him along the dim corridor and into the courtyard, and then they were out on the track again and walking in the undiminished sun towards the harbour.

Arnold was thinking about the Bey and about the Bey's prisoner. It was settled, then. "Dispose of him—finally." Both the Bey and Tarollier liked that word dispose. It didn't sound so bad in a way, and scarcely suggested "kill" or "murder." He saw that Tarollier was looking at him, his eyes intent and oblique, like little currants stuck in a round pudding. Tarollier was working something out. Everything was silence but the faint scrape of shoes on sand.

Soon the silence began to gnaw inside Arnold's head. He said, "So the Bey doesn't like the idea of an air base here."

"Apparently not."

"Or French rule either."

Tarollier grunted. "He is a fanatical nationalist. He was the same in the war. But he controls the district and appears to have a few armed men around him, and so we have to co-operate. I knew that he would allow us to do what we wanted to do, at a price. A stiff price."

The Frenchman stared moodily ahead. Sun, sand, silence, the scattered rocks beside the track, the deserted plantations. For Arnold it was not too soon when they came to the junction of the road that led to the airfield. "We part here, then," he said.

A slyness slid across Tarollier's face.

"No, my friend, I do not think so. . . . In my hurry to see the Bey I forgot something. We must go back to the boat—together."

"Why?" Arnold was suddenly alarmed. Tarollier must not find the girl, not yet. Would she still be in the little room, as he had ordered? "You must go back to the airfield. . . ."

"Soon." Tarollier cut him short. "But there are more immediate things. First things first, as you say, eh?"

Arnold said sulkily, "I thought that was the first thing."

"You are wrong. The first thing, my friend, is to ensure that your boat leaves at the right time, and not before. There are, too, some further instructions which I must give you."

Arnold knew that it was useless to argue. His heart pumped hard and unevenly as he thought of the coming night. Tarollier was going to bring this pilot to his ship and murder him, and Tarollier would do it without a second thought. No one would do it easier than Tarollier. When he had spoken about the captain before there had been pleasure on his face, pleasure that had made Arnold feel sick. Arnold was not concerned so much with the man's fate as with his own and that of the girl. But as they neared the harbour his vacillating spirits all at once began to recover something of the puffy assurance of the weak; suppose the man was dropped overboard, uninjured. It was unlikely that a body would ever be found after being dumped in the middle of the Mediterranean. Even if it was it would only be that of a drowned man, and there would be nothing to show how he had been drowned. . . .

They descended the last slope to the harbour. With a surge of relief Arnold saw that there was no one on deck but Manuel in his accustomed sprawl beside the forward hatch. He followed Tarollier as the Frenchman swung himself over the rail and suddenly lurched along the deck towards the cabin.

Tarollier sat down heavily on one of the seat lockers which ran the length of each side of the cabin, and Arnold tried not to show that he was listening for sounds from the alleyway which led to the room, only a few feet distant, where the girl and Pedro were. But Jo would have sense enough to make no sound, knowing that it could not help her if she did. The seconds ticked by. . . . Nothing. Why must the fat fool come into the cabin at all?

Tarollier was saying something; better listen. "We shall need your help now, as the Bey won't give his."

Arnold had to swallow a couple of times and moisten his lips before he could speak. He said, "Well, what do you want me to do?"

"Collect the food and water. I expected that you would be low on provisions. These last few days I have been—scrounging, you call it?—scrounging supplies from the camp stores which I have hidden by the road that leads to the airfield."

"How shall I carry them?"

"We are fortunate to have a jeep at the field which I shall have to—well, borrow." The word seemed to amuse Tarollier. "Some time this afternoon I shall load it with these stores. As soon as it is dark you will go and find the loaded jeep about half a mile along the airfield road. It will be near a tall conical rock on the left as you go towards the field—a safe place, but you will find it easily enough because you are certain to see this rock. You will drive the jeep here and put the stores on board the boat. Then you will wait for the truck. It is very simple. Do you understand?"

"I understand." Arnold could not stop a nervous glance along the alleyway. Could she hear? It would make no difference if she could. . . .

"Good. Now—to get the whole thing clear. After you have done this you wait here to help when the cargo arrives, at about eight-thirty. Meanwhile I shall go to the palace, pay the Bey his protection money, collect his truck with our captive captain in it together with the two guards, and go to the hiding place and load up. From there we cannot be seen or heard by the crew who will be guarding their precious machine by the tents, nor will the others be . . ."

"Others? What others?" Arnold's mouth was a gaping rent across his face, the words spilling out like grain from a torn sack. "There were only three of you, weren't there? Garraud, Richer and yourself—that's three. . . ."

Tarollier looked at him. "Your arithmetic is perfect, my friend. I forgot to mention Mr. Smith. He came only yesterday, in the plane."

"Smith? Who is he?"

"He is a weather man, a meteorologist. It seems that someone in Paris or London decided that weather observations were necessary. So—here is Smith."

Arnold jerked out, "I don't like all these people being here. Is he all right?"

"As far as I know," Tarollier said shortly. "He sends up his little balloons and seems to know what he is doing. Well, I don't like all these people here either, but . . ." He shrugged. "We shall go ahead."

"This crew—won't they signal for help if their captain doesn't return?"

Tarollier scowled, the peculiar eyebrows making a knot of sandy hair at the top of his nose. "You are raising a lot of dangerous points, my friend, but I think that we have taken care of them all. The crew will send no signal because we shall have seen to the radio. That is all right. Now, I was saying . . . The stuff will be loaded and brought straight here. We stow it and the captain on the boat, and then it is goodbye to Faruda."

Now Tarollier was confident, anticipatory, small eyes bright.

"We should be ready to go by about nine-thirty or ten o'clock," he said, "and be well out to sea by dawn. We attend to the captain, and then our troubles are over."

Over, Arnold thought; perhaps. He wished that he could be as certain of that as the Frenchman seemed to be. Again he licked dry lips, and his hoarse voice came from them. "What happens at the other end?"

Tarollier laughed. "Do not worry, my friend, it is all arranged." He rose suddenly, looking at the door that led from the cabin to the engine room. "Now—one little task before I go back to the airfield."

The small engine room was stuffed with the sickly stink of hot oil, thick and ineradicable despite the open skylight above. The two powerful diesels lay side by side flanking a narrow steel platform, and control rods ran up from the throttles and clutches through the forward bulkhead to the wheelhouse, so that the motors could be operated from there as well as from below. Tarollier stood on the platform for a minute, bending his head beneath the skylight and looking at the squat engines, and then he turned to Arnold who waited uncertainly in the doorway behind him.

Tarollier said softly, " I know a little about diesels. The fuel injectors. . . . Take out the main feed valves and give them to me."

Arnold looked at him, and Tarollier's eyes were almost closed and the small mouth was tightened up and Arnold thought stupidly that it looked like a red rose. The hand was in his pocket again.

Slowly and unevenly Arnold said, " It—isn't—necessary. But if . . ."

He knew that he was going to do it even before he took the spanner. He unscrewed the unions of the main feed pipes to the injectors and removed the spring-loaded brass valves from their housings. The mucous trickle of black oil that dropped from the pipes was the final, impotent dribble of his resistance and manhood. Tarollier wiped the valves on a piece of cotton waste and put them carefully in his pocket.

" Thank you," he said. " We will replace these when I arrive tonight." He pondered for a moment. " Well, that is all, I think. You understand what you have to do, eh?"

" Yes."

" Good." Tarollier smiled gently. " There will be no mistakes. We are in this, together. You will expect us at eight-thirty."

Arnold nodded silently, and Tarollier pushed past him into the cabin. Arnold watched him go up on deck, watched his lurching walk across the quay and up the track until the big figure disappeared round a bend between the rocks, and then he turned and went to the locker inside the cabin door.

His hand trembled as he took the full bottle of brandy and removed the cap. This pilot. . . . It was decided now, the disposal, and he was in it. And Jo—what would they do to her when they found her? Didn't she know too much, like the pilot? Why had he been such a fool as to bring her?—but he knew why, and it was too late now to do anything about it. They couldn't move now. The drink was long, from the bottle, and he felt the spirit raw and hot in his throat before the comfort of it began to caress his heart. He placed the bottle on the locker top and looked in the misty mirror nailed to the wall above it, and he combed his thick wavy hair carefully, admiring it in the glass, before he moved towards the little room where the girl was.

Smith waited for Tarollier to pass some way up the track and then he left his hiding place on the outcrop and followed leisurely; he found no difficulty in keeping out of the Frenchman's sight on the winding, rock-strewn track. Even tailing these two almost up to the gate of the Bey's palace had been pretty easy. Smith felt hot and tired now, but he was whistling to himself very softly as he walked in the pestilence of the sun, and he was like a man whose schemes are working smoothly towards the destinies which he has planned.

* * *

David Tarrant sat in his place at the radio table, staring at the transmitter and the receiver which stood side by side upon it. At his left elbow the little window showed not a clouded drift of land or sea, not a bold horizon as he would have wished, but a baked and dusty patch of concrete. Grounded. . . . Why was it that motors always picked the most miserable and outlandish places in which to spring leaks and generally go sick?

In here the stagnant heat was a vice gripping body and mind, crushing them to a single wedge of craving for air and relief. There was nothing to do outside, but he did not know why he had come into this hot, dead cylinder. There was nothing to do here either. It was a useless thing now. The black transmitter box before him with its dials and knobs of startling colours—that was useless too, with no power or height to drive it. They could hear, but not speak. Across the gangway Harry's navigating instruments were dead, and the massive panel that told Gleason the story of flight was without a flicker or wink or pulse of life. Forward, the two control columns leaned, needles drooped, the safety belts hung forlornly from the seats. An empty flight deck was a weird, unnatural place, Tarrant thought; why had he come here?

He rose, stretching his arms in the gangway, fingers sliding on the plastic roof insulation above. The morning had been a prolongation of weariness, its time heat-clogged, braked by boredom. He saw that it was a few minutes after twelve-thirty, and something in the way of food ought to be appearing before long.

His footsteps echoed, metallic in the empty cabin. Susan Wells was standing in her galley, watching him as he approached. She smiled, her face pale but still composed. It was her usual serene smile, but there was a new spontaneity and warmth in it, and Tarrant realised suddenly that it was the first time she had smiled at him like this, as if she welcomed him. He felt strangely glad; strangely, because he had not thought much about Susan Wells and her smiles or their absence had meant nothing to him. He'd supposed that she was a nice, pleasant, capable girl, a stewardess. First a stewardess—and that didn't encourage anyone to think of her as anything else. But when she smiled like this it was different.

He stopped, his eyes meeting hers. She said, " I was just checking on our food. There isn't much left." The way she said it made things seem almost desperate. " The catering people at Westonmills didn't expect us to be away more than a few hours."

" We didn't expect it either. But we'll be off this afternoon."

" I hope so." Her composure sagged momentarily and then recovered. " I was wondering about lunch."

" The Frenchmen—won't they be giving us a meal?"

" I suppose they will, but I don't know whether we ought to take their food. . . . Captain Kingsley didn't say anything before he went off."

" Isn't he back yet?"

" I haven't seen him."

" Well, he can't be long." Tarrant paused, watching her. She was running her hand backwards and forwards on the smooth edge of the refrigerator, a controlled yet apparently unconscious movement. Her well-brushed hair was darker than the khaki uniform, fine and shining. She had a very pleasant, English, serviceable sort of face, Tarrant thought, and he thought it kindly and in no mind of disparagement, a face which could stand a lot of emotional punishment and show no defeat; a face that would absorb and hide the marks, as perhaps it had absorbed some already. Her figure was unremarkable, but right—it had everything in the right proportion, and she did not wear her womanhood obtrusively. He thought of another stewardess he had gone about with for a time; Jill's physical charms—and there had been few of any other nature—had been flaunted as a banner, a challenge and a lure, and the most conspicuous finally exposed as an inflated fraud. Susan Wells was nothing if not real and wholesome, and she was different.

He realised that qualities such as these would not have interested him greatly a year or two ago; he must be growing up, surely. Wholesome, serviceable—hardly romantic adjectives to apply to a girl, but if they meant that she was different from the others he had known he was glad that this was what she was. She was something else too, something new and undefinable and linked with sorrow and kindness.

He said awkwardly, wanting to talk with her a little longer, "Tell me—do you like this, being a stewardess?"

"I like it," she said, smiling again, and her hand ceased its oscillation. "It's work that's useful and interesting, sometimes with a stimulating flavour of excitement. . . . Yes, I like it."

Pinkly serious, Tarrant announced, "The stewardess is the busiest and most necessary member of any crew. You've only to ask the passengers."

"The busiest. . . . Well, not always. Not on this trip."

"No, but this one—well, it was different, right from the start. More so for you, I suppose."

"Yes, it's been a new experience," she said thoughtfully. "But that first one. . . . I didn't tell my mother about it. You know . . ."

"I know. You were really wonderful then, I thought."

"You spoke to me, didn't you? You said, 'You're all right, aren't you?' and it helped me. I wasn't wonderful—I was sick and frozen with fright and it was all through me, a cold sickness."

"But you flew again."

She glanced up at him, a faintly surprised and annoyed look.

"That's my job, isn't it? Anyway, I've got over it now." She paused and touched the refrigerator again. "But I—I wouldn't want it to happen any more."

"It's not likely to." That was true, thank God. None of them wanted *that* to happen again.

She said suddenly, "Last night was the first time I've ever slept in a tent. I dreamed that it was a flying tent, and that I was flying to Faruda in it over the sea—so low that I could see each little fleck of foam and fishes swimming in the clear water. It was afternoon, and so hot. . . . I landed, and there was no one but Garraud here, and he said, ' They have all gone home. They were tired of waiting for you.' And then he disappeared and I didn't see him any more."

"What then?"

"I don't know. It sort of tailed off, and then it was daylight and I was awake." She laughed shortly. "My dreams are always like that, pointless and unfinished. I came to Faruda but I didn't get away. I hope that doesn't mean you'll forget me when you go."

Tarrant smiled. "All or none, that's our motto. How could we forget the most useful member . . .?"

"I thought radio operators were the most useful members," she said, and there was an unusual mockery in her eyes. "All those I've known have told me so."

"I could never be so immodest. The hardest worked, yes —stewardesses always excepted. If I'd known two years ago what the job was like I might not have been so keen to have it."

"Two years—is that how long you've been a radio operator?"

"That's all. I'm pretty new."

"Well, I'm even newer. Six months."

Somehow Tarrant felt that this shared inexperience was a bond between them. He said, "I thought that you must have been a stewardess for a long time. You always look so —well, composed and capable, practised."

"Do I?" A closed, defensive expression crossed her face. "I think it helps, perhaps, to look like that."

"Helps? Your work, you mean?"

"Yes—my work, and other things." She shrugged, and smiled faintly. "Anyway, I'm old enough to be able to *look* capable, I suppose. If you can't do that by the time you're twenty-five it's best to give up trying."

Tarrant said automatically, "You're a year older than I."

Something like surprise, or derision, flicked for an instant in the stewardess's eyes. "We seem to be getting down to vital statistics, Mr. Tarrant."

"Couldn't you call me David now? It would save you a couple of syllables, if nothing else."

Hesitantly she said, "Well, in the circumstances—perhaps I could." Then, suddenly, she was more willing. "And it would be ungracious not to reciprocate with Susan, wouldn't it?"

"I like Susan," he said frankly. "Susan . . ."

All at once she laughed, looking directly at him, and he had never heard her laugh in such a free and genuine way before. It was a delight to listen to this sound—so many women cackled, screamed or seemed to think that laughter was either indelicate or bad for the complexion. His artless face showed pleasure, glowing, and Susan Wells thought that it was the healthiest-looking face she could remember having seen.

It was then that she felt the waiting heat strike at her like a cowardly enemy, and she knew that she would have to leave the galley. Tarrant saw her face go taut and white, and he took her arm and led her out, watching as she descended the ladder. In the broad shadow of the tail he was gentle with her, seating her in the canvas chair which they had used when on watch the previous night; she lay back with her eyes closed, feeling shivery and faintly sick, her head aching. But she knew that it would pass, it would be better soon. It helped to have him there, but she wasn't built for the heat.

To Gleason the sun was no more than an inconvenience, or he would have passed out hours ago. He wore an ancient uniform cap with a handkerchief stuffed in the back to cover his neck, an oil-stained singlet and slacks. His arms were strong and brown in the sun, lightly shaded with dark hairs. His face was solemn, sweaty and patched with oil, the black smudges shining on the clear wet skin, eyes intent on the spanner which he was turning. His wrist ached.

Silent, inflexible, beautiful, the engine smelled interestingly of metal and hundred octane and oil. Oil was everywhere —dripping, black, filmed, warm, sticking; inside stuff that should never be seen like this. It should be prisoned like blood, doing its good work below the surface. But even with blood on its face the motor was beautiful.

That was why it was entitled to be perverse, as all beauty was entitled. Perversity had made it spring the leak in almost the worst of places. Gleason was not angry now as he twisted the hot, slippery spanner, his wrist one glowing ache. It was no use to be angry, and a real engineer never was, knowing perversity rightly as a challenge to his skill. And he knew that anger turned motors sour, and a sour motor was an unresponsive lump of trouble for ever.

If he wasn't exactly enjoying himself on the hot and lonely top of this ladder, Gleason knew that he wasn't too unhappy either. Not about *this*. He wanted to go home, all right, but this was work—it was what he was here for, and now it rested with him when they should all go home. He had plenty of time to think up here, and he'd never minded being alone, except sometimes. . . .

Except sometimes. Last night was the second time in a week that he had disappointed Della. He couldn't help it, and she would say that she understood, but another little bit of resentment would tick up in her mind. He knew that, and he knew too that she would never marry him, not now or any time; he didn't think that Della was going to marry anyone until she was much older, when desire was ebbing and the empty future lurched nearer like a drunken man coming down the narrowing alley of the years.

At first a fierce but not unexpected disappointment had filled him at her refusal. What did he feel now? Gleason hardly knew how he felt now, but at least the disappointment had gone. In its place was something that was both resignation and relief, though yet he scarcely recognised it to be this; but his need of her had not decreased, and it was still his only fear that one day he would come back from a trip to find that Della was gone. He knew it was going to happen one day—one day there would be no soft and splendid body next to his own, no passion before the resting blankness of mind and the warm sleep which followed. And there would never be another Della, never another like her.

All at once the spanner slipped and his knuckles scraped on the rough metal of the filter housing. He felt nothing; at that instant something in his brain was preparing him for Della's leaving, and it seemed to say that if he did not go home that night he would not see her again. It was when he was away that she would go, and they should have been back yesterday. Another two hours, he thought, readjusting the spanner, that should fix it. He forced his aching wrist to turn again, and blew a sweat drop from the end of his nose. They must get back tonight.

Below him, in the broad black blade of shadow thrown by the wing, Harry Barthell looked first at his watch and then turned his cheerfully ugly face towards that of the co-pilot, which was pop-eyed and gloomy behind his limp whiskers. They had just moved again to keep out of the sun; it was past its zenith now, but this was the hottest time, when the sky was like a silvered reflector of the glare, a burning-glass directed upon the pinch of dust that was Faruda.

Cummings was resting between searches. Muttering for the tenth time that day, "I'll never find it—same colour as the sand," he gazed hopelessly across the immediate concrete.

Barthell groaned, hunching his muscular shoulders.

"Forget it, Lester. You ought to be thinking noble, improving thoughts, not worrying about a lousy rabbit's foot."

"Nobody understands," Cummings said despondently, addressing the distance. "Everyone thinks I'm crazy. And so I am—with fear that Flo's foot has gone for ever. I know we shan't get anywhere until I find it."

"If you wander about that apron any longer the only place you'll get will be in hospital—with heat-stroke. Lay off."

"All right, all right. Instinct shall defer to blind and arrogant reason. But"—and Cummings raised an admonitory finger—"you must admit that we've had nothing but trouble since I lost that limb. In a final effort to avoid any explosions or other unpleasantness on the way home this time, I shall make one last search before we go."

Barthell looked hard at him. "You really do believe this, don't you, Lester?"

"Harry, I do."

The navigator paused, still staring at Cummings, opened and closed his mouth a time or two and then said slowly, "Well, I've heard of crazier things, after all. You know—perhaps I might help too, just to ease your mind."

Cummings's grin managed to look wolfish, surprised and gratified at the same time. He said pontifically, "It is the wise man who is not afraid to change his mind."

Another silence fell, the latest of a hundred in that scorched morning. They sat as still as possible, trying vainly not to sweat. Now the heat had a smell, a stink of putrefaction. It was the festering breath of this place which crawled under the contemptuous sky.

Idly Barthell noticed that Tarrant and the stewardess were together beneath the machine's tail. His habitual optimism was beginning to wear thin under the press of heat and the enforced delay. He said, grunting, "Wonder where the skipper's got to. It's one o'clock—he's been away two hours."

The co-pilot brushed his ginger whiskers tenderly. "Don't get lost, he says, then goes and does it himself. Well, you know him—he just can't resist poking about in strange places. He'll turn up in time for lunch. Which reminds me—I'm hungry."

Barthell nodded. He looked across to the tents and saw Richer's thin body bent over the oil stove under the tarpaulin.

"Looks as though a meal might be coming up before long. How are you doing up there, Bob?" he called to the engineer.

Gleason's quiet voice sounded hollow and distant from inside the engine cowling. "About two hours should see it fixed, Harry. Sorry to be so long, but things aren't as accessible as they might be."

"Can we do anything?"

"Not just now, thanks. I'll let you know."

The occasional rattle of Richer's pans was all that broke the silence. Barthell stared round him yet again at the dusty emptiness of this place and for the first time an icicle of apprehension touched his heart. Where was the skipper?—he ought to have been back before this. And Tarollier? The

Frenchman had disappeared too and Barthell suddenly could not recall having seen him since soon after breakfast. And the man Smith had been missing from about eleven. Where were they all?

Faruda gave no answer as he scanned the dreary, amorphous plain on which the airfield lay, and Barthell shifted uneasily in the wing's shadow. A thought stabbed at his mind. Supposing that Kingsley hadn't come back by the time the motor was repaired; someone would have to go and look for him, and they couldn't go without him, anyway. I shall go, Barthell told himself, because he is my friend as well as my captain. And if . . .

The sound of a motor made Barthell raise his head again, and it was made by Garraud's jeep coming along the runway towards them. With a pang of angry disappointment he saw that Garraud was alone in the vehicle—for a moment he had cherished the hope that Kingsley might have met the Frenchman and gone with him on his job of surveying the airfield, to pass the time while the engine was being repaired.

Garraud stopped the jeep beside the tents and stepped down, walking with his characteristic eager alertness to have a word with Richer before coming to where the aeroplane stood. The battered sun helmet lay on the sliced-off top of the right ear, and Barthell thought that he seemed on edge and even angry, but was keeping a tight hold on himself. The gold tooth was hidden, and the nervous muscle in his jaw twitched and jumped regularly.

"So you are not gone yet, eh?" Garraud said, glancing up at the exposed motor.

"Not yet," Barthell replied gruffly. He looked directly at Garraud. "Have you seen Captain Kingsley this morning?"

Garraud looked puzzled. "Captain Kingsley?" He repeated the name as though he had never heard it before. "No, I have not seen him since I left to start my morning's work. Is he not here?"

"No. We don't know where he is. He went off to have a look round two hours ago, and he hasn't shown up yet."

"I expect he will be returning soon," Garraud said briskly. He removed the helmet and wiped his forehead, brushing back the pointed line of hair. "Perhaps he has gone down to the village. But I have not seen him—I have been working over that way today." He waved his arm towards the west.

"It's not like him to be late," Barthell said uneasily.

Garraud shrugged, and the navigator saw that he was not very interested in Kingsley's absence. Or was he only *trying* to appear so? There was something on Garraud's mind, something that made him both alarmed and angry, and now he was lighting a cigarette nervously and kept glancing over his shoulder in the direction of the control tower and the track which led to the village.

Avoiding Barthell's eye, he said suddenly, "You will be off when Captain Kingsley returns?"

"And when the motor is repaired."

"Of course. Will that be long?"

"About two hours."

"Sometimes," Garraud said, "it is lonely here. . . . It will be when you are gone. You will have lunch with us, please?"

"Very kind of you. Are you sure . . .?"

"It is nothing." Garraud's hand sliced the air and then was still, outstretched. He was staring towards the tower.

Near it the lumbering figure of Tarollier was approaching. At once Garraud threw down his cigarette and walked rapidly in Tarollier's direction, and when they met about a hundred yards from where Barthell was watching Garraud stopped the other and appeared to be speaking earnestly to him before they both made for the tents. Tarollier's flat face was expressionless, betraying nothing.

Barthell had no idea where Smith had come from or how long he had been back on the airfield, but all at once the weather man was standing beside his tent, a slim, alert form in a white shirt and well-pressed slacks; there was an evident calmness, a sureness, about him. As Barthell saw him there he thought suddenly and illogically that Smith would be a better man to have on your side than on the other.

Kingsley had not arrived when Richer signalled that lunch was ready. Barthell, as he walked towards the mess tent followed by the rest of the crew, had made up his mind that it would be better to eat before doing anything about the skipper. They could give him a bit longer, even up till three o'clock, for after all Kingsley knew that Peter Easy wouldn't be ready until about three, and it might be that he hadn't felt like any lunch. Barthell wondered if he was worrying over nothing. But it was strange that Kingsley should stay away so long, and nobody seemed to have seen him go or had any idea in which direction he had left the airfield—if he had left it at all.

Neither Smith nor Garraud's assistants had any news of him. The meal was not a cheerful one, and apart from the crew speculation over Kingsley's absence seemed to interest only Tarollier and Smith. Tarollier appeared anxious to appease their growing fears, making plausible suggestions to account for the captain's disappearance and watching carefully for their effect on his hearers.

But Barthell was watching Smith. When Smith first realised that Kingsley was missing his thin face was suddenly drained of its colour, and there was an unsteadiness to his hands which was unusual for this silent, collected man. Soon he was calm and controlled again, but Barthell knew that he had been concerned for Kingsley's safety. Why? It was an uneasy, silent company after this. Garraud, at times, had what seemed like a glow of fury in his clear eyes. Richer's skinny form drooped above the trestle table and he ate little; despite the heat he still wore the old khaki sweater over his shirt, the sleeves pulled down to his wrists. Occasionally he glanced at Garraud with a kind of sad querying look, his taut-skinned face solemn and waiting. Towards Tarollier he never looked at all.

After lunch Garraud went off immediately to continue his work, this time on foot in the direction of the control tower. The crew resumed their places under the plane's wing, the engineer climbing up again to number four motor. When Garraud had disappeared behind the tower the empty deadness of Faruda, outside the desperate little oasis of tents and aircraft, was complete and final.

They were all uneasy now.

"Not what I'd call a jolly meal, that," Cummings said out of the silence. "Don't know why our friend Garraud invited us—he wasn't exactly the genial host."

The stewardess smiled faintly. "We shall have to rely on him to feed us if we stay here much longer," she said. "There's very little in the galley."

Cummings eyed her, his moustache lifting crookedly. "My dear young lady, we shall be leaping into the air in just no time at all." He paused. "That is, if . . ."

Barthell's glare silenced him. Tarrant was shifting his feet uncomfortably, his face anxious. He looked from the stewardess to Barthell and then said suddenly, "I've got a feeling, Harry. Something funny is going on here, I know it is. The skipper wouldn't stay away so long—not unless he had to."

"He should have been back long ago," Cummings muttered. "It's time we did something about it. . . ."

Barthell was staring across the field, not saying anything or moving, and they began to think that he wasn't going to answer. His face and body was all muscle, adamantine with final resolve when he spoke at last.

"Yes, I'm worried. . . . You're right, David—the skipper must have run into trouble somehow."

"He may have had an accident. What are we going to do?"

Barthell said slowly and decisively, "You're going to stay here, and I'm going to look for him."

"Alone?"

"Yes. Bob must finish that motor, and I want you, David, to send a signal yelling help if either of us hasn't come back in—well, two hours. I don't think we should send one any earlier in case it all turns out to be a false alarm. And if you have to send the signal, do it yourself, whether Richer likes it or not." Barthell squared his massive shoulders, and his strength came out to them. "Lester, you'd best stay close to Miss Wells and the kite—we don't want anything happening to either of them. . . . Have you got it?"

Susan Wells was pale and calm, her round eyes fixed on the navigator. Cummings said jerkily, "Someone ought to go with you. What about one of the others—Smith, or . . ."

"No." Barthell's gentle smile sought each face. "I would sooner go alone. Somehow I don't really trust any of them."

"Where are you going?" the stewardess asked quietly.

"These buildings first, and then I'll go down to the village. Those are the most likely places."

Without Kingsley it was automatic and accepted that Barthell was the leader. His decision was made, and no one could challenge it. He said, "I'm taking one of the guns, and I suggest that you keep a couple handy too. Nothing like being prepared—though for what I'm not sure yet. All right?"

Cummings nodded, chewing his whiskers. "All right, Harry, if that's how you want it. But look after yourself."

"I will."

Barthell climbed the ladder into the machine and came out with an automatic pistol holstered and strapped to his waist. The others felt suddenly lonely and apprehensive as they watched him go, and moved closer together under the wing. Barthell waved to them and set off towards the sagging control tower, and as he passed the tents he saw Tarollier there, motionless, watching him.

He came to the tower. Inside the two lower rooms the sand was thick and undisturbed, open to the sky. Between here and the hangar the sand was too hard for any footmarks to show; the silent, rotting hall was empty but for an old wheel-less tractor and some burst packing cases and rusty girders.

"Skipper!" he called loudly. "Skipper!" A sullen silence answered.

Fear drew its snagging barbs through Barthell's mind, a sudden fear more acute than anything he had felt since the skipper had gone, and at that instant he knew, though without any sign or reason, that Kingsley was in extreme danger. Instinctively he dropped his hand on the gun, feeling its solid reassurance, but it was not enough to smother this new dread for the captain. . . . The huts too were empty, and it seemed that no one could have set foot inside these desolate ruins for years past.

There was nothing else here—the airfield held no more cover for a man. Barthell moved from the door of the last hut and walked beside the decaying wooden wall towards the little depression in the dunes which carried the track to the village.

It was then that he remembered the jeep—why hadn't he thought of it before? He could borrow it to go to the village.

Swiftly he changed his course away from the dunes, round the far end of the hut. And as he turned the corner he almost fell over something in the black shadow under the wall, and he stopped dead. Suddenly his chest was all heart, a great pounding engine which left no room for breath as he stared at this thing in the shadow.

What he saw was the body of a man, hunched low and leaning as though for protection against the wall, very still.

For a time there was no power in Barthell to lift his feet. Then he snatched air and moved forward a slow step, seeing the dark stain on the sand and the carved metal handle of the knife which protruded from the man's back. He bent down, warily touching the body, and the head with its red face and sliced-off ear rolled over like a doll's which has come loose, the mouth open as though in awful laughter and the gold tooth shining.

The body was still warm, nearly as warm as in life, but life for Garraud was ended.

CHAPTER VII

THE AFTERNOON

DONALD ROGERS stared for the third time in half an hour at his watch, and then through the small round window at the looped mountains and slashed valleys of the Cevennes below.

His thick body was hunched in the cabin seat and he felt hot and uncomfortable, beads of sweat starting continually on his forehead and pink bald scalp to be swept away impatiently with a large handkerchief. Flying as a passenger he loathed as mightily as he loved it as a pilot—or as he had once loved it, for now the captain's seat had given way to the managerial chair, the symbol of a more remunerative but less satisfying existence. Even nearing fifty the feel of a stick in one's hands, he thought, was as good as it had been twenty-five years ago, but it wasn't often now that one got the chance. Pity. . . . He looked down at his generous waist-line, frowning; the office chair was to blame for that, too. He tried not to remember how thin he had been once.

Nearly two-thirty—it was late enough. He didn't want to be hanging around Istres for a night if he could avoid it.

The still form of the accidents inspector from the Ministry lay stretched out in the seat beside him, a form which uttered snores with metered regularity. Genteel, delicate snores, Rogers thought, suitable for Mr. Brant who, in his formal black jacket, striped trousers and wing collar, still nursing his monogrammed briefcase, seemed unaffected by the stale heat of the cabin. Some people, Rogers told himself, would wear stiff collars and black suits at the equator.

He wished he could have left for Istres a day or two earlier but he had been forced to wait for Brant and there had been a back-log of important work at Westonmills which could not be held over. At one time he had not expected to get off even by today. It seemed that the French authorities had made some inspection of the machine, and they had reported that the cause of the explosion and subsequent crash of Peter Fox appeared to have been petrol vapour, ignited by a means unknown. A spark, set up by friction from the control rods, as Kingsley had suggested? Rogers sighed heavily, suddenly feeling that perhaps this was the cause and that he was wasting his time in flying out here hoping to find another. He was still hoping, for somehow this explanation had never satisfied him; anyway, he had to see the wreck and report on it to the Company whether he and the inspector found fresh evidence or not.

Kingsley and his crew. . . . There was news for Kingsley. It was a pity that they had been forced to stay at Faruda last night, with a dud engine. Since this business started they had collected all the bad luck that was going. Rogers turned over in his mind the events of the last twenty-four hours. Kingsley had reached Faruda without mishap, but then last evening the signal had come to say that he would not be leaving until the following afternoon; he should be getting under way any time now. There had been no further signals that morning before Rogers had left Westonmills early for London Airport to catch the B.E.A. plane to Istres. If everything had been going well it was probable that Kingsley would not send another before taking off for home—he had always been economical with signals.

But a tiny, nagging doubt in Rogers' mind would not be stilled. He stared from the window, trying to trace its cause. Did it spring from the crash of Peter Fox last week, the holdup at Faruda yesterday? Or was it somehow bound up with Faruda itself, a place about which they knew almost nothing, in a country where discontent simmered dangerously beneath a stretched veneer of authority? And these Frenchmen. . . . Garraud, for instance; recalling the details of his brief acquaintance with Garraud, Rogers scarcely knew what to make of him. He had left the impression of being anxious to get to Faruda—in fact it appeared now that they all had. And what about Richer? Why had Richer invented this story of the lost briefcase? At Westonmills he had been explicit in denying that he possessed such a thing, and it seemed that he had made up the yarn as an excuse to visit the flight deck, but for what purpose no one but Richer knew. Certainly the intrusion could have had nothing directly to do with the crash. What else was there? Smith—his arrival had been unexpected, especially since they had been told that there would be no more passengers after the first trip, but . . .

The cultivated and impersonal voice of the stewardess interrupted his musings.

"Fasten your safety belt, please, sir," she said. "We shall be landing at Istres in ten minutes."

Rogers nodded, drawing a long breath of satisfaction. They were arriving sooner than he had expected. He touched Brant on the arm and the official awoke with a start, blinking owlishly, stretching his lean body.

"Are we there, Mr. Rogers?" His voice was thin and precise.

"Just about. We're going in to land now."

"Excellent! We shall be able to inspect your machine straight away, what?"

"I hope so."

"Good, good. Nothing like getting on with the job in hand, eh, what?" Brant gave a humourless cackle and began to rub the palms of his hands together as though they were frozen, looking eagerly through the window.

Half an hour later Rogers and Brant were met at the Customs barrier by a small and dapper man who introduced himself in ornate English as a "sub-inspecteur of hazards of the air" attached to the civil aviation department of the French Air Ministry. Brant blinked at his French colleague, a slightly scared look of amazement on his face as the little man led them, talking and gesticulating without pause, to where Peter Fox was lying.

Brant's eyes lit up when he saw her and he rubbed his hands again, the briefcase dangling from a short strap. His thin voice was animated and almost enthusiastic as he said, "Ah! A nice little job. . . . Very nice. I like to see them all in one piece, eh, m'sieu?"

"Ah, yes, it is better." The Frenchman laughed gaily and spread his hands. "Sometimes they are all in bits, and it is not so good."

"Or they burn. That is no good either. I like a nice *clean* crash, what?"

Rogers stared at the two men, pressing his lips together, and then looked sadly at the wreck of what had once been a proud machine. Peter Fox lay beside the runway on the field's bare, red-brown plain, and the sunlight played mockingly on the broken silver body. When they reached her he detached himself from the inspectors and stood beside the torn fuselage and the silent engines with their twisted propellers.

She was as Kingsley had left her when he and his crew escaped the crash. She had been examined, the little inspector said, but nothing had been moved or taken away. The engines could be salvaged, Rogers thought, and most of the fittings and instruments saved, but would the rest of her be worth trying to repair? There might still be unsuspected fractures in the wings or body caused when the undercarriage folded and she hit the ground. A nice, clean wreck, eh? To Rogers any crashed aircraft, apart from the death or injury it might have brought, was a grievous thing, like a strong man suddenly crippled.

The inspectors disappeared into the great hole below and forward of the tail. Gloomily Rogers made a complete circuit of the machine, noting the gashed metal under the body where she had skidded, the smashed landing gear and splayed-out wheels with their great black tyres, the turned-back blades of the screws.

"What a mess." His mutter was sad and angry. "What a hell of a mess!"

He climbed to the flight deck through the open escape hatch near the nose. As he had expected, the controls and instruments gave him no information. He tried the stick but it wouldn't move. He stood there for a long time, his eyes going slowly and carefully over every small dial and switch and lever, over the floor and walls and the insulated roof, and then he moved back down the empty cabin. It was warm and silent, smelling only of that special odour which aircraft have and which does not leave them even in death. There was nothing here.

The inspectors passed him on their way to the flight deck, the Frenchman talking earnestly and Brant looking profound.

He came to the great hole in the machine's side, near the tail. The afternoon sunlight streamed through, lighting the dismal wreckage within. Rogers saw that the torn edges of the hole were bent outwards, indicating an interior explosion, and he stared incredulously at the tail plane, now almost resting on the ground, and wondered by what miracle it had not parted from the body of the machine.

Aft, the galley bulkhead had been smashed back by the uppercut of the explosion, but—strangely—the cargo doors opposite the hole had remained fast closed. This was where the petrol had been stowed; even now there was still a faint smell of it. Below the torn galley floor he saw the buckled arm and loose pivot which controlled the elevators, and then he looked carefully at the twisted ribs and stringers inside the shell of the machine. Near the edge of the hole, low down on the inside of the skin, was a black, greasy mark. He rubbed at this with his finger and smelled it, frowning.

Going down on his knees he examined the gashed floor. In two separate places the metal had been blasted open, revealing the skin below, and here this was intact. So were the control rods beneath the floor, although one was bent. Rogers knelt thoughtfully beside the holes. Surely, if the petrol had seeped below the floor—as Kingsley had surmised—and collected inside the curve of the skin the explosion would have occurred there, not almost three feet higher and level with the floor as it appeared to have done. At least there ought to be evidence of burning; but the skin below was smooth and bright.

Rogers took a flashlight from his pocket and poked it through one of the holes, thrusting his head down inside to get a better view. The control rods were correctly in their guides, and these were tight and well greased, like the wires which worked the trimming tabs for rudder and elevators. There could have been no possibility of a spark originating here, he thought. He moved his light slowly in the cavity, picking up and examining one or two loose pieces from the great hole above.

It was then, as he was about to rise, that he saw something —something different. He bent lower, stretching down his arm to its fullest extent, and grasped the little coloured fragment which had lain almost hidden behind one of the ribs at the very bottom of the fuselage, then straightened up, his face scarlet with exertion.

Between his fingers was a small square of red fibre which carried two brass studs, and these had short, burned-off stubs of wire depending from them. Attached to one stud was a thin brass strip to which a tiny gear wheel had been sweated. Rogers turned the little wheel and the strip rotated, making contact with the second stud. Then he smiled slowly and grimly, nodding his bald head, and smelled the small object long and with care.

His smile became more grim. This was it; it was all that was left, but it was enough. Donald Rogers knew then that the explosion which caused the crash of Peter Fox and almost cost the lives of her crew had been anything but accidental.

* * *

Barthell stared down at the twisted body of Garraud. Now the silence deafened.

And then it was as if some waiting shadow, beyond the body, had needed this moment to achieve substance and life. Gently, it moved in the silence, and the silence was not disturbed. Barthell found himself looking over Garraud to the wire-taut man who stood by the far corner of the hut.

" Garraud."

Smith uttered the one word, his head seemed to nod wisely as the sound hung like a cold blade above the dead and the living. There was no surprise, no horror in it, and the sharp face wore no distinct expression. But Smith's body had a sort of wary stoop, like that of a man who waits for treachery.

Smith moved towards Garraud, bending over him, and he looked very carefully at the body and then at the hard sand beside the wall. The examination was unhurried, somehow practised. Barthell watched him, waiting, and his hand was on the gun.

" Stabbed in the back, eh?" Smith's voice was calm; he straightened up, and Barthell saw that the lids had dropped lower, hiding his keen eyes. " What do you make of that?"

" Murder, Mr. Smith," Barthell said quietly. " What else?"

Smith nodded. " Murder, all right. No wound in that position was ever self-inflicted. I didn't think . . ." He stopped speaking, his mouth shut tight.

Harshly Barthell said, "Half an hour ago Garraud was

alive, as we all know. . . . Somewhere, not very far away, there is a murderer."

"Looks like it," the weather man said casually, staring at the hut wall.

The off-hand tone caused a sudden fury to rise up in the navigator. Angry-voiced, he said, " Murder—and you behave as though it's some sort of game. Strange things are happening here, Mr. Smith—things I don't like. . . ." All at once Barthell's voice was soft. "What are you doing here, anyway?"

Smith was smiling. " If it comes to that, what are *you* doing?" he said evenly.

"You know well enough. I'm looking for Captain Kingsley."

" I am just—looking," Smith said. They eyed one another over the body of Garraud, and Barthell was wondering if it was Smith who had murdered him. Surely the face of a killer could not be so calm, the eyes so steady. Looking at Smith, Barthell suddenly thought that his was the face of a hunter ; a killer would hunt his victim, but there were also hunters of those who killed. . . .

"That is a common type of Arab knife," Smith said. He gestured with his foot towards it. " You see the carving on the handle?"

" I see it. But . . ."

" Arabs may have killed him," Smith cut in quickly. " It is possible, the way things are here. He had no time to use his gun—it's still in the holster."

Barthell said quietly, " Wouldn't an Arab have taken it ? And he doesn't appear to have been robbed. Strange, isn't it?"

Smith shrugged, his head turned to the body. " How can we tell? The desert people do strange things."

" Garraud told us the local people were friendly—or at least they did not interfere."

" That still doesn't let them out," Smith said. " Garraud may have quarrelled with them for some reason. And then there are wandering Bedouin. . . ."

Barthell moved his strong shoulders impatiently. " All this —in a few minutes? And there is no sign of a struggle—no footmarks."

"The sand is very hard here. It would show no marks." All at once Smith's voice was strained and angry. "It could have happened that way. What reason could anyone here have for killing Garraud?"

"I don't know," Barthell said coolly. He felt himself collected now, his mind clear. "But someone had a reason, someone close."

"I know one thing—two things," said Smith. "One is that you didn't murder Garraud, and the other is that I didn't. And that's all." He brought the palms of his hands together hard as if he was trying to crush something between them. "Well, standing here won't help, and we can't let him lie all afternoon. Give me a hand to carry him back to the tents."

Together Smith and Barthell bore the dead man across the hot sand to the camp. While they placed him inside one of the tents and covered him with a blanket Barthell was wondering what Smith had been doing by the huts and why he was so quickly on the scene of the murder—if he had not done it himself. Why had he appeared so casual at first, and just now suddenly angry and even faintly scared? But somehow Barthell's strongest feeling was that Smith had spoken truly when he had denied killing Garraud. Then where was the killer now—who was he? As he left the tent these thoughts were blasted instantly from Barthell's mind by a new, cold fear of his own.

Kingsley—was he already dead?

He still had to find the skipper, before anything else. Richer was beside the mess tent. When they told him about Garraud the stretched panels of the Frenchman's face seemed to turn more yellow and his deep eyes, already bright, glowed as lamps turned to full brilliance. His hands trembled, and the sweat stood icily on his high forehead.

"Who could have done this? I do not understand. . . . My poor colleague."

Smith was looking hard at Richer. He said, "You have no idea who might have done it?"

"None at all. There was no quarrel between us here." Richer was agitated, his glances straying. "*C'est terrible.* . . ."

"It might have been someone—outside," Smith suggested quietly. "From the village, perhaps."

"Yes, yes—I was going to say that. Now there is a murderer at large. I must send a signal at once. We may need help, and there is no one to carry on the work. . . . I must send a signal."

Barthell shook himself, thinking of Kingsley. He saw Richer go and speak to Tarollier who was working at the food store nearby, and Tarollier did not appear to say anything before Richer hurried on to the radio tent.

Gleason still worked on the plane's motor, and beneath the wing Cummings and Tarrant sat, each with a Sten close at hand. They looked up, surprised and apprehensive, when Barthell approached.

"Harry! What's happening?" Cummings's face was pale and strained as he saw the navigator's grim expression. "Have you found the skipper?"

"No. Where's the stewardess?"

"In the galley. Why have . . .?"

"Listen. I didn't get off the airfield. It's Garraud—I found him by one of the huts. . . . He's been murdered."

They stared at Barthell, faces collapsed and foolish with incredulity.

"Murdered? But—he was here, at lunch."

"He was, and then we saw him go towards the huts. A few minutes later he was dead."

Tarrant said hoarsely, "Why? Why should anyone want to kill Garraud?"

"That's what I'd like to know. I'd no sooner found him when this Smith appeared on the scene. . . . He suggested that wandering Arabs or someone from the village might have done it. Well, I suppose they *might*—Garraud was stabbed in the back with an Arab knife—but so could I, or Smith, or anybody else in Faruda. Who?"

Barthell lifted his hands, leaving the doubt hanging in the hot air like a threat.

They were silent then. Etched deeply into their consciousness now was the certainty that the threat was real and close. But it was because it seemed blind too, purposeless and indiscriminate, that the death of Garraud was linked in their minds with Kingsley's unaccountable disappearance. There might be a hundred reasons for the Frenchman's murder; but there was no cause why Kingsley should not have returned long ago, had he been free to do so. They looked at one another, thinking of Garraud's swift and silent fate.

"What now?"

Tarrant was holding his Sten, and for the first time his boyish face was set in a mould of anxiety which lent him a curiously mature and responsible air. By unspoken consent both he and the co-pilot appealed to Barthell, as by consent they had given him the place of command now that Kingsley was not there. His square and muscular frame and the ugly, rugged face inspired comfort and a vague confidence that, somehow, he would see things through. He was not the insensible man who had never known fear, but one who, feeling it, could conquer by patient courage and determination. It was Barthell who had crept back through the roaring, trembling shell of Peter Fox after the explosion over France, crept to stare down through the yawning hole to the dark valley below, he who had told them that they could get down though he himself did not believe it.

And in this still and torrid afternoon of the desert, where suddenly danger had entered the silence and fused with each grain of sand and particle of the enamelled sky, it was he who had elected to go alone and search for Kingsley.

For a time Barthell said nothing, staring thoughtfully at the dusty tarmac. His chin was a crag, clouded by muscled cheeks and heavy brows.

Then he said, "Richer is sending a signal now. It may be as Smith says—a wandering tribe—anybody—could be hiding in the dunes over there, and we may need help." He paused, looking from one to the other of the set faces before him. "This Smith—he's a strange bird. Lunchtime he seemed to be worried over the skipper, and just now he got mad when he thought I was doubting his theory of Arabs being responsible for killing Garraud. But if he's right about the Arabs, what motive could they have?"

Chewing his moustache, Cummings said, "Garraud may have crossed swords with the local people. A lot of them are full of ideas about self-determination and so forth and take a poor view of the French and any interference from them.

And Garraud looked the kind of man who wouldn't take kindly to opposition of any sort."

"But he seemed rather to sympathise with the local people when we talked to him last night. Anyway, he's dead now, poor devil. We put him in the sleeping quarters—the far tent."

"Are you suspicious of anyone, Harry? Smith?"

Barthell laughed shortly. "I don't know if I am or not. He acted a bit queerly just now, and what was he doing so near Garraud's body? Later, I thought he looked almost scared...."

"Of what?"

"I don't know. Unless it was of—of whoever killed Garraud."

"If there's any connection between Garraud and the skipper going missing," Cummings muttered, "it could be Smith or Tarollier. Both were away this morning and out of sight for a short time after lunch. Richer was here all morning—he couldn't have had anything to do with the skipper's absence."

"No—at least, not directly."

Tarrant said, "Harry, it's worse now.... Are you still going to the village, alone?"

"Yes, but I'll take the jeep."

"It's dangerous."

"It's dangerous here," Barthell said, his mouth hard. "I've got to go. You two must not leave the kite whatever happens, d'you understand? I still think we should send that signal, despite the fact that Richer is sending now."

"You don't trust him?"

"I don't trust anybody after this. Make it an hour and a half from now, David, if I'm not back with the skipper." Barthell glanced at his watch. "Hell! It won't be all that long before dark, and I must find him while the day lasts. There's still a chance that we may get away before nightfall."

"A pretty slim one now," Cummings grunted.

"But still a chance. Remember—whoever killed Garraud can be lurking about and may attack us too. If any strangers come nosing round, Arabs or otherwise, shoot first and ask questions afterwards if they look the wrong sort."

"Haven't seen the ghost of a native yet—that's one of the creepy things about this place." Tarrant stared round anxiously, fingering his gun. "It's too damn quiet and deserted by far."

"I'm going now." Barthell's voice was calm and soft, and he smiled slowly. "There's no need to tell the stewardess about Garraud, eh? And don't forget that signal, if . . ." He left the sentence unfinished, raised his hand in a brief farewell and began to walk towards the tents.

"So long, Harry. Watch out, and good luck."

The jeep stood where Garraud had left it close to the mess tent. As Barthell was about to climb into it Tarollier appeared at the entrance to the tent and called to him. He waited impatiently while the big man lurched up to the vehicle's side where he stopped, a kind of scared calculation in his little eyes. Barthell caught the pungency of stale sweat, of the large wet patches on Tarollier's shirt under the arms and the streaks of it on the chest where it had run down his body.

Tarollier looked quickly towards the aircraft before he spoke, his small red mouth round and moist.

"This is bad, m'sieu," he said, a high sound.

"About Garraud?"

Tarollier nodded and Barthell watched narrowly, weighing him. The Frenchman's pale, squeezed-up features registered an expression of flabby anxiety. What was Tarollier's part in the strange happenings at Faruda—why had he been so much away from the airfield? Until he appeared at lunch there had been no sign of him that day, or the previous evening. There might be a simple explanation—a woman in the village, or it could have been Tarollier's job to keep in touch with the Bey. He did not look very intelligent, Barthell thought, but there was something like a sullen determination about him.

"Yes, M. Garraud. He was a good man. Who could have done this?"

"I don't know," Barthell said briefly. "Mr. Smith thinks he may have been killed by Arabs."

"It is very likely—there are some lawless tribes in this region," Tarollier said. He leaned forward. "You are wanting the jeep, now?"

"I am taking it to look for Captain Kingsley." The navigator looked directly at Tarollier. "Have you seen him today?"

"No, I have not seen him." The reply was quick, the eyes unwinking on Barthell's.

"Where were you this morning?"

"I had to take a message to the Bey for M. Garraud. I went to the palace, but I did not see the captain. He could have gone to the village. . . ."

"You know it, this village?"

"Yes, I have been there once or twice since we came to Faruda." Now Tarollier's eyes shifted, he smiled slightly and there was a cold eagerness in the smile. "Why do you not take me with you, and we can look for your captain together? Richer and Smith—they will be safe here with your crew."

Barthell hesitated. He did not know if Tarollier was all right, but it would be useful to be accompanied by someone who knew his way about. And he could look after himself anyway, against half a dozen Tarolliers. The only test was —would it help in his search for Kingsley to have Tarollier with him? He decided that it would.

"All right. How far is it to the village?"

"Not as much as three miles."

All at once Barthell was uncertain about the village. Why should the skipper go there? But he had to look somewhere for Kingsley, and with nothing to go on this was the most likely place. A wave of bitter hopelessness rose in Barthell and he said harshly, "Let's go, then." Suddenly he had felt it was useless to go.

"I am not afraid of being murdered by Arabs," Tarollier said with something like a sneer in his voice. "Shall I drive, as I know the way?"

"Yes. Now, let's get moving." He'd feel better moving.

Tarollier started the engine and the jeep swung round on the tarmac, leaving a horizontal cloud of fine dust behind it, and Barthell waved to the two figures beneath the aircraft's wing as they sped away.

Although he was not favourably impressed by Tarollier, Barthell was glad now that he had someone with him who knew the road to the village and the surrounding district; it would save time, and as a passenger he would be able to see more. The jeep swept past the control tower, leaving the concrete and bumping over the hard-packed sand near the huts where he had found Garraud, and then they were in the little depression which cut through the loose, low mounds of sand that hid the airfield from the sea.

Barthell was surprised at the extent of the dunes. The undulating hummocks, shaped into fantastic patterns by winds which must sometimes blow in Faruda and here and there ribbed like the skin of a whale, bordered the track on both sides for perhaps half a mile after they had left the field. The road snaked between them, but its general direction was north-easterly, where Barthell knew the village lay in relation to the airfield. In several places loose sand had piled in the road but the jeep ploughed through it determinedly when Tarollier went into low gear. He drove in silence, his eyes under the peaked cap always on the way ahead.

Barthell scanned the track and the rolling dunes anxiously for any sign of Kingsley having passed this way. His heart sank as they went on and he saw nothing. The walls of sand were smooth and untouched; there was no sign, no help from them. And even now the sun was beginning to drop low to their left, fire in the metal sky, and he knew that they must hurry.

Soon the dunes became flatter and receded a little from the track, so that it ran across the floor of a shallow valley which was scattered with wind-eroded sandstone boulders, like strange little houses in the valley, Barthell thought, like the homes of a people who were never seen. How many of these unseen, hiding people were here? Suddenly it seemed that there were eyes behind every rock, balefully watching as they passed.

The jeep slowed and stopped, Tarollier pointing to the fuel gauge.

"*Tiens!* We are nearly out of gas," he said, snapping his thick fingers and climbing down from the driver's seat. "But it will not take a moment, m'sieu. Wait there while I get the spare can."

Barthell sat staring moodily at the sandy waste around them

while Tarollier moved behind to unstrap a jerrican from the back of the jeep. The late afternoon was still, the air a little cooler already and silent with the terrible, potent quiet that was the symbol of this place. Barthell reckoned that they were about a mile from the field now. Beside the road he saw a sort of cairn of sandstone blocks piled roughly together, perhaps the mark of an Arab grave.

Behind him Tarollier did not touch the petrol can. He was looking carefully at the back of Barthell's head, measuring the distance, and a little smile of pleasure was on his small red mouth. His hand closed on a heavy metal wrench which lay in the back of the jeep, and he felt its smooth weight lovingly, bracing his arm.

"Hurry," Barthell said. Now he was looking down the dusty road ahead.

"I am coming," Tarollier replied softly.

He leaned across the vehicle, his arm raised, and the wrench came down.

Barthell heard it but had no time to move. It hit him behind the ear and he fell soundlessly, sideways across the steering wheel, his head smacking against it, and then he slid back slackly over the seats. Tarollier threw down the wrench and the smile was still there on his mouth as he saw what he had done. A slow trickle of blood began at the wound in Barthell's head, dropping to the canvas covers of the seat.

Tarollier looked quickly up and down the track. Nobody. . . . He showed no effort as he picked up Barthell and laid him face downwards on the sand. There was cord and cotton waste in the jeep's toolbox, and he tied Barthell, hands and feet together and then the feet back and up to the bound hands, and the cotton waste was stuffed into his mouth and tied there. Tarollier grunted this time as he lifted Barthell and carried him to the pile of stones beside the track.

It was lucky, Tarollier thought, that he had remembered the old well. It was disused and dry now, only a few feet deep, but it would serve the purpose of hiding the meddlesome navigator until they were gone from Faruda. He raised his burden, balancing it on the low wall before he pushed it in. The slack body fell down the shaft and hit the bottom with a hollow thud, and the sharp rattle of loose stones dislodged came after, sound-children following a parent.

Tarollier gazed down at the huddled figure for a moment and then went back to the jeep, moving quickly. There was much work to be done, and it was getting late. The track was empty, soundless. He poured the contents of the jerrican into the jeep's tank and jumped into the driving seat. It was time the food and water were loaded, ready for the man Arnold to collect after dark.

He let in the clutch and drove on down the road, and he did not turn to glance at the old well. Then he remembered that in his haste he had not taken the navigator's gun. It was too late now; but it would not matter. They would be gone before he could free himself—if he ever did free himself.

Tarollier smiled at the road ahead, licking his red lips with sensual pleasure. In spite of the setbacks, it was going well.

*　　　*　　　*

Tarrant was alone under the wing when he saw Susan Wells come down the ladder from the cabin. He frowned, watching her; somehow he didn't want to see her now, and she would be safer inside the machine. He wanted to see her when they were all on their way home, all together again going home. Now it seemed that they might never be together any more. Cummings was wandering aimlessly on the tarmac nearby, a tall, shuffling figure in the sun.

As the stewardess walked under the machine's belly she was looking not at Tarrant but at the Sten on his knees. She came and sat beside him and put out her hand to touch the gun.

" I remember seeing my father with one of those, in the war," she said. " He never had to use it in the Home Guard. I hope you won't have to use it."

He nodded, suddenly awkward, wondering what to say. " Don't touch it. They go off easily."

" If you use it, it will only be because you have to, won't it, David?"

" Only because I have to," he said. " Are you feeling better now?"

"Yes, thank you. It's cooler. . . . When will it be dark?"

"In about two hours, more or less. I think you ought to stay in the kite. It's safer there."

"I'd rather be here." Her voice was a whisper which he could scarcely catch even in the silence.

She sat with her hands clasped before her, pale, her calmness gone, suddenly looking very young. Then she raised her eyes for the first time to his face, thinking that it was a boy's frightened face, and she smiled a little to help him. Then she thought that it did not look so much like the face of a boy at all, except for the young unlined flesh of it, because the eyes were different. They were scared, but older now with this experience and an effort to control it was there, showing that there was no defeat. No defeat yet. She was glad, for she felt that something else had happened, something evil and mysterious.

He said, trying to find hope for them both, "Bob has almost finished. When Harry comes back with . . ." He stopped, feeling all at once that each lame word was adding height to the dark hills of doubt and anxiety which surrounded them.

"We can only wait," she said steadily, "hoping that they will come back soon."

It was then, unexpectedly after the steadiness, that she began trembling, slow ripples starting from some point of agitation inside her, spreading out and shaking the clasped hands and the smooth brown hair. It hurt him to see it, and he put out his hand to hers. As the hands touched her trembling ceased.

"David, I *am* afraid of something here. We don't know what it is."

"It will be all right soon. Don't be afraid, Susan."

"I'm trying not to be. I've been trying for a long time. . . . Fear does funny things to people, doesn't it?"

"Sometimes it opens their eyes," Tarrant said quietly.

"Yes, it opens their eyes," she said, looking at him gravely. "I know now. It started with the explosion in Peter Fox —but this is different from the kind I felt then. That was sharp and deep and quick, and it was there. This is slow, waiting, and we don't know where the danger lies, only knowing there is danger. It's worse, this kind."

His hand still lay on hers.

"There's something else. It was not long ago. What was it, David?"

"Nothing," he said slowly, avoiding her eyes, "nothing that concerns us—the crew—directly. . . ."

"All right," she said. "If it's something like that perhaps I'd better not know." She smiled faintly. "But ignorance isn't bliss, David. It would be wonderful just to go home—all of us together."

"It would be the most wonderful thing in the world now."

"Yes. . . . Let's hope for it."

"You look like a little girl," he said. "You're not calm and capable and distant any more."

"I don't feel it, either. Faruda has done that for me."

"I'm glad it has."

"Because it shows that I'm human after all?"

"It shows that you have a heart." He smiled. "Once—I thought you hadn't."

"Stewardesses are better off without hearts," she said. "They're waitresses, nurses, cooks, helps, messengers, companions. Not women."

"And you were always so much a stewardess."

"Why not?" she asked in a low voice. "It was my shield. . . ."

"Against what?"

"Against—being hurt. I didn't want to be hurt, not any more." She looked away, over the plain towards the far southward hills, and when she spoke again the words came tumbling out as though a dam had broken, releasing not only words but pain. "I think you'll understand," she said simply. "I loved a man, I believed he loved me, and we were going to be married. And then—I found that he didn't want to marry me after all. That was it—an ordinary little story that must have been told thousands of times before, only when it's yours it's not ordinary, or little. I was young then, when these things hurt so much more . . . And I thought I could still be hurt, afterwards, by someone else. I felt that I had to shield myself."

"I'm sorry," Tarrant said. "I hadn't guessed. . . ." He hesitated. "This man—do you still love him?"

"No, I can't, I suppose. I don't think about him very much now." She looked up into Tarrant's face. "Once—not very long ago—I'd have died rather than tell this to anyone. But now—I want to tell you, and I feel better and not ashamed." Her eyes were very bright, but no tears fell.

"There's nothing to be ashamed of," he said gently. "I'm glad you told me, and I'm glad you weren't really just a stewardess."

"I suppose some women wouldn't have made such a fuss about it. But I'm afraid I'm one who takes these things seriously—too seriously, perhaps. It's a disadvantage when your hopes don't materialise. Anyway, it's over now."

"Yes. . . . And you couldn't have gone on being a stewardess all the time."

"I know, but I wasn't looking very far ahead. I daren't. I was only trying to protect myself from the daily, immediate contacts. But now I realise that I saw danger everywhere because I was so afraid of it, even where there was none. I saw it in everyone new. I saw it in you."

He was silent, watching her face.

"Now I know it was never in you—not for me. These physical dangers that we have gone through together and are still going through—they have shown me that it wasn't there, David. Perhaps if we had been in England, doing the ordinary, everyday things, I might still have been suspicious of any friendliness of yours, and I would have been even more a stewardess to you. Now . . ."

"Now you're a woman, not that cold wax model of efficiency any more."

"If being scared means I'm one, then I am. But at least it's a relief to be able to show it after trying not to show anything for so long." She smiled softly into his eyes. "You've never had to worry about that, have you, David—trying to blank yourself off from other people? You wouldn't do it. It's cowardly, really. I'm glad you wouldn't do it."

"There's another thing I wouldn't do," he said gruffly, and he was thinking of this other man. "I wouldn't hurt you, ever."

"I don't think you would," she said, and she was still smiling, but a sudden shyness had entered her round eyes. "Isn't it strange that Faruda should have done this to me —the hot, dusty, forsaken place where we are. Will I still be changed, afterwards?"

"I think you will," he said. "I know you will, if you want it. It's a little world here, but it's not *another* world, it's a part of ours, a little part of our lives. What it does to us will last if it has opened our eyes and our hearts."

There was surprise on her face, but it fled as she looked at him and saw his conviction.

"I believe it now," she said. "Let's stay together until we go home."

Gleason secured the last clips holding the cowling of number four motor and wiped his hands on a piece of waste before descending the metal ladder. She was fixed now, he'd beaten her. A smile curved upward on his firm mouth as he looked at the power-egg, its silver skin bright and faintly touched with gold in the sun's declining beams. She was finished, but there was no hurry. The skipper and Harry weren't back yet.

They wouldn't come now, not before dark. Somehow he knew they wouldn't.

He was suddenly sullenly angry with the motor as he looked at it, with the machine. Peter Easy had always been a bitch, a sly and cunning bitch who took delight in her caprice so that you had to nurse and tend and beat her. There were kites like that, with bitchiness built into them, just like some people. . . .

She would be all right now, but they wouldn't get home tonight. And Della wouldn't be there when they did. He knew that too.

He couldn't care so much about Della now; which showed, he thought wryly, that he had never loved her, had only wanted her. But there would be time enough to regret Della's going when they got home, and there were other things to think of here; Harry and the skipper. It surprised him how easy it was to put Della into the background of his thoughts.

Something must have happened to them—to the skipper anyway. Harry had not been gone long yet. But—Garraud. . . . Lester had told him about Garraud. The sullen anger in Gleason all at once focused into a cold fury against Faruda and the unseen menace of the place. The motor was finished and he could do something. The hard streak of determination in his character, the refusal to be baffled or beaten, was uppermost in him now. He'd been thinking about what he could do while he was working on the motor, especially since Harry had gone. Harry had taken Kingsley's place; who would take Harry's, if Harry didn't come back?

The first thing was to get the motor run up and ready in case they came soon, then to send the signal if they didn't. After that—well, who knew what?

He descended the ladder and laid it on the tarmac, stretching his compact body which was stiff from the cramping positions it had been forced to assume throughout the scorching day, and looked at the others. Cummings had just joined the stewardess and Tarrant, and his pale, thin face seemed to have shrunk, leaving the eyes more prominent than ever and the great red moustache with a new and grievous droop. They sat silent beneath the wing, waiting.

"Nothing happening?" Gleason asked quietly.

"Nothing."

"I wish to God something would," Cummings said jerkily, nursing his gun. "Something—anything. . . ." His breath hissed out, whistling. "And no foot. It's gone."

"Oh, to hell with your foot!" Tarrant burst out. "What does it matter . . .?" He checked himself as he caught Susan's eye, and she smiled wanly.

"How long is it before we have to send the signal?"

"Half an hour."

Gleason looked towards the north-east. The line of dunes was sharp against the bright sky, but darker now before the quick evening's coming. It was a clean and uninterrupted line, and it seemed changeless as the configuration of a place where no human had ever trod. No returning jeep emerged from the little cleft near the huts—there was nothing but the hopeless plain and the decayed and useless works which, long ago, men had placed upon it. Looking at it Gleason felt the weary anxiety in him as he wondered how the mystery of Faruda would be resolved.

Now only an hour of full daylight was left. It had been a long, long day, and in their hearts the four people by the lonely aircraft were preparing themselves, each in his own way, for the night. And the night would be longer. But they must be ready, Gleason told himself again; if their faint hopes were realised and the skipper and Harry came back they might have to get off in a hurry.

"I'm going to run her up," he said.

"All right, Bob. Don't be long."

"Five minutes."

He climbed the ladder at the cargo doors and the others moved clear of the propeller. In a few seconds the blades began to revolve, stiffly and reluctantly like the clogged steps of an old man; the motor cleared its throat, coughing and banging before it belched blue smoke and awakened, roaring rage. Heavy brown dust clouds swept back from the flailing propeller, and the thick silence of Faruda was shredded, destroyed at last by the motor's huge storming voice. It thrummed and chattered with mimic life through the bodies of the people who listened there, and in it was hope and despair. It rose and fell—rose, fell again as Gleason moved the pitch levers, screaming a defiance at the desert, the propeller not metal now but a disc of translucent, shimmering light. For three or four minutes the sound blasted over the hot sand; and then the return of silence, the propeller clacking away in slowing silvery revolutions until it stopped to point a broad finger at the sky.

Tarrant said, "They'll know the job is finished now. . . . Wherever they are they ought to have heard that."

Cummings wiped his face with a soiled handkerchief, pulling at his moustache. "Why don't they come?" he muttered. "What's to stop them now?" His voice rose querulously to a sharp, thin sound.

The engineer emerged from the machine and came to stand beside them. He had changed from his working clothes into a clean shirt and slacks, and he brought out the remaining Sten.

"She's all right now," he said in his usual restrained manner, staring up at the now silent motor. "No sign of any more leaks and pressure is well up to scratch, so we're ready."

"Ready for another night here by the look of things,"

Cummings said glumly. " By the way, has there been any reply to Richer's signal? Where is he?"

" Don't know." Tarrant peered over his shoulder as though Richer might be there. " Now I come to think of it I haven't seen him since he left the radio tent about an hour ago. I suppose the signal went. . . ." He hesitated, wondering whether Susan was going to ask why Richer had been sending signals. " He'll be about somewhere."

" And Smith?" Gleason was standing beside Cummings, and he looked alert, expectant.

" Smith asked me some time back if I was sending a signal," Tarrant said. " I told him I was, if the skipper hadn't turned up soon. He said he thought we should ask for help immediately, and then he suddenly nipped off towards the tents and disappeared. I haven't seen him since."

" He's been popping up and disappearing all day," Cummings grumbled. " Queer sort of weather man, if you ask me."

" The big man—Tarollier—went with Mr. Barthell in the jeep," Susan said, gazing in turn at each of the still faces before her. " That leaves M. Garraud. Is he still working somewhere?"

Gleason answered. " Yes—working." She would have to know soon, he thought; she wasn't the kind you could hide things from very easily.

" The longer I stay here the less I like it." Cummings stared round him uncomfortably, a sickness on his face. " I don't like it now—not a little bit." His voice began to rise as the first mad stirrings of panic touched him. " This waiting. . . . Where is the skipper? He was only going for a walk—what's happened to him?"

" All right, Lester." Gleason's voice was quiet and his hand steady on the co-pilot's shoulder. " Don't get worked up about it. There may be quite a simple explanation—the jeep may have broken down. . . ."

" I suppose there's a simple explanation for Garraud too!" Cummings laughed shrilly. " Or perhaps we just dreamed that bit. . . ." Suddenly the sound of his own words seemed to sober him, and his voice dropped, muttering. " I'm sorry. . . . I didn't mean to say anything about that."

Gleason saw that the stewardess's face was white, and she was gripping Tarrant's arm. He said flatly, "Tell her, David." It would be kinder to tell her, and she could stand knowing about Garraud as well as some of them. Cummings was still being sorry but he looked better now. "It's this waiting," he said. "I seem to have been sitting under this kite for days—waiting. It caught up on me. . . ."

"Yes." Gleason was quietly patient. "Now, listen. It's still possible that both the skipper and Harry may be back soon. But in case they're not, we must decide what we're going to do."

"Harry wanted us to stay with the machine."

Gleason was silent for a time. Then he said, "Yes, I believe we ought to stay together. Things will soon start moving at Westonmills when they get David's signal, even if Richer's hasn't started something already. But if we're going to need help it can't reach us until dawn—at the earliest. We'd all better realise that.

"So, if we have to, we must stick it out until the morning," Gleason said. "We can take watches to guard the kite." He laughed shortly. "Rogers will be furious if we lose another."

Then Tarrant said, "While we're together, here, we seem to be safe. Nobody comes, nobody touches us. We weren't disturbed last night. But when anybody leaves the field something happens. The skipper, then Garraud, and now . . ." He stopped short, staring down at his gun.

"All right," Gleason said quietly. "Until we know what's going on we stay here." He looked at his watch and then out over the empty and mocking spaces of the field. No one came. "I think you'd better go and set up the transmitter and get that signal off, David."

"There's still ten minutes before Harry's time. . . ."

"Never mind. There's no one coming, and I don't like it—none of us does. Send the signal, then we'll all feel better."

Tarrant rose and Susan's eyes moved up to him. "Shall I go with you, David?"

"No—better stay here with Bob and Lester. I won't be long."

He moved off to the radio tent. The two men and the girl sat silently, staring in the direction of the little depression where the road to the village began, the way that Barthell had gone and the skipper too, perhaps, the way from which they had not returned. They strained their ears, hoping to catch the sound of the jeep's engine, but there was nothing. Instead the awful silence, rotten with evil, drummed maddeningly in their heads.

And this silence, this utter negation of life, was suddenly a thing against which they could no longer strive. It was the badge of an enemy which was always unseen, always beyond reach, intangible as a shadow. How could shadows be fought? It seemed that the enemy had won, that their defeat was acknowledged in the signal which Tarrant was about to send. They knew then that Faruda was an enemy too, that all the time it had been waiting to destroy those who invaded it, those who had tried to pierce its tough skin of loneliness and silence with roaring machines. It hated them. . . . For years it had been dead, returned to the desert from which it had been wrested only under the compulsion of war; and that was how it wanted to stay.

They looked at one another, each knowing what the others were thinking, each knowing at last the power and dread of the place where they were.

Now the sun was a huge scarlet ball, sliding quickly down the sky's perimeter, soon to darken in crimson fire before plunging to its evening death in the low western plains. And then Tarrant suddenly appeared again beside them, and his young face carried the pale, sweated wash of a new fear.

He had not sent the signal; they knew it before he spoke.

His voice was hoarse, stumbling. "The transmitter—it's useless. I can't—can't send any signal. . . ."

"What's wrong with it?" Gleason grasped the radio operator's arm, searching his face with bright and anxious eyes.

"There's been a short somewhere. I think the main transformer has burned out, and there are blown fuses all over the place."

Their silence was overlaid by the darkening shadow of despair.

Cummings said slowly at last, "The damage. . . . Was it —did it look like an accident, or . . . ?"

"I don't know yet. I haven't looked closely enough. But why should it have happened—now?"

"Can't you do anything about it, David?"

"I'll go back." Tarrant tried to smile at Susan. "There may be some spares in the tent. I'll try it, Bob."

He turned quickly away. Again the three who were left looked at each other, and their eyes were weary of searching for the silent danger that was never seen.

It must have been deliberate, Gleason thought. He stroked the smooth barrel of his gun. Richer—he was last in the tent. Where was he now?

"Richer," Cummings said, an echo to the engineer's thoughts. "Richer—or Smith. . . . Either could have wrecked the transmitter, and gone. It would be easy for anyone to slip away behind the tents."

Susan said, as if to herself, "If the radio has been wrecked deliberately it was to stop help coming. Whoever did it would have sent no signal—nobody will have heard us." Her hands were clenched in her lap, her big eyes on the radio tent.

"It could have been someone else," Cummings muttered. "Why should Richer or Smith want to harm us? And Garraud . . .?"

"It might be someone else," Gleason said softly. "It might . . . Why should Richer kill his chief? They were working together in a strange place, among strange people—enemies perhaps. It would be to their advantage to preserve one another. . . ." His voice trailed away, smothered by the silence.

They knew that unless Tarrant could fix the transmitter their hope of rescue was gone, and rescue was what they needed now. Salvation had dangled on the frail wires in that tent, and now the wires were severed, melted, dashing their faith to the dust. Was it Richer who was the hidden menace of this desolate place? Or the silent and watchful Smith? Or was it some other, unknown, who had been stealthily at work while they guarded the machine? There was unrest here in Africa; here there were men who would take the law into their own hands to gain their ends. . . .

With an effort of will Gleason forced the crowding fears

from his mind. The machine's transmitter? But no—there was not enough power in the batteries, and all of what there was would be needed to start the motors; there had been a heavy drain on them already, starting up number four. Besides, there was no height to carry the range of any signals, even if they could be sent by this comparatively weak transmitter, beyond the radius of a few useless miles where there was no one to hear. The faint dots and dashes would perish in the heedless desert, drown in the uncaring sea. Gleason cursed below his breath as he stared at the slender voiceless mast beside the tent. It stood, a folly and a monument to disaster. And yet . . .

Suddenly his whole body grew taut; a challenging, excited look lit up his handsome face.

He said urgently, "There might be a way, even now. Keep your eyes open, Lester, and look after Miss Wells. I'm going to see David."

"What's happening?"

"I don't know if anything *will* happen. But there may be a chance to get that signal off after all. I've just got a feeling that whoever blew up that transmitter, if it was blown up, may have made a little mistake. I must talk to David."

It was cool and dim inside the radio tent. Tarrant was on his knees, rummaging inside a wooden box with the aid of a flashlight, and he was muttering furiously to himself. The black face of the transmitter with its coloured knobs and dials stared contemptuously from a trestle table; an open signal book and a pair of headphones lay beside the morse key.

"It's hopeless!" Tarrant almost shouted the words as he saw Gleason in the entrance. "There are no spares here— no fuses, no transformer, nothing. It looks as though the place has been cleaned out."

He stood up, pointing unsteadily at the transmitter.

"We can't send any signals. This thing is so much scrap, and I can't do anything about it."

"Then it's not an accident . . .?"

"Accident? Not a hope. Look at this." Tarrant held up a small piece of metal about three inches long. "This was across two power terminals. See how it's been burned? That's what blew her up."

"Whoever did it knew what he was doing, then?"

"I'm sure of it. It just *couldn't* have been accidental." Tarrant's voice shook. "Someone is after us, Bob. This proves it."

"Take it easy, David." Gleason stood motionless, brooding, over the transmitter. "Richer and Smith," he said, as if speaking to himself. "Both are radio operators. But . . ."

"The set's ruined, which means we're sunk. Sooner or later, if they don't hear from us at Westonmills, help will come—but then it may be too late." Tarrant passed a hand over his pallid and suddenly sweating face. "All these people —disappearing or murdered, one after another. . . . What can we do now?"

"There are things we can do, perhaps," Gleason said in his unobtrusive voice.

"What things? What . . .?"

"Listen, David. First, while there's still some daylight left, we'll search the camp in case there are any spare radio parts stowed away which might get this set going again. We'll have to work fast." Gleason paused briefly, his eyes bright with a new resolve. "And if we draw a blank we may yet be able to send that signal."

"How? The kite's radio is useless while it's on the ground —there's no power and no aerial. I can't use the trailing aerial on the deck, can I?"

"No, you can't." Gleason moved quickly to the entrance and pointed upward to the tall mast outside. "But—you could use this one."

Tarrant stood beside him, staring up at the mast from which a long wire ran down to a wooden post beside the tent. From the base of the aerial a cable had been led through a hole in the tent roof to connect with the transmitter.

"I might," Tarrant said doubtfully, "with a long wire from the machine. But there's still the power. . . ."

The engineer was eager, near to triumph. "Power! Isn't that what a generator is for? Don't you remember the generator we brought on the first trip? It's here—look!"

The little portable generator stood behind the tent, roughly protected by boards torn from a packing case which had once contained tinned food, and it appeared to be undamaged.

Tarrant bent over it quickly, and as he turned to face Gleason his eyes held something of the engineer's own hope and determination. This little thing, resting on the sand on its two legs and rubber-tyred wheel, this could be their answer. And even at that moment Tarrant was conscious of new and half-formed but urgent reasons for their safe deliverance from Faruda. Now it was he on whom they must rely—all of them, and Susan.

He said, " Perhaps we can do something, Bob, after all. . . . We shall need some cable to connect it and to hook up the aerial."

" The kite's not many yards from this mast. We can wheel the generator across. Do you think you'll be able to transmit then?"

" I think so. I don't know what the range will be, but it's worth trying."

" It's our only chance, David. They'll be listening for us at home, but if they don't hear it may be days before anyone wakes up to the idea that there's trouble here."

" Yes. We've got to transmit somehow. I saw some cable in the tent. Let's get . . ."

" Wait a minute!" Gleason grabbed the radio operator's arm. " If we can find any spares it will save a lot of time. Better search the other tents first."

" All right." Tarrant was unhappy, looking at the far tent. " That—that's where Garraud is, isn't it?"

" Yes, but we'd better do it, David. Come on."

Tarrant nodded, squaring his shoulders, and Gleason said, " I'll tell Lester."

After Gleason had spoken to the co-pilot he and Tarrant moved off to the mess tent. The quick, sub-tropical dusk was beginning to gather over the dun wastes of the airfield, and now the sun's bloody sphere was touching the westward horizon. Suddenly, it was cold. And then already the first faint star was in the east, winking its greenish light as it pricked through the mid-blue of the sky, a snapping, mocking eye from a vast outer and untouchable world, precursor of a million other taunting eyes. The breath of night, still and fear-haunted as that of day, could almost be seen rising from the desert beneath this star, exhaled by the mysterious and infinite sands far beyond the small compass of the field. They could feel it, even before it came, cold and sullen on their faces.

Their sick anxiety for Kingsley and now Barthell multiplied the potentialities of danger that darkness could hide. It would be long, silent, lonely, more evil than any night they had known. Whatever happened, there could be no help before the day came. Gleason almost laughed out loud when the thought that he might have been in bed with Della crossed his mind. But there was nothing to laugh at here, nothing. And Smith and Richer and Tarollier—where were they? Had any of them met death like Garraud, met his senseless and horrible end which seemed to be a madman's work? And they would see Garraud soon. . . .

Gleason fought grimly against these clamorous fears as he walked, gripping the butt of his gun more firmly; but what use was a gun against nothing, or bullets when there was no target?

They came to the mess tent in the growing dusk. Inside it was just as it had been when they left it after lunch—the trestle table and the folding chairs, the oil lamp hanging from the tent pole. There was a square cupboard at one end of the table, like an old-fashioned meat safe with a wire gauze door, but it contained only some plastic cups and plates, cutlery, three bottles of red wine and a few cans of meat and vegetables.

Under the tarpaulins outside they examined the insulated food containers and the piled cases in which the unused stores of the expedition to Faruda were packed. There was only one box of radio spares. It had been opened; the only object inside it which might have been of use was a small hand-operated transmitter of the kind carried in ships' lifeboats. When Tarrant tried the handle it would not move.

"Thorough, aren't they?" he muttered. "But that thing would have been no good to us anyway."

The little tent that Smith occupied yielded nothing.

"Looks like we'll have to try the generator after all," Tarrant said quietly.

"We'd best make sure." Gleason drew a deep breath. They were talking in whispers now. "Let's do the last tent."

"All right—if you insist. I'm not keen on viewing corpses tonight, but I suppose we ought to do the job properly." Tarrant shook himself, half angrily, half in apprehension. "When I joined this outfit nobody told me there would be times like these."

"Nor me. Come on."

The last tent was a drab olive green, slack guy ropes allowing the ridge to sag wearily like the spine of a broken-down hack. The flap was closed. A vision of the murdered Garraud rose before Gleason's eyes as he fumbled at the laces; he set his teeth, all at once tugging savagely at the ropes, and the flap opened.

He dropped on his knees to enter. And then, as though a curtain had been drawn, darkness came.

Gleason turned to the suddenly dim figure beside him.

"Give me the torch, David."

"Here . . ."

Gleason took the lamp and crawled through the flap. The beam of light illuminated the musty-smelling interior of the tent, revealing the three low camp beds, the tumbled blankets on them and the suitcases beneath, the wash basin in its metal stand and the odd pieces of clothing and toilet gear strewn on a big wooden box which served as a table.

The three beds were empty. The body of Garraud was gone.

CHAPTER VIII

THE EVENING

"So—you're going through with it," the girl said.

Her eyes despised the man who sat on the other side of the table. Heat swam about them in the little cabin.

Arnold did not look at her as he pulled hard on his cigarette and gulped down smoke as though it was food for his empty belly.

"I have to," he said.

"You wouldn't have had to—if you'd turned back outside."

"I've told you before. The trip took longer than I expected because of the storms and we've almost nothing to eat or drink. I couldn't turn back, Jo. You know it."

"I only know how I hate you for bringing me here." The cold contempt in her voice cut into his heart like a keen blade. "What is it?"

"What d'you mean?"

"You know what I mean. What have you come here for, Jim?"

"Listen, Jo. It's just another job. Why can't you forget it?"

"Because if it was just another job you'd tell me what it was, like you told me about the others—the Tangier jobs." She looked at him and still he avoided her eyes, his brown hands moving nervously on the smooth surface of the table.

"I can't tell you," he said. "Don't ask me."

"Don't you think I'll find out, some time before I leave this boat?"

"There's no reason why you should."

"It's big stuff, isn't it?"

"All right, then it's big," he said loudly. "So what?"

"And it's hot."

She saw him stiffen. He said nothing, and his hands stopped moving on the table. The little locket he wore was outside his shirt, swinging on its gold chain above the table.

"I'll tell you something, Jim. You're afraid of this job

—you've been afraid of it since we left Algiers. That's right, isn't it? And you're afraid of the people who are with you. You don't want to go through with it now, even less than you did this morning." Her voice dropped, floating on slow breaths. "This man who came today, the big man. I saw him on the quay. He told you something you didn't like. Is he coming with us?"

"Yes. . . . He's coming."

"What did he tell you?"

"Never mind what he told me." Arnold seemed to speak from behind some obstruction. "That's my business."

"And mine too, now."

All at once the man's jaw fell oddly, as though a set of facial muscles had gone, and a trickle of saliva started at the corner of his gaping mouth. His smoke-stained fingers let the cigarette fall to the floor and suddenly he began to talk very fast, the slack jaw jerking up and down like a puppet's.

"All right, Jo. You've a right to know what I've come for and I guess you'd better know now before you find out some other way. You won't like it and I don't. I didn't want to tell you—it won't help between us to tell you, but . . ."

"But you will."

"I will. It's drugs. Morphia and cocaine."

The girl's face showed no surprise, no fear, but very slowly its clear, clean lines began to sag in the first crumblings of a vague decay. Her eyes closed.

"Well—aren't you going to say anything?" Arnold's voice was still quick, but defiant now. "You asked for it, didn't you?"

"I thought it was something like that," she said tonelessly, opening her eyes. "Drugs. . . . So you're the kind who would do even that. I'm glad you told me now, Jim, so glad. . . ."

This voice and the face tortured him.

"Don't say it like that, Jo. Not like that!"

"Why not?" she asked. It was like an image speaking. "Why not? You wanted me to say something."

"Not like that—not from you. I had to do it, Jo. Can't you see I had to do it?"

"You didn't have to bring me into it though, did you? I'm

glad I've found out what kind of man you are." She smiled a little. "I suppose I should have guessed, but I didn't—not until today. If I'd known what you were going to do I'd have died first, even in that stinking hole you took me from, rather than come with you."

"I didn't want to do it, but I was broke. It's big money and I need it. That's all."

"Big money. . . ." She looked at him with a kind of sick curiosity, as at something unusual and strangely vile. "Yes—I suppose that's all that matters to people like you. What doesn't seem to matter is the lives you'll help to ruin, the disease and suffering you'll spread. Have you ever thought what a really filthy racket it is, Jim? Have you?"

"I've got to have the money," he whispered.

"I've seen some of them on the stage, the addicts," she said. "The old ones—they're pretty horrible to see when you get up close to them. It's as though there's nothing inside them, some of them are like that, and some are like sort of papery shells which if you poked them with your finger would let out some slimy putrid stuff. Do you want to . . .?"

"Shut up about that," he said very softly.

"All right." Her face was controlled now, beautiful again. "You knew I'd feel like this, and yet you brought me. You're keeping me on your boat against my will now."

"I'm sorry, but you'll have to stay."

"I suppose I shall." She stood up, staring from one of the little ports at the still, closed harbour, the deserted houses, the cruel sky that watched them. "I was a fool to come with you," she said quietly, and it seemed as though she was speaking to her mirrored self which looked back faintly and inquisitively from the glass. "But I really hadn't much choice, had I?" She turned quickly to face the man, a fierce and even proud movement. "And I thought I had fallen in love with you too. I wanted you as much as you wanted me, did you know that? I wanted you too, beside my desire to get home. . . . And now—now look what you have done to me."

He was silent, staring at the floor, hearing her bitter laugh.

"No, you don't want to look, do you, Jim? You haven't left very much to look at if you look deep enough. You've taken me, taken my self-respect—I had some once, not so long ago—you've kept me on board your ship and because you couldn't trust me set a stinking Spaniard to leer at me and make sure I won't escape, and now you've mixed me up in a filthy game of drug-running. And after all that, I'm farther from home than when I met you. Do you expect me to love you now?"

Arnold raised his shoulders wearily, and let them fall.

"I can't make you love me against your will. There were things I had to do but I didn't want to do. I did them because I wanted you and wanted to help you, but there were other things which I didn't know about. I *will* take you to Malta, as I promised, afterwards. . . ."

"Afterwards!" She almost spat the word at him. "Do you think there will be any afterwards, with this man? I heard him in the cabin this morning. What will he do when he finds me aboard, and what will he do to you when he has finished with you? Do you trust him even to give you your money?"

He leaped to his feet, his eyes staring fearfully and his hands trembling in a sudden access of rage and terror.

"Shut up!" he shouted. "Shut up, can't you? I can take care of both of us. I will, I tell you! I'm not afraid of any of these scum. I'm the captain of this ship, and they'll obey my orders at sea." He sat down slowly like an old man, licking pale lips, and his eyes crept towards the gangway leading to the deck.

The girl sat too, saying nothing. She knew he was afraid now, terribly afraid. His weakly handsome face was pallid below the fair wavy hair of which he was so vain, and the coating of sunburn gave the skin a curiously glazed and muddy texture. She saw that he had been drinking; a bottle of brandy, half emptied, stood on the cabin table, and there was another opened bottle on the locker by the gangway. Would he keep sober enough to get them out of this hole in the rocks without wrecking the boat? He was all right now, but soon he would reach that maudlin, drink-valorous stage when he thought he could do anything, and that no one could stop him doing it.

She was thinking about this slack and emptily defiant hulk

which leaned across the cabin table. She knew him now, and the confinement and intimacy and monotony of these long days and nights on the great, lonely ocean and under the wide sky had revealed him to her as little else could have done in such a short acquaintance. He had his good points—he had been kind and loving to her, and in the storms which had delayed them he had shown calmness and ability, for he was a fine seaman and navigator. Whatever else he was afraid of, he was not afraid of the sea. He had taught her some of these things which he knew so well, taught her about the stars and how to recognise the great navigating constellations, to identify the various kinds of cloud, to use a sextant and keep a course by the compass. And she had come to believe, as he did, that the sea was hostile only to those who would not take pains to know it, those who were contemptuous of its vast and hidden power.

But, in dealing with men stronger than himself, he was weak and frightened and malleable, and any prospect of easy money could submerge altogether the waterlogged remains of his self-respect. She knew that for a long time he had been smuggling American cigarettes out of the international port of Tangier to France and Italy, but she did not know that he had also run arms and criminals escaping from justice across the Mediterranean, or that this was not the first time he had carried drugs.

This job was different, and he was afraid of it; it was big, dangerous, and there must be a cunning and utterly ruthless brain behind it. Arnold was only the carrier, and since the morning the girl had sensed this powerful and controlling force which directed him, a force which was driving on over all obstacles to its goal. Was it centred in the big man whose accented English she had heard faintly from the cabin, whose lumbering form she had glimpsed on the quay from the little window of the room where she had been locked with Pedro? Somehow she did not think so—he did not look like the man she was imagining. Her hearing was acute and she had caught snatches of his talk, enough to know pretty well what was going to happen tonight. There had been something about " attending to the captain " as well, but she didn't know what that meant; she would have to think about it.

She realised that Arnold could not have wanted this man in the cabin, but there had been no way of stopping him without giving away her presence on the boat. How much did he think she had heard? But he would not care now; he was too frightened to care. . . .

Although the skylight was wide open it was still very hot in the cabin. For some reason which was not clear even to herself the girl had changed from her brief shorts into dark blue slacks and sweater, and as Arnold looked fully at her for almost the first time since she had entered the cabin it did not strike him as strange that she had done so. Her young figure under the simple clothes was beautiful and disturbing, but the red mouth was pressed into a hard, determined line, and the wide blue eyes which were more shadowed with experience than they should have been seemed now to be measuring some prospect, coolly and with an almost serene detachment.

Suddenly and deeply, Arnold envied her. She was calm, poised, now. She was afraid of nothing. This cool woman could not have overheard Tarollier talking of what he was to do to this poor devil of a pilot. He shuddered. And Jo —what would they do to her, afterwards? He had got her into this, selfishly and cruelly, because he had wanted her for himself, ignoring the warnings of a rusty conscience that she would hate him for what he was going to do at Faruda. Somehow he must protect her after they had sailed, keep her presence from these men as long as possible, or at least convince them that she knew nothing of their cargo or of this pilot.

She was beautiful. . . . His eyes lingered on the glowing red-brown hair, the firm outline of her breasts and the slim waist. Might there still be a chance to keep her, to persuade her not to leave him when all this was finished? He had never wanted any woman in his life as he wanted her. He knew that she was only a dancer in a cheap touring revue which had gone bust, but she had not hidden this from him any more than she had hidden the fact that her real name was Joan Briggs and not Jo Fanshawe, and that she was a docker's daughter from Stepney. She was straight, all right. And then the sick urgency of events at Faruda crowded into

Arnold's mind, shutting the door through which his thoughts were escaping towards her.

She said at last, quietly, "You see, if I had known about this in Algiers—it might have been different. Perhaps I could have done something. But now . . ."

"I've told you. . . . I was afraid you wouldn't come with me. But I didn't know it was going to be like this, Jo."

"Like what?" she asked sharply, watching him.

He gnawed at his lip. "Because we're late, there are . . ." He checked himself. "Oh—what does it matter? It's too late now."

"Too late for what?"

Arnold laughed without mirth. "Too late for everything."

All at once he leaned across the table towards the girl, looking directly into her eyes.

"Jo. . . . I would go now, as you want me to, if I could. I would cut the cables and go."

She knew that he was in earnest. Never before had she seen such desperate pain and truth in a man's eyes.

"Then why not, Jim?" she asked softly, and she touched his hand as it lay on the table. "Let's take a chance, and go, go together. Forget this filthy business. We can hoard our food and water—make for the nearest port. . . ."

"No!" He snatched his hand away and struck it against his head. "Jo—we can't!"

"Why not?"

"Because—this man who came aboard, he didn't trust me. . . ." Arnold's voice sank, whispering. "He took the main valves from the fuel injectors away with him. Until tonight, when he comes back, we can't move."

It was too late, then. She stared at him, her eyes large and dry and dark with this final destruction of hope, for until then she had kept alive the faint belief that he might be induced to get out before the drugs were put aboard. Even now she was not afraid. But they were caught in this thing, and it was something worse than Arnold would admit.

"He wanted to make sure I didn't run out on him," Arnold was mumbling. "I couldn't stop him. . . . There are a dozen ways he could have immobilised the ship." He pointed at a bunch of keys hanging from a hook above the engine room door. "He could have taken those keys and locked the fuel tank valves, put the compressed air bottles out of action, opened the sea cocks and flooded us—anything. But we can't move...."

"You didn't *try* to stop him," the girl said accusingly.

"He was armed. I wasn't. How could I have stopped him?"

She said nothing, watching him, despair mounting within her.

When he spoke again it was with a kind of sulky defiance. "Well, there it is—we have to go on. I need the money. I may as well have it."

Still she did not speak, the contempt slowly returning to her eyes.

"If you do as you're told, you won't be hurt," Arnold said, avoiding this cold, steady gaze. "But there's one thing . . ."

"Well?"

"It's you I'm thinking about, Jo. I hope you'll believe that, because it's true. Later—at sea—if this man finds you on board, you know nothing about this job, do you understand? Nothing."

Her nod mocked him. "I understand perfectly."

"It's for your own safety, Jo."

"I know. And it's for yours too. There will be no 'if', Jim. He's bound to find me sooner or later. You can't hide anyone on a boat this size for days on end."

"We can try," he said sullenly.

"Don't be a fool! It's impossible. He won't be very pleased with us, will he?"

"I'll take care of him. I'll tell him nobody knows anything about the job but me."

"And you hope he'll believe it?" She laughed contemptuously. "Will he be alone?"

"No—there will be another man."

"Is that all?"

Arnold's eyes shifted away and he tried desperately to stay the trembling of his hands.

"Yes. . . . Yes, one other man. That's all."

He felt her cold stare upon him, but he dared not look up. A thick, stifling silence fell in the small cabin, and

Arnold reached out suddenly for the bottle of brandy, almost knocking it over with clumsy, inert fingers before pulling out the cork and taking a long draught of the spirit. The girl watched him, her eyes hooded, waiting in the stillness.

At last she said, " What have you to do, before we go?"

The brandy was warm and comforting in his chest; he could breathe more easily now and gradually, under its emboldening influence, he was beginning to feel more confident, more in control of these dire problems which Faruda had so unexpectedly raised. He wiped his lips with a clean handkerchief which he folded carefully and replaced in his pocket, and then his comb came out and he drew it slowly through the wavy yellow hair.

Somehow, as she watched him, this action made a sudden sick fury rise up in the girl's breast, almost choking her.

" Stop that!" She was screaming at him, her face twisted in despairing rage. " You swine! You got me in this—and you comb your damned hair!"

She jerked forward and snatched the comb from him and hurled this thing which seemed to have become the futile symbol of her contempt and desperation furiously out of the open skylight. Arnold sat still, looking at her, a foolish smile on his handsome face.

" I've got another," he said.

She lay back, her breast heaving, her anger crystallising slowly into a weighted ball of hatred where her heart was. She hated him now, this weak adventurer who had tricked and betrayed her into danger, into becoming an accomplice in this despicable trade which spread human depravity and misery, disease and corruption. She stared with loathing at the stupidly smiling face opposite.

And then, at that moment, the embryo resolve which was already formed began to grow within her.

" You asked me what I have to do before we go," he said. He was casual now, almost airy. " As soon as it becomes dark I shall go up the track which leads to the airfield—did you know there was an airfield? Half a mile along this track a jeep will be waiting, loaded with food and water. I shall drive it here and put the provisions aboard. And then I shall wait for the cargo to come. That is all I have to do until we go."

"When will that be?"

"The cargo comes at eight-thirty—perhaps it will take an hour to load. We replace the injector valves, and then it's goodbye to Faruda."

"So you're going to leave this harbour in the dark?"

Some of the man's new assurance abruptly left him.

"It's narrow," he said uneasily. "But I'll make it."

"Not if you have any more brandy," she said scornfully.

"I've taken my ship through more difficult channels than this in my time." He was trying hard to regain his poise of a few moments ago. "And on darker nights than this will be, without scratching her paint. You'll see."

"Where did you go this morning, with this man?" Her voice was careless, but her eyes watched him.

He smiled. "Just for a little walk. . . . To see a friend of his—a big man in the district."

"Is he mixed up in this too?"

"Perhaps." Arnold lit another cigarette. "Why do you want to know?"

The girl's mouth made a sardonic upward twist, but she did not answer.

She stood up again and looked from the port across the small harbour. It would not be long before the dark came. The two stubby black fishing boats lay alongside one another against the opposite quay, silent and still, mounted on their own reflections in the calm water, lateen sails furled; there seemed to be no one aboard. Behind them the few houses stared at her with dead and hollow eyes, like homes abandoned long ago and left to rot in the decay which fell hotly from the sky above this place. The rough stones of the quay against which their own boat lay were dusty and cracked; she saw the leaning tin shed and the track which led up through the low plateau above it towards the west. She knew that the man Pedro would be watching from somewhere on the fore deck which was hidden from where she stood.

There was no wind, and the sun still blazed down from the sky's brassy container, bringing the torment of heat which had been painfully borne since they left the open sea. The sweater stifled her, but the night would be cold. It was as well that she had dressed for it. She had not known then why she was dressing like this; but she knew now.

They had a silent and frugal meal in the cabin. The food was running very short. It was when they had almost finished that the girl heard the noise. In this blaring silence it came as a quivering shock, electric in the thin air, cored with hope and yet hopeless. It grew from a sad mutter to a low-pitched roaring that trembled distantly from the desert. She listened carefully, recognising the sound of a plane's motor, and it seemed to come from the south-west. It lasted for several minutes, rising and falling, before it faded slowly to be killed by the universal silence.

She saw that Arnold was listening too, and his face was oddly crumpled, grey with a new fear.

As the afternoon began to close towards the cool, quick evening, Arnold's nervousness increased. He sat moodily silent in the cabin, chain-smoking American cigarettes and taking occasional pulls at the bottle. Half lying on the seat opposite the girl watched him covertly, and her big eyes were veiled, hiding the speculation in them. Once Arnold rose with jerky, mechanical movements and went on deck, and she heard him speaking in low and rapid Spanish to Pedro. Soon, she knew, she would be confined again to that fetid box with this unwashed ape. . . . She shuddered, pressing her hands to her temples with a desperate, unconsciously tragic gesture. She saw Arnold walk along the quay to where the narrow cleft of the harbour entrance was slashed through the brown rocks as though by the blow of a great axe, and he stood looking at it for a long time before walking slowly back to stare up the track at the harbour's landward end, and then he climbed back aboard the long grey ship.

The evening was time stretched into a tense, twanging agony. It was so deep and so nearly beyond all bearing that the girl found herself praying that the night should soon come, the night which might put an end to this awful silent waiting, while she yet knew that it would cloak dangers greater than any she had dreamed of or known. Steadily the light faded, and no more sound came from the airfield. . . . Arnold sat, half drunk, staring at some fixed and invisible point far outside the cramped cabin, at some focus in the terrible unknown that was closed round them.

At last the sky became slowly pearled with coming darkness, and the direct sunlight had gone. There was a brief orange glow in the west, bright and harsh on the edge of the sky, and then the spangled night strode above like a cool deliverer from heat and pain.

Without speaking Arnold rose, a dim shape uncoiling, and switched on the cabin light. The small yellow glow made his face look suddenly old and drawn. He passed down the alleyway which led aft to his room, ignoring the girl.

She watched him go, tensely still on the seat, and heard his door close behind him. She moved then, rising quickly and clutching something from the locker beside her, going silently on her rubber-soled shoes along the alleyway to the room opposite Arnold's.

She was back in the cabin again when his door opened and he returned along the alleyway. He had put on a dark sweater and he carried an electric torch. He stood for a little time, still, looking down at her.

"I'm going now," he said at last. His voice was thick and unsteady. "You—you'll have to stay in your room again, with Pedro. I'm sorry, Jo, but it's got to be done."

Their eyes met for an instant before his flickered and swung away.

"All right," she said, without emotion. "I'm cooked. I know."

He turned quickly and climbed the gangway to the deck.

She said something very quietly and sadly, something he did not hear. In a few seconds Pedro came down the steps and stood before her, and she rose silently and moved along the dark alleyway.

*   *   *

Between the hangar and the dunes Smith stood motionless, alert, his head thrust forward as though he was listening for the silence to speak. What now?

He didn't know. Anything might happen now. But the stuff was somewhere around here, everything indicated that. And wherever it was, his man would be there too.

His controlled fingers touched the gun in his pocket. And then the idea which had been so elusive, the important idea, came to him as he stood beside the curved and pitted wall of the hangar, and new light entered his sharp eyes. Garraud's death. . . . Why hadn't he thought of it before in this connection? It had looked like Arabs at first—it was meant to look like Arabs. But it wasn't. Although the Bey was in this, obviously since Tarollier and Arnold had been to the palace this morning, it seemed that he had warned off his people altogether from the harbour and the airfield until Arnold's boat finally left.

Garraud could be the key. Smith's lean face was hard, his eyes screwed up to little lenses which gleamed with a kind of wary triumph. Why had Garraud been murdered? Not for nothing. Had he interfered with these men, was he becoming dangerous to them?

Or was he about to find the drugs?

It's not so good for me now, Smith thought. These people were going to stop at nothing, not even murder. He hadn't reckoned on that. And why had Kingsley allowed himself to be caught? He must have been caught, and Tarollier must have caught him, before Tarollier went to the village to meet the boat. And Kingsley had the letter.

He knew that if he was taken by surprise now his life might depend upon whether or not Kingsley had been searched. They might not have found the letter, but if they had they would be after him. His brain sent out its coldly warning message once more. Better watch out, Smith. . . . Now you know they're far more dangerous than you thought.

It had not been a good afternoon's work—the morning's was much better. He had been obliged to keep up some pretence of weather observation and this was a handicap, but he had made too many mistakes, and mistakes were always expensive. He was appalled and ashamed as he added them up, for most were due to nothing else but underestimating the enemy's qualities, and he'd enough experience to know that this was the last thing anyone in his work should do if he wanted to keep his health. He knew that he should have warned the plane crew about these people instead of trying to carry the whole fight himself, but he had been afraid of scaring them off and he'd got to find out where the stuff was and what had happened to Kingsley and the letter. Garraud's life might have been saved too if he'd been a bit quicker off the mark. And then he had been too late to stop Tarollier slipping away in the jeep with the navigator, and that was bad—not least for the navigator.

But the letter—that was sheer bad luck. It was a better way of sending his information than by radio, or so he'd thought. His presence in the radio tent might have given ideas to the wrong people, and if only the repairs to the plane hadn't taken so long the letter would have been safely away by now.

It was comforting to know that the crew radio man must have sent a signal before this. Unless these people had thought of that too. . . . A faint sickness stirred in Smith's belly then as he stared across the cooling sand.

And now he had lost sight of Richer. There must be some hiding place nearby, perhaps the very place he was looking for, and to find the drugs was the main reason for his being here at all, or had been. Now it was to find Garraud's killer too, but he was almost certain who that was. Playing a lone hand had forced him to give them all plenty of rope because he had to find out just where this place was, and they might yet lead him to it. He wondered whether he should have got to the radio first, before Richer. But he could not have done so without making them suspicious, for Richer was the official radio man and he'd dived into the tent pretty fast after Garraud's body was found.

That was something else he had been forced to take a chance on, but he was a fool to let these men out of his sight to go prowling round the huts and hangar looking for a sign that might show him where the drugs were hidden. And it was because he had not credited them with such a capacity for bold and swift action or with their inflexible determination to carry it all through that he had seen no sign, and he had wasted a lot of time since coming upon Barthell and the dead Garraud. It was late now. These people—Richer anyway —must have been watching him. How else could they have moved between the tents and huts, as they must, without being seen themselves?

Where had Garraud's body lain? It was beside the hut, the far hut nearest the dunes. In any case it would be as well to take another look, for there might be something which he had missed earlier, and he had not examined this one very closely because it was the most remote from the tents and he was trying to keep an eye on the tents too. And like anyone else who attempted to be in two or three places at once, he knew he hadn't succeeded very well. But the man he wanted must be here. Would he have seen the letter?

If he had, Smith thought, then I am not so much the hunter as the hunted.

It would be dark very soon now, and they were sure to be leaving tonight. His body grew more taut, his eyes more wary as he gripped the gun's hard butt and moved from the hangar's side across the open sand towards the hut, the dunes on his left. He stepped lightly, the old hat pulled down low on his forehead, and although he looked straight ahead he seemed to be watching sideways and backwards too, listening to everything but the faint crunch of his feet on the sand. He felt better, moving.

The hut's long shell was before him, its walls warped and blistered, punched with staring ragged holes which had once been windows, and the holes looked down on the sand like blinded eyes. Thirty yards away the dunes rose, hollowed and bulged and silent. Garraud had been here, against the wall. Here was the stain, binding the sand together in a little brownish cake.

Was there anything else? He must hurry, before it got too dark to see. The sand was hard and smooth here, unmarked but for the blood, and its secrets were locked in the packed grains. Smith knew a sudden wave of anger and futility, and he felt then that the airfield had defeated him, that there was nothing left but to go to the plane's crew now and tell them what he knew before leading some kind of assault on the boat. An attack there might well succeed; after all, Arnold was the weak spot—he knew Arnold.

Smith sucked in a long breath, trying to crush the seeds of failure that were germinating in his mind. The wall? Its desiccated wood was rough and splintered, paled by the blaze of Faruda's constant suns. He leaned closely towards it, searching, touching the harsh surface with the tips of his long fingers, moving slowly along the wall.

And there was something—a tiny thing—impaled on a splinter almost directly above where Garraud had been lying, so small that it was no wonder that he had missed it before. His heart stopped, then seemed to convulse in his chest. On the splinter was a minute strand of wool—khaki wool.

Smith straightened up, and there was a little sour smile on his thin mouth, but only watchfulness in his eyes. Now, from here . . .

The darkening hills of sand behind him spoke very quietly. It seemed to be the voice of all the desert which spoke, in words that would not need an answer; there was no answer. . . .

"Put your hands up, Mr. Smith," it said, "*now*. Come here, Mr. Smith."

Smith's wary eyes froze, and he turned his head slowly towards the dunes. And then, his hands aloft, he moved with a kind of delicate deliberation nearer to the man with the gun.

Behind the weapon this figure seemed incredibly tall against the dunes' grey battlements, an attenuated threat; and it moved back as Smith advanced, back beside the dunes to where a bulge hid an inner slope of them, and suddenly within this slope there gaped a square black hole, a pit in the wall of sand.

So—it was here . . .

"Ah, Mr. Smith. . . . Keep your hands up, please." Richer's voice was deep, soft, expectant. He stepped aside from the hole, moving behind Smith. "Your gun. . . . That is better. Now go in."

Smith felt himself stiff with a cold and leaden fury. To be caught like this . . . But almost at once his drilled mind rose out of sterile anger and began to adjust itself calmly, making his eyes ready to observe and his ears to hear. He bent and entered the low doorway, hands outstretched, stumbling down into the blackness below. Richer was behind him, switching on a torch, his feet falling with sure and triumphant steps, and he closed the wooden door of the cell silently behind him. All the time his gun was steady on Smith's back.

Smith had stopped in the middle of the underground room, and now the torch lit it with an eerie, liquid glow. He saw the piled boxes round the walls, the black boxes with their stencilled letters and numbers and the emblem like that on the canister he had found in the Frenchmen's tent. But this was big, far bigger than he had imagined then. If they got away with all this . . .

Richer faced him, his large head thrust forward. At first, blinking in the light which shone at him, Smith could see only the yellowed face and the bright eyes behind the glare —and the gun held still as death by an arm which was covered to the wrist by the sleeve of a khaki sweater. . . .

"I think this is what you are looking for, Mr. Smith?" Richer said very quietly. "Yes—this is where our cargo is kept. There is quite a lot, eh?" He moved the light, and all at once Smith saw the awkwardly crumpled mass in the corner.

The silence lasted only a second, and then Smith said evenly, "You keep other things here too, I see." He watched Richer, his lips barely moving as he spoke. He was sure then that Richer knew all about him, and Richer was going to talk. Richer was the kind of man who would talk when he'd got someone who had to listen.

"Ah—Garraud. . . ." Richer frowned, and Smith could see that his sucked-in lips twitched and curled in a sort of annoyed distaste.

"You killed him, didn't you?" Smith said.

"It was unfortunate." Richer spoke with no emotion at all. "I was sorry about Garraud, but he was becoming a nuisance, and today he almost found our cargo. He would not mind his own business, like some others, Mr. Smith. He was a difficult man to reason with, and unpredictable. That was why he was so dangerous. It was unfortunate. . . ."

"So you brought his body here, from the tent?"

"Yes—it took me not much more than a minute. The crew could not see me, and you were busy behind the hangar." Richer paused, and a strange look, feral and mad, momentarily crossed his face. "It was not necessary to remove him, perhaps. I acted on the spur of the moment, and I am a tidy man, Mr. Smith—I do not like to leave bodies lying about, and crimes are always more difficult to prove when there is no—no solid evidence, eh? Especially—murders." He didn't seem to mind the word, Smith thought; most of them would never use it. "As a policeman you know that very well, don't you, Mr. Smith?"

Smith smiled rigidly. "Policeman? How did you work that one out?"

"I apologise." The gun moved slightly. "Of course, no member of your exclusive organisation would care to be addressed as a policeman. . . . Why do you think I am telling you all this about myself and what I am doing here? Because I know all about you, and I want to satisfy your curiosity about me. I think you are entitled to know about me after all the trouble you have taken to find out. But I know you, Mr. Smith. . . . Have you forgotten the letter —the letter you wrote and gave to Captain Kingsley, which unfortunately he could not deliver?"

Smith was silent, and for an instant the sickness he had known by the hangar passed through him.

"Yes, the letter," Richer said softly. "I found it here this afternoon. It must have dropped from the captain's pocket when Tarollier surprised him this morning. It makes interesting reading, your report to your Air Ministry on my activities here. . . ."

Richer smiled in the dimness behind the light.

"You know, I had a feeling that someone might be sent out to watch me. On my way here I made up a story about a missing briefcase. It was a trick—a somewhat hasty and clumsy one, I'm afraid—to try to find out from the radio man if anyone might be following." Richer stared into Smith's taut face. "And you came on the next flight. At first you nearly fooled me with your little balloons and your barometers. . . ."

Smith said coolly, "I fooled you until you found the letter."

"Perhaps you did." Richer was suddenly snarling, trembling as fury destroyed his control. "But now—*now* I know all about you, my friend, and why you came to Faruda. It was not to watch the weather, but to watch me. You were sent here because the Paris police suspect me of being a big man in the drug business there. . . . And somebody thought it a good idea to send an Englishman—a member of the Air Ministry special investigation branch—instead of a French *gendarme*, eh?—thereby hoping to allay any suspicions I might have. So they chose you, Mr. Smith. . . . You had your little lessons in meteorology, and then you came to watch me. . . .

"It is all in the letter, is it not?" Richer went on. "How you searched our tent and found a sample of the drugs under my bed, and the newspaper I was a little foolish to bring, with the account of a Paris drug ring, as they call it, on the front page. . . . 'An early arrest is expected.'" Richer laughed quietly. "I am so sorry to disappoint everybody."

Smith said nothing. He stood motionless, his body poised. His eyes were narrowed on the dim figure behind the light; he could see it better now.

"The letter told me that you know far more than is good for you, Mr. Smith," Richer murmured. "What else do you know?"

There was no point in not telling Richer what he knew, Smith thought, about Tarollier and the boat, and he had to play for time—only time could help, or a mistake by Richer. But Richer didn't look like making a mistake, not yet. When Smith spoke, his words were quiet but they seemed to be magnified, rebounding from the close walls of the cell. He drew a deep breath, and what he took in was stale, poor stuff, as if breathed too much already.

"I know a little," he said slowly, taking his time. "I've been getting around since I came here. I like exercise. And I was interested in Tarollier's absences—it occurred to me that they might have some connection with you. . . . I followed him this morning, or rather I went down to the village after I had made sure he was not at the airfield, and was in time to see him meet the boat."

"Ah—so you know about that too?"

"Yes. As a matter of fact I know your man Arnold. He happens to be an old friend of mine whom I helped to put away for a couple of years just after the war. He was gun-running then. . . . Well, I'd a good idea what was going on when I saw him here this morning, Richer."

"This is very interesting," Richer said. "Go on, please."

"There isn't much more to tell. I saw Arnold and Tarollier visit the Bey's palace, and that explained one or two little points which had been worrying me. What I didn't know was where your cargo was, or how it came to be here. I decided to say nothing to the crew of the plane but to watch you, hoping that you might lead me to it. . . ."

"I see. But you were caught instead."

Smith's still face smiled slowly, but the watching eyes did not change.

"Perhaps I underestimated you, Richer, but I was also a little unlucky. I was just too late to see you kill Garraud —there is a piece of wool from your sweater on the hut wall. . . . Also I could not stop Tarollier leaving with the navigator in the jeep."

"You are right—you underestimated us. You did not think we would go so far as to kill a man to make sure of our cargo, eh?"

"No—I admit that. I thought at first that it must have been Arabs who killed Garraud for some reason—perhaps the Bey's men."

"You did not think that we would act so fast, or so boldly." Richer's voice purred, and Smith saw the vanity shine like false jewels in his deep eyes. "But we did. You did not appreciate one vital thing, and that is I am determined to take these drugs away whatever happens—*whatever happens*. Nothing shall stop me now."

Smith's words were loud in the dim room. "You can't get away with it, Richer."

A spasm of wild laughter gripped the Frenchman's body. It passed quickly and he gestured with the gun, moving a step nearer to Smith.

"I suppose you are thinking that this crew will have signalled for help." Suddenly Richer's face was pitiless, like yellow stone. "You fool! You are still underestimating our abilities. I sent no signal this afternoon—I suppose even you must have realised that by now. But I did something, Mr. Smith. . . . I wrecked the transmitter. You did not expect me to do that, eh?—under everybody's noses. They can send no signal."

The time of deepest despair was the time to fight hardest

against it. Smith drew back his shoulders and his head went up with an oddly proud lift of the chin.

He said, a taunt in his voice, "I say you won't get away with it, Richer."

"I won't?" Richer was almost screaming. "Oh yes I will, my friend. And you—you will pay for your interference and your mistakes, like these others." Suddenly his voice dropped, coiling down to evil softness. "Soon Tarollier will be here to collect the cargo. Garraud and this captain—they will go with it, and we shall rid ourselves of them at sea." He paused, a faint smile on his yellow face. "One more will make no difference, Mr. Smith, no difference at all. . . ."

The threat hung, foul and thick in the little cell; the gun glinted, blue in the torchlight.

"Sit down, Mr. Smith." Now Richer's voice was a whisper. "Make yourself comfortable. You have not very long to wait."

*   *   *

The darkness was whole, stained blacker with impalpable menace.

In a single quick, fear-motored movement Gleason backed from the tent and stood up. Tarrant's vague figure loomed close and urgent, muttering.

"What's wrong?"

"Garraud. . . . He's gone."

Tarrant did not recognise the shaken whisper as belonging to the engineer. He stared, eyes glittering dreadfully from his night-clad face, knowing that his mind was clutching at reason.

"Gone? He's dead, isn't he? Dead men can't . . ."

"The tent's empty, David." Gleason waited, trying to recover himself. "Someone must have taken him away. It couldn't have been long ago."

Tarrant was shivering then, his stare leaving the engineer to strike anxiously into the plain's darkness.

"How do these things happen? How do they happen like this? People spirited away—one after another. . . ."

"If we can find that spirit we shall know all the answers." Gleason did not move, but his mind was trembling. "All the answers."

Tarrant said, " It's uncanny how it all happens under our noses, and there's never a sound, never a sight of anyone. Someone is watching—watching all the time. . . ."

Gleason bent down to retrieve the torch which he had dropped coming out of the tent. Somehow this simple action seemed to condition his brain, steering it back towards the fine balance of normality.

" Let's get back to the kite," he said calmly.

The co-pilot's edgy voice challenged them as they passed across the silent tarmac. Susan was there beside him. Gleason told them quietly of the disappearance of Garraud's body, and Susan was whitely still as she listened, looking up at Tarrant who stood beside her, but Cummings was all jerks and starts, pulling at the ends of his bushy moustache and moving his body in sudden involuntary spasms.

He said hoarsely, " This gets worse. . . . Will any of us be left by morning?"

" I hope so." Gleason frowned at him but his level tones did not change, and his calmness helped them. " It won't do any good to worry about what may or may not happen to us."

" It's easy enough to say that, but . . ."

" I know it is. But don't you see, Lester—the skipper and Harry, wherever they are, they're depending on us. We've got to help them and help ourselves, not sit and wonder what'll hit us next."

Lester's sliding, Gleason thought; anger against the co-pilot stabbed at him, then was gone. Lester had the hardest job, sitting inactive by the machine, with too much time in which to build up his fears. But the girl's position was worst of all, and she was afraid, but she didn't complain. And then Cummings was looking at him, his head up, taking a new grip on his Sten.

" You're right, Bob," Cummings said, and now there was purpose in his voice. " Anyone who can't identify himself and comes too close had better watch out. What's the form now?"

" We've got to send a signal, and there's no time to lose. We found no spares in the tents, but we think we may be able to rig up the mobile generator and hook up the radio mast to the kite's transmitter. It will take two of us, so you and Miss Wells will have to stay on watch together."

" All right."

" For God's sake keep your eyes peeled, Lester, and shout if anything funny happens."

" You bet I will," Cummings said grimly.

" Come on, David. Where's that cable?"

" In the radio tent. Susan . . ."

" I'll be all right," the stewardess said. " Can I do anything?"

" No. Better stay here." Tarrant touched her shoulder and turned sharply away, following Gleason across the tarmac.

Inside the tent Tarrant collected the big coil of rubber-covered cable, then joined the engineer who was pulling the covers from the portable generator outside.

" Help me wheel it across to the kite, David. It's pretty heavy."

Tarrant said urgently, " Hadn't we best put it inside the cabin? These things aren't exactly quiet, and if it's heard running someone might . . ."

" Try to interfere? Right—inside. That will make it easier for Lester to listen too."

Gleason felt a power now, even an elation, as he threw aside the last board which had covered the generator. This was work, the medicine for fear and desire, whether it was successful or not. . . . They each took a handle and lifted. The single wheel sank into the yielding sand, making it difficult to move the generator, and despite the coolness of the night they began to sweat, but it was easier going when they reached the edge of the apron near where the aircraft stood. They pushed wildly now, half running, and when they got beneath the cargo doors they leaned heavily against the ladder for a few moments before Gleason scrambled up it into the cabin.

He switched on one of the small cabin lights and swung out the jib of the crane, dropping the hook to Tarrant. The generator came up very slowly as he turned the crane handle, bumping against the side of the machine, and it seemed an age before it was level with the door. Gleason swung the jib again, inwards, and released the handle, and the generator dropped clattering to the metal floor. Tarrant climbed in and they wheeled it along the empty cabin as far as the door leading to the flight deck. It was too big to go through.

"Right." Tarrant straightened up, and he was panting as much with excitement as from his exertions. "Leave her here, Bob. I'll connect up." He felt better now, a new decision in his voice and movements. "Now—take this cable and join it up to the aerial lead-in at the top of that post by the tent. Make sure it's a good contact, and bring it back here through the escape hatch by the nose. There ought to be enough on the reel. Got it?"

"Yes. I'll be as quick as I can."

"Okay. It will take a few minutes to get this generator hooked up."

Gleason almost fell down the ladder from the cargo doors, the coil of cable on his arm. The stars' faint light shone eerily over Faruda, a ghost-light illuminating a throbbing silence. The dim outlines of Susan and Cummings watched, and the co-pilot said, "All right, Bob?" and Gleason gave a brief answer as he passed.

At the foot of the mast he fumbled for his pocket knife and, finding it, slashed at the thick rubber of the cable, baring a few inches which he wrapped round the aerial lead.

As he did so Gleason was suddenly struck by a terrible and despairing uncertainty. All at once these desperate improvisations seemed ridiculous and futile, foredoomed to dangerous and inglorious failure. How was it possible that anyone, hundreds of miles away, could hear a call from such a contraption as they were preparing? He stared at the cable in his hand despondently, and then shook himself in a sudden access of savage anger. Why not?

"You fool, Gleason," he muttered aloud. "Get going."

A strip of insulating tape was attached to the end of the cable. He wound this tightly round the joint he had made on the aerial lead and then backed towards the aircraft, paying out the cable as he went. He was almost under the machine's nose when the end of the cable slipped off the reel.

Again a black hopelessness seized him.

"David." He called the name softly and the radio operator's head appeared in the escape hatch. "It's too short. Here!" He held up the end of the cable.

"All right," Tarrant said. "Wait."

He withdrew his head and in a moment returned, dropping a snaking wire to the engineer.

"Connect it up with that, and make it tight."

Gleason breathed his relief. Again he sliced away the rubber insulation and joined the wires. They pulled on the long cable until it came clear of the ground and Tarrant secured it to a bracket inside the hatch.

"Nearly ready now," he said.

Gleason ran beneath the machine and re-entered the cabin. He stood at the door to the flight deck and watched Tarrant adjusting his transmitter, this magical box in which might lie salvation; now the generator was connected to it with black wires, filaments of hope.... A single dim light shone down, and the flight deck was a strange, awful place, peopled with weird and groping shadows.

It seemed hours before Tarrant, earphones in place, slewed round in his seat and said briefly, "Right—start her up."

The engineer bent and swung fiercely at the generator handle. It felt stiff and unresponsive, and the motor coughed hoarsely, spat and died. Again he swung, and again. At the third attempt the engine fired into throbbing life which seemed to fill the aircraft with terrible reverberations, roaring ever louder as the sound hurled and multiplied itself between the imprisoning walls. He stared in fascination at Tarrant's still figure, bent over the transmitter. Would they be heard?

Suddenly Tarrant's hand reached out and he began to tap at the morse key with a tense and final rapidity. Gleason stepped in beside him, closing the sliding door so that as much as possible of the generator's exhaust would be excluded from the flight deck, and he waited, scarcely breathing, afraid to hope.

Beneath the machine Cummings sat, alert with apprehension, fondling the Sten, his eyes sweeping the dim expanse of the field. Susan Wells was beside him, silent, her pale face tilted up at the black hulk above. He knew that she didn't want to talk, and he knew that if he talked it wouldn't help her. Already the night was a merciless suspense—a continuing threat. It was cold now, and nothing moved in this coldness which crawled over his skin like a slow reptile.

The sky was a bright multitude of stars. They seemed to be lower than the shattered blackness above, as though they were hanging on invisible threads just above his head, and he felt that he could have clutched a handful by raising his arm. They spread their faint silver light over Faruda, and he could see the tents clearly, and farther off the vague shape of the control tower and the hangar's bald skull. He was in shadow, beneath the broad blade of the wing. A star lay at the wing-tip, and Cummings thought inconsequently that it was like the navigation light he had seen there so often when flying at night; or it was a ray of deadly atomic light, needling his brain. It was queer, the strange thoughts which crowded into the mind here in this sterile desert—strange mental visions, transient and disconnected. . . . Was he going crazy? He shook himself, gripping the gun. This waiting. . . .

He thought about their danger, and was ashamed for being afraid and for having shown it. He had felt better for a time, but now he was afraid again. Were the others afraid as he was? He was ashamed of himself for not having gone down to the village with Harry to look for the skipper; he could have gone with him instead of the Frenchman, but he was more afraid of the unknown village than the known airfield. Garraud's murder had scared the last spunk out of him and he hadn't wanted to go, hadn't wanted to do anything, and he had been relieved and glad that Harry had gone with the Frenchman. He knew he was a coward, and cowards did nothing if they didn't run away and there was nowhere to run to, and when he felt like that he didn't want to do anything at all. If only he could conquer this inertia, or find Flo's foot, he'd feel a whole lot better.

Yet again he stared round, straining his eyes. There was nothing. And then he heard the noise of the generator starting up inside the machine, muffled by the cabin's shell. The signal . . . ?

He tried to attune his ears so that they would shut out the baffled hum and hear only movements from the darkness outside. Already his eyes were beginning to ache from constant peering into the shapeless void of the field.

Once he thought he saw a shadow move beside the control

tower and he held his breath, half raising the Sten. He must be careful—it might be Harry or the skipper. . . . But there was nothing now save the tower's blurred smudge. Had there really been a movement beside it? He shifted his eyes slightly, remembering that objects could be seen better in the dark if they were not looked at directly, but a little to one side. No. . . . He blinked. Was the signal being heard now, in the far place called home? Let it be heard!

There *was* a shadow, and it moved.

Cummings's breath stopped, and he lifted the Sten. Where was Bob? He opened his mouth to call out but no sound would come, and he did not realise that Gleason could not have heard him above the noise of the generator. The shadow moved again—it was nearer—a single figure, soundless, appearing to float over the sand. It was suddenly close. . . .

Cummings found his voice.

"Get behind me," he said to the stewardess, "quick!" Then he called out harshly, levelling the gun. "Get your hands up or I'll shoot! Who is it?"

The shadow was very still now, and clear, a thin dark body with arms raised stiffly above its head. A strange, high, sexless voice answered him.

"Don't shoot!" it cried. "Don't shoot! It's a friend."

"Keep your hands up, or I'll fire. . . . Come on."

The figure advanced. Cummings moved slowly to meet it, his finger curled round the gun's trigger, and now he felt a sudden and unexpected steadiness inside him.

They came together, and the gun was only a yard from the stranger's chest. Cummings heard a kind of stifled sob, and he peered closely into the shadowy face.

The gun almost dropped from his hands.

"Good God!" he said aloud. "It's a woman!"

CHAPTER IX

THE NIGHT

CUMMINGS stared stupidly at the girl, his mouth open.
"Please," she said at last. Her voice trembled. "Please.
... Can I put my arms down?"

She was young and lovely, and he could see what looked like a white and exhausted relief on her face. She wore a dark sweater and slacks, a scarf over her head. They stood like uncertain adversaries, and then Cummings stepped back a pace, watching her.

"All right," he said. "But don't try anything."

"I can't. ... I haven't any gun."

She dropped her arms and suddenly began to cry, standing quite still and gazing at him from large bright eyes while the tears welled in them and rolled down the white face. Somehow her sobs seemed to him more the product of exhaustion than fear.

Cummings spoke over his shoulder to the stewardess. "Fetch the engineer," he said, not taking his eyes from the slender crying figure.

"Who are you?" he asked harshly when Susan had gone. He was foolishly angered by this sobbing. "Where have you come from?"

"A boat—in the harbour." All at once her crying ceased.

"A boat? What boat? What are you doing here?"

"I've come because I wanted to escape, because ..."

Gleason's voice was sudden and alarmed from the door of the machine.

"Lester! Who's that? Are you all right?"

Still looking at the girl, Cummings said loudly, "Yes. We've got a visitor." Gleason came up and peered at her, a look of almost comical incredulity on his face.

She said wearily, "It's all right. I'm real."

"She's come from a boat in the harbour, so she says." Cummings thrust his face close to the girl's, gesturing with the Sten. "Come on—spill it. You're just another queer episode of the last few hours here, and we're getting a bit tired of them. . . . What's the game?"

"Listen," she said desperately. "I'm on your side—you've got to believe me." She stared over her shoulder in the direction of the control tower as if evil might be at her heels and the sobs began again, deep and slow and dry now, and it seemed that they were necessary to rid her of pain and memories. But she did not look afraid.

"Sit down," Gleason said quietly.

The girl appeared to collapse on the sand like an empty sack, her head bowed. Presently Gleason dropped on one knee beside her, watching; he was wondering what was going to happen next in this strange and awful place. A girl— here! He looked up warningly at the co-pilot. It was just as well that he had told the stewardess to stay with David in the aircraft, in case this was a trap. Could it be one—set by the unknown enemy?

Somehow, then, he didn't think so. Whoever she was, the girl was exhausted, and she seemed like someone who had reached safety after danger. He said, "Now—what's the story?"

She looked up at him, her big eyes luminous in the pale face, and her sobbing died.

"Listen to me," she said. The words began to tumble out, and Gleason caught the faint Cockney flavour in their urgent accents. "I believe one of your crew is in danger—or all of you. The captain. . . ."

Gleason said sharply, "What about the captain? What do you know about him?"

"I heard talk about a captain on the boat. I was thinking about it after I heard your engines this afternoon. Are you the captain?"

"No." Gleason reached out and grasped the girl's shoulder. Her flesh was soft under his fingers. "Our captain is missing. What did you hear?"

"Missing?" Her voice hurried on, breathless with anxiety. "Then they *were* talking about him. They said they were going to attend to the captain. It sounded bad, the way they said it. He's in danger—I know it now. I . . ."

"Take it easy," Gleason said. She did know something,

he could see it in her eyes. He dropped his hand. "Take it easy. Why not start from the beginning?"

She nodded slowly, only taking her eyes from his face to glance again towards the tower.

"I came on a boat to Faruda this morning," she said, still talking fast. "It doesn't matter how I came to be on it. The skipper is a man called Arnold, who is a smuggler. He's come to take away some drugs."

"From Faruda? How can there be drugs here?"

"I don't know, but there are." All at once she was more composed. "There is a big man here—a Frenchman I think —who has these drugs."

"A big man? What is he like?"

"I didn't see him very well, but he is tall and heavy, with a little pale face, and wears a kind of peaked cap."

Gleason and Cummings stared at one another. "Tarollier. . . ."

"And Harry's gone with him." Gleason leaned down. "Go on," he said softly.

"This man came aboard the boat to see Arnold as soon as we got here this morning," the girl said. "Arnold didn't want him to see me, and so he locked me up on board while the man was there, but I could hear something of what they were saying. The Frenchman said they would attend to the captain. I didn't know what he meant then, but later I could see that Arnold was frightened by something the man had said or done." Suddenly the girl clutched Gleason's arm. "I've been thinking about it since then. I know that the Frenchman and Arnold are smuggling drugs, and I believe your captain must have interfered with their plans somehow, and they may even be going to kill him. . . . Otherwise why should Arnold be so frightened?"

Gleason gave her a long, intent stare. She wasn't lying— there was too much urgency and desperation in her for that.

He said, "You think our captain is this man Tarollier's prisoner, then. Where?"

"I don't know. But Arnold and Tarollier went ashore this morning to see someone—a big man in the district, Arnold said."

"A big man . . ."

"The Bey?" Cummings muttered. "The skipper could be there, in the palace."

Gleason nodded, speaking to the girl. "What else did you hear?"

"That the boat was leaving tonight. Arnold told me. He said the drugs would be loaded at eight-thirty, and a little more than an hour later they would go." The girl's mouth was suddenly hard. "But they won't—perhaps they won't go at all...."

"What do you mean?"

"I locked the fuel tanks in the boat's engine room and turned all the wheels I could. I was trying to let the sea in."

Gleason looked at her, and beyond his wonder and anxiety there was a dawning admiration. If this was true the girl had guts, and she was beautiful too. "Then you think they won't get away," he said, "or at least not for some time?"

"No. Even if I didn't sink her the locks on the tanks are very heavy. I threw the keys in the harbour." Hatred came to her face, smearing the beauty there. "I hope she sinks— I hope she sinks deep."

"How many crew are there on this boat?"

"Two besides Arnold," the girl said. "Arnold—he's scared to death of this job now. He's not the same type as the Frenchman."

"How did you know we were here?"

"Because of the noise of your plane being tested this afternoon—it helped to guide me here. Afterwards I heard no more, and so I knew that you must still be in Faruda."

Gleason leaned forward. "You said you were locked up on the boat when Tarollier went aboard. If Arnold took that kind of precaution, how was it that you were able to do all this in the engine room and then get away?"

"Arnold was ashore when I did it, but I made up my mind to try to escape some time before. You see, Arnold had been told by Tarollier to go and collect a jeep loaded with food and water as soon as it became dark and drive it to the boat. He locked me in my room with one of the crew and went ashore to get the jeep." The girl gave a little bitter laugh. "That was the second time today he made a prisoner of me.... Arnold likes his brandy, and he left a bottle in the cabin. I was able to smuggle it into my room—he never missed it because he'd been swallowing brandy all afternoon and was half drunk by the time he left. So was the man who came to guard me, and it wasn't very difficult to get him even drunker. I only had to take the key off him and get out. . . . The other man was asleep on his bunk, so I immobilised the boat and came up here."

"Did anyone see you?"

"I don't think so. There was nobody about in the village. On the way I heard the jeep coming and hid behind a rock while it went past, towards the harbour. Arnold was in it, driving like a madman. He didn't see me, I'm certain."

"Our navigator went with Tarollier in that jeep this afternoon, and he hasn't come back," Gleason said grimly. "Did you see anyone else?"

"No. Arnold was alone, and I saw nobody else."

Gleason nodded slowly. She's telling the truth, he thought. But why had she come here? Why had she been on this boat in the first place if it wasn't to go smuggling with Arnold, and what was her relationship with him? Arnold had told her they were leaving with drugs that night—despite this story about escaping from his boat could he have sent her to the airfield for some reason? He stared at her curiously; she reminded him of someone, he thought. Who was it?

"I want the truth about this." His face was hard and determined. "Are you in on this smuggling with Arnold? Did he send you here?"

She threw back her head. "No! I wouldn't be in on the rotten job for all the money in the world. And he didn't send me—I told you I escaped, and it's true."

"All right. Then why did Arnold tell you about the drugs? Why were you on his boat at all if you didn't want to be involved in what he was doing?"

"I didn't know about the drugs when I went with him—I didn't know about them until this afternoon," she said simply and patiently. "He told me about them only because I insisted on knowing what I was being let in for. He didn't want to tell me, but I broke him down."

"I see. . . ."

"There were a lot of reasons why I had to find you," the

girl said hurriedly. "I had to warn you about the captain, to escape from being mixed up in this business, to get away from Arnold. I hate him now for what he has done to me. . . ." She paused, her head bent. "It will all be clearer if I start from the beginning. . . . I'm a Cockney, as I suppose you've guessed, and my name is Joan Briggs. On the stage it's a bit more classy—Jo Fanshawe. Back home I was a dancer on the halls until a couple of months ago when I came out with a scruffy touring revue to North Africa. We got to Algiers, and there the show went broke and I was stranded, broke as the show. Well, I met Arnold there. He told me he was going to Malta where it happens that I have friends, and promised to take me there—I've no one in England who could help me. . . . I went with him."

She spoke in a low, flat voice, as though she was neither glad nor sorry about her story.

"I'd no idea he was coming here and had no intention of going to Malta until after this job was done. I knew he was an adventurer and a smuggler, but I thought he never carried anything worse than cigarettes—like he did on the Tangier racket he told me about. That just shows the kind of fool I was. But he didn't tell me about Faruda because he knew I'd never have come with him if I'd known what the job was, and he wanted to keep me." She was whispering now. "I don't have to tell you what we were to one another, do I? He wanted me. . . . But when we got here instead of Malta he had to tell me why. And that's why I hate him."

"That's the reason you came here tonight?" Gleason's voice was sombre. "And to warn us too?"

"Yes. And—don't you see?—he hid me from Tarollier because he was afraid of what Tarollier would do if he knew I was aboard," the girl said quietly. "But he couldn't hide me for long on a small boat like that. What would have happened to me, once we got to sea? I'm sure that Tarollier would have killed me, as I believe he will kill your captain, because we both know too much. I had to escape to save myself."

"And Arnold—still he would have held you?"

"He wanted me so much," she said unemotionally. "Because of that I don't think he ever really considered what might happen afterwards."

Gleason said thoughtfully, " By now he must have discovered your absence. What can he do about that?"

" I don't think he will or can do anything, and I have an idea that the Frenchman will be too busy now to look for me."

" Besides Tarollier and Arnold, is there anyone else in this?"

" There is another man, but I don't know who he is. I remember now that I heard Tarollier say something about the Bey being paid and sending guards. It looks as though the Bey may be providing transport for the cargo and also an escort for it."

" This other man could be the Bey himself then?"

" I suppose he could."

" Did you hear Tarollier or Arnold speak of any other person at all?"

" No."

" Do you know where the drugs are hidden or how they got there in the first place?"

" No. All I know is that there *are* drugs, cocaine and morphia, somewhere in Faruda. I don't know where the boat is taking them, and I don't think Arnold knows yet, either." The girl paused, and then said desperately, " Isn't there anything you can do? Your captain. . . ."

" We're trying to signal for help now." Had their call been heard yet? There was no sound from the machine but the steady, muffled note of the generator. Gleason stood up and faced Cummings. " It looks like this to me, Lester. . . . Possibly because the skipper found something out on his wanderings this morning, Tarollier got him. It seems that Tarollier is in with the Bey, and so the skipper and Harry may be at the palace and the drugs may be there too, and Tarollier is going to load them all on the boat tonight. If so, we've got to do something about it before it's too late."

" I hope it's not too late already," Cummings muttered.

" We all hope so," Gleason said briefly. He tried not to think of Garraud. The girl was watching him and he said to her, " How far is it to the harbour?"

"Two or three miles, I should think." She pointed to where the track left the field beyond the control tower. "It's a clear road, even in the dark."

"Couldn't you have got help in the village before coming here?"

"How could I have made Arabs understand all this? Anyway, there was nobody about—I never saw anyone all day, and if the Bey is mixed up in this it's not likely that his people would have helped me."

"No. . . . And perhaps that's why you saw no one. What is the harbour like?"

"It's very small, almost square. The track leads directly to it. The boat is tied up on this nearer side—the western side—and there are two small fishing boats at the opposite quay where the houses are. I think the entrance is difficult —it's very narrow with a sharp bend in the middle. Arnold seemed worried about getting out in the dark."

Gleason was silent, thinking. The girl's story was true— it must be true, and if they wanted to save the skipper and Harry they had to accept it. But he himself had no doubts —a desperate, naked truth lay in her eyes and her voice rang with it. There was little more than an hour now before Tarollier was expected at the harbour with his cargo. A cold fury expanded, convulsed in Gleason as he thought of the pale, fat Tarollier. Was it Tarollier then who had killed Garraud and removed his body? And was he the answer to the disappearance of both Richer and Smith as well?

He said slowly, "This must have been carefully planned, and Tarollier must have been embarrassed by our presence here today. If we'd not had trouble with an engine we should have gone home yesterday, leaving him a clear field."

The girl frowned, clasping her hands together. "But it wasn't planned for the boat to arrive today," she said. "We are two days late because of bad weather."

"Two days late?" Gleason paused and then looked sharply at the co-pilot who had been anxiously watching the dark field. "Lester! Two days ago was the twenty-sixth—the day we were originally due back here until Peter Fox's crash caused the trip to be delayed twenty-four hours. . . ."

Cummings stared. "Well, what does that tell us?"

"It tells me that there might be another reason for that explosion. Look at it like this. Suppose there was somebody here who, knowing we were short of kites at Westonmills, wanted to stop us—or anyone else—returning to Faruda on that particular day. . . . And supposing he was determined and ruthless enough he could have done it by planting something in Peter Fox. . . . A bomb, for instance."

The co-pilot's stare was a gape now. "He—he could, but . . . Do you think that's what happened?"

"It could have happened that way." Gleason was grim, tight-faced. "All at once that explosion is beginning to look just a little too coincidental. . . . And I'm thinking now that if it *did* happen that way—well, anyone who doesn't hesitate to blow up a kite and its crew will certainly stop at nothing afterwards. We'd better remember it."

"I'll remember," Cummings muttered, feeling sick.

The girl said, "In any case Tarollier must have been pretty mad to see you here today. Why hasn't he tried to prevent your getting help?"

"He has—or someone has. Someone's wrecked the ground radio." Gleason stared up at the machine; the generator droned on. David was a long time in there. . . . "There's just a chance that we may be heard with this makeshift gadget we've rigged up, but whatever happens we can't expect any help before dawn at the earliest."

"Let's hope someone hears," the girl said uneasily. Again she looked back, shivering a little in the cool night. "But —the boat. . . . It may not be held up for long. What can we do?"

All at once the thing was simple and clear to Gleason.

"I'm going to the harbour." He said it quietly, almost offhandedly. "The boat must not sail—because I believe that Tarollier will try to take Harry and the skipper with him. I believe it even more now since I got this idea about the explosion. And even if they're not with him, we must get Tarollier. . . . Lester, while David is trying to send the signal you'll have to stay on guard."

"But—what can you do, alone?"

"I don't know, yet. But I may be able to hold things up until help comes." Gleason looked at the girl. "And if the boat is out of action already so much the better. There's sure to be a chance of some kind."

Cummings was eyeing him uncertainly. "I don't like it much, Bob," he said. "Don't you think I'd better come?"

"No. Someone must guard the kite. David may be some time up there."

The girl stood up suddenly between them, facing the engineer. She was as tall as he, her figure lovely and firm and slim and he smelled the fragrance of her, and even in the darkness he knew that her hair was a deep, warm colour, and if she removed the scarf it would fall in a fine and glowing cascade to her shoulders. He had never seen such big eyes —they were bigger than Della's—Della who would be gone when he got home. If he had wanted another woman she could be something like this one, but he didn't. He was pretty sure he didn't.

"I'm coming with you," she said.

"You? You can't...."

"I'm coming."

She was very close to Gleason, and her unwinking gaze flooded over him like a warm moon in the starlight. She saw him and knew that she must stay with this man with the handsome, determined face which had oil smudges on it, this man who was strongly and neatly built as a man should be. The other with the whiskers and the popping eyes was no more than a quivering toy in the hands of fear; she could not stay here. If this man was going to the harbour, she would go with him. She knew that he was a man, and she wanted a man beside her tonight.

"I'm rested now," she said almost defiantly, "and I know the way. I'm not afraid to go."

Gleason returned her stare and knew that she was not afraid. It seemed to him then that she had never been afraid in her life, and now he felt no fear for himself, only for those whom he was going to seek.

He said, his voice strangely harsh, "Do you *want* to go?"

"I want to go, if I can go with you."

He wanted her to go too, then. "All right," he said, still roughly, "all right. We're going. I'll take a Sten."

"You're both going?" Cummings sounded faintly angry

behind his surprise. " But there may be trouble. . . ." He saw their faces and suddenly knew that there was nothing more for him to say, except to be careful. " For Heaven's sake watch out, Bob."

" I will. At least we know what's going on now. Wait here while I tell David about it and see if he has any news."

Tarrant was still bent over his transmitter, his young face drawn and weary in the cone of light which shone down to the table where his hand was tapping feverishly at the morse key. Susan stood beside him, her face tight and exhausted of all but a final hope. He looked up at the engineer, removing his earphones and shaking his head despairingly.

" Nothing—nothing at all. . . ."

The generator whined and shuddered behind them, and despite the open windows here and the closed door to the cabin its fumes were beginning to foul the air. The flight deck was a dim, trembling place, grey with the waiting. Gleason bent down and spoke loudly above the noise, telling them briefly what the girl had said.

" I'm going to the harbour. Lester will keep watch. Don't give up trying, David, and if you get through tell them what's happened—and tell them to hurry."

There was no argument, nothing else to be done.

" I will. Good luck, Bob."

Gleason left the machine with the Sten and three clips of ammunition and a torch from the spares box. The girl was waiting at the foot of the ladder, and as they started across the apron he raised his hand briefly to Cummings whose pale, intent face watched from the dimness under the wing. Silently and lightly beside him the girl moved, as if she had found a new and buoyant energy, as if she was happy. They walked quickly towards the control tower, turned the corner beside it, and the small oasis of security which seemed to have surrounded the aircraft was blotted out behind them. They were alone now.

If only Westonmills had heard the signal, Gleason thought, if only they could have started out knowing that help was already on the way. . . .

All round was darkness, silence. The tower, the huts and

hangar vaguely to their left, the dunes—all slept deeply under the stars. Ahead the track opened, beckoning to danger.

"I was afraid you would leave me." The girl's voice was soft as starlight falling. "I didn't want to stay there."

"I know you didn't," he said. "But why not?"

He felt rather than saw her smile.

"It was something I had to do. I couldn't have waited there with the other man, and I wanted to help you. . . . Did you want me to come?"

"It may be dangerous," he said quietly.

"I know. But waiting and wondering can be even more dangerous. Did you want me to come?"

"Yes. You shouldn't have come, but I knew I couldn't stop you. And I'm glad now."

It was true. He couldn't have stopped her, she knew what she was doing, and he had felt far more hopeful and confident since she told him that she would come. Suddenly he knew that she reminded him not of anyone he had met but of some deeply imagined woman whose form had lain long in a remote fastness of his mind. It was not even Della of whom she had reminded him, though he had been measuring her against Della. . . . And he was glad that it was this girl and no one else, unknown as she was, who walked beside him tonight, for he knew that she could aid him more than any other woman, or many a man. A strange elation took him, focusing his strength and resolve, and he felt alert and without fear.

"Your eyes are blue," he said.

She nodded, smiling again, and they went on close together, silent now.

Beside the track which was clear in the starlight, the dunes lay softly shadowed against the sky, the low walls of a little valley. Gleason held the Sten ready before him, his eyes searched the way and his ears were attuned for any sound that was not of their own making. But there was nothing —only the empty silent road and the blue-black sky with its huge and pendent stars contained in a thousand galaxies of snapping and wondrous brilliance.

Soon the track bent slightly to the right, and then the walls of sand fell back from it so that it ran over an undulating plain which rolled, open to the sky except towards the west where the straight ridge of a low hill was just visible. Here and there on the plain isolated hummocks of rock or sand rose in strange and tortured lineaments. Gleason looked at his watch; we must be about a mile from the airfield now, he thought, nearly half-way. Under foot the sand was hard and level but scattered fairly thickly with loose, sharp stones that they did their best to avoid; they did not want any noise. It was then, while he was staring at the ground a few feet ahead, that his quick eye caught the odd shape of something lying there, and it was not a stone.

He saw almost at once that it was a metal wrench, long and heavy. Involuntarily Gleason grasped the girl's arm, stopping her.

"What is it?" she whispered.

"Look!"

What was a tool like this doing here? Could it have fallen from something?—the jeep, this afternoon! Gleason peered round before bending quickly and switching on his torch, shielding the light with a cupped hand.

There was a black stain on the head of the wrench, and he touched it gingerly. And as he touched he knew what it was; dried blood.

The girl heard the sound first; she was pointing, and then he heard it too, a sort of scraping noise followed by a sharp click as though two stones had been knocked together. He had not noticed the dark mound of rocks beside the road —a mound with a certain decayed regularity, not of any weird eroded form. The sound came again as they watched, louder now, a longer scraping and the tap of loose stones. Gleason straightened up slowly, snapping off the light, facing the shadow beside the track.

"Someone's there," the girl murmured. "Be careful. . . ."

He nodded. It might be a snare; but why—here? The gun was hard, cold and comforting in his hand. Tarollier? —no, at the Bey's palace now. The wrench. . . . Harry was with him. Harry . . .?

"Stay here. I've got to look at this."

"Careful. . . ."

The clicks had watered his blood and the scraping pared his muscles to threads, but something still moved him. He began to go forward, slow and crouching, the Sten thrust before him, a probing threat. The noises had ceased now, and all the dreadful silence of Faruda was about him as he moved to the cairn. No, not a cairn—a low, roughly circular wall, enclosing a blackness; a hole—with someone or something in it.

He jumped then, torch and gun shoved over the piled stones. Light sprang with him, shattering the blackness inside.

"Harry!"

The hunched and feebly jerking shape of Barthell lay on dry rubble in the hole a few feet below.

Harry—at least he was alive. Gleason did not hesitate before leaping down beside the navigator. A knife.... He had one—yes, here. He fumbled with it, then sawed furiously in the torchlight, first the gag and then the cords on Barthell's hands and feet, and he could see the raw weals in his flesh where they had cut and all the time Harry's eyes were staring at him like polished buttons, fixed and intent.

"It's all right," he called, loudly enough for the girl to hear. "Our navigator."

Was it all right? Barthell was free then, sitting on the rubble, moving painfully.

"Harry—how are you? Can you ...?"

"Soon," Barthell muttered. "I'll be okay soon." He groaned a little. "How long have I been here?"

"Since this afternoon when Tarollier took you in the jeep."

"The jeep.... I remember now. I'm so bloody stiff—help me get up."

Relief ran like wine in Gleason's veins. It seemed that Harry was not badly hurt after all. Barthell was straightening himself, working his arms and legs in slow, awkward motions. Now the girl's head was over the edge of the wall above, watching them, a dark moon against the sky.

"All right," Barthell said after a time. "All right.... Let's get out of this."

Gleason climbed out first, helped by the girl, and together they gripped Barthell, heaving, half dragging him from the well. At the top the navigator leaned against the wall, panting, his face white, and he was staring at the slim shadow beside Gleason.

"Who's this? A girl...."

"She's with us," Gleason said quickly. "She came to warn us about Tarollier. There's no time now—I'll tell you later."

"Tarollier.... Wait till I get my hands on him," Barthell muttered, feeling the back of his head. "He hit me with something and threw me in there...."

"We know about Tarollier. That's why we're here."

"Know about him? How?" Barthell eyed the girl suspiciously. "What brought you here?"

"Later. How are you feeling now?"

"Like hell.... But I'm all right."

"The wound isn't bleeding any more," Gleason said, holding the light close to Barthell's head. "It looks pretty clean. Listen—do you feel well enough to come with us to the harbour, now?"

"I think so. Yes...."

"If you do, it will make all the difference. You've still got your gun?"

"It's here. Tarollier was in too big a hurry to remember it, I guess. What's going on, anyway?"

"The skipper's in trouble. I'll tell you on the way."

"All right. Just let me have a minute."

They waited while Barthell rested against the wall and flexed his thick arms and legs, and then they went on down the track which soon began to drop gently as they neared the coast. As they walked Gleason told the navigator quietly of the girl's arrival and what she had said, of the wrecked transmitter and their efforts to send a signal for help. Barthell listened in silence, his broad, ugly face growing darker with anger as the story unfolded. Gleason, for his part, felt a new hope now that he and the girl were no longer alone. Barthell's courage and massive strength—these were a comfort and an assurance; and this strength was making it possible for him to throw off the effects of an attack which might have injured seriously anyone of less rugged construction.

"So Tarollier has got the skipper too, then." Barthell's growl when Gleason had finished was a muted threat. "He'll be sorry for that.... What's the programme when we get to the harbour?"

"Main job is to get the skipper—we think Tarollier will be bringing him to the boat with the drugs and two of the Bey's men as guards. I don't know just how we're going to do it, and we'd best go carefully when we get near the village. . . . If we can only stop the boat leaving, help is bound to come soon."

"We mustn't do anything that would be bad for the skipper's health," Barthell said. "That's why we can't ambush the whole outfit on its way to the harbour. Best thing is to see how the land lies before we decide what to do."

"All right."

They went on in silence, ears and eyes alert for any dark outriders of the danger into which they were heading. The flat, sloping plain was drained of everything but the shadowy stillness and the dull silver of starlight lying eerily upon it. Barthell looked up at the pole star's pin-point, a dim guide among the brighter stars and planets, and saw that their way led a little east of north. But soon, on the left, they noticed a white stone beside the track and another road leading off towards the west, while their own bent sharply to the right and soon began to descend more steeply.

"That must be the road to the Bey's palace," Barthell muttered. His head still ached cruelly, but he could feel his strength returning with almost every step.

The girl said, "We'd better be careful. It's not far to the harbour now."

She was calm, moving beautifully in the faint light, and even the self-reliant Barthell was somehow glad that she was there. Ragged sandstone outcrops rose beside the way, making a narrow valley of the road as the dunes had done near the airfield. They went on more warily, keeping as well as they could to the shadows beneath the rocks and trying to make their advance as soundless as possible. After a few minutes they felt rather than heard something from the west, behind them; it was a noise, a low and distant throb.

They stopped, listening. It was the sound of a heavy car, or a truck.

"Tarollier—leaving the palace," the girl whispered. Her steady hand touched Gleason's arm.

"It's not yet eight. . . . He's early."

The sound came nearer, a growing throbbing hum—hesitated, and then began to fade.

"It's going towards the airfield," Gleason muttered hoarsely. "Why . . .?"

Barthell's forehead was creased in anxiety. "I don't know, but I don't like it much. . . . Anyway, we can't do anything about that now. Let's take a look at this harbour."

Again they moved on cautiously for what Gleason thought would be four or five minutes, and then the girl said suddenly, "It's here." All at once the track dropped yet more steeply and round the shoulder of a rock there was the velvet glimmer of starlight on water, the vague white shapes of houses beyond. The village. . . .

They halted. Barthell said, "Now what? We mustn't be seen, and we'd better keep clear of the houses."

"The boat's tied up on this side, just round the corner," the girl murmured.

"We can't wait here. . . ." Barthell had been staring up at the rocks which frowned above the track. They were twenty or thirty feet high at this place, not too steep, and scored by little fissures and gullies. "Look—if we can climb these rocks we should get a view of the whole harbour from the top. . . . Once we have the general set-up we can decide what to do."

The girl said, "It should be a good place for watching the boat. I can climb."

"It doesn't look too difficult. All right, then? Don't make a noise."

Barthell went up first, his burly figure scrambling on the rock's worn face. Gleason gave the girl a start and she climbed nimbly, long-legged, like an agile boy; he slung the Sten by the strap from his shoulder and followed. Once his foot slipped on the sandy surface and only by clutching desperately at a projection did he save himself from falling. A dislodged stone bumped dully down the rock face with a noise which seemed to them thunderous in its magnitude, and they waited half-way up, scarcely breathing, expecting discovery to be inevitable. But the brooding silence was vast and unbroken. On they went over roundly eroded surfaces which made foot and hand holds so insecure until, suddenly, they were at the top.

They stood on a little rock-strewn plateau which was slashed by the black scar of the track down which they had just come. All at once there were sounds here—sea sounds, slowly coiling airs; and a short distance away on the right the plateau's edge, the straight dark line of it fused indissolubly to the night sky. Bent like infantrymen advancing under fire they half ran, half walked towards it, and at the edge lay flat and peered cautiously over.

Barthell warned softly, " Mind your heads—we're on the skyline."

The harbour and village lay below, and seemed to sleep. It was all silent and motionless in the dim light, a ghost village by a ghostly enclosure of still water in which the reflections of the stars were deep and clear. Not a light showed anywhere. The girl pointed silently, and close and directly beneath where they lay they saw the black shape of a shed, the rough quay, the boat. . . . Barthell and the engineer stared at this boat, and it was long and narrow and powerful in its rakish set on the water, a drab and uniform colour all over. The ready and seaworthy appearance of it struck like a knell into Gleason's heart.

He felt the girl stir angrily beside him. She whispered, " Then I didn't sink her. . . . Why didn't she sink?"

" Never mind." His murmur was consoling. That the boat hadn't sunk was bad, but not disastrous, he thought, not yet.

Barthell was muttering, " I can't be sure, but I think there's a man in the wheelhouse and another beside the forward hatchway. . . ."

" That's Arnold in the wheelhouse," the girl said, " waiting for Tarollier, and I bet he's scared."

Gleason nodded silently, trying to resolve the boat's shadows into their correct identities. The jeep stood on the quay below them, in front of the tin shed. Across beneath the sightless eyes of the few houses the fat black shapes of the two fishing vessels lolled against the opposite quay, side by side. Seawards a compressed channel seemed to leave the harbour only to stop in darkness below a cliff; the entrance, narrow and sharply bent. Staring at it Barthell knew that the bend must be there, where the cliff appeared to stand athwart the channel; it would be difficult enough for a boat the length of this one to pass through even in daylight, and more so now. . . .

Could it be made more hazardous yet—even impossible? Suppose that the girl's attempts at scuttling were to fail, as it seemed evident that they had already, and that the locking of the fuel tanks was a failure too, then the boat would be off in little more than an hour. There was not much time if they were to act. But if things worked out well they might not only get the skipper but Tarollier and the drugs as well. Barthell was hopeful that Kingsley would not be harmed until the boat was at sea, unless they were panicked into killing him before.

Turning his head towards the girl Barthell said, "Did you see the entrance when you came in this morning?"

"I was locked in my cabin then, but I could see that it was very narrow—a cleft in the rocks, and I could almost have touched them at times. Arnold had to go dead slow to get in, and the boat only just got round the corner."

"How steep were the rocks there?"

"Not too steep to be climbed, I should think, but not easy either."

Barthell nodded, and looked long and calculatingly at the narrow channel, and then across at the houses and the fishing boats. From these his eyes travelled slowly over the dim slopes which rose in gradual elevations behind the village, slopes which enclosed the whole harbour and made a shallow bowl except by the sea cliffs and on the side where he lay with Gleason and the girl on the lip of the little escarpment. The slopes were sown thickly with sandstone outcrops and eroded chunks of rock. There would be plenty of cover. . . . It would mean going back and climbing down to the track again, crossing it, scaling the far side and working round behind the houses. A risk, all right, but what else could they do? When the boat went the Bey's guards would go back to the palace, and they were the main obstacle. But we have to chance being seen, Barthell thought, by Tarollier's gang and also by the village people; though there was less risk of being spotted from the boat if they waited until the loading started, when everybody would be occupied with the cargo. Fortunately there were some deep shadows under the cliffs on the far side, near the harbour entrance. What about the girl? She would have to come with them—anyway, she looked ready enough and she must have guts. Something told him that she would be all right whatever happened.

Should they jump the boat—now? No—even that was too dangerous for the skipper's health. The safest way was to stop the boat leaving Faruda.

Gleason moved restively beside him. " I hope everything is all right at the airfield. What are we going to do? Tarollier will be here soon. . . ."

" I know. Listen—the boat *may* be immobilised, but we can't rely on it," Barthell whispered. " The scuttling seems to have gone wrong, though the fuel locks may hold it up for a time. It's probable that they won't find out about the locks until they try to start the motors."

" Well?" The girl was gazing silently at each man in turn, waiting.

" If my plan succeeds it will stop them leaving the harbour all right and it will avoid a clash with the Bey's men, but it depends upon our not being seen. That's why I think we ought to wait until Tarollier comes before we try it, when they're busy with the loading—if we start now those two on the deck or someone in the village may spot us, and that will kill it. Besides, I want to get a good look at these people on the truck, and we shall have a clear view of the performance from here. Tarollier isn't alone, and we must know the whole set-up. What about Richer—and this bird Smith? How do they fit in with this?"

" I'd almost forgotten them. They both disappeared this afternoon, and Garraud's body vanished too."

Barthell checked an exclamation of sheer incredulity.

" Garraud—vanished! What d'you mean? How . . .?"

" I don't know how. All I know is that he wasn't in the tent when David and I were searching for spare radio parts just before dark. But it looks to me as though Tarollier is at the bottom of all these disappearing acts. Anyway, what's this idea of yours?"

Barthell nodded towards the far side of the harbour.

"See those two fishing boats alongside the opposite quay? Now—if we could get across there and untie one we should be able to tow it round under the cliffs and block the harbour entrance. They're quite small, and the entrance is only a few feet wide. D'you think we could do it?"

"I think so." It was the girl who spoke, and her voice urged them.

"It's no more than a slim chance." Gleason was cautious.

"But one that could come off. If they hit the boat hard enough it should sink and that will be the end of friend Tarollier's hopes. We may even be able to scuttle it. From that quay to the entrance is only a few yards, and mostly in shadow. You two could stay on board to keep the thing from bumping against the cliff while I pull."

"What about the moorings?"

"We've both got knives to saw through any ropes it's tied with. You don't find this kind of boat moored by wires."

"How are we going to get aboard without being seen?"

"This is how," Barthell whispered. "Look—we go back down to the track the way we came, cross it and climb the far side. Then we can skirt round behind the houses and down the slope, taking advantage of the cover given by all those rocks. Now there's a little alley between two of the houses almost opposite where the boats are lying—see it? Through that and straight aboard the first one. The other is tied outside it—that's the one we'll take."

"Cut the mooring ropes, leaving one for you to tow her?"

"Right. With any luck the people in the houses will be asleep. . . . I shall go back ashore and pull the boat along the quay and then under the cliff—it's not too steep for a foothold." Barthell's low, rumbling voice was fiercely determined. "I'll get her in the entrance even if I have to swim with the rope tied round me."

Gleason had no fear of this plan of Barthell's, but he felt bound to point out some of its disadvantages; he even smiled a little then, for knowing Harry they would probably do what Harry wanted in the end. "Suppose there's someone aboard," he murmured.

"That will be too bad—for them," Barthell said coolly.

"We've got to risk that. We must put the boat across the entrance a little way from where it opens into the harbour—see where it looks narrowest and darkest?—fix her there somehow and then attempt to scuttle. When we've done that we'll climb ashore and wait for Tarollier to sail out."

" If we can."

" We must choose a place where we can."

" What then?"

Barthell stared at the dark harbour. " It depends on what happens with Arnold's boat," he muttered. All at once he seemed uncertain and even empty of hope. " But this—this will delay them until help comes. . . . It's got to."

" That won't be before dawn, even if David gets the message through. It's a long time, Harry."

" I know. But if they do leave in the night we'll have a chance of rushing the boat and grabbing the skipper while they're wondering what's hit them. If only the skipper wasn't being guarded by these thugs of the Bey's we could jump this truck and get him. But you can bet your life the guards will have orders to shoot him at the first sign of trouble regardless of whether they get shot themselves, because the Bey won't chance the skipper talking about his part in this game. We can't risk it."

" No. . . . I suppose that's out."

Barthell's short loss of confidence was gone; he was sure of himself again now. He said, " I should guess that the guards will stand by until they see the boat away, and then return with the truck. After that there will be only Tarollier and his pal and the crew to deal with when they come out, and the odds will be that much more in our favour." Barthell paused, then went on quietly, " I've got a feeling they'll do anything while there's a chance of getting away with the drugs, but once that chance has gone they'll be more likely to fold up. That's why I think we should do it this way."

A silence. Gleason looked at the girl, and she was already watching him, her face speaking to him. He said, " All right, Harry. It's probably the best we can do."

" I think it is. We have to play for time. The longer we can delay things the nearer we are to getting help."

The girl said in a low voice, staring down at the boat,

"Arnold will be half dead with fear now he's discovered I've gone, and when Tarollier finds out—if he does—there will be big trouble on board."

"So much the better—there's nothing like having a disorganised enemy."

"Arnold is the weak link," she murmured. "He's dead scared too about your captain—he doesn't want any part in a killing. I think he'd surrender if he got half a chance."

"That might help. . . . Now—are you willing to try this with me, both of you?"

Gleason looked at Barthell's resolute face, again at the girl's. She was half smiling, her eyes bright, and he knew that she would be ready to go with them.

"Yes, let's try it," he said, and his voice was firm.

"Good. We know what to. . . ."

"Listen, listen!" The girl had grasped Gleason's arm and her head was turned towards the west. "It's the truck—now!"

They heard it then, the faint sound of an engine coming over the plateau. Barthell eased himself round, listening, as the noise grew steadily louder from the dark slash of the track behind them. It floated in the silence, passing the point where they had climbed from the road, there was a second of stillness while the vehicle turned the shoulder of the plateau and then they saw it bump across the quay, carrying no lights, to stop with a faint squeal of brakes directly below where they lay.

The truck was a big open one, almost new. It was loaded with a stack of black boxes, and beside these the dim figures of two men squatted. Barthell could see the long-barrelled rifles against the background of the harbour's starlit water.

As soon as the truck stopped a man got down awkwardly from the driving seat, a big, lumbering man, and Barthell's breath hissed in through his teeth as he recognised the shape of Tarollier. The Frenchman moved to the back of the truck and released the tailboard and the two guards jumped down, never relinquishing their hold on the rifles.

Barthell did not see the other man leave the cab, but suddenly he was there beside it, a tall, stooping figure, a skeletal large-headed shadow in the darkness. Richer; then it was Richer and Tarollier together. . . .

Two slow shapes detached themselves from the waiting stillness of the boat's deck and climbed the rail to the quay. With his peculiar lurching walk Tarollier went to meet them and began to speak in tones which Barthell and his companions could not hear, gesturing towards the truck, while Richer and the guards stood silently beside it. The men from the boat were almost unnaturally still while Tarollier talked with them, and Barthell could have sworn that he felt a sort of telepathic terror emanating from their rigid bodies before they went to the truck, reached into it with reluctant hands and dragged out something heavy and unwieldy—something like a long sagging bundle which they held at each end and carried slowly to the boat. There was a uniform, the whiteness of a face. . . .

"The skipper!" Gleason's voice was low but hoarse with fury. "Come on—let's go now."

"Wait!" Barthell gripped the engineer's arm with powerful fingers. "I want to see where they put him. . . . Better wait till the loading starts before we move."

Richer was standing by the tail of the truck, watching, his thin body bent forward in a kind of impatient expectation. Now the two men were carrying Kingsley along the after deck, and they disappeared with their load down a companionway near the boat's stern. Barthell switched his gaze to Tarollier, and the big man was pulling something else from the body of the truck, a smaller mass, shapeless and inert, that seemed to be wrapped loosely in some dark material, which he slung easily over his shoulder and carried to the rail. The two men emerged from the companionway and took it from him, bearing it below as they had borne Kingsley.

The watchers on the low cliff looked at one another with silent and awful certainty, for they knew that this thing was the corpse of Garraud.

But Tarollier was reaching yet again into the truck. . . . Another shape, like Kingsley's, the head rolling slackly as it was carried to the boat.

Barthell found something like a voice. "Smith! It must be Smith. They've got him too. . . ."

"Is he dead?" the girl whispered. "Like—like . . ."

Nobody answered. Then all at once the waiting figure

of Richer seemed to leap into motion as though some powerful spring inside him was unlatched, as though the removal of these dreadful shapes had been but a trivial preliminary to real and urgent issues, and he climbed with spider-like agility over the side of the truck and began to lift the boxes from the top of the stack and drop them by the tail. He seemed to hug them to his chest, his thin body bent painfully under the weight.

"So—it's Tarollier and Richer," Barthell muttered. "Now we know. Come on—let's get going."

Gleason looked at the girl. "All right?"

She nodded. "I'm ready."

They crawled back from the edge of the escarpment, and when it hid them from the harbour they began to run, crouching, to the cleft where the track was. Afterwards Gleason remembered only a breathless bumping slide down the rocky wall, the sandy surface stinging his clutching fingers, and then a jarring shock as his feet hit level ground. He followed with the girl as Barthell darted across the track and began to clamber up the rocks on the far side, and this climb was no more difficult than the descent had been. In a few moments they were at the top, on a great flat slab of rock, boulder-strewn, which almost immediately began to slope downward as they moved over it. They went in a wide sweep over the tilted side of this bowl which enclosed the village, moving as quickly as they could from the shadow of one boulder to that of the next, often having to scramble awkwardly over sandy ridges and leap across small fissures in the rock.

As they approached the rear of the village Barthell slowed his pace in order to avoid making unnecessary noise on the ragged surface, and when they came directly behind it and about fifty yards away he halted for a minute, looking carefully down at the ground before him. He was relieved to see that the backs of the houses were nearly all flat white walls, unbroken by more than one or two of the black rectangles that were doors or windows; there was the chosen alley between two houses. . . . Now, away on the far side of the harbour, he could just see the long blackness of Arnold's boat.

Motioning to the others he moved forward again, bent low,

stepping carefully in the shadows of the scattered rocks. The houses loomed palely, the dark alleys which divided them like black bottomless pits, silent with evil terrors. Now Gleason felt his breath coming fast, but it seemed that he could never draw enough into the throbbing constriction of his chest. He wondered how the girl was feeling; she said nothing, but moved easily over the rough slope in Barthell's wake. And then, after what was like ages and miles of stumbling, crouching advance, they were together in one of these dark pits between the houses, the walls leaning close and threatening above their heads.

A sudden new strength, a faith, lay upon Barthell as he stood in the silent alley. Now he no longer felt the ache of the wound in his head, or even any misgivings over what they were about to attempt. There was no turning back. He knew too that this strong hope had touched the others, and because of this there was no one he would rather have had with him on this night.

"All right?" he whispered. "If there's anyone aboard, hit him—hard. Now into the first boat—then the other. Keep low."

The fishing boat nearest the quay was not thirty feet away, its rail less than a yard above the rough stones over which they had to go. Barthell peered round the corner of the house, and then forsook the darkness of the alley to dash across the open quay and almost roll his body over the gunwale, the girl and Gleason following together at his heels. They dropped beside one another to the wooden deck and knelt there, sweating and listening in the sudden reek of decaying fish and in the eternal silence. . . .

There was no sound, even from the farther quay; the houses stared down but did not recognise them, their pale faces expressionless. They crawled across the stinking deck and over into the boat alongside, and it was theirs alone.

After another listening pause Barthell said softly, "Okay —I don't think we've been spotted. The ropes. . . ."

Gleason nodded, gesturing to the girl to stay where she was. He crawled aft, keeping his head below the top of the gunwale, and Barthell moved towards the blunt bow. The decks were a litter of rope ends and wooden stays, iron belaying pins and the gluey and decomposing carcases of long-dead fish. With the tense care of desperation they picked their way over the debris, knowing that a sound now must inevitably mean discovery and failure.

The boat was tied carelessly by a single weedy rope fore and aft, the worn strands parting easily under their knives, and soon they were together again on the deck, and Barthell had a length of rope in his hand.

" All right now," he whispered. " I've tied this to the bow. I'm going ashore to tow her under the cliff, and you fend her off the rocks and give a shove when you can."

" Right. Be careful."

Barthell swung himself over the gunwale again and crawled across the deck of the inner boat, dropping his rope over the bows, and Gleason and the girl began to push their boat along, crouching beside the rail, and slowly it moved forward, timbers scraping faintly on the side of the other. If Tarollier and Richer saw it moving, now. . . . Barthell had jumped down to the quay and had the rope over his shoulder, bending forward and pulling with all the power of his muscular body. The boat slid silently in the water, slowly gliding in a terrible suspense between stars and reflected stars, and every second they expected shots from the far quay or shouts of alarm from the quiet houses.

But none came. And then they were clear of the quay and in the grateful shadow of the cliff which protected the harbour from the sea, and Barthell was scrambling over the slippery rocks below it, hauling the boat in close, always pulling.

Now it was only the boat's length from here to the channel's mouth. Barthell stumbled doggedly over weedy ledges and into cold pools, and once he had to go up to his thighs in water, feeling his way round a projecting boss of the cliff face. He reached the corner where the channel began and here the rock was almost vertical, offering no hold for feet or hands, and he knew the water would be deep. He gave a great heave on the rope and scrambled aboard as the boat slid past. With finger tips digging at the rough cliff they edged it slowly forward until Barthell was able to find a secure hold from which to pull it round the corner, and the boat drifted at a maddening snail's pace along the channel. Fear clawed at their backs.

They searched the steep walls for a place at which the entrance might be blocked; it was growing darker and more narrow as their vessel advanced until, just before the sharp bend that hid the sea, the channel's width was no more than twice the beam of the boat. The black gash of a small gully cut deeply into the rocky wall on the left side, and seeing it Barthell knew suddenly that this must be the place. He called softly to the others and they reached over and clutched at the wall, their fingers lacerated by sharp projections, and gradually the boat lost way and stopped. It floated on a dark, still pool of awesome silence.

"I think we can get her across here," Barthell said. "See that little gully? We could jam the stern in there and try to get the bows tied on the other side. Even if she moves they can't get past—it's too narrow."

"All right. I've found a boathook. We must try to scuttle her too, after she's in position. It looks possible to get away by climbing up the gully from the stern."

"I believe we can. Okay—here we go."

Barthell took the rope again and scrambled over the side on to a small ledge jutting out from the cliff. He held the bows while Gleason pushed with the boathook and the stern moved round slowly, putting the boat squarely across the channel. Inch by inch Gleason worked the stern into the base of the gully until it came up solidly against the gully's side.

"She's in," he called quietly.

Barthell scanned the rock on his side but could find nothing to which the rope might be secured except a small crack and he wedged it into this, stamping it in firmly with his heel, and then he clambered back over the bows.

"That's the best we can do. Now—let's see if she can be sunk."

"There's a sort of hold here," the girl said, "and a ladder. . . ."

"We'll try it. Got the torch?"

"Yes." Gleason pulled the lamp from his pocket. "Stay here and keep your eyes open," he said to the girl. "We'll make it quick."

Barthell had picked up a belaying pin from the deck and he followed Gleason down a rickety ladder into the hold. Down here the darkness was complete and evil-smelling. When the light stabbed into the blackness they saw the bare wooden ribs of the boat and the tarred timbers, and several inches of filthy water swilled gently round the keel board and one or two dead fish floated whitely in it. The timbers were old, but thick and strong, reinforced in places with square iron plates.

They stared round the hold for some time, eyes following the bright circle of light, before Gleason suddenly cried out, pointing at the hull near where the surface of the bilge water touched it.

"A plug!" Barthell's voice carried overtones of triumph. "I'll knock that out somehow—whether we're heard or not."

He struck the wooden plug a mighty blow with the pin, and then another. The dull sounds boomed between the walls of the hold in sinister thunderings, made louder by confinement. Four times he struck, and with the last blow a jet of clear water shot up from the hole where the plug had been, striking him full on the chest. He laughed out loud, throwing down the pin, and they scrambled up the ladder to the deck.

They found the climb up the gully less difficult than it had looked from below, and the rocks were no more than fifty feet high at this point. The girl went up after Barthell, Gleason last, and she was sure-footed and nimble as before, asking no help from either of her companions. At the cliff top they stood and watched the black shape below settle slowly in the channel. Now they had to wait for Tarollier and Richer—or for the help which they hoped might come first.

"We can jump them from here if necessary," Barthell said quietly. He touched the gun at his waist, and he was grinning now with a furious and savage anticipation. "We'll hear them coming, and when they realise they can't get out —that's our chance."

He began to pace up and down on the flat top of the cliff, trying to generate heat to keep the coldness of his wet clothes at bay, but it was the great hope inside him that warmed more than movement and which smoothed away physical discomfort. Gleason and the girl sat down to rest, listening. She was hunched beside him, knees drawn up to her chin, and her great eyes were on the dark cleft below.

"Are you cold?" he asked softly.

She looked at him. "A little."

Instinctively they drew closer together, and Gleason put his arm about her shoulders. She seemed to be part of him then, a calm, strong, waiting part without which he was not whole.

* * *

How long have I been here now? Tarrant wondered. Thought was a vague and weary labour, leaving only pain in his head. The throbbing chatter of the generator from beyond the closed cabin door came to him as a diffused hum, muffled by his earphones. How long? He knew that Susan stood beside him and it was as though she had always been there, watching, a silent and supplicating novice at some futile ritual; he looked up at her and she smiled wanly and touched his shoulder. At least they were together. . . .

In spite of the open flight deck windows the fumes from the motor which had crept past the door were beginning to make their heads ache. The transmitter's flat black warty face seemed to leer mockingly as Tarrant tapped away with desperate concentration at the morse key; his wrist and arm were one consuming pain which spread out into all his body, filling it with a numbing weariness; and the mansions of hope which their minds had built were crumbled now almost to nothing.

But yet again he adjusted the dials of the receiver, straining his ears. Nothing. . . . The signals must be too weak. He had heard Westonmills calling faintly just after Gleason left for the village. "Westonmills to Peter Easy. Are you airborne yet?" And they had said they were listening out. Airborne! Tarrant's face grimaced wryly. At this moment they had as much chance of becoming airborne as the Albert Hall. . . .

Once more he tapped out the despairing call for help and swept the receiver's tuning dial. Among the ceaseless babble of dots and dashes which tormented the ether there was no word for them. He set the dial to Westonmills' frequency and lay back in his seat, closing his eyes in utter weariness and dejection.

He seemed to have been asleep when Susan's voice came to him, floating, quiet-tongued.

"Try again, David," she said. "Keep trying."

He nodded, opening his eyes with an effort and reaching again for the key. But before he could touch it the sounds were there, meeting and echoing within his brain. He sat up, grabbed at his pencil and poised it over the signal pad. The call-sign—theirs!

It was twice as loud as the weak signal from Westonmills had been. It came from *Marseilles*. . . . Why . . .? His hand moved fast, scribbling.

"Signal received. . . . Two military aircraft with troops. . . . Arrive at dawn. . . . Rogers will accompany. . . . Call again on frequency of 6850 kilocycles. . . . Keep end up. . . . Listening out."

CHAPTER X

AND THE MORNING

RICHER entered the wheelhouse, stooping low to pass through the doorway. He stood there, looking at Arnold and Tarollier, and nobody spoke.

In the dim light of the single bulb which burned from the wheelhouse roof Richer's face was closed and still with an inward, monstrous triumph; the lipless mouth and pared moustache, the black pile of hair thick on the great head, the yellow, stretched skin—all were but a frame for his eyes. Deeply from their sockets the luminous pools shone to a ferocious and anticipatory gloating, fired with light that seemed strong as the lamp above. Under the clinging khaki sweater the fleshless, stringy body was consumed by a strange and rapid trembling which was almost vibration and the long hands moved, jerking, twitching, never at rest.

Close to Richer at last, Arnold was emasculated by him, knowing a fresh and plunging terror. He wanted to scream something, to ease his fear by letting it fly howling into the night, but he could make no sound nor move a muscle of his body. In his goaded brain there was nothing now but the fear that Richer had put there, for cold murder had been done by this thin, quivering man; and even that was not enough, for tonight, on his boat, there would be massacre. . . .

Richer, voice purring, was saying something. "At last, then, it is safely aboard." It? The cargo. Richer was thinking only about the cargo. The lives of these men meant nothing to him—less than nothing. Arnold felt his guts freeze as he saw Richer's face, deadly currents sliding like glaciers through all his body. Painfully, grinding, his mind began to move. When he had known Richer before he was not like this— an ordinary enough man then, of the scheming and furtive kind that Arnold was used to dealing with in his trade, but now. . . . And suddenly Arnold knew that Richer was still that kind of man, but there was a revealed determination in him, towering and absolute, to allow nothing whatever to stand in his way; it was not that Richer had wanted to kill, but that having been forced he had done so with no more compunction than he would feel in kicking a stone from his path.

"You were slow," Richer said, looking from Tarollier to Arnold before the heavy eyelids all at once dropped, hiding the light beneath. "The loading should have been finished before this."

"There were a lot of cases," Tarollier muttered. His head was bent and he did not look at Richer. "And they were heavy. . . ."

Arnold stared at Tarollier, and with a surprise that was like a blow he saw that the big man was shuffling uncomfortably and that there was dread in his beady eyes. The knowledge that Tarollier too was afraid of Richer twisted the agonising sword of fear in Arnold, and the sweat stood in white blisters on his bloodless face; now the yellow hair was no longer combed but dank and in disorder, like some grotesque wig on the head of a clown. Would they find out about the girl too, and that she was gone?

"You were slow, I say." Richer turned to look at the quay where the empty truck stood, and beside it the two guards still squatted, rifles across their knees. His eyes came back to Arnold. "The captain," he said, soft-voiced, "and the man Smith. . . . Are they safe?"

Arnold said thickly, "Yes. Locked in the lamp room aft."

"It will be better for you that they should be safe." Richer leaned forward, and Arnold felt anew the awful power of him. "Nothing will go wrong now, my friend. I have had enough of things that go wrong."

"There are three now," Arnold whispered. "Three. Why . . .?"

"You knew about the captain. But our colleague Garraud —it was unfortunate. A little amateur politician, a pale Red, eh?" Richer smiled, shrugging. "It is ironical that one such as he should be chosen to survey an airfield of the free nations, but convenient for me. He was a worker, that one, whatever he may have thought of the job he had to do. Perhaps he was working for Moscow, eh? We may indeed have struck a blow for France, for which she should be grateful. . . ." Richer's voice grew suddenly harsh. "If he had not been so inquisitive about our movements I think he would still be alive. And Smith—he was also inquisitive, and very dangerous."

"Why bring them to my ship?" Arnold burst out hysterically.

"Because it is the best and safest way of dealing with them," Richer said evenly. "Soon there will be no evidence, no one to speak against us, no bodies. You understand?"

Arnold opened his mouth and the weird, high sounds shuddered from it. "There were to be no killings! I thought this was just another job. . . . Now we shall all be murderers." He was shouting at Richer now. "Murderers! And you don't care!"

Richer seemed to sway forward, and he hit Arnold in the face, once, and then stood still with his arms down, watching. Arnold fell back against the wheel, a red mark glowing on his cheek where the blow had struck.

"You will keep your mouth shut and listen to me," Richer said. A slender and desperate control lay upon him. "Whose fault is it that these disposals are necessary? I will tell you—it is yours, my friend, because you did not arrive on the appointed day."

"I couldn't help it," Arnold whined, and his hand groped at his cheek. "The storms. . . ."

"The storms!" All at once Richer was shaking, more deeply than before, the veins on his neck and forehead swollen with fury. "You fool! Did you not realise that everything depended on your getting here on the right day? Because you were afraid of the weather all our plans were upset." Richer turned his great rage-filled eyes to Tarollier, and the big man seemed to contract beneath them. "What fools I have with me! You too—you must lose your thick head when the captain discovered our hiding place, when a little explaining might have satisfied him and saved us so much trouble."

Tarollier was silent, awkwardly shuffling, waiting for Richer to speak again.

"Everything has gone wrong from the beginning," Richer went on more quietly. "This crew—due back here on the twenty-sixth, the very day we had chosen for our job of work. . . . Even the little present which I put aboard their plane failed to do its job properly, and they returned only one day late with a man who had been sent to watch us. Bad luck, eh? Then their motor was sick and they had to stay the night. More bad luck, because after that their captain stumbled on our hiding place. And in the middle of all this you came, M. Arnold, two days late. It is what you would call a chapter of accidents, eh?"

Again no one spoke, and Richer said, "Therefore it is easy to see where the blame lies for having to take these people aboard, my friend. . . . Now, you will assist us on this trip in anything we require you to do—*anything*, you understand?"

Arnold was cowering, clutching the wheel to support his quivering body, and again he was empty of all but fear of Richer and what Richer was to do. His mind drifted, with no power of its own.

He muttered his defeat. "I—I understand. . . ."

"Good." Richer stepped back and clasped his thin hands together as though holding something infinitely desirable between them, and he seemed to be savouring each moment of a triumph that was still secret and magnificent. "I have overcome all these difficulties, my friend, and I am not to be beaten now by you—or anybody. And, perhaps you are not so indispensable as you think, either. Now, it is time we were going. Is the cargo properly stowed—safe?"

"Yes, it is in the big storeroom below us here."

"And the food and water?"

"Also in the storeroom."

"Ah, that is good. Now, when you have left the harbour you will steer a north-westerly course, round the west of the island, at full speed."

Arnold nodded mutely.

"You will receive further instructions later. We must get as far as possible from Faruda before dawn."

Tarollier reached into the pocket of his drill trousers and took out the two fuel injector valves which he had removed that morning. He looked at Arnold, holding out the valves. Without a word Arnold took them and went out along the deck towards the engine room gangway.

Arnold was trapped into this thing now, finally, and he knew it. These men would stop at nothing. He had been afraid of Tarollier this morning, but now he was far more afraid of this thin, empty man with the blazing eyes. He thought, the girl has escaped too, this was the extent of her hatred for him, and he knew that he would never see her again. What a fool he had been to get half drunk and leave brandy lying about—Pedro could never resist brandy. These men might find out soon about the girl, from Pedro or Manuel. . . . But if they put to sea quickly and got away with the drugs they might not worry about her then. It was only he who would know the gnawing loneliness, the desolation of life without her.

He felt the smooth round pieces of metal in his hands; Richer had trusted him to fit them, he thought stupidly, and he could throw them over the side, now. But he knew that he would not, and Richer knew it too, and at that moment he would have fought to the end of life to keep those bits of metal. Descending the gangway steps, he entered the warm and oily darkness of the engine room. There was a faint and unusual noise from somewhere inside it—a sort of bubbling sound which came from the port side, low down. He took a step forward on to the control platform, groping for the light switch on the bulkhead, and his foot went up to the ankle into wet coldness.

The lights came on. A dark, oily mass of water lay over the engine room plates, sucking at the sides of the diesels. Arnold stared at it, dully uncomprehending, stared down at his ankle which still stood in the black flood. And then the sudden realisation came upon him. Jo—Jo had tried to scuttle his ship. It could only have been Jo. . . .

A bursting desperation seized him. He sloshed forward in the water towards the sea-cock valve and shut it. It had only been partially opened or the boat must have sunk. His eyes darted fearfully in the direction of the gangway, and he was cursing himself for not having gone down to the engine room while waiting for the truck after he had discovered that the girl had gone; but he had not thought of this, and his dark and inward anxieties had so encompassed all his senses that he had not heard the faint sounds of moving water there, nor noticed the almost imperceptible settling of the boat.

Suddenly Arnold was galvanised by fear into maniac action. The pumps! There would be only the hand pump until the motors were started. He snatched a spanner and began working furiously to replace the injector valves. The water was cold and slimy on his ankles, foul-smelling with filth from the bilges. One of the valves dropped from his uncontrollably trembling fingers and he had to grope for it in the flood and clean the water from it before again attempting to screw it to the injector.

He had just completed the replacement of the first valve when the lights went out.

Almost immediately Arnold heard Tarollier's high voice from the engine room skylight above. "*Tiens!* What is happening? What are you doing down there? The lights have gone."

"I know that. There is water in the engine room—it must have got to the batteries."

"Water? How is that? How . . .?"

"I don't know." Arnold was shouting. "Call my two men—they will have to pump."

Tarollier's voice was suddenly frightened. "Pump? Are we sinking?"

"No, but this water must be pumped out. Call them!"

The two Spaniards came down the gangway into the engine room, Pedro surly and red-eyed. Arnold lit a storm lamp and by its light the men began to work at the handle of the bilge pump in a slow and spiritless manner which signified that their interest in the boat's departure was not worthy of too much exertion. Tarollier watched from the skylight for a time, and after several minutes it seemed to him that the level of the water scarcely dropped at all.

"Can't they go any faster?" Still his voice held a note of fear. "We shall be here for hours at this rate. How did this happen?"

"I don't know," Arnold lied. "It looks like a faulty seacock. We can't leave with all this water in her. I'll get the motors started as soon as I can, and then we can use the electric pump."

"Hurry, then," Tarollier snarled. "Already we are late. Now—this." Arnold was bending over the second diesel, screwing in the injector valve, and the Spaniards still pumped with sulky and unhurried strokes despite Arnold's orders to work faster. This was a task they had not expected and did not like; moreover the captain owed them many weeks' money, and Pedro had been cursed for a fool for getting drunk and allowing the girl to escape. But the water fell slowly as the long minutes ticked by until, at last, it was below the level of the control platform.

Arnold adjusted the throttles of the diesels and primed the injector pumps, making sure the clutches were disengaged. Now all was ready. He opened the valves of the compressed air bottles and pressed the starter button, and straight away the first motor jumped into life with a healthy, clattering roar. He started up the second, and the little engine room was filled with the loudness of them and with the sickly smell of fuel oil. Arnold stood motionless on the platform, listening to the engines' voices.

And as he listened they both suddenly coughed and died, together; the unexpected silence was more profound than ever it had been before. The Spaniards had stopped pumping, and they stood indifferently, watching Arnold in the lamp's dim glow.

Tarollier was squealing from the skylight.

"What are you doing now? When are we going to move?"

Arnold did not reply, bending over the motors. He tried the starters again and the diesels turned but would not fire. The fuel—it must be the fuel. . . . He examined the injector pumps, and the little glass tubes which measured the cylinders their ration of oil were not the black and shiny columns that they should have been. They were empty.

He stared unbelievingly at first one pump and then the other. Both were dry. He could not remember having turned off the fuel—had he shut the locks while he was half drunk earlier? Snatching the lamp from its hook he carried it behind the motors. The heavy steel padlocks which he had fitted on the delivery pipe cocks as a precaution against the theft of his boat were closed. He *must* have locked them. No! The girl. . . . He swung round and ran back through to the cabin, holding the lamp aloft before him, and there he saw that the hook where the keys were hung was vacant.

Tarollier's voice came thinly, as in a dream.

"Why do you not start the motors? We can pump out when we get to sea."

"I can't start them!" Arnold cried shrilly, stumbling back to the control platform. "The keys. . . ."

"What keys?"

"The keys for the fuel locks—they're gone! Someone has taken them."

"Someone? Who? Are you playing a game with us, my friend? If you are . . ."

"No! I swear I'm not. This . . ."

Richer's gaunt figure, stooping, suddenly appeared at the door from the cabin. He stopped there, hands behind his back.

He said, deeply and quietly, "What is the matter now?"

With a great effort Arnold nerved himself to become calm, trying to loosen the clenching terror at his heart.

"We're in trouble," he said hoarsely. "The keys for the fuel locks are missing."

Richer was staring at him intently with a fixed and almost hypnotic gaze. "Missing? And who could have taken them, M. Arnold? There has been nobody on board but you and your crew, has there?"

"No, no. I—I can't understand . . ."

"Nobody, eh? Then perhaps you can tell me how this came to be here."

Richer held up a black plastic handbag towards the light, a cheap, shining little thing, and Arnold recognised it immediately. His leaden face sagged, and a new and violent trembling took pitiless charge of him.

"I found it just now, under the cabin table," Richer said softly. "Well?"

"There was a girl on board," Arnold muttered, and then the words came tumbling out, a babbling rush. "She was with me—I locked her up in a room with one of the crew but she escaped. I thought it was all right—it wasn't my fault. She . . ."

"So—a girl. . . . Then it was she who sabotaged the boat?"

"It must have been, while I was fetching the stores. I took all the precautions. . . ."

"You fool!" Suddenly Richer was screaming, and Arnold's knees buckled as he shrank from the fury before him. "You take a woman on board when there is a job like this? And you allow her to escape and almost wreck the boat! You're mad! You shall pay for this—afterwards." He moved slowly towards Arnold, and now his voice fell to a whisper. "Yes—you shall pay. But nothing shall stop me now, do you understand? Whatever this woman has done or to whom she has gone—these things will not stop me. The cargo will go with me—or die with me. . . . Now, if you have no keys you will break the locks and we shall go."

Arnold sucked in air which rasped his throat, and there was no stilling of his body's awful shaking. His words came out at last, muttered, slurring from his tongue. "They are very strong—I can't break them or the pipes will burst. They will have to be sawn through."

"That I shall leave to you," Richer said, and still his voice was only a sibilance of breath. "But you will remove them somehow, and quickly." He turned on his heel and went back through the dark cabin and Arnold heard him climb to the deck.

There was only one hacksaw in the boat, and this Arnold took himself while Pedro began to scrape at the other lock with a file. He worked with desperate haste, spurred by his terror, holding the lock with one hand and sawing with the other until his arms ached cruelly and he sank even more deeply into despair as he saw how small an impression on the tough steel the blade was making.

He cursed his own prudence in selecting such heavy locks; after half an hour's toil the cut was no more than an eighth of an inch deep. It was like trying to fell an oak tree with a pocket knife. After a time he changed the blunted blade and carried on, and then Tarollier came down to take his turn at the sawing but after the first few slashing strokes he broke the blade. Arnold fitted another, telling the Frenchman to work more carefully, and stood nursing his throbbing arms.

A great weariness fell upon him, and he heard the slow, menacing footsteps of Richer on the deck above, but all at once he could not care so much, for fear was crammed so tightly in him that it was liquefying into a kind of cold indifference. Again he took over from Tarollier, and now he worked more slowly at the gradually deepening cut. The minutes ticked away, multiplying. . . .

On the deck Richer was holding his impotent fury under iron control, but he could not stop it mounting. His great eyes were black with the force of it as he listened to the steady scrape of the hacksaw from the engine room below, the scrape that seemed as though it would go on for ever. All else was silence, nothing moving but the stars in their slow and mighty swing across the flossy sky. The woman, he thought, this woman who had escaped—she could do nothing, and the Bey's guards still waited. . . . He touched the gun, heavy in his pocket, and pulled down the wrinkled sleeves of his sweater. It must be a long time since he had looked at his watch—he had tried to make it a long time; he peered at the luminous face.

Now it was only three hours to the first light.

At this moment the strained bonds of his rage all at once snapped, and above the engine room he screamed down dreadfully at Arnold and drove his clenched fist through the skylight, smashing the glass which fell with an icy tinkle to the steel floor below.

From then until two hours later when both locks had at last been sawn through and the fuel valves turned on Richer strode the boat like a madman, raving terribly and screaming his blind fury at the four men in the engine room. All the time the two Arabs squatted on the quay, watching, motionless and silent as figures cut from the coat of night itself, and the bound Kingsley struggled weakly and in vain at his cords in the little oil-smelling room where he had been locked with the unconscious Smith and the corpse of Garraud. . . .

Arnold dragged himself heavily to the control platform and once more primed the fuel injectors. The diesels started easily when he pressed the buttons, their chattering clamour filling the engine room with pulsating tremors, and he switched on the auxiliary pump to clear out the remaining water in the bilges. Still there were no lights.

He stumbled up on deck and into the wheelhouse. Richer

and Tarollier waited there. Richer seized him by the arm, his long fingers biting deep into Arnold's flesh; there was blood on the fingers where the skylight glass had cut them. His rage had long since reached its saturation point, and now it had crossed some dark, lunatic fringe within him, somehow bringing a strange and flickering calm.

Thinly Richer said, "Are we ready, at last?"

Arnold nodded dully. He could feel no fear now, only an incredible weariness. "Yes, we are ready."

Richer dropped his hand and Arnold spoke briefly to the Spaniards. They cast off the ropes fore and aft and the boat lay there, free of the land.

It was very dark now. The stars had paled, and Arnold could only just make out the slash in the cliffs where the channel lay. It was madness to attempt to get out in darkness such as this; but he could not care any more, for all was futility weighted with aching fatigue. He engaged the port clutch and spun the wheel. The boat trembled with familiar life and began to move forward slowly, her nose swinging from the quay wall. Behind him the Frenchmen stood, tense and silent, threatening shadows in the dark wheelhouse.

Motors dead slow, Arnold eased her carefully into the black cut that was the harbour entrance. When the sides of it were pressed about them the darkness was intense—thick treacly stuff which seemed to cling to his eyeballs, making sight dim and painful. The rock walls passed slowly by, each a fuliginous threat, very close. Dead slow, just a touch of engine now and then to keep the way on her, slow, the strip of sky above the only sign that this was not some smoking tunnel. The boat's length inside now, and soon they would be at the bend. . . .

He thrust his head from the window to call to Pedro in the bows to switch on his torch so that he could see better where the turning point lay, but before he could utter the sound a grinding, splintering shudder seemed to ripple along the boat from bow to stern and it stopped dead. The three men in the wheelhouse were thrown forward violently against the bulkhead in a disordered and sprawling heap.

Arnold struggled to his feet and freed the clutches, shouting to Pedro. The Spaniard had been hurled to the deck by the collision and had only saved himself from going overboard by clutching at a stanchion. It was Richer who ran forward and snatched the torch from him and flashed it over the bows into the channel's dark pit.

Only the mast and smashed gunwale of the sunken fishing boat showed above the water's oily reflections. Richer stared at these black, mesmeric objects for perhaps half a minute, then gave out a long, wailing scream and stumbled back along the deck to the wheelhouse. He stood there, rocking on his feet and staring with wild, mad eyes at Arnold and Tarollier. The big head lolled oddly, and he seemed to be fighting for breath through a mouth which sagged open and still screamed.

And then, as the first faint lightening of dawn touched the eastward sky, Richer moved. Jumping forward he hurled the stupefied Arnold from the wheel, putting the motors into reverse. Arnold was thrown violently into a corner, and nothing could have given him the power to interfere with this madman who was now hunched, crazily screaming, over the controls. The boat slid astern. . . . Then Richer suddenly reversed the propellers again and opened the throttles wide. The diesels howled, screws thrashed the water into a phosphorescence of foam which boiled against the channel's rocky walls; the boat stopped—hesitated—moved forward, gathering momentum. Faster it moved, and then again the sharp stem crashed against the sunken wreck with a jarring shock that shuddered through every timber and rivet of the vessel, stopping it dead.

Again Richer threw the screws into reverse, at full speed, but it was some time before the bows would free themselves from the wreck's drowned yet sucking grip. Sweat poured from his haggard face as the motors raced; then somewhere there was the sudden gunshot splintering of wood and she came free, backing. Now it was light enough to see the lumpy upperworks of the fishing boat and the ragged hole in its side where Richer had rammed; and all at once its mast began to lean, wavered, and then fell quite slowly with its furled sail across the channel.

As he rammed again Richer was screaming continuously now in a thin, wailing voice which sounded weirdly above the noise of the motors and the crash of rending timbers. His face was chalk-white and glassy with running sweat, his eyes great balls of black fire in the whiteness, staring wildly while the foaming mouth hung open and the awful crazed sounds came from it in endless howling. Arnold crouched, frozen with renewed terror and watching Richer, and Tarollier stood with naked fear in his small eyes, clutching at the doorway for support.

They did not see and could not hear the two aircraft which flew in from the north-west as the first scarlet arc of the sun burned its release from the sea.

Kneeling on the cliff top above Barthell knew that it was time to move. Stiff and cold though he was, he did not feel the clammy press of his wet clothes now, for the moment of action was here. The three watchers had seen the long black shape slide into the channel to a mutter of diesels; was it good fortune for them and for the prisoners on board that its departure had been so long delayed? But it must mean that help was so much closer. . . . They had heard the first splintering crash as the boat struck the wreck and Richer's screaming, and now, as the quick daylight grew and the eastern sky was suddenly aflame with red and orange suffusions, they saw in the still crepuscular valley below that it was going astern for a third attempt to break through the barrier which they had placed there. And they knew then that it would not get out—even now the bows were a mass of shattered timber and seemed to be down in the water. They could make out the deathly mask that was Richer's face in the wheel-house, staring ahead and mouthing at some crippled Olympus beyond the sea.

It was time. Barthell had risen, the gun in his hand, and as he stood now on the cliff his burly frame seemed to be fashioned of iron in the weak light. Gleason was on one knee, the Sten cocked; the girl was to stay on the cliff top.

No help yet, Barthell thought, knowing that he had never expected it. Right—move now and move quick, while they're still surprised.

"It's our show, Bob." His voice was quiet, unhurried, and he did not turn his eyes from the boat. "Ready? You know what to do—drop anyone who tries to shoot or leave the wheelhouse."

"Ready. . . ."

Gleason gave one look at the girl and her head was lifted in the direction of the sea; he swallowed the foul-tasting stuff which had collected in his mouth and moved away, but the girl suddenly raised her hand in a curiously imperious gesture. Before the men, her quick ears had gathered the tiny sound from the sea, even before the twin specks had left their bed on the dawn's contracted horizon.

"Planes!" she said. "Coming this way. Wait. . . ."

They all heard it then, the drone of hope. Barthell halted at the cliff edge. The specks appeared, growing low over the sea in steady formation, one higher and a little behind the other, and they were flying directly at Faruda. . . . Beneath them a thick yellow cloud suddenly erupted from the sea, coiling and drifting up in the almost windless air; a smoke float.

Not far from the coast the aircraft banked hard over, all at once turning eastward; they were big, four-engined transports marked with the French roundels, and near the tail their cargo doors were open, square black holes in the silver flanks.

Gleason's weary face had been alight with a joy and thankfulness which was suddenly stricken as the machines turned away.

"Is it help?" the girl asked, and for the first time her lips quivered and despair sounded in her voice.

"I don't know. . . . What are they doing?"

Barthell had been staring at the aircraft, his eyes pinched small in muscled cheeks.

"I think they're coming round again. . . . Look—look at this!"

The machines had banked a second time, pivoting about wing-tips in the quick turn; now they flew a little inside and parallel to the coast at about fifteen hundred feet, heading straight for the harbour.

"They're not making for the field," Barthell said. Suddenly he was shouting hoarsely, waving his gun. "A drop! I know now—it's a drop!"

From the first aircraft, even as he shouted and as it flew towards them a little curled-up bundle fell. Then, while this seemed barely clear of the tail plane, a red canopy was spewed out, billowing from it like a great flower opening, the bundle dangling beneath; then another, and another, until nearly a score of coloured parachutes drifted down in the new light of the sun, and the little bundles were given life by it and became men. The second machine came in on the same track as the first, dropping from almost the same point in the sky, and the warming air was all at once filled with these huge blossoms floating slowly to earth.

The morning was so calm that the placings must have been judged without difficulty, and the drop was perfectly executed, the men coming down in a small area around the village. Three dropped within fifty yards of where Barthell and his companions stood, and they touched, knees bent and rolling over, and almost at once the parachutes collapsed in the still air and they had released themselves. They wore French uniforms under their jumping smocks and carried automatic guns.

Gleason found himself waving furiously, shouting, and the men came at a stealthy trot, grim and crouched behind their ready weapons. One was a tall young lieutenant with a tigerish face.

"Name!" the lieutenant called in sharp English. His eyes were on their airline uniforms. "What are your names?"

"Barthell—Gleason. . . ."

"All right."

When they were close the officer gestured to his men and they stopped, watching. Barthell began to speak, pointing to the channel below, but the lieutenant cut him short and said crisply, now with a noticeably American accent, "We know about this. Got your signal. Let's go."

Barthell stared at him for a second, stupidly, but the officer was peering down the gully and at the boat. As he began to scramble down the slope followed by his men Barthell's mind and body clicked into action and he descended at their heels, and after him the engineer.

The deep cleft below was still shadowed with the dregs of night. Now the boat was stopped, its bows resting on the wreck, and Barthell knew that it must be jammed there for the propellers were racing in a mad turbulence of foam. The three men in the wheelhouse, in their narrow rock-bound cavern which was filled with the roar of the boat's motors and Richer's thin screaming, had not heard or seen the aircraft; even yet they had no hope or thought for anything but the dying chance of reaching the open sea.

As the five descended the gully, their guns ready, Pedro who was still crouched on the fore deck looked up and saw them. The Spaniard stared, his bristly face a smeared white and his eyes popping, and then slowly raised his hands above his head. It was like a performing animal making some well-rehearsed and yet uncertain salute. It seemed to Barthell that some time elapsed before the men in the wheelhouse recognised the significance of Pedro's attitude; and then, all together, they turned their faces upward to where the lieutenant was now nearly within jumping distance of the boat's deck, eyes and mouths open in the paralytic imbecility of surprise.

Barthell knew that the screws all at once stopped their churning and the lieutenant shouted something, levelling his automatic. He saw that Richer was the first to move, dropping suddenly to his knees below the wheelhouse window.

Again the lieutenant shouted, calling for surrender, and at the same moment Richer's white, glassy face which was like a grotesque and furious mask raised itself above the sill and his shot whined over the lieutenant's head and struck the rock near the feet of one of the soldiers behind. The lieutenant fired and the bullet cut a furrow across Richer's right cheek and the blood spurted and ran down over his jaw. Richer was screeching unintelligibly, a mad and disembodied head in the window.

It was Tarollier who first hurled himself from the wheelhouse, throwing up his arms in capitulation as a shot from one of the soldiers hit him in the shoulder, and he was followed at the opposite door by Arnold who in his stumbling haste fell prone on the deck and lay there, his mouth pressed and sucking at the boards so that his cries were distorted strangely into pleading, desperate echoes. "Don't shoot! For God's sake don't. . . ."

Richer did not move from the wheelhouse. His bloody face screamed at the men on the cliff as he shot, wildly and furiously, to the end; it came soon, when the screaming stopped suddenly, choked off in one great sob unheard among the shots which poured into the wheelhouse. The smeared white mask made a strange, tired grimace of something which was like disgust, and then slid quite slowly out of sight below the window. Silence then. . . .

The wheelhouse was splintered and riddled with bullet holes and there was blood on the shattered compass and on the wheel when the lieutenant and Barthell entered. Richer was lying on his side, still clutching his gun, his face turned upward and the great eyes staring, but they no longer held the deep and glowing lustre of life, for Richer was dead.

There was a thick quietness now in the channel and over the stranded boat. Tarollier and Arnold gave no trouble, for they had known the end of hope when they saw the soldiers on the cliff; and Tarollier had recognised defeat in his first sight of Barthell—Barthell whom he thought securely out of the way in the dry well on the road to the airfield—and now he stood under the paratroopers' guns holding his wounded shoulder, trembling, fear and pain on his little, compressed features. And terror laced with a shuddering relief that it was all over at last had reduced Arnold to a mumbling wreck incapable of independent thought or action.

Barthell led the lieutenant aft and they unlocked the door of the lamp room with the key which Arnold had given them. Here were Kingsley and Smith, both heavily bound, sitting in the floor's oily filth, jammed together by the close walls which preserved the fetid breath of confinement. It was some time before Kingsley could move at all freely, for he had been in bonds almost continuously since his capture by Tarollier the previous morning; Smith had not long recovered consciousness from the blow which Richer had dealt him in the airfield cell when Tarollier arrived to take away the drugs. And there too Garraud's body had been thrown like a bag of potatoes, into the tiny room with its single half-shut ventilator and screwed-down port, the teak door locked on the dead and the living. . . .

Later, with Smith, Kingsley and Barthell, the lieutenant questioned Arnold and Tarollier in the little cabin while Gleason went back up the cliff to the waiting girl. The demoralised Arnold especially was eager to answer anything put to him, and the trembling yet surly silence which Tarollier at first maintained was broken by some thinly-veiled threats from the lieutenant, and Tarollier all at once crumpled into an abasement as complete as that of Arnold. Then, unfolding in sporadic rushes and hesitations, the story of the two men whose fear-stained mutters filled the cabin was told, but it was really that of another man, one whose cunning, resource and ruthless determination had carried him over all obstacles to the very gates of triumph.

When Kingsley with Smith and Barthell left the boat to return to the airfield they saw Richer's body still lying on the wheelhouse floor, still the awful glazed eyes stared, and even in death the febrile passion of the man which had once moved his gaunt frame seemed to be there, waiting only for sleep to end.

CHAPTER XI

THE CHANGED PEOPLE

FARUDA's silence was gone. Now the airfield was busy with soldiers guarding the transports which had landed there, Arnold's stranded boat was occupied and a party had advanced on the palace of the Bey who, realising the folly of resistance to armed men who might speedily be reinforced, offered no opposition.

At the field Kingsley's crew, Smith and Rogers, all except the stewardess and Jo who were resting in the machine, sat round the table in the mess tent; a group of weary but thankful men, infinitely glad that the night of suspense and danger was over.

Now that they were together again as once they had scarcely hoped to be, it seemed suddenly that too much had been endured for any of these experiences to be revealed, too much had been changed both in them and in their relationships to one another. Kingsley thought this as he looked at his crew. They were silent, reflecting on shared dangers; but he knew that soon they would talk, and then there would be no stopping them.

Cummings passed round cigarettes. Sitting next to Tarrant, Gleason spoke first, running a hand over his unshaven chin as he said quietly, "So you got through after all, David. When?"

"About an hour after you left for the village with this girl. I'd really given up hope long before. . . ." Tarrant's grin was tired. "But our contraption worked in the end."

Rogers had been stroking his globular head and smiling round the table, the merest hint of smugness in his eyes.

"As it turned out," he said, "we were coming anyway. But now I know that without your signal we should have been too late to help—if the boat had been able to break out of harbour."

"We're glad to see you, Don," Kingsley said simply. His long face was lined with weariness. "Smith and I weren't giving much for our chances by the time the troops arrived."

"No. . . . And I don't mind telling you I had a few bad moments myself before I got things moving. Anyway, what's been going on here?"

"Well, plenty, but I think we ought to have your story first. We want to know how you laid on this trip with the paratroops."

Someone said, "Yes, what's the dope about that, sir?"

"Ah—well, all right. It begins with the explosion in Peter Fox last week," Rogers said weightily. "Somehow I didn't like the smell of that right from the start, although I had no reason to suspect anyone, of course. When I heard about it I couldn't get it out of my head that something funny might have been going on, in spite of the likely explanation of the leaking petrol cans and the spark from the control rods. . . .

"In any case I had to take a look at Peter Fox and I knew her so well that I had hopes of discovering something which the official inspectors might have missed." Rogers paused deliberately. "Well, to come to the point, I found something right enough. It was part of the timing mechanism of a bomb."

Gleason said grimly, "Richer's handiwork. He planted the bomb when he was working in the machine, unloading the stores. Unfortunately—for him—it failed to kill us all as he intended."

"But why . . .?"

"We were due back here on the twenty-sixth. Richer knew that. He was unfortunate again, for this was the very day he had arranged for Arnold to arrive at Faruda, and he wanted no interference on that day. He also knew that we were short of crews and machines at Westonmills, and therefore if he got rid of Peter Fox and us he could expect a clear field here until he got the drugs away."

"We surprised and annoyed him by not only surviving but by turning up on the following day," Barthell grunted. "Bad enough, though worst of all Arnold was delayed and only arrived yesterday."

Kingsley looked at Rogers. "Go on with your story, Don."

"Well, you can imagine how I felt when I found this bit

of the bomb," Rogers said. " I knew then that a deliberate attempt to kill you had been made by someone—someone who was at Faruda. All at once the fact that you had been held up overnight with engine trouble began to assume pretty ugly proportions."

He went on, " I got a message off from Istres to Westonmills right away asking about you, and Westonmills replied that they had heard nothing since your morning signal which said you hoped to get going that afternoon. There wasn't much comfort here, so I got Istres to radio Faruda direct. No reply. By this time it was nearly dark and you should have been well on the way home, but Istres could make no contact on your frequency. I was thoroughly frightened then and rushed round like a lunatic with my bit of evidence. At first nobody seemed very interested, but I persuaded them to listen out and getting on for nine o'clock they at last picked up Mr. Tarrant's faint signal."

" This gingered things up wonderfully, and they decided to send me to Air Force headquarters in Marseilles to argue it out there. I'll skip the talking and telephoning that had to be done before I finally convinced the air chiefs that you were in a bad way and that after all it was French responsibility to protect you. It's enough to say that they were convinced at last and then things moved very fast indeed. The C.O. decided to lay on two of his own transports, two officers and thirty men to be dropped over Faruda if necessary, and allowed me to go with them. We took off soon after midnight, and got here at first light.

" When we were within range I spoke to Mr. Tarrant on the radio telephone and he told us what was going on at the harbour. The officer in charge of the paratroops therefore decided to drop over the village as soon as it was light enough, and—well, that's about it." Rogers paused, smiling. " Now, just satisfy my curiosity over what's been happening here."

Kingsley sucked at his pipe. " The first night we were held up," he said, " nothing happened except that while I was on watch Tarollier came sneaking back from what I thought was some village jaunt, but now I know he had been looking out for Arnold. It was next morning that things began to bubble.

"Wandering round the field to pass the time while the motor was being fixed, I accidentally stumbled on this hoard of drugs. Tarollier must have been keeping an eye on me, and he laid me out with his gun. It wasn't a very clever thing to do—I'd have thought it easier for he or Richer to try to explain the stuff away somehow rather than have me on their hands. But it might have been difficult to satisfy Garraud about it. . . . Anyway, Tarollier hit me, hard.

"Next thing I remembered was being in a little dark room in a house which I know now was the Bey's palace. I was kept bound all the time except when an old Arab with an escort came and fed me dates and sour milk. And there I stayed until I was put in a truck and taken back to the hiding place where the drugs were loaded and Smith and Garraud thrown aboard with me. And then to the boat."

Kingsley passed a hand across his face.

"It seemed years before we moved," he said. "Then—the boat crashing against the wreck. . . . We heard Richer screaming, the shots. . . . And suddenly it was all over, and we were safe."

"Daren't jump the boat," Barthell said gruffly, "in case the guards or Richer got at you first—Richer didn't care what happened so long as he got his cargo away. By blocking the entrance we hoped to delay him until help came, or at least it might give us a better chance of pulling you out. We were just going for Richer when the drop started."

Barthell told of the crew's anxiety at Kingsley's absence and how he had found Garraud's body. Thinking of his past suspicions, he grinned apologetically at Smith who sat quietly smoking at the end of the table.

Cummings said breathlessly, "It—it was Richer who killed Garraud?"

Smith's eyebrows went up, wrinkling the high forehead, and his keen and not over friendly gaze rested on the co-pilot as he said evenly, "Of course. Garraud was becoming much too inconvenient and inquisitive for Richer's peace of mind, and yesterday I believe that he was on the point of finding the drugs. Moreover, Richer needed Garraud's jeep, and no doubt he would have been difficult about that."

Barthell nodded. "Whatever Garraud was and whatever

he believed—he seems to have leaned towards communism at any rate—he was keen on his job and wasn't the sort of man to allow any funny business while he was in charge here. Tarollier said that Garraud was the boss, and he and Richer had got to remember it."

Somewhat shamefacedly Barthell told them how he was knocked out by Tarollier. "Seems to be a hobby of his," the co-pilot remarked; and then Gleason told his story, beginning with the discovery of the wrecked radio and the disappearance of Garraud's body, and ending with his journey to the village with the girl and how they had found Barthell and had all watched the boat before blocking the harbour entrance.

"Did Richer move Garraud's body from the tent?" Tarrant asked.

"Yes," Smith said, his sharp face expressionless. "He did it while you were running up your motor—Garraud was a small man, and it was easy enough for Richer to carry him to the cell where the drugs were stored, keeping out of sight behind the tents and huts."

Smith paused. "Richer was fortunate—clever perhaps—not to be caught in the act of killing Garraud either by Mr. Barthell or myself. What I think happened was this: after lunch Richer followed Garraud behind the huts, and believing that Garraud was about to find the drugs Richer found it necessary to kill him. He may have had other reasons too for wanting to be rid of Garraud—we don't know. Meanwhile I'd been trying to do my weather stuff and keep an eye on Richer as well, but when Mr. Barthell and I got to Garraud Richer was creeping back to the tents. Then after we had put Garraud in the sleeping quarters and broken the news Richer feigned surprise and shock—and very well he did it—and pretended to send a signal. He wrecked the transmitter instead. He knew you could send no signal from your grounded machine, but he forgot the generator and the aerial."

Smith stubbed out his cigarette with an impatient jab. He said coolly, "I have to apologise for a great many mistakes. . . . One was that I did not expect Richer to be bold enough to wreck the radio under all our noses or to snatch Garraud's body while no one was looking. I'd better explain the real reason why I am in Faruda—as Captain Kingsley and Mr. Barthell learned on the boat this morning, it was not to study Faruda's weather. . . . I am attached to the Air Ministry's special investigation department, and by arrangement with the French police I was sent here to watch Richer who was suspected in Paris of being the head of an organisation for the distribution and sale of narcotics."

"Before you go on," Rogers interrupted, "*why* did Richer move Garraud's body?"

Smith shrugged. "I believe he did it on impulse, acting on the assumption that it is difficult to prove murder where a body cannot be found. And although there were half a dozen people who knew that murder had been done, Richer still thought it best to drop the body in the middle of the Mediterranean, from where he had strong hopes it would never be recovered. That, of course, was also to be the fate of Captain Kingsley and myself."

A corroding silence filled the hot tent. Smith lit another cigarette, drawing the smoke deep.

Presently he went on, "The first night of my arrival, while Garraud and Richer were in the radio tent, I searched their sleeping quarters, and hidden beneath Richer's bed I found two very interesting items. Yesterday morning I saw the boat come and watched Arnold and Tarollier visit the Bey. After this I was sure that there was a store of drugs somewhere in Faruda and that Richer and his associates had come here for them. Therefore it was essential that my first task should be to find these drugs, for they were the key to all Richer's actions, and so I spent most of yesterday afternoon searching for anything which might give me a line on their whereabouts.

"Rather belatedly it occurred to me that Garraud, if he had been about to find them, might have been murdered close to where they were hidden. I went to the spot beside the far hut. I suspect that much of the time Richer had been playing hide and seek with me and—well, Richer won." Smith's lips twisted, rolling the cigarette neatly to the corner of his mouth. "He got me just where he got Garraud.

"I didn't have to look for the drugs any more," Smith said dryly. "Richer took me to them. . . . You see, he knew all about me then because I had reported to my department on what I had found in the sleeping quarters the previous evening—the report was in a letter which I gave to Captain Kingsley to deliver, and through his capture it fell into Richer's hands. Richer kept me in the cell until Tarollier arrived with the truck."

Tarrant said, "Just where is this cell, then?"

"In the dunes behind the farthest hut—it's an old underground storeroom. There could scarcely have been a better place for Richer's purpose—it is well concealed, out of sight of the apron and too far away for a truck's approach to be heard there. It was only because Richer was careless on one of his visits and left footmarks that it was discovered at all."

Rogers nodded ponderously. "So the Bey is in this too?"

"Yes," Kingsley answered, "and Tarollier was the link between the Bey and Richer. Yesterday was a busy day for Tarollier. He fixed me in the morning, met the boat, returned to the palace with Arnold to make final arrangements for departure, knocked out Harry in the afternoon. Then he loaded the jeep with provisions stolen from the camp and hidden somewhere on the road and left it for Arnold to collect after dark. In the evening he went again to the palace, paid the Bey something for his assistance, then drove the Bey's truck with me and the two guards in it to the hiding place where Richer helped him to load the drugs. . . ."

With a sudden impatient movement Rogers said, "Yes, but what about this drug question?—they didn't just grow here. How did Richer and Tarollier know about them?"

Everybody looked at Smith. Still his face was closed and expressionless, and when he spoke it was with a curious disinterest, almost as though the subject bored him.

He said, "It all began when Faruda was an operational airfield during the war."

"Yes?" Rogers leaned forward attentively.

"Tarollier, not Richer, is the man who started it. Tarollier was then in the Free French Air Force and was stationed here for much of his service, right up to the end when after the armistice the place was finally abandoned. Faruda was the main depot for all medical supplies over a large area of North Africa, and he was the man in charge of them. The most valuable part of these stores consisted of drugs, chiefly morphia and cocaine, and for a long period Tarollier was systematically stealing them, knowing that they would be worth a fortune on the post-war dope market. He'd no idea then just how he was going to remove them from Faruda, but he was hoping that some means would present itself eventually.

"Because Faruda was often bombed by the enemy Tarollier was able to convince the authorities that all his large stock of drugs had been destroyed. It wasn't difficult, he said, and in fact on one raid the sick bay where the drugs should have been stored—but weren't—was blown to bits. Tarollier also appears to have been in sole charge of the underground storeroom which, being close to the sick bay, made things all the simpler. He was almost the last man to leave Faruda when it was abandoned, and this was done without the drugs being found or their presence even suspected by anyone else."

Smith paused, then said sombrely, "God knows how many poor devils suffered through lack of drugs while the fighting was going on here, but that didn't worry our friend Tarollier, apparently, nor was he much concerned with what could happen to those whom they might eventually reach. . . . What did worry him was that he could find no way of taking such a large quantity with him when he left, and he was forced to go without them.

"However, they were all in sealed metal boxes, the storeroom was dry and he had piled tons of sand over the door, and so he comforted himself with the thought that his loot should remain in good condition and undiscovered for a long time. And it did."

Smith indulged in a sardonic smile.

"Since then, for various reasons, Tarollier was never able to return here and had no means of removing all the drugs could he have done so. He was meanwhile drifting into and out of a variety of jobs until about a year ago he got a temporary post with the French Air Ministry in Paris, and there he met Richer."

"Ah—so the association begins then?"

"Yes. Richer was a radio operator as he had been during the war, though why he continued to work at this trade when presumably he was making large profits from the distribution of drugs I don't know. Anyway, there he was. Garraud, an airfield engineer and surveyor, was also employed at the Ministry and knew Richer."

Smith went on, " The possibility of Faruda's re-opening began to be talked about in the Ministry, and as soon as Tarollier heard this he saw his opportunity to return there. But, even if he did return, there was still the problem of getting the drugs out.

" As the time approached when it was obvious that something was really going to be done about Faruda Tarollier grew desperate, and he hinted one day to Richer—from the start of their association each appears to have known that the other was a bird of like feather—he hinted to Richer that there might be big money for someone who could help him get to Faruda and arrange for a boat to go there too.

" Well, as it happened he couldn't have chosen a better man than Richer for the furthering of his plans. Richer had qualities of intelligence and determination which Tarollier lacked, and moreover in his collection of crooked acquaintances was one Arnold, a professional smuggler who owned a sea-going ex-torpedo boat and who might be persuaded to carry a cargo from Faruda. Incidentally, Arnold is an old friend of mine whom I helped to put away for gun-running soon after the war. Well, in short, Richer did contact Arnold, and Arnold agreed to do the job."

" Garraud knew nothing of this?" Rogers asked.

" Nothing. Eventually it was Garraud who was picked to survey the airfield, and somehow—since both he and Richer are dead we shall never know exactly how—somehow Richer prevailed upon Garraud to include himself and Tarollier in the party as radio operator and general handyman respectively. This suited them better than travelling with Arnold as it would take some time for the drugs to be made ready and moved to the harbour and there was always the Bey to be fixed before anything was possible at all. Also they didn't want the boat to be at Faruda longer than necessary, as this might have attracted unwelcome attention.

" It so happened that when it was time for the party to leave there was no suitable French plane available and the work was given to your Company. This was unexpected, but made little difference to the plans of these two. They went, fully equipped for anything that might happen, as evidenced by the bomb which nearly blew you out of the sky and by the money necessary for the Bey's co-operation—dangerous items, these, but being on an official mission they correctly anticipated little trouble from the French or British Customs. . . . Right. Arnold was to be at Faruda on the twenty-sixth which was the soonest he was able to arrive, his boat first having to undergo some repairs in Algiers. This, however, is where their luck began to fail, the twenty-sixth being also the day of your return here with further stores.

"You will see," Smith said evenly, "that as the plans of Richer and Tarollier developed, so too did Richer's emergence as leader."

"Richer was in charge from the moment they got to Faruda, anyway," Barthell broke in. "I think he might even have done away with Tarollier if he could, but Tarollier was indispensable."

Smith nodded. "Tarollier knew Faruda, knew just where the drugs were hidden, knew the Bey during the war and had guessed that the Bey's nationalism and greed would smooth their way—if it was made worth his while. The Bey had no use for the drugs, but the money which Tarollier brought could be very useful indeed.

"It was Richer who obtained the money, and I've no doubt that it came from the proceeds of the drug traffic which he controlled in Paris. Although under police suspicion he could not be prevented from going to Faruda and no one guessed the real reason for his journey. However, later on it occurred to someone that he might be worth watching and it was thought that if an English 'meteorologist' was sent out as a kind of afterthought it would allay any suspicions Richer might have about a newcomer. And so this was arranged between the French police and the Air Ministry on the one hand and my department on the other, and the job was given to me."

"Your weather recording foxed me, anyway," Kingsley said, grinning.

"It might have foxed Richer too, but for his finding of the letter I gave you. My job was to keep an unobtrusive watch on him and report anything interesting. As I told you, I found something interesting almost immediately, when I searched the sleeping quarters. Under Richer's bed there was a canister of morphia and a Paris newspaper folded back at a column describing the latest developments in the hunt for the leaders of the drug ring. Because of its war-time markings it was the canister which first opened my eyes to the possibility of drugs being here in Faruda. Arnold's arrival next day left no room for doubt."

For a time Smith was silent, his face dark and brooding.

Then he said, "When you meet such ruthless cunning and determination as Richer showed you may be sure that it is not being applied for any but an evil cause. Undoubtedly he was a far stronger character than either Arnold or Tarollier. Arnold—a weak, vain adventurer, easily frightened, vulnerable to both women and drink to the extent of allowing them to interfere with a job the size of this. Even Tarollier despised Arnold. And Tarollier himself—an unscrupulous ruffian, not averse to murder if he thinks he'll get away with it and it will do him any good, something of a sadist because I think it gave him real pleasure to crack Captain Kingsley and his navigator on the head. . . . But Richer—he was different.

"I believe that almost from the start both Arnold and Tarollier were scared stiff of Richer and realised his terrible determination to secure these drugs," Smith went on, now with some emphasis in his voice. "At the end he was in such complete control that even Tarollier didn't know what arrangements had been made for the cargo after it left Faruda. Such was Richer's power over these two—power born of a resolve so great that it drove him to murder one man and to attempt the murder of many more. . . . He was determined that nothing, short of his own death, should take away what he had so cleverly schemed to possess."

Rogers shifted his heavy body. Wonderingly he said, "Some men will do anything for money. If . . ."

Smith's short laugh interrupted him.

"Money? Arnold and Tarollier—yes, they wanted money. But it was not only money with Richer."

"Not. . . . Why?"

Smiling very faintly, Smith said, "Don't you see? Richer was an addict."

Rogers stared, his mouth open. "Then—then is that why he was so desperate, why he wouldn't stop even at murder?"

"Yes. He'd got to have his morphia. When I found the canister under his bed I saw that it had been opened and some morphia removed. Richer took it—for his own use. This trip came as a godsend to him, for recently the Paris police seized a big dump of the stuff and it's possible that Richer was running short.

"After we were released today," Smith went on, "I had a look at Richer's body. There was a bottle of morphia in his pocket, a hypodermic syringe in a case, and a patch of little punctures on his left forearm. He always wore an old sweater with long sleeves to conceal the marks made by the needle."

His voice hung about them, imprisoned by the drooping canvas.

Then he said, "The strange thing about this is that both Tarollier and Arnold were unaware that Richer was an addict. Not being over-intelligent, they ascribed to him only that motive by which they themselves were activated—gain. It's true that this was a *part* of his motive, but the main force which drove him on even to murder was the craving for morphia—morphia for himself. . . .

"After what I heard this morning I believe that it was Garraud who guessed the truth about Richer, who became suspicious of Richer's behaviour here and was determined to find the cause as the responsible man on the spot. He paid for his determination with his life."

They all sat quietly then, each occupied with his own press of thought. Now they saw one another almost as strangers, but strangers who were bonded more closely than the friends they had once known, for they had all been changed, whether they yet knew it or not, changed by this place of sand and heat.

At last Rogers spoke, and his was a voice calling them back to another and all but forgotten world. They looked up, surprised, seeking confirmation on other faces, beginning to remember.

"Well, it's all over now." Rogers expelled a long breath

and looked at his watch. "Time we were thinking about going home."

Suddenly Tarrant smiled, and from him the smile spread round the table like a flame leaping and lighting each face; home—it was not so far away now.

Smith rose stiffly and went out. When he had gone Kingsley felt that he too must get into the open—all at once this tent was grey and airless, like his prison room of yesterday. Rogers was looking at Kingsley, a smile on his face as the captain got up quickly and went outside.

Kingsley re-lit his pipe. In spite of his weariness the noon heat rested lightly upon him. Here was Faruda, sand and blaze and decay. . . . The same, yet not the same, for Faruda had changed even as he had changed. He saw this place, and beside Peter Easy the two French transports stood, soldiers patrolling beneath them. From the tent behind him voices came indistinctly, urgent and excited. The silence and the loneliness had retreated now and even the decay was no longer permanent, and then to Kingsley it seemed that one day this could be again a busy airfield, again a strong base in freedom's defence. And he felt too that all they had been through since their first flight here had not been endured in vain and that a recompense lay in the future, here in Faruda where corruption would be swept away by fresh and thriving growth.

Rogers was beside him. The operations manager was eyeing him with a sideways look, his face red as raw beef.

"How d'you feel, Bill?"

"Not bad." Kingsley made an effort to straighten his lean body. "Not all that good, either."

"What about the trip?"

Kingsley smiled faintly. "You think I shouldn't take her, eh?"

"Take her if you're fit enough. Are you?"

All at once Kingsley knew that he was not. He said, "I'm pretty tired—perhaps you'd better take her, Don. You don't get much chance to drive airframes nowadays, do you? You take her."

Rogers beamed. "You're sure . . .? Well, all right—you can catch up with some sleep." He was serious almost immediately. "Bill, I've been waiting to get you alone to tell you this. I thought you'd want it that way. . . . I've got to congratulate you—you're a father."

Kingsley stared, the pipe loose in his teeth.

"Everything's all right," Rogers hurried on. "Heard just before I left Westonmills. . . ."

"What is it?" Kingsley's voice was loud. "What is it?"

"It's a girl."

"A girl. . . ." The prominent bones in Kingsley's face seemed to soften, sagging. "A *girl*. . . ." He drew a deep, slow breath. "It's early. How's Carol?"

"She's fine and sends her love. I—I made some excuse about your not being home. . . ."

"I wanted to be home for this," Kingsley said. He paused uncertainly. "We were both hoping for a boy."

Rogers looked at him. Slyly he said, "Well, Bill, you know what to do about that."

Kingsley was silent, and Rogers went back to the tent. A girl, Kingsley thought, and then he was angry that he had not been at home. He must go now, go home where he belonged and see his wife and daughter. And then suddenly and clearly he knew that this thing, this completeness which he had never been able to feel, had been there all the time, waiting in his own house, but he had not sought it with his heart as well as with his mind. A family was a complete thing, a creation of new life, and to create new life was the consummation of man.

A girl. . . . Kingsley smiled slowly, turning the word and the image in his mind. And then he was glad, a burst of light and wonder possessing him, a thankfulness. He must get home quickly to this completeness which had always been waiting there, to this tiny life which he had made, to Carol. The boy would come one day. They could wait, the three of them. . . .

He turned back to the tent. Smith was walking towards it from the apron and they went in together.

Smith said, "I have seen the French officers and there is no objection to your going home now. I shall return in one of their machines and see our two friends and the drugs handed into safe keeping. If you should be wanted later the

Ministry will let you know, or I shall see you at Westonmills. . . ."

"What—what about the girl?" Gleason asked awkwardly.

"We have made arrangements to get in touch with her in England. She can go with you."

Barthell said quietly, "I know we're all very grateful to her. I'm glad she'll be with us."

He spoke for them all. Each man shook hands with Smith, solemnly, and he gave every one the same painful little smile and nod as they left him, a taut and lonely figure in the empty tent. Going out Barthell was thinking that even now they could not have met the inner Smith, for they knew nothing of him but what the shallow and perilous acquaintance at Faruda had afforded. He was still the same withdrawn man, cold and faintly mysterious, who had come to Westonmills two days before. Alone of those who had flown to Faruda, Smith seemed to have changed not at all.

Gleason walked ahead of the rest, his grave eyes on the machine that contained the girl to whom they all owed much for their safety. She was going with them. . . . In his heart anticipation stirred with vague regret. Della was gone, he knew that she was gone. And here was another ready to take her place, a fearless woman almost as lovely in her less obtrusive and disturbing mould; he did not know if there was a heart and mind there beneath this fine and balanced form, but what he did know was that he would need a woman now that Della was gone. It was no more and no less than this, perhaps for him it never would be, for this was only what he asked for or deserved.

Behind him Barthell and the co-pilot walked together. Barthell's strong, flattened face was eased by a smile which was half content and half thankfulness. So much for which to be thankful, he thought, and now they were going home. He was always glad to be going to his cheerful and noisy home, as he was always happy to leave it. There would be other trips after this, to new and better places, with the skipper and the others. They had been together a long time, and now a still closer coherence had sprung from common dangers; comradeship was as necessary to a man as his clothes.

Suddenly Cummings said, "Well, I found it." His voice had a note of hollow triumph.

Barthell looked up. "Eh? Found what?"

"Flo's foot. . . . Found it under the nose wheel this morning."

"Well, I'm glad, Lester," Barthell said. "Honest—I know how much that thing means to you."

A kind of defiantly sheepish look made its furtive appearance on Cummings's face and he tugged at the red moustache.

He said, "Ah—I've been thinking, Harry. Somehow it doesn't mean so much now. That is—it didn't pull us through last night, did it? Perhaps I . . ."

"What?"

"Perhaps . . ." Again Cummings hesitated. "Oh, hell! —last night taught me that lucky charms and all that stuff don't count as much as plain guts. . . . I've slung it away."

For a second Barthell stared at him and then burst into a vast rumble of a laugh. The co-pilot's embarrassment faded, and soon he began to laugh too, whiskers lifting unevenly and eyes popping; he felt better now than for a long time back—it was a relief to be able to laugh and to be rid of self-built fears and superstitions, to carry no longer the burden of mockery from others, to be equal.

Kingsley and Rogers followed close behind, and last of all came Tarrant, alone; and Tarrant, because he was full-living and the youngest of them all, knew with youth's certainty that he was also the happiest. Already the tormenting night was a bygone time, small among the broad delights of life, though in it he and Susan had recognised one of danger's many faces, as they had seen another on that terrible evening above the Rhône. The face had leered through the swollen hours and they had been afraid, but they were together and suddenly it had backed into the shadows, hesitated, and was gone. They would know it if it came again, and each time their fear would be a little less.

He stood at the foot of the ladder while Kingsley went up and into the machine. Susan was at the door, and her soft eyes smiled down at him as she held out her hand. He began to climb up to all the world's beauty and love which waited there in a metal frame.

As Rogers turned on to course, Peter Easy's silver body gleamed in the sun above Faruda. The dusty flange of desert merged gradually into the afternoon haze, melted and failed, then became haze itself. The machine climbed over the sea, alone and powerful, a solitary bird soaring towards the immense sky.